BLOOD MAGICK

BLOOD MAGICK

This is a work of fiction. All characters, organizations and events in this novel are products of the author's imagination and are not to be construed as real. Any resemblance to persons, living or dead, is entirely coincidental.

Blood Magick

SUZAN HARDEN

More Books by Suzan Harden
(Each series is in suggested reading order)

Bloodlines

Blood Magick
Zombie Love
Zombie Confidential
Zombie Wedding
Amish, Vamps & Thieves
Blood Sacrifice
Love, War & a Bulldog
Zombie Goddess
Ravaged
Sacrificed
Reality Bites
Ghouls in the Grocery
Resurrected
Bloodlines Shorts Anthology
Bloodlines: The First Boxed Set

Seasons of Magick

Spring
Summer
Autumn
Winter
The Seasons of Magick Anthology

Justice

Sword and Sorceress 28
("Justice")
Sword and Sorceress 30
("Diplomacy in the Dark")
Justice: The Beginning
A Question of Balance
A Modicum of Truth
A Matter of Death
A Touch of Mother
A Twist of Love
A Virtue of Child
A Hand of Father
A Measure of Knowledge
A Hint of Thief
A Cup of Conflict

The Justice Thalia Stories

Snowfall
Murder Most Fowl
The Sweetest Poison
A Granddaughter of Mine
Too Many Fish in the Sea

Tales of the Twelve

*The Trickster Priestess and the
Demon*

Crossover Worlds

Invasion!

888-555-HERO

Hero De Facto
Hero Ad Hoc
Hero De Novo
A Very Hero Christmas
Hero De Jure
Hero In Camera
Hero Amicus Curiae
A Very Hero Wedding
A Very Hero New Year
Hero Ad Litem
Queer Eye for the Super Guy

Solar System Services, Inc.

Alone Is Not Lonely
Halloween Harvest
("A Place at the Table")
A Place at the Table

Millersburg Magick Mysteries

Spells and Sleuths
Fae and Felonies
Magick and Murder
Feline Navidad

Soccer Moms of the Apocalypse

Pestilence in Pumpkin Spice
Famine in French Vanilla
War in White Chocolate
Death in Double Mocha
Demons Run at Halloween

Miscellaneous

Sword and Sorceress 31
("Pig-Headed")
Sword and Sorceress 32
("Unexpected")
Practical Witches
Revenge Served Hot
The Yule Switch
Chocolate for Dinner
Silver Shoes and Pigs' Ears
Snipe Hunt

For updates, news, and giveaways, join Suzan's mailing list at suzanharden.blogspot.com/p/contact-me.html, or visit her website at www.suzanharden.com. You can also check her out on Facebook @SuzanHardenWriter.

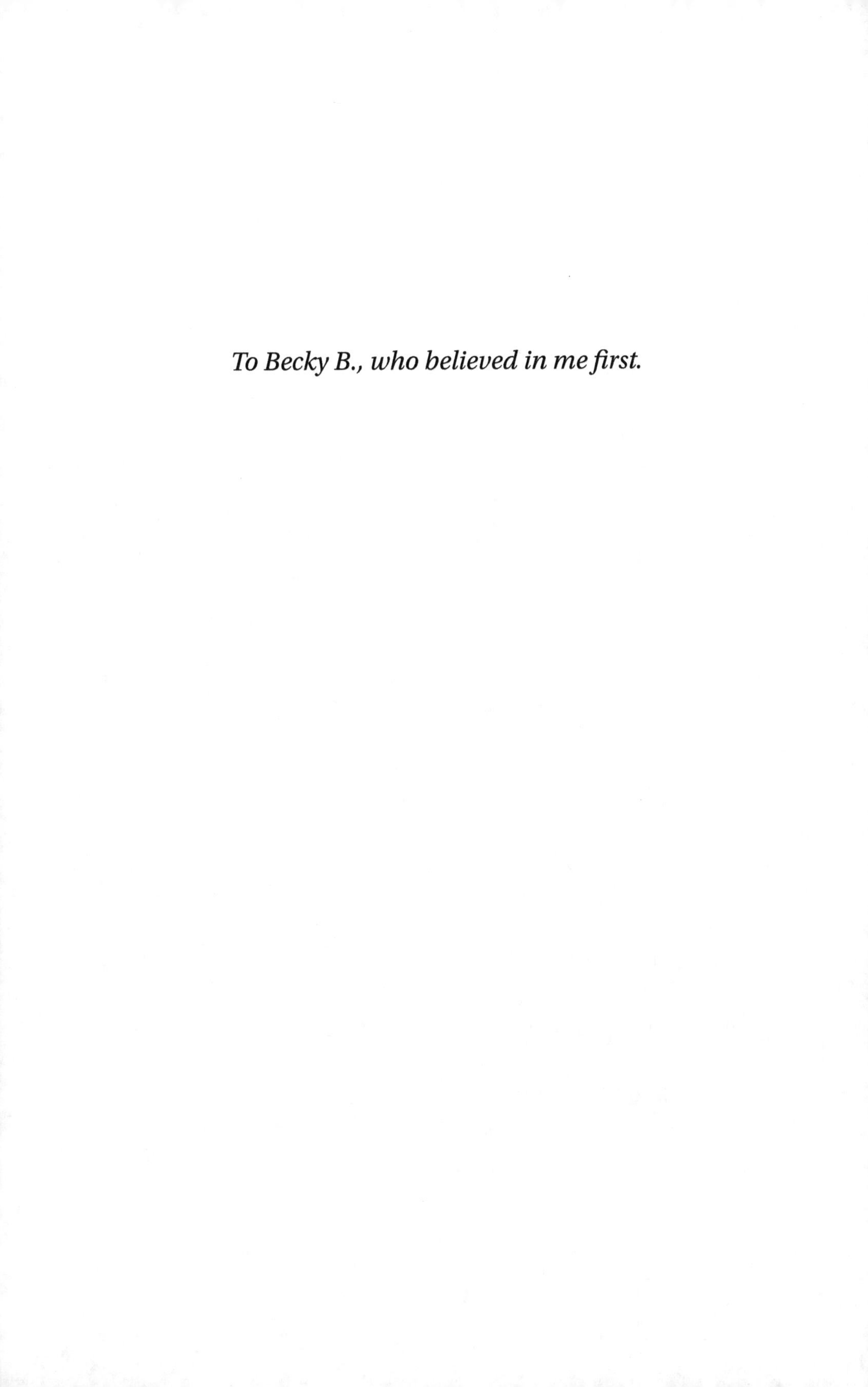

To Becky B., who believed in me first.

Chapter 1

The bang of the auctioneer's gavel sealed the fate of Grandma Petrov's wardrobe. "Sold! To Bidder 665!"

Another wave of grief overwhelmed Dr. Bebe Zachary, not so much at the loss of the furniture, but from missing Grandma. Why had she let things between them fester for so long? Why hadn't she answered Grandma's last letter? She wouldn't be in this mess if she'd simply swallowed her pride.

No great revelation answered her guilty conscience as the auction house staff scurried to roll the huge wardrobe out of the way for the next piece. Soft coughs and murmurs interrupted the stark silence of the exclusive facility, but the heavy burgundy drapes covering the walls muffled even those slight noises.

Swallowing hard, she glanced at the man two rows down who had outbid her. Striking, with olive skin and dark, wavy hair trimmed in a conservative style, he gave her a mock salute. The glint of an overly sharp canine in his smug grin confirmed her suspicions regarding his aura.

Vampire.

Damn. One more problem she didn't need. How was she supposed to get Grandma's Book of Shadows now?

Apprehension sizzled across her nerves. She ignored him and turned her attention to the next item in the catalog, a milk can once used by Harry Houdini. Grandma's quirky obsession with Normal illusionists never ceased to amaze Bebe. Why bother when a witch had real power at her fingertips? But all the magick in the world hadn't changed Grandma's fate.

If only she'd learned of Grandma's death before the human probate judge had ordered Grandma's estate into receivership, an act for which she could thank her asinine cousins and their petty squabbling. Little did the judge know the real fight was over the coven leadership, not the estate assets. Ironically, the half-elven attorney appointed to oversee the estate knew exactly what he had been dumped into. He'd contacted this auction house, since it specialized in serving supernatural folk.

And supernaturals comprised the majority of bidders. The smattering of humans without abilities, aka "Normals," was most likely Family, scoping the estate for their supernatural relatives.

After another half hour, the auction of Grandma's possessions ended as quietly as it had begun. No other members of the Petrov clan had bothered to show. Probably a good thing since Bebe had the urge to turn every one of them into newts.

Grief mingled with anger and regret in her heart as she dodged the confused milling of the crowd after the auction. A quick glance assured her no one watched her while she sidled next to the wardrobe. She could cast a blurring spell to cover her, but the receiver had boasted that the auction house carried the best spell-detection charms available. Jail time and losing her medical license on a possible fraud charge wasn't worth testing the power of said charms.

She eased the door open, and the silky grain of the wood triggered old memories. Years ago, it had been her favorite place to hide, especially after her parents' deaths. The pain had been too much for a child to bear. Now, Grandma was gone, and old wounds she thought long buried ached with fresh agony.

Anger flared again at both Grandma's stubbornness and her two cousins' greed and lust for power. She had been close to both of her cousins once. Damn their idiocy that had forced her to return to San Francisco. She didn't want to be here. She didn't care about the family fortune or about power within the coven. She wanted to be back in Africa. At least Doctors Without Borders didn't consider her a pawn in some stupid game.

She ran a hand along one of the doors smoothed from generations of use and tugged it open. Someone had to retrieve the ancient tome secreted inside the wardrobe. If Grandma's Book fell into the wrong hands, the results would be disastrous—for everyone, not just her family. She stooped to disable the spell that secured the secret compartment at the bottom of the antique.

"What are you doing to my furniture?"

Bebe lost her balance at the unexpected tenor behind her and fell on her butt. Following the gray pinstripe-encased legs upwards, she met the eyes of her bidding foe. Pressure caressed her shields and receded. The weasel had been trying to read her mind the entire auction.

She climbed to her feet, her movements awkward in the straight navy skirt. "If there's something you want to know, then ask me," she snapped.

One of his raven eyebrows rose in amusement. "I believe I did."

She took a deep, nerve-calming breath. "I was examining the piece."

"And why would a White Rose witch be so interested in the interior of her high priestess's wardrobe?"

Oh shit, he knows! I should just go back to the hotel and wash the day away with a bottle of Jack Daniels.

Instead, she shot back, "Why would a West Coast vampire care about a witch's furniture?"

He shrugged, the motion displaying powerful shoulders. His thumb stroked the onyx ankh set in the heavy gold on his left ring finger. "I liked the piece."

"So did I." Tears threatened. Thanks to her family, she had nothing left to remember Grandma except for the photos in her scrapbook.

He sobered and studied her. Again the pressure of his mind against her shields. A tiny thread of triumph ran through her. It would take a master vampire to shatter her protections. Her secret was safe.

He nodded at the wood behind her. "I'll let you buy the wardrobe."

Shock and mistrust ran along her frayed nerves, seasoned with a healthy dose of fear. Bargaining with a vampire was a dangerous proposition. Since her cousins and the coven elders admitted they didn't have Grandma's Book of Shadows, it must still be in the secret compartment. Bebe didn't dare let anyone get his hands on it, including this guy. Of course, his offer to negotiate could be a ruse.

She suppressed a shiver. "And your price?"

"Dinner with me."

She shook her head. Dangerous proposition was an understatement. She could be dinner for him for all she knew, though he didn't come across as a rogue. If he'd been anything but a vampire, she'd be tempted to take him up on his offer. She couldn't remember the last time she'd been on a real date. "How about my last bid and a couple of cover spells for your coffin?" she countered.

He chuckled at her forced attitude, the timbre sending a shiver of awareness down her spine. The bastard couldn't seduce her if he couldn't get past her shields, and she wasn't about to do something so monumentally stupid as drop her mental barriers.

He pulled a gold case from his coat pocket, withdrew a business card and held it out to her. She matched his unblinking gaze, her arms firmly at her sides. No power on earth could make her take that damn bit of cardboard.

One heartbeat passed. Then another.

Why wouldn't he leave so she could retrieve the Book? All she needed was a few seconds.

With a faint quirk of his full lips, he slid the card into the vee formed by the buttons of her tailored blouse, brushing the crest of her breast with his fingertips. His brazenness shocked any comeback right out of her head.

"If you change your mind, call me." He nodded and sauntered off into the crowd.

She turned back to the wardrobe, only to see the auction house staff cart it into the back in preparation for shipping. There was no way to access the compartment now, not without a lot of questions. Frustration at her lost opportunity welled up inside her.

She pulled the vampire's card out of her shirt with the intention of ripping it to shreds. Horror engulfed her at the name engraved in raised black ink. Caesar Augustine. Not any vampire, but the freakin' master of the western half of the U.S.

She squeezed her eyes shut. Both she and the rest of the witches were royally screwed.

Chapter 2

Caesar Augustine stood back while the movers unwrapped the antique cedar. He inhaled the spicy odor of the wood. Unmistakably Lebanese. Pieces like this weren't crafted anymore. Hades, trees like this weren't even grown anymore. He dismissed the workers with a wave. The men snatched their straps and quilts and scurried out of the room.

He shook his head at their anxious haste. *Normals.*

The polished surfaces gleamed under the recessed lighting in his office. Anticipation racing in his blood, he opened the doors. The little witch at the auction house had been interested in something inside, but the interior of the wardrobe was bare. Not even the faint scent of Natasha Petrov's favorite lavender perfume graced the wood.

He quelled the brief swell of grief at Natasha's death. She had been one of the few people he had called friend. He ignored the tiny voice that reminded him she was one of his few friends in the two thousand plus years of his existence. Not for one moment did he believe her overdose of heart medication was accidental. And if what he suspected were true, the killer would be after the named heir to Natasha's position within White Rose, her granddaughter Bebe.

He released the breath he had been holding as he ran his fingers over the interior wood. There wasn't a whole lot left in this gods-forsaken world he cared about, but he owed Natasha. For her efforts in finding a cure for his blasted disease, if nothing else. A disturbing thought wormed its way through his consciousness. Had the witch at the auction been searching for Natasha's missing notes as well?

No, he couldn't dwell on such selfishness. Honor demanded that he pursue Natasha's murderer. And the minimum he could do for his friend was protect her granddaughter from the assassin, even though he hadn't seen the child since the day of her parents' funerals.

At least, the child had been able to go to her parents' funerals. At least, her parents had the grace of dying by someone else's hand instead of their own. At least, little Bebe had someone who gave a fuck about her instead of being handed over to a sadistic bitch—

He shut down that line of thinking with practiced effort. His parents and half-brothers had been dead for over two millennia. Dwelling on it wouldn't help him locate Natasha's granddaughter or discover what the witch at the auction was trying to do.

He sucked in a breath when he found an indentation in the wood. No, the dip was a worn spot from decades of use.

Air whistled between his teeth in exasperation over his current dilemma. Tracking Natasha's estranged granddaughter down was proving problematic with the current unrest in Central Africa. He'd ordered his sister, Selene, to send her hired eclectic, Lucien, in the hopes the girl would be more receptive to another witch, even if he were covenless. But so far, Lucien hadn't found the girl.

Maybe he should have shown his hand and asked the little witch at the auction.

The woman had been the only White Rose member to bother showing up at the sale of Natasha's estate, the silver flower-shaped stud in her right ear the only sign of her affiliation. He couldn't tell if she was one of the conspirators that Natasha had suspected, but she was definitely one of Natasha's students. He hadn't been able to penetrate her mental shields even with direct eye contact.

He smiled at the scene she had made when he caught her, firm heart-shaped behind in the air as she poked around the bottom of the wardrobe. She wasn't a classic beauty, but her bosom had complemented her behind. And she had blushed when his fingertips had grazed her breast when he placed his business card inside her shirt.

The fact she was flustered by his touch coupled with her un-enhanced breasts amazed him. Few women were that innocent and real in this day and age. The desire for more than the brief touch of her soft skin caught him off guard.

Pushing thoughts of the little witch out of his head, he knelt and ran his hand along the bottom. Nothing unusual presented itself to his touch, only cedar smoothed from years of use. He frowned. She had definitely been looking for something. He knocked on the bottom panel, but no echo indicated that a hollow space lay beneath.

Sitting back on his heels, he stared at the piece. The dark interior of the wardrobe sucked all light out of the room. Even his virus-enhanced vision had difficulty distinguishing individual boards. Good thing he had anticipated such problems.

Grabbing the flashlight and toolbox from his desk, he crouched before the wardrobe again and aimed the light inside. With a careful touch, he probed the wood. No catches, but who knew what booby-traps Natasha may have set. The woman had grown cannier with each passing decade. Pushing his head and chest further into the interior, he ran the beam over each seam and peg.

"That's an undignified position for a prince."

Caesar jerked at Ptolemy's voice behind him and banged his elbow against the right door. Unfortunately with vampire speed and strength, the heavy cedar whiplashed into his right temple as he tried to extricate himself. Rubbing his head, he sat back and glared at his snickering brother.

"Glad I'm entertaining you." Annoyed, Caesar rose and brushed packing dust off his polo and khakis.

Ptolemy's snicker turned into outright laughter. "Better than any gladiator. Did you find anything?"

Caesar shook his head. "Not yet. This was the only piece the White Rose witch at the auction was interested in." He cocked an eye at Ptolemy. "Please tell me you've identified her from the photo I e-mailed you." Hellfire, what he would've given for a smart phone camera centuries ago when he was in Rome.

Ptolemy's expression grew serious. "You aren't going to like this."

"We've got a potential coven war brewing. I already don't like it," he snapped.

"She's Bebe Zachary."

Caesar clenched his fists. "When did she get back in the country?"

The last time he had seen her, she had been a child of eleven. Still, he cursed himself for not recognizing the fiery woman at the auction house.

Ptolemy shrugged. "Don't know. She didn't fly in, or she would have shown up on the Homeland Security airline database. She had to have crossed the Mexican or Canadian border by car. With the paperwork backlog at the crossings, she may have been in the country for up to three weeks."

Caesar groaned. Not only had he made a pass at Natasha's granddaughter, now he couldn't even protect her as he had promised because he had no clue where she was. "Have Anne start working the streets. Send anyone we can spare with her. And have Stan come see me before he leaves for the night."

Ptolemy pivoted on his heel and left to execute his orders.

Caesar closed his eyes and whispered a prayer that his people found Bebe before Natasha's assassin did.

Chapter 3

Bebe eased the dingy hotel curtain aside and peeked out. Night fell early this close to Yule. Red and green lights twinkled in counterpoint with blue and silver tinsel in the shops across the street from her hotel room, the color a half-hearted attempt to drive away the desperation that seeped into the very air of this downtrodden section of San Francisco. Tiny, who had followed her all evening, crouched in the alley between two of the storefronts with her shabby coat pulled tight against the winter chill. The vampire girl couldn't have been much more than sixteen when she was Turned, and Goddess only knew how long ago that had been. Only the faint red haze overlying Tiny's natural green aura gave any indication that she was a vampire and not one of the homeless kids roaming the area.

Bebe let the yellowed fabric drop back into place. The tail didn't make sense. If Augustine had Grandma's Book of Shadows, why bother with her?

A small quiver of relief rippled through her. He hadn't found it yet. Or else hadn't figured out how to open the compartment without destroying the contents.

The furniture in her one-star hotel didn't leave much room, but she paced the four steps. Walking helped her think, and she definitely needed to plan her next step with care. Between the little vamp today and the brown sedan that shadowed her yesterday, she felt wanted in her hometown.

Not.

She rubbed her temples at the growing tension headache as she tried to work out her plans, cursing the nightmare of Grandma trapped somewhere, screaming for help, that had awoken her before dawn. What she needed was to focus on her real problem, not some stupid dream resulting from her own guilt and remorse. If Augustine's people knew she was here, she needed to find a new hotel before she tried to retrieve Grandma's Book. She sighed in exasperation at yet another delay.

Bebe glanced at the real estate records and building plans on the utilitarian wooden desk. Breaking into a vampire's estate was not the brightest of ideas. She would have to do it in the morning while the vampire household slept. The trick would be getting past the daytime guards. And she hadn't been able to discover what the guards were yet, though fae magic lay thick around the estate. It didn't make sense given the Cold War situation between the fae queens and the Vampire Nation.

Too bad it wasn't Girl Scout cookie season. If she had an excuse for ringing the front doorbell, checking the aura of whoever answered would solve the question.

Reaching over her shoulder, she dug her fingers into the knots at the base of her neck. If she didn't get a grip on her fear, all of the vamps and weres in San Francisco would be pacing outside her window. Goddess, she wished she could contact a friendly face for help, sympathy, anything. But everyone she knew was either too scared or making their own bid for power.

When applied pressure didn't relieve her headache, she rooted through her shoulder bag. Yes, peppermint oil.

A sharp rap at the door sent already fried nerves haywire, and the small vial flew through the air. Before she could search for the oil, a rich, heady essence slammed into her shields, one that seemed very familiar.

Standing on tiptoes to peer through the peephole, her heart stopped. Caesar Augustine raised his fist to knock again.

Frantic, she searched for a weapon. Any weapon. The fiberboard chair wouldn't hurt him. Everything else was bolted to the floor or walls.

Another knock, more insistent than the last. "Dr. Zachary? It's Caesar Augustine. I know you're in there."

A polite vampire. The world really was about to end.

Damn, surrounded and no way out. Even if her acrophobia allowed her to try the fire escape, Tiny would grab her before she climbed down one floor.

His firm knocks grew louder. "Dr. Zachary, would you please open the door? I only wish to speak with you."

With a deep gulp of air, she concentrated until a decent-sized fireball glowed in her hand. She flung the door open. "Make it quick or I'm having barbeque for dinner."

As impeccably dressed as yesterday, he eyed her with obvious amusement in his expression. "So if I don't make it quick, you're accepting my invitation?"

She glared at him.

"The hotel sprinklers will be set off in another minute if you don't put that out."

She hated to admit he was right. Displaying her abilities in public was never smart. Grandma had drilled that into her head for the entire twenty-eight years of her life. She clenched her hand to extinguish the witchfire.

He brushed past her into the room, acting like royalty. Very good-looking royalty, with a vampire's signature sandalwood scent drifting in his wake. Not for the first time, she wished all the myths about vampires needing an invitation were true. Vampires were jerky, conceited, and dangerous, but not true supernaturals. A freaking virus from 10,000 years ago had created them, not magick, but lack of the occult arts didn't make them any less deadly a foe. He paused at the token desk.

Oh, shit!

The bottom dropped out of her stomach.

He shuffled through the diagrams of his estate lying on the desk then glanced up with a smirk. "If you want to see something, just ask me."

Her eyes closed in resignation. Her marvelous plan for B&E had crashed and burned because she was too damn tired and panicked to think clearly enough to shove some blueprints under the bed.

He didn't wait for her reply. "You really should stick with practicing medicine, Dr. Zachary. I don't believe you're cut out for espionage."

Her eyes snapped open. "Thank you, Mr. Augustine. I'll take your career advice under consideration." She waved toward the door she still held open. "Now that you've done your civic duty, why don't you find someone else to annoy?"

Ignoring her, he flipped through what passed for the room service menu before tossing it back on the desk. "I'd prefer a private venue for our discussion, but I will not subject a lady to swill." He picked up her coat lying on the bed and held it open. "There's an excellent restaurant a few blocks from here."

"I am not going anywhere with you," she said and tried to look as stern as possible. Normally, she could hold her own with anyone. She wouldn't have survived medical school otherwise, but this man's audacity rivaled her worst professor's.

And she wasn't about to go anywhere alone with a vampire. Especially not a conceited, rather attractive . . .

She squashed that disturbing thought.

Her nerves were so wired she jumped when his jacket pocket emitted soft beeps. He frowned, jerked out an older model cell phone and barked, "What? When?" before snapping it shut. He thrust the old gray trench coat at her. "Get your coat on now, Doctor."

"No." She shook her head. "You can't order me around like I'm one of your minions."

Pressure smacked her shields. He wasn't even pretending to be subtle. "Get. Your. Coat. On. Now."

"And I said no." Her arms crossed over her chest of their own accord. Between her family and the Council of Elders, she'd had more than enough of people trying to bully her.

Big mistake. Augustine stalked towards her. There was no time to conjure a fireball, but she could deliver a mean kick if she had to. She shrank against the open door, but he poked his head through the doorway instead. He muttered something under his breath she was pretty sure translated to "manure" in Latin. Wrenching the door from her death grip, he slammed it shut and pushed her towards the window.

"Out the fire escape." When she hesitated, he roared, "Now!"

Blood hummed in her ears, and she scrambled around the bed. When she bent to push up the sash, the pane exploded in a storm of shards.

Caesar shoved her down in the middle of broken glass and filthy carpet and threw himself on top. She opened her mouth to yell at him. Then she realized the muffled thuds and grunts were bullets hitting him.

Terror ripped through her as easily as the glass slicing into her palms and knees. Her attempted objection to his rough handling morphed into a scream. One of this stupid vampire's enemies had to have followed him, and now she'd be the innocent victim of some screwed up vamp vendetta.

The firecracker sounds paused. In one fluid motion, Augustine was on his feet and lifting her through the ruined window. She peered back. Holes winked at her from what was left of the hotel room door.

She didn't have time to think about who was shooting from the hallway. Augustine threw her over his shoulder. Vertigo roiled her empty stomach, not aided by the fact she was hanging upside down. Damn, where was her peppermint oil when she really needed it? He climbed down the escape so fast, all she could do was squeeze her eyes shut, hang on to his coat and belt for dear life, and pray she wouldn't puke on his custom tailored suit. She sure couldn't afford to replace the darn thing.

A solid jolt popped her eyes open. They were on the pavement, but Augustine didn't stop. He raced down the street. Each step rammed his shoulder into her already protesting stomach, but the shouts from above froze her blood.

I'm going to get shot in the back while hanging upside down from an arrogant asshole's shoulder.

As if reading her mind, one more bullet pinged off the pavement. She glanced up to see Tiny running behind them. Except the female vampire didn't have a gun.

Bebe's chin smacked Augustine's back at his abrupt halt, making her bite her tongue. He tossed her across the seat of some large vehicle before throwing himself on top of her once again. Tires squealed as whoever drove sped away from the hotel.

The adrenaline surge eased off, but her attempt at a deep, calming breath was impeded by the hunky vampire splayed over her chest. "You can get off of me now." She shoved at Augustine's chest, but she could have been pushing a granite boulder for all the good it did.

"I don't know. I rather like this position." He rose slightly to look at her. His eyes gleamed fluorescent yellow in the darkness.

Her heartbeat tripped double-time at the sudden awareness of his body against hers. Nipples tightened from the press of his chest. Liquid warmth pooled where his thigh lodged between hers. Breath caught in her throat, refusing to fill her lungs for fear he'd realize his affect. His lips were so close. All he had to do was . . .

"Hey, if you two are going to mack in the back, can you wait until Anne and I are out of the Hummer? I *don't* need the PDA tonight."

She reached out mentally. The harsh coppery texture of his shields and the rich scent of sandalwood confirmed the man guiding the Hummer through the streets was another vampire. Underneath the copper was a burnt toast taste, the vamp's personal signature, but she couldn't get past his shields to pick up specific thoughts.

Augustine chuckled and pulled her up with him, somehow managing to sit her so she didn't give the driver a Sharon Stone in the rearview mirror. Why the hell hadn't she put on jeans when she returned to her hotel room earlier?

"How many times were you hit, Caesar?" The tiny vampire, who must be Anne, peered over the front seat.

"I lost count," he said with a dry tone.

"Oh, damn," Bebe muttered. Under the passing streetlights, she realized his cashmere turtleneck was no longer the pristine cream it had been in her hotel room. She ran fingertips over his chest, ignoring the blood, and searched for exit wounds.

She gasped when Augustine grasped her hands tight against hard muscle. "Sweetheart, as much I love what you're doing, trust me. Most of the bullets are still in me." A wicked smirk lit his face. "And with my blood covering you, you make too much of a tempting snack as it is."

She looked down. The blood staining her navy sweater was invisible in the darkness, but the sticky wetness against her skin gave her no doubt that her bra was ruined as well.

Her gaze returned to the glowing eyes that regarded her. "We've got to get them out." She wasn't a weapons expert, but she had done her stint in an ER during med school. If Augustine's enemies had shot him with some kind of explosive bullet, even the vampire virus wouldn't be able to heal him fast enough. The metal obviously wasn't silver, or he'd already have gone into anaphylactic shock.

"Do you have a safe house?" she asked.

Anne answered. "We have an adequate medical facility at the mansion." When Bebe twisted to face her, the female's eyes were glowing gold as well and her fangs were fully extended. A quick flick of her gaze to the rearview mirror revealed the driver in similar straits. Augustine's wounds were triggering the bloodlust of every vamp in the vehicle. And she was the only tasty treat inside.

Self-preservation overrode her desire to render medical aid. She silently berated herself for forgetting who she was with as she inched towards the door.

Augustine's hand shot out and grabbed her wrist before she could lunge for the handle. "We've gone to a great deal of trouble protecting your cute little behind. I would *not* appreciate you killing yourself by jumping from my SUV."

She hissed in pain, not so much from his strength but from his thumb grinding into a cut on her palm. He yanked her palm closer to examine it, and the pressure of his thumb eased from the sliced skin.

"Shit," he muttered. Faster than she could follow, he seized her other hand as well. "You're going to need stitches yourself, Doctor."

Shit was an understatement. She had been touching his chest. His chest with his contaminated blood . . .

Anne leaned over the seat to study her hands and wrists as well. "It doesn't look like you severed any tendons or ligaments." The smile Anne gave her would have been sweet if not for the fangs. "We'll make sure there's no shards still in the cuts and get those cleaned up in a jiffy."

Her words jolted Bebe out of the threatening bout of panic. Jiffy? What kind of vampire says jiffy?

Nothing was making sense anymore. The vampires she rode with hadn't attacked her despite the blood oozing from both her and Augustine. He still held her hands, and his gentle strokes sent strange tremors through her body. Her stomach clenched with nausea that had nothing to do with her vertigo. She may have contracted the vampire virus in the last few minutes. Then there were the gunmen at the hotel. If they were after Augustine, why did he bother taking her with him?

His earlier words about saving her hit her addled neurons like a Mack truck. "Those men were after you," she said. Passing streetlights revealed no change in Augustine's stoic expression. Two more blocks passed before she gathered the courage to add, "Weren't they?" She loathed the quiver in her voice, but it was more desirable than tears.

"No, Doctor, they were after you."

"But why?" she squeaked. "And why do you care?"

He exhaled, a long drawn-out affair, and shifted to stare at the traffic. Her father had made the same sound when he prayed for patience after she'd done something particularly annoying. The sharp pain at the memory of her parents jabbed through her soul as it always did. Ironic that she sat in a vehicle with creatures just like the ones that had killed them.

When he faced her again, his eyes had dulled to a faint amber. "You already know why those men were trying to assassinate you, Doctor, so please don't play coy with me. As for why I care—"

He drew a sharp breath as if pain racked him.

"It's because Natasha asked me."

Chapter 4

Bebe wouldn't have been more shocked if Augustine claimed he was the pope. Her grandmother's given name from a vampire's lips? And he spoke as if he and Grandma were more than acquaintances. "I–I don't know what you're talking about."

"I said don't play games—" Another shudder racked Augustine. "I said—" The whispered words barely made it out of his mouth when the convulsions took him.

"Caesar?"

Bebe glanced at the rearview mirror. Raw fright shone from the driver's eyes, matching the gruff tone of his voice. "How close are we?" she asked.

"Another couple of minutes," Anne said.

Years of training took over. She pulled Augustine over her lap to keep him from further banging his head against the reinforced doorframe. She'd never seen a vampire choke on his own vomit, but she struggled to turn him over anyway. Seeing what Bebe was trying to do, Anne single-handedly flopped Augustine on his side.

"What's wrong with him?" Panic scarred the driver's voice.

Horns blared, and Anne yanked the steering wheel hard to get the Hummer back on the right side of the street. "Dammit, Ptolemy, pay attention!"

"He's going into shock. The bullets may be time-released with some kind of compound." Experience forced Bebe to shove her personal feelings aside. She pressed her fingers against Augustine's neck, seeking a pulse. A faint rhythm existed but it was far too erratic, even for a vampire.

Tires screeched in protest as Ptolemy whipped the vehicle into a long driveway. Bebe winced when the barely open gates caught the sides of the Hummer with a nails-on-chalkboard screech. Augustine's seizure stopped as they cleared the ornate ironwork.

A shiver of fear ran through her. What would the other vamps do to her without their master to keep them in check?

The unconscious vampire's weight was the only thing that kept her in her seat when Ptolemy slammed the brakes once the vehicle was inside the attached garage. He was out the door and pulling Augustine from her lap before the rebound bounced her against the back of the seat. After an instant of hesitation, she scrambled out and followed the vampires into the main house. She couldn't violate her Hippocratic Oath even if the patient was a blood-sucking fiend.

Who happened to save her life.

"What in tarnation!"

Another male vampire jumped up from the table where he'd been sitting when the little group charged through the huge kitchen. Bebe spared him no more than a cursory glance. She followed Ptolemy down a hallway into a brightly lit room. The infirmary was small but well-appointed, the equivalent of the after-hours clinics scattered throughout the city.

He laid Augustine face down on the exam table, his manner gentle despite the fear rolling off him. Anne was already cutting away the ruined sweater. Their practiced ease scared the daylights out of Bebe.

The new vampire pushed his way past her. Tall and blond, the vampire had probably used his looks and Texas accent to lure many women to their doom.

Damn. She should leave now while the three vampires were occupied with Augustine's injuries. She bit her tongue. Augustine had saved her life from the gunmen. She couldn't leave, not until she knew he'd be okay.

The new vamp seized a metal probe off the instrument tray. "Shit, I thought y'all were just taking the witch out to dinner."

"Some hitters had other ideas," Ptolemy said.

The new vampire chuckled. "You've watched *The Whole Nine Yards* one too many times." He surveyed the damage to Augustine and glanced up. "Your brother will be fine, Ptolemy."

That explained Ptolemy's excessive worry. Biological siblings in the vampire community were rare, but they did exist. And they didn't take a family member's death lightly. Another shiver of fear gripped her.

The new vampire eyed her before he grinned. "I'm Alex, by the way." He turned back to his injured master and poked the probe into Augustine's shoulder. "This is going to sting." He eased out the first bullet and frowned at it. "Not silver. Why's he out cold?"

Bebe edged closer to the table. "Probably laced with garlic. He went into convulsions on the way here." At her words, another seizure racked Augustine. This one lasted barely a minute.

"Fuck," Alex said under his breath. A new sense of urgency flared in his voice. "Ptolemy, you're going to have to hold him down, or I won't get these blasted things out in time."

"I can help." She stepped forward and reached for another set of instruments, only to hiss in pain again as Ptolemy grabbed her injured hand.

"Let me see." Alex examined her sliced up palm when Ptolemy yanked her closer to them. Alex looked at her with a strange mix of worry and admiration. "The last thing you need is to mix his blood with yours and accidentally Turn."

She met his gaze and sighed, resigned to her fate. "It's a little late for that." If she were infected, if she survived the transformation, she'd probably wake up a raving lunatic.

"Aw, shit." Alex closed his eyes for a split second. "Anne, get her washed and stitched up." Before Bebe could protest, he added, "And find her some of those latex gloves. I'll need the help." His blue eyes carried a naked mourning as he regarded Bebe. "Might as well make the doc's last hours with the living useful."

Despite his pronouncement of doom, a prickle of pride ran through her. Someone here took her seriously.

With terrifying strength, the tiny vamp tugged Bebe over to the sink. The warm water stung almost as much as the anti-bacterial soap Anne lathered over the main slice in Bebe's right palm and the multitude of tiny nicks on both hands. Anne peered at the cut. "No foreign objects and the blood's still flowing." She smiled at Bebe, a small hopeful smile. "There's a good chance you haven't been infected. We can test you in the morning."

Bebe snorted. "Assuming I don't go into a coma tonight."

The vamp shrugged and turned off the faucet. "There's that possibility."

Bebe ran through the initial symptoms of the vampire virus: dizziness, irritability, nausea, and abnormal pain and tenderness around the entry site of the infection. That pretty much ran the gamut of what she was feeling now. Goddess, she didn't want to think about what she could turn into. The vampires may not have a choice about killing her.

She blinked in surprise and looked down at her hand. Anne was already tying off the final knot. With precision, the vamp clipped the suture and handed a pair of surgical gloves and goggles to Bebe.

Anne rummaged in the cabinet before pulling out a bottle of Midol. "I'm afraid this all we have in terms of over-the-counter pain relievers."

Bebe cocked a puzzled eyebrow at the vamp, who shrugged again and smiled, this time in true humor. "They're not mine. Tiffany left it here when she came up during summer vacation." When Bebe's other eyebrow rose to join the first, Anne said, "Tiffany's Family."

Family with a capital "F." Bebe considered Anne's words as she snagged the pair of pills from the vamp's hand and swallowed them dry. So a member of Augustine's coven was young enough to have living Family running around. What surprised her was that the girl was allowed to associate with vampires. Someone needed to have a long talk with her parents. She pulled the goggles over her eyes.

"Are you two finished? We need some help here!"

Another seizure gripped Augustine, so strong that the two male vamps were having trouble keeping him on the exam table. Anne rushed over and flung herself on the unconscious Augustine's legs.

Bebe snapped the gloves on and snatched the bloody probe that Alex had dropped on the tray. A quick count showed he had extracted ten bullets. "How many more?"

"Four." Alex grunted, doing his damnedest to keep Augustine's right shoulder down. "Watch it. I found two explosive rounds."

Her night was getting *so* much better. No, she should count herself lucky. The damn things could have blown up already. And she'd been in close proximity to Augustine the whole time.

One entry wound was uncomfortably close to the lower spine. If he was a normal human and this was a real hospital, she'd send him up to surgery. A little anesthesia would do wonders. But no, she couldn't get that lucky.

The holes where Alex had already removed the bullets were trying to close, but the healing was slow compared to the usual vamp's ability. Sucking in a deep breath, she dealt with the most difficult one first. The metal instrument struck something hard, and she pulled it out.

Damn, a bone fragment.

She dropped it in the tray with a clatter. Augustine's thrashing did not help her concentration. Chewing on her lower lip to distract her from the aches in her hands, she reached back into Augustine's mangled body with the probe. This time there was a definite metal-on-metal clink.

Careful, careful.

She eased the bullet out, and she nearly choked on her own spit. The explosive round was unmistakable. Gently, she set it in the tray.

"Come on, Doc. You've got three more to go," Alex muttered.

"She's taking too long."

She looked up to see Ptolemy glaring at her, eyes still glowing and fangs halfway extended. His partial vamp-out didn't help her nerves at all.

"Do you think your virus will repair all the damage if one of those things goes off inside him?" Bebe snapped.

"With all due respect, Your Highness, shut up and let her work." Anne's tone was polite even if her words to Ptolemy weren't.

Ignoring the vamps, Bebe felt inside the next bullet wound. Bingo.

Working methodically, she removed the last two. Augustine's body gave one last shudder and stilled. She laid two fingers on Augustine's neck. He had a slow, weak pulse, but he had one.

She met Alex's worried gaze. "Do you have any epinephrine?"

"For the anaphylactic shock?" He shook his head. "Nope. Stuff doesn't do jack for us. All we can do is remove the problem and hope for the best."

"And you'd better pray to your gods that my brother survives, witch." The expression on Ptolemy's face promised her hell on earth if anything happened to Augustine.

Swallowing her own fear, Bebe met his threatening stare. "I didn't invite him for a social visit, Your Highness."

Her sarcastic edge on his title wasn't lost on Ptolemy. His eyes, so much like Augustine's rich brown ones, narrowed, but he remained silent. That scared her more that any verbal threat he could deliver. No one outside of these vampires knew where she was. She could be drained before she could blink, and nobody would ever find her body.

"Now, Ptolemy, play nice and use your company manners for once," Alex said. He turned and winked at Bebe before he headed to the sink to wash Augustine's blood off his hands.

Ignoring Ptolemy's menacing stance, she turned to Anne. "Do you have a pressure cuff?"

The girl nodded and pulled one from another cupboard.

Girl. Bebe winced at her assumption of the vampire's age based on her appearance. Anne was hardly the homeless waif she appeared and could be thousands of years old for all Bebe knew. The last thing she needed was to underestimate these people.

Bebe gingerly pulled off her gloves before she took the cuff from Anne's outstretched hand and wrapped it around Augustine's well-formed bicep. She shoved away the memory of that arm wrapped around her, protecting her from the hail of bullets. She sighed in satisfaction when his blood pressure registered normal. Well, normal for a vamp. She reached for his neck again. This time his pulse was a strong, steady forty.

Without the garlic-laced bullets to impede the virus, the holes sealed themselves in four minutes. By five, not even a scar showed on his skin. She shook her head in amazement.

Alex eyed Augustine's back as he wiped his hands with a towel, then grinned at her. "Good work, Doc." He held out a platter-sized palm.

She gave him an apologetic smile and displayed her stitches. "If you don't mind, can we pass on the high-fives for a couple of days?"

"Sorry." He bent closer to examine her stitched cuts. "Anne does a mighty fine job with a sewing needle, doesn't she?" He waved Anne closer. "Let's roll him over, or our boy's going to wake up with a mighty stiff neck."

"You'll take him to his room," Ptolemy said.

Bebe had forgotten he was in the room though she wasn't sure how. "No." Maybe medical ethics overrode her common sense, but Bebe didn't back down from the haughty glare Ptolemy gave her. He was no longer the scared kid from the Hummer, but someone who expected his orders to be obeyed.

"Lady's right, Ptolemy. Why don't you two get some rest? We'll keep an eye on him and holler if there's a problem."

Ptolemy stiffened. "I don't take orders from you, Stanton."

Bebe shifted her gaze between the two men. Now, she had a last name to go with Alex. And by his relaxed stance, he didn't seem all that intimidated by the other vampire's posturing.

"No one's ordering you, Your Highness." Anne's soft voice sounded as if she had to smooth ruffled feathers on a regular basis. "Dr. Zachary has the medical expertise, and Alex can advise her on any peculiarities regarding our physiology."

"Very well. Keep me apprised." Ptolemy shot Bebe another nasty glare. "You would best hope that Stanton's faith in you is not misplaced." He turned and stalked out of the room. No if-then threats from this guy. He probably got that lesson from his brother.

Anne gave her an apologetic look and mouthed, "Thank you," before following him out of the room.

Bebe sighed in relief. Maybe she'd survive the night after all. She turned to the remaining vampire. "By the way, Alex Stanton, I'm Bebe Zachary. Nice to meet you." Not that he didn't already know who she was, but a few manners never hurt.

Alex grinned in response and gave a mock tipping of an invisible hat. "Pleasure, ma'am."

After waiting a few heartbeats to make sure vampiric hearing outside of the room wouldn't catch her next words, she whispered, "Does Ptolemy always have a broomstick shoved up his ass?"

Alex laughed, displaying very sharp and very white canines. " 'Fraid so. Hope he didn't offend you too much. He tends to act like a real pisser when it comes to his brother." He placed his fingers against Augustine's neck. With a satisfied nod, he crossed to the mini-fridge and pulled out a plastic pint bag of blood. With a practiced manner, he set up the IV and inserted the needle into his master's arm.

Remembering his earlier skill, curiosity burned in her. "Where'd you go to medical school?"

He glanced up, surprise on his face before he resumed taping down the IV tube. "I did a year at Johns Hopkins, but medicine wasn't where my heart was." He chuckled and waved at the IV. "Of course, medical school was nowhere near as complicated back in 1876."

"You're young for a vampire," she commented.

Alex shrugged. "All depends on your perspective. Anne says I'm ancient because I remember the Civil War." He grinned at the unconscious Augustine. "Caesar here thinks I'm a snot-nosed brat because I haven't had a personal conversation with Jesus Christ."

Bebe returned his smile. "And he has?"

Alex shrugged again and checked the IV line. "Claims he has. I wasn't there."

She looked down at the unconscious vampire. Augustine's aquiline features could be Roman. He definitely had a Mediterranean cast in his coloring. He wasn't drop-dead gorgeous by today's blow-dried and gelled standards, but he was . . . well, compelling would be the best way to put it. In sleep, he had a certain serenity. "Shouldn't he be awake by now?"

She glanced up when Alex snorted, anger surfacing on his face.

"Between the blood loss and the tissue damage, I'd expect him to be out for a couple of hours. With the garlic, it'll take a hell of a lot longer. All we can do is give him a couple of pints and see what happens," he said, concern softening his tone.

"Don't you have a, um, vampire physician to consult with?"

"Darlin', I'm pretty much it." Alex laughed. "Besides, unless our heads come off or we get staked through the heart, there ain't too much we don't recover from."

"What about explosive bullets or dirty nukes?" She smiled sweetly.

"Well, there is that," he conceded with another chuckle. "Why don't I show you a room, and you try to get some sleep?"

Bebe shook her head. "I'll stay here. Not that I don't trust you—" They both smiled at her obvious lie. "But I'm the closest thing you've got to help right now."

He nodded in acquiescence. "I'll go find us a couple of decent chairs."

Waiting for his return, she paced next to the unconscious Augustine. She should leave now. The smart thing would be to slip out of the mansion, head back to her hotel and try to retrieve her purse. Augustine's place was in a decent neighborhood. She could probably get a cab despite the late hour.

She wrapped her arms around her. No, she couldn't leave. At least, not yet. This would be her only chance to search for Grandma's wardrobe and retrieve her Book. Now that the vampires knew who she was and where she was, she wouldn't get another opportunity.

She glanced at the man on the table and tried to quell an even more disturbing thought. He had saved her life tonight. She had a duty to make sure he survived—beyond her Hippocratic Oath, beyond his brother's unspoken threat. Pretending that her motive was purely selfish did no good when strains of the Stones' "Sympathy for the Devil" ran through her head, mocking her.

Caesar awoke with a start. The dim bedside light could have been a million-watt halogen thanks to the obscene headache that pounded his skull. He checked the luminous display on the clock next to his bed. After sundown, but sundown on what day?

He peered through squinted eyes around the room. He was in his own bed in the San Francisco mansion. Better than dead and the flesh melting from his bones. Instinct warned of another presence. Then he noticed the glossy dark hair that flowed across his comforter.

He frowned and reached for the locks. The muscles in his arm burned like they had in the old days after one of his older brother's taxing sword lessons. Brushing the silky curls aside, the face of Bebe Zachary appeared, her cheek resting on her crossed arms. The rest of her remained in the chair pulled close to his bed.

In sleep, she looked innocent and peaceful, not the frightened, angry and very stubborn young witch who seemed hell bent on making his life difficult. He smiled and continued to stroke her hair. She was so much like Natasha, but there was an emotional vulnerability in her that her grandmother had never possessed. On the other hand, she couldn't have moved him from the Hummer to his bedroom by herself, so presumably she hadn't fried the rest of his household.

Big, brown eyes blinked open, and Bebe jerked herself upright. She wouldn't meet his gaze while she smoothed her wild mane out of her face. "How are you feeling?" Not even waiting for his reply, she busied herself with the blood pressure cuff.

He missed the texture of her soft hair against his fingertips, so he settled for drinking in the sight of her. Instead of the blood soaked clothes she had on earlier, she wore gray sweats and a white t-shirt obviously borrowed from Ptolemy. Her figure was too full to fit into any of Anne's clothes. Not that he objected. Interesting how her nipples perked under his gaze. It was all he could do not to reach for her assets dangling right in front of his face.

Ignoring her question, he asked one of his own. "I take it you don't normally sleep in men's beds?" His teasing was worth the slow blush that crept up her neck and flooded her cheeks. If it wasn't for his enhanced physique, she would have cut his arm off when she yanked the cuff tight. He grunted but managed to keep the smile plastered to his face.

"I'm surprised my people let you stay in here alone."

Still no answer from Bebe, who stared pointedly at her watch as she squeezed the bulb for the cuff.

"I am sorry our dinner plans were interrupted." He gave an exaggerated sigh. "If I'd but known it would be this easy to get you into my bed—"

"You think this is funny?" She ripped the cuff off and impaled him with a ferocious glare. "You think your vampire charm will save you the next time some jerk-off shoots a full clip of garlic-laced explosive bullets into your ass."

"Bet you had fun digging them out." He teased her even though her revelation had his mind churning. The assassins weren't taking any chances. Why else use garlic bullets? Or did they know about his promise to Natasha? Was the culprit one of Natasha's suspected conspirators, or worse, a leak in his own coven?

He needed to keep Bebe out of sight until he knew for sure from whom or what the danger came. And by the way she clenched her fists, keeping the doctor hidden was going to be a problem.

Something was up in that head of hers because she forced herself to calm down and her hands relaxed at her sides. Hades, what he wouldn't give to penetrate her shields. Despite his aching body, his cock stirred at the image of penetration of another type. He blew out a frustrated breath and banished the thought. Fun and games with any non-vampire was definitely out of the question. Bebe might as well have been locked in a chastity belt with the key at the bottom of the Pacific.

"Look, Augustine," she said, totally oblivious to the direction of his mind. She glanced south for an instant before continuing to berate him. He couldn't help the wicked smile that spread across his face. Maybe she wasn't so oblivious after all.

"I appreciate your help last night, even if it's some misguided debt to my grandmother." She crossed her arms over her chest. "If you knew my grandmother, why didn't you introduce yourself at the auction?"

"I wasn't sure who you were. It's not like I could read your mind." And he didn't dare force an attempt now, not if he wanted her trust. She wouldn't accept his protection if she didn't trust him, making an already difficult task a total nightmare. He levered himself slowly into a sitting position, as much to keep from startling her as from the lingering pain from the garlic working itself out of his system. "Once I found out you were Natasha's heir, I tracked you down."

She smirked. "You mean you had Anne track me down."

He nodded. "She's very proficient at finding people who wish to disappear."

Her expression changed to something sad and something else unreadable. What he wouldn't give to know what she was thinking, but he didn't dare touch her body, much less her mind. Not that he feared retaliation at the intrusion, but it would destroy the tenuous link developing between them. The best he could do for the moment was be honest with her.

"If you were that close to Grandma, then you know I refused to be named her heir," she finally said, not meeting his eyes.

Hades, the girl's ignorance of politics was exasperating. He swallowed his irritation. He dared not lose his temper with her. She'd try to run if he did, and the last thing he wanted was to keep her here against her will.

"Did you think it was that simple?" he said, striving to keep his tone even. "Did you really think that denying your heritage would negate your responsibility?" He barely kept himself from cringing when he realized he echoed the same words his twin sister had thrown in his face two millennia ago.

Ire flashed in Bebe's eyes when she met his gaze. "It's not my fault my mother died." She jabbed a finger in his direction. "At the hands of your people I might add. It's not my fault Grandma refused to accept my decision." She dropped the accusing finger and stepped closer to him. "And it's not my fault she didn't name another heir before she died."

An avalanche of resignation crushed Caesar. As much as he hated destroying Bebe's innocent view of the world, some truths needed to be told. "And which one of your cousins was she supposed to trust, Dr. Zachary? The one who poisoned her or the one who tried to shoot you last night?"

Chapter 5

Bebe stepped away from the bed, rage seething through her. No. The bastard was lying. Vampires lie. That was as much a law of nature as the sun rising in the east.

She wasn't about to let him manipulate her. "Is this how you get your jollies, Augustine? Spreading vicious rumors to see what trouble you can cause?" Anger shook her voice despite her efforts. Besides, he was crediting William with lifting a lazy finger to do something. An obvious falsehood.

"I'm not lying about this," he replied with a quiet conviction.

"Both of my cousins know I'm not accepting the leadership of White Rose coven. I've already tendered my formal withdrawal to the Elders. There's no reason to kill me." She couldn't stop the venom in her voice. She shoved her hands into the soft fleece pockets of her borrowed sweatpants to squelch the urge to fry Augustine in his cream silk sheets.

"A withdrawal the Elders refused to accept."

Her face heated at his blatant statement of fact. How the hell had he known about her encounter with the Council of Elders? Had he slipped into her thoughts when she'd fallen asleep? She checked her shields then breathed a silent prayer of relief that they were intact. So how had Augustine discovered what happened between her and the Elders?

More anger flared at the memory of their bullying tactics, and she lifted her chin. "They can't force me to accept responsibility for our coven, so there's no motive for either William or Alice to want me dead. Care to revise your story, Mr. Augustine?"

Dark circles swam under his hazel eyes, and he released a weary breath. "What about your grandmother's suspicions? Natasha contacted me when you refused to answered her letters. She had reason to believe that someone was trying to kill both her and you in an attempt to seize power within your coven."

Sure, Bebe had some close calls over the past few years. The epileptic driver that nearly mowed her down at UCLA. The snapped cable in the elevator in New York, which hadn't helped her fear of heights one bit. Heck, even the Frisbee that gave her the concussion at Golden Gate Park had all been accidents.

Except there had been more accidents lately. The kid who mugged her at the Nairobi airport. The bus from Mexico losing its airbrakes pulling into San Diego.

Oh, Goddess, now she was beginning to be as paranoid as Grandma Petrov!

Deliberately forcing down her anger, she considered her options. Maybe sheer logic would shake Augustine. "My position with Doctors Without Borders is risky in itself. Grandma blew stuff out of proportion every time she read about a terrorist attack or another civil war breaking out. Has it occurred to you that Mom and Dad's deaths messed with her head? She saw assassins under every bush. Their deaths were the result of sloppy governing." She yanked a hand out of its pocket and jabbed a finger in his direction again. "Which, I might add once more, was your fault for not keeping control over your people!"

"I am sorry rogues killed your parents."

Her accusing finger dropped and clenched into a fist with the rest of her digits. How could he sit there so calm and not even apologize for screwing up his job? She held her breath, but he said nothing else.

"Is that it? Is that all you can say? You're the fucking coven master! It's your responsibility to police any rogues!"

He blinked, but otherwise his face remained as impassive as ever. "I'm not disagreeing with your assessment. I dealt with the problem as soon as I learned of the incidents."

Her fingernails dug into her palms. Goddess, she never wanted to hit someone so bad in her life. "Incident? Is that what you call my mom being gutted, my father ripped limb from limb? In front of my face!" Her chest heaved, desperate for oxygen. The memories of that night swam in her vision.

"You may not remember but I visited your grandmother the night after your parents died." He gave her that same pitying look that everyone who knew the truth had given her for the last seventeen years. The look that infuriated her. "You hid in Natasha's wardrobe and refused to come out. I offered to erase your memory—"

Bebe gasped at his audacity. There had been someone at the mansion. Someone she'd referred to over the years as the Dark Man because his face had been hidden by shadows. Someone who had promised to take the pain away. Someone Grandma said didn't exist. Grandma had to have mentioned the story to Augustine, but before she could bitch him out for trying to use a childhood fantasy against her, he continued.

"Natasha would not allow me."

"Damn straight, she wouldn't! Assuming you're telling the truth, how could you even think of doing that to a child?"

"And it was better to leave you in that much pain? Pain you're still feeling? Pain you can't let go?" Something twisted in Caesar's expression. Not the fake sympathy everyone else gave her, but almost a shared experience.

For once, she cursed her lack of knowledge of the local vampire hierarchy. Dealing politely with the bastards was one of many reasons she loathed stepping into Grandma's position. "And you think Grandma let go of her pain? What the hell do you think killed her?"

"I think that she was far too young to die of heart failure."

Somehow, Augustine's calm demeanor unnerved her more than his flirtatious innuendos or even his previous attempts to slip past her mental shields. "Grandma was 102."

He gave her a small, sad smile. "And the current life expectancy for your people is 160. Natasha was hardly ancient."

Bebe bit her lip. Damn, he had her there. Defiant, she lashed out. "Grandma's health was never the best as long as I can remember. She always tired easily. It wouldn't take much for her to forget she'd already taken her nitroglycerin."

"Natasha was hardly that incompetent." For the first time, an edge appeared in his tone. "Do you really believe she would have forgotten that she took fifty pills instead of one?"

"What are you trying to insinuate, Augustine? Grandma was many things, but suicidal wasn't one of them."

"For once, we agree, Doctor," he said, dry irony filling his voice.

"Oh goody, that made my day." Bitterness flooded her. "Assuming you're correct and the overdose wasn't accidental, it doesn't mean the guilty culprit was one of my cousins. Grandma had enemies out the wazoo, not to mention so many secrets she couldn't keep track of them all." *Grandma wasn't the only one*, her personal nag reminded her. Ignoring the voice, she continued her rant at Augustine. "She wouldn't have dared to show weakness. Knowing her, she could have hidden how bad her cardio-pulmonary problems really were from everyone for years until they finally caught up to her."

He looked away as if praying for strength. When he turned back to her, his gaze contained an odd combination of steel and sympathy. "Bebe, we both know the real cause of her health problems was her incarceration at Auschwitz. And you're right about one thing. Her work against the Nazis earned her a lot of enemies, but the only ones to profit here and now by both her death and yours would be your cousins."

Her breath whooshed out of her lungs, his words a sucker punch to her psyche. Her memory tumbled back to the awful day of her parents' funeral. She reached for the chair where she'd kept her daylight vigil over Augustine, collapsing into it as her knees turned to rubber.

"I—suspected she'd been in a concentration camp," she said, unable to meet the vampire's eyes. The morning of the funeral, as Grandma brushed and braided her hair, Bebe had seen the blue-tinted letters and numbers tattooed on the soft flesh of her grandmother's inner arm. When she asked Grandma what it meant, the blood drained from Grandma's face. Despite all the disagreements they had in the successive years, it had been the only time in her life that her grandmother had ever truly raised her voice to Bebe.

Bebe never saw the tattoo on Grandma's arm again. She almost sure she had imagined it until she saw another, similar one on Grandpa Petrov's arm after her grandparents had divorced. By then, a classmate's grandfather had spoken at her middle school about his experiences in the Nazi concentration camps, so she knew what the tattoo meant. Grandpa had admitted being imprisoned in Auschwitz, but he steadfastly refused to discuss the matter. Afterwards, she subtly examined Grandma's arm and detected the small cosmetic glamour.

Was that the reason for the arranged marriage Grandma had tried to force down her throat? A tortured woman's attempt to keep her family line alive?

She raised her eyes to meet Augustine's, twisting her entwined fingers until her knuckles cracked. "It would seem you know more about her life than I do." The confession tore at her.

"I'm sorry, Bebe. I assumed that she would have discussed such matters with you." His expression belied his words though. He schooled his emotions until only the harsh face of a vampire coven leader remained.

How dare he? The problems between her and Grandma should have remained in the family. Now he claimed an intimacy with her based on his knowledge of Grandma. Him. A vampire. Resentment grew until her head ached.

"So now we're on a first-name basis, Mr. Augustine?" Irritation crawled along her nerves, the itch so bad that she didn't wait for his reply. Sucking in a deep breath, she shoved her emotions aside. She needed to deal with one problem at a time. "What proof do you have that my grandmother was killed? And why do you think those men blasting my hotel room were after me? They could have just as well been your enemies, not mine. I don't need a garlic-coated explosive bullet to kill me."

"No, the regular variety would do the job just fine." That annoying smirk of his twisted his lips. "Obviously, someone close to one or *both* of your grandmothers knew they had asked me to become your guardian in the event something happened to either of them. Your assailants came prepared last night."

No!

Her hand flew to her mouth. Augustine *had* to be lying. Fury burned past the numbness in her veins, and her hand dropped.

"A vampire? My guardian? Neither of my grandmothers would have done such a thing to me," she snapped. "Not after my parents—" The surge of anxious energy spurred her feet into action. She jumped up to pace back and forth at the foot of his bed. Granny E. wasn't as anal as Grandma Petrov, but for all her easygoing nature, there was a reason she was the Los Angeles coven's high priestess.

No, not even Granny E. would have sold out to a vampire.

"They didn't inform you of that little decision either." His words were a statement, not a question. He let out a deep, heartfelt sigh and turned to arrange the pillows behind him before leaning back against the ornately carved headboard. "I'm sorry this comes as a shock, Bebe."

"It's Dr. Zachary to you!" But her words came from very far away. She couldn't catch her breath. Something sucked all the oxygen out of the bedroom. Spots swam in front of her eyes. "They wouldn't do that to me," she whispered. Images from that awful night flashed through her brain. Mom shoving her into the entertainment center as Dad's blood splashed across them . . .

She felt rather than saw Augustine climb from his bed. When he tried to wrap his arms around her, she struck at the blurry vision of him. Despite his weakened state, he easily pulled her into his lap as he dropped to the edge of the bed. He rocked her, his hand stroking her wild curls as Grandma Petrov would have done after one of her frequent nightmares. She loathed admitting, even to herself, that his actions were soothing.

Too soothing. A warm tickle of another kind started in her belly and worked its way through her veins. With an awkward reluctance, she leaned away from his hard chest and eyed him. "Why would either one of my grandmothers trust you? Especially after what had happened to their children?" The skin around her eyes tightened as she eyed him. "Let me see the Blood Seal." The magickal oath mark on his skin would confirm his story.

He shook his head. "I don't have one."

"Really? How convenient. Do you expect me to believe that either of my grandmothers wouldn't take steps to guarantee your performance on this alleged promise to protect me?"

"I expect—"

The bedroom door popped open, Alex poked his head around the edge. His good-natured grin faded when he saw them together on the bed. "Good to see you awake, boss. Uh, everything okay in here?"

Bebe slid off Augustine's lap and took two safe steps away before she turned and crossed her arms. "Everything's just fine." She imagined how the picture of her sitting on Augustine's lap appeared to the younger vampire. Heat seeped into her cheeks.

"Uh-huh." Alex flicked his gaze to Augustine and cocked an eyebrow.

"We're both fine," Augustine said.

For once, the bastard didn't make any cracks at her expense. She breathed a silent prayer of thanks when Alex merely nodded and left, shutting the door behind him. She pivoted back to face Augustine.

He remained silent, his expression again an odd mix of concern and wariness.

"Look, you want me to trust you, then you've got to come clean," she said. "Why would my grandmothers come to you without making you take the oath?"

He sighed and ran a hand across the stubble of his beard before giving her a wry smile. "The enemy of my enemy is my friend."

She rolled her eyes. "In English, please."

He sobered. "We had mutual objectives. Your parents weren't the only ones murdered that night. Others were killed by the rogues as well, including some of my people."

"Your people?" Her eyes narrowed. "You mean other vampires?"

He nodded. "And weres and Normal relatives as well."

"Why?"

Augustine shrugged. "Either an attempt to start a race war or an attempt to seize power. We're not sure. None of the culprits were taken alive."

She crossed her arms. "Once again, how convenient."

"Feel free to confirm my story independently."

His story made sense, but why the hell hadn't Grandma Petrov ever told her any of this? The urge to do something, anything, grew overwhelming. "I need to go to L.A." Granny E. would tell her the truth. Give her a direction in this mess.

"I would like to discuss the incident at the hotel with your paternal grandmother as well."

"Where's your phone?"

He gestured toward the modern set sitting on nightstand.

She ignored his smile at her blatant faux pas. The lack of sleep definitely affected her reasoning capabilities. She reached for the handset and started punching in Granny E.'s number.

"You do know she won't be back from Europe until Friday, don't you?"

Irritation washed over Bebe at Augustine's words. "And how would you know this?"

"I called Los Angeles yesterday once I had located you. The housekeeper informed me she would return on Friday."

She couldn't summon the energy to feed the annoyance she should feel towards him. Exhaustion tugged the edges of her mind.

He grinned when she could no longer resist the huge yawn that threatened to crack her face wide open. "However, I think you could do with some more sleep before we fly down. Why don't you lie down in my bed?"

Yeah, right, the spider said to the fly. The man had sported a woody simply from having his blood pressure taken.

"I managed not to contract the V-virus last night. How, I'll never know. Let's not put my luck to the test." Too much was happening, and not just Caesar's continuous flirting. She shook her head at the thought of the last twenty-four hours. If she didn't get a break soon, she might go bonkers.

He rose from the bed, his Road Runner pajama bottoms still freaking her out as much as they had when Alex put them on the unconscious Augustine last night. "Sorry, Dr. Zachary," he said stressing her title. "I wasn't planning on joining you." He gave her a top-down perusal that would have been promising if he weren't a vampire. Then he flashed a wicked grin. "Next time perhaps?" He snagged the rich velvet bathrobe off the trunk at the end of his bed and shrugged it on. "I'll be in my office making flight arrangements for Los Angeles if you need anything."

The bedroom seemed oddly empty after Augustine strode out the door. Bebe glanced between the closed door and the bed. A bed still rumpled from its owner. She squelched the thought that sent tingles through her nerves. He was a vampire, damn it!

A check of the clock showed she had slept maybe twenty minutes before the touch of his hand had woken her. Her scratchy eyeballs reminded her how crappy pulling a thirty-six hour shift felt. Cursing what was probably another stupid move on her part, she crossed to the door and locked it. The heavy click of the deadbolt was only slightly reassuring.

Climbing between his silk sheets, Bebe snuggled in and inhaled the spicy scent of Caesar, sandalwood and something indefinably masculine. It was almost as good as having his arms wrapped around her.

Once in his office, Caesar paced in front of Natasha's wardrobe, cursing the old witch, cursing the Fates, and most of all cursing himself. After five minutes, his body reminded him it was still recovering from last night's experience at Bebe's hotel, and he sank into the soft leather of his desk chair. Two seconds later, there was a quiet knock at his door.

He wanted to ignore Alex in favor of wallowing in his own self-loathing. Despite Caesar's silence, the Texan strode in balancing a tray with two mugs of warm blood. Mugs that bore the logo of Little Caesars Pizza.

The boy did not know when his perverse sense of humor crossed the line. Waking in the cartoon pajamas Tiffany had given him as a Winter Solstice present last year had been bad enough. He had to assume Ptolemy had already left for the evening and had not seen the mugs. Otherwise, Alex would be nothing more than a puddle of goo with a wooden stake lying in the middle.

Alex finally acknowledged the death glare Caesar aimed at him. After placing one steaming mug on the desk and setting the tray on the credenza, he crossed his arms and said, "If you wanted privacy, you should have locked the door."

"Like that ever stopped you." The familiar surge of thirst made Caesar reach for the mug, but he hesitated at the odd odor. He took another careful whiff before raising an eyebrow. "What the fuck did you put in my cup?"

Feigned innocence spread across the Texan's face. "It's prime Angus. Your favorite."

Not in the mood for the younger vampire's games, he bared his canines.

Alex spread his hands in a defensive motion. "I added a little barbecue sauce."

Caesar narrowed his eyes, and Alex's eyes glowed electric blue in response to his threat.

"It's the only thing that covers the bitterness of liquid ibuprofen. I figured you might be a little sore this evening. No one else knows." Alex held his hand over his heart. "I swear," he finished.

Caesar relaxed a fraction. While he trusted his immediate household, the sheer nature of both ancient Roman and modern vampire politics made him reluctant to show any weakness. Not that passing out in his own Hummer and being dragged into the house wasn't a dead giveaway. He gulped half the mug in two swallows, then grimaced and set the giant-sized cup down. "Next time use chocolate or vanilla instead. Your homemade sauce sucks."

"Har-de-har-har," Alex said. "By the way, you want to tell me why Dr. Z is sound asleep in your bed?"

"Yes, brother dear," a soft voice purred from the doorway. Caesar twisted to see Selene leaning against the frame. "Why *is* a witch sharing your bed?"

Alex pursed his lips before giving Caesar an apologetic shrug. "Also, your sister's here to see you."

Chapter 6

The vampire virus eliminated nearly every form of ailment that plagued Norms, but stress migraines were not unknown. And a doozy began pulsing behind Caesar's left eyeball.

"Why, Selene, to what do I owe this unannounced pleasure?" He didn't bother rising, and his twin sister didn't bother crossing the room to kneel before him. Gods forbid she might get lint on her black designer slacks.

"Passing my respects to my coven master, of course."

Her sly smile didn't fool him for an instant. He gave Alex a measured stare. "That will be all."

Alex frowned, but then he nodded and backed out of the office, closing the door behind him.

Selene crossed the room and nestled in the brown suede couch. "So tell me more about your new pet. And why is *my* eclectic still stuck in Africa?"

He wiped a hand down his face. "Why Dr. Zachary's here is none of your concern, Selene. And I told you a couple of days ago to recall Lucian." He reached for his mug, wishing that the ibuprofen were opium. Sometimes progress wasn't all it was cracked up to be.

"Do you have any idea how hard it is to get a last minute flight out of Chad? If I'm lucky, he might be back in the U.S. before the end of the week." She crossed her arms and glared at him. "Don't tell me you're getting us in the middle of the White Rose succession."

He smiled, deliberately displaying his canines. "As you wish."

She leaned forward, elbows on her knees. "What in Isis's name are you thinking? Finding the girl for Petrov is one thing. Involving us in a witch war is totally different. This is why you got your ass shot up, isn't it?"

He took a sip before answering her. "And you came here hoping I had brought Duncan to San Francisco with me, not out of any concern for my well-being."

The faint pink that flooded her cheeks was the only indication Caesar had nailed her real purpose for the visit. Selene's obsession with his Chief Enforcer knew no bounds. She had Turned the man without his consent, then couldn't understand his rejection of her. Five centuries after the fact, she still pursued him. Gods above! For an intelligent woman, Selene did some damn stupid things.

She cleared her throat. "Of course, I'm concerned, both as your sister and as your second-in command. Ptolemy called me last night. Very upset about you getting shot, I might add."

He had to give his twin credit. She could dissemble better than anyone he'd ever known. "He didn't need to call you. As you can see, I'm perfectly fine."

One of Selene's slim black eyebrows flicked upward. "Really? Then why was he rambling about garlic-laced explosive bullets?"

Caesar took another sip of the doctored blood and decided to ignore the issue with Duncan for now. "Ptolemy blew things out of proportion. I wasn't shot in the ass, and I'm fine. Thank you for asking."

"Ri-i-ight." Selene pursed her lips and nodded. "I'm sure that's why Stanton is serving you Advil-laced blood."

He sniffed the cup again. "You can smell it over his nasty barbecue sauce?"

She gave him a 'duh' look. He shrugged and downed the last of the cup before trading it for the second one.

Frowning, Selene sat back and crossed her arms over her ample chest again, which pulled her black turtleneck even tighter. Her move was so instinctual when she dealt with men. She probably didn't realize the effect was wasted on her brothers.

"Let's go back to our original topic," she said. "Want to tell me why you're dragging our coven into the middle of the White Rose succession?"

He needed to have a word with Ptolemy about the kid's big mouth.

He matched her frown. "I'm not dragging the coven anywhere. This is a personal issue. Natasha Petrov was my friend."

Selene snorted in disgust. "It becomes a coven issue when you start imitating Swiss cheese. It becomes a coven issue when your second-in-command gets frantic phone calls in the middle of the night that you're in a coma. It becomes a coven issue when you've got the new White Rose High Priestess sleeping in your bed." Her lips curled in a nasty snarl that would have scared the crap out of anybody with common sense.

"Bebe hasn't been confirmed by the coven Elders yet." He started to take another drink and looked down in surprise. He'd already drained the second cup during Selene's rant.

"So what in Hades is she doing here?" A suspicious glint flared in her deep brown eyes. Her arms dropped and she slid to the edge of the couch. "You're not trying to Turn her, are you?"

"Turning the unwilling is your department."

Her eyes glowed neon yellow. "That's a really shitty thing to say, even for you."

Ancient guilt sprang up. When Octavian's army camped outside of Alexandria's city gates, their mother had made Caesar promise to protect Selene and Ptolemy. And here he was, throwing insults without any care. He sucked in breath to calm himself.

"I'm sorry. And no, I'm not trying to Turn anyone. Assassins were after Bebe, and I—" He gave her a wry smile. "—got in the way."

She relaxed slightly but remained perched on the end of the cushion. "It sounds like they were gunning for more than witch."

He shrugged. "Maybe they were simply taking precautions. We would do the same in a similar operation."

She cocked an eyebrow. "So what *is* she doing here? Why not hand her over to the White Rose Elders?"

Caesar propped his elbows on the desk, his fingers steepled. As much as he loathed asking Selene for more help, he needed it if he was going to keep Bebe alive. "Natasha asked me to protect her granddaughter. She believed there was a conspiracy within her coven to assassinate both her and Bebe."

Selene jumped to her feet and threw her arms in the air. "Isis, help me! Since when do we get involved in internal witch politics? In case you haven't noticed, we're vampires!"

"And that's your excuse for letting an innocent woman die?"

"You said Petrov's heir hasn't been confirmed by the White Rose Elders yet." She started pacing, the sharp stilettos on her sandals poking holes in the plush of the beige carpet. "Then it's not *our* concern. Are you even considering the ramifications of your actions? The witches will have a field day if *you*, a vampire master, champion one candidate over another in a succession contest. Not to mention the sanctions the International Council will impose on us." She whirled and pinned him with an irritated glare. "Have you even discussed this with the other North American Masters?"

"No, I have not. As I said, this is a personal matter." Caesar leaned back into his chair. Selene's anger spiked her normal sandalwood into burnt ash. The acrid odor caused the pounding behind his left eye to escalate.

"Good, good," she murmured and resumed her pacing. "If no one outside your immediate circle knows about this, we have a chance at damage control. We'll return your little houseguest to her Elders and no one will be the wiser. Damn, how can we spin this?" She raked her hands through her hair, mussing her stylish black tresses.

She was so intent on her plan she didn't notice Ptolemy slip through the door. He shot a grin at Caesar while she continued her mumbling. "She was mugged, you rescued her, we alter her memory—"

"Are we giving that butt-ugly wardrobe back to the witches, too?" Ptolemy asked.

Her head jerked up at his words and the furrows in her brow smoothed. She walked over and gave him a quick hug. "Thanks for calling me last night."

"Glad you're here." Ptolemy shot a thumb in Caesar's direction. "I just hope you're talking some sense into him."

She snorted and smiled as she looked up at Ptolemy. "Like anything I say has any effect on him."

"So are you going to send that atrocity back with the girl?" He pointed at the corner between the couch and the built-in bookshelves where Caesar had placed the wardrobe.

She tilted her head to examine the piece and grimaced. "Where did that come from?"

"He bought it at the old witch's estate auction."

She crinkled her nose. "Why, in Isis's name, would he do that?"

"You know, I am in the room." Caesar tried to give them his most menacing scowl, but the effort was wasted when all three of them cracked up. Damn, it had been too long since they had been in the same room. And even rarer still since they had shared any laughter. Gods, he missed the old days.

Once the last chuckle died, Selene turned serious again. She strode to the front of his desk and crossed her arms. "We have to send her back to her people."

Ptolemy stepped forward, shoulder to shoulder with Selene. "She's right. I know you're concerned about the witch, but it's not our problem—"

Caesar slapped the desktop, hard. His siblings jumped but didn't back down. "No, it's my problem. This about a promise I made."

Selene leaned forward and slammed her own palms on the hard cherry wood. "To a dead woman who probably wasn't in her right mind when she extracted that promise."

Caesar rose and dipped down until his nose was millimeters from his twin's. "We are *not* turning her over to anyone, Selene."

"Damn it, Alexander Helios Antonius!" Her eyes flashed gold. "For once in your misbegotten life, listen to me!"

"Uh-oh," Ptolemy muttered and backed away from them.

Caesar's pulse pounded a rhythm to match his rage, and the tips of his canines pressed into his lips as they elongated. "Don't you *ever* call me by that name again." The cold calm in his voice contradicted the red that swam in his vision. "That man died the day Octavia sent her immortal pets to assassinate us. Or don't you remember, dear sister?"

Selene deliberately lowered her hard stare and took a hesitant step away from the desk. "I meant no disrespect, Master."

Fire roared in his ears. "You both need to leave." He clenched his fists in an effort to get his blood rage under control. The last thing he needed right now was to lose it and attack his sister. He felt rather than saw Ptolemy take a tentative step forward.

"Do you need more blood—"

"Now!" he roared.

His siblings scrambled out the door. His chest ached as he forced slow, steady breaths. In. Out. Gods, he couldn't let Bebe see him in this way. Her emotional state was questionable as it was, and any connection he had with her tenuous.

In. Out.

He dropped into his chair and concentrated on the cool leather against his overheated skin. Why in Hades did Selene have to bring up the past tonight? Selene's husband, Juba, had done his best to protect him and Ptolemy, but it hadn't been enough to stop Octavia's bitterness. He forced the memory of that terrible night aside.

In. Out.

Caesar wasn't sure how long he sat slumped in the chair before the red haze cleared from his vision. He rose and stretched. The aches in his body intensified, no longer the dull throb now that his temper-fueled metabolism had burned off the painkiller.

Selene wouldn't assist him in protecting Bebe. She'd made that perfectly clear. Not that she was likely to be in a gracious mood after his temper tantrum if she weren't already dead set against getting involved in White Rose's problems.

He shambled up the hand-carved staircase towards his bedroom with the intent of getting some more ibuprofen and then sleep. The earlier talk with the witch flared to life in his brain. Crap, Bebe was still in his bed.

As much as crawling in next to her held its fascination, getting fireballed in his own bed didn't have the same appeal. And Bebe needed the sleep as much as he did. He had the impression she had stayed up all night and the following day to keep an eye on him.

He'd just grab some more painkillers from his bathroom rather than suffer the torture of making his way back downstairs to the infirmary. Then he'd fall onto a mattress in one of the guest bedrooms. Yes, that'd work. Especially if he didn't look at the bed or touch its occupant. He eased the door open.

Just one problem with that plan.

His bed was empty.

Chapter 7

Guilt and worry stuck to Bebe's consciousness, preventing sleep despite the fatigue plaguing her limbs and eyelids. Rolling over on her back, she stared at the blue glow from the alarm clock reflected against the ceiling. She couldn't wait for morning to search for the wardrobe and retrieve the Book of Shadows. Augustine probably had a private jet, which meant he could come upstairs anytime to collect her for the flight to L.A.

The doorknob rattled. Her breath hitched in her throat, and she mentally reached out. A vampire was on the other side. Alex, from the fruity cereal taste of his surface thoughts. The deadbolt slid back, and she closed her eyes and deepened her breathing to feign sleep. No shuffling foot steps on the carpet. Her willpower hammered to keep her breaths slow and even.

Seconds later, the door clicked shut, and the deadbolt gave a soft *snick* as it locked again.

Bebe opened her eyes and stared at the door, but no other sound came from the other side. Now what the hell was that all about? She swung her feet over the edge of the mattress and eased over to the door to listen. The fruity cereal taste receded down the hallway towards the main staircase when she reached out with a psychic probe.

Goddess, she truly was becoming as paranoid as Grandma Petrov. Alex had probably come up to check on Augustine again. If the Texan were one of Augustine's enforcers, he'd have a key to every door in the mansion. Most likely, when he realized his coven master was up and about, he went looking for him.

Concentrating, Bebe leaned her forehead against the door and reached past the hallway. No one upstairs.

Stretching, she pressed her thoughts further through the house. The rich, beefy taste of Caesar fired through her nerves. He must be weaker than he let on because she didn't get a reaction from her slight intrusion.

She breathed a sigh of relief. No taste of spinach and dandelions, which meant the two half-elven day guards had left for the evening. And no burnt toast or cotton candy meant Ptolemy and Anne were gone as well.

Confirming that Caesar and Alex were still downstairs, she cast a blurring spell around her before she twisted the lock and crept through the door. Not true invisibility, a blurring spell merely kept the casual observer from noticing someone or something was out of place. Once the vampires realized she wasn't in Caesar's bedroom and started a thorough search, she was screwed. She prayed that she'd been in enough rooms during the day that any previous scent would cover her most recent passage. Keeping her own shields tight, she began a room-by-room search through the second floor. The ambient light from the security lamps outdoors guided her way.

Emerging from the fourth bedroom she checked, Bebe cursed softly to herself. The wardrobe had to be downstairs in one of the rooms she hadn't visited. Even with vampire strength, she couldn't imagine the practicality of hauling it up to the attic or down to the basement. And from the functionality and simplicity of every piece of furniture and art, if Caesar Augustine was anything, it was practical.

She jumped at the soft chime of the front doorbell, her elbow knocking into the urn of daisies at the head of the stairs. She snatched the crystal, which she sensed was Anne's touch, before it could crash to the floor. Tension scraped her nerves as she settled the flowers upright and crouched down.

Soft voices drifted up from the foyer, but the hint of anger in Alex's was unmistakable, even if she couldn't make out the words. Dropping to her belly, she crawled to the edge of the landing to peer down through the banisters. The voice of the woman Alex spoke with carried an air of amused arrogance at his irritation. After another exchange, he gestured for her to wait by the entrance before he stalked off toward the kitchen.

Instinct warned Bebe this woman was not someone to screw with. She didn't dare reach out with a mental probe.

The dark-haired woman paced back and forth in the foyer, impatience in every click of her designer shoes. Her skin-tight turtleneck was not something Bebe would have dared wear, much less with the heavy gold jewelry that drenched the woman. The slacks, that had to have been spray-painted on her ass, screamed sex with every twist of her hips.

The woman's head jerked up, and for an instant Bebe would have sworn they locked eyes. How the heck did the bitch see through her blurring spell? Was she a vampire? Bebe couldn't tell by scent when sandalwood odor from the other vampires filled the house. If she weren't a vampire though, who else would be visiting Caesar?

Bebe's heart banged an obscenely loud rhythm the woman probably heard despite the magickal shield. From the hard look on the woman's face, this was not someone who would cut anyone slack for sneaking around the mansion. Bebe bit her lip, clenched her fist and started to summon a fireball. Energy tickled in her fingertips.

The woman's sharp gaze shifted across the banister and flicked across the high windows of the foyer. Bebe stopped her incantation and tracked her line of sight. What was she looking at?

The visitor's eyes settled on the security camera lodged in the corner of the entrance's cathedral ceiling. Her sharp canines gleamed under the chandelier when she smiled at the camera and blew it a kiss. Okay, that came under the heading of weird behavior, even for a vampire. Then the female vamp pivoted and sauntered down the main hallway until she disappeared under the landing.

Bebe held her breath until the clicking of the vamp's heels disappeared. The air in her lungs escaped with a *whoosh*. She glanced again at the security camera. While the blurring spell worked against electronic eyes the same as organic ones, she needed to be more careful not to set off any other conventional alarms.

Last night, when she had questioned Stan Gryffudd, one of the half-elven day guards, about magickal security measures, he had snickered and told her it was none of her Morrigan-damned business. In her experience, that statement meant Stan and his partner, Harry, knew the most powerful spells a half-elf could wield. If their techniques were anything like White Rose security, their spells focused on keeping intruders out, not preventing someone from snooping inside.

In a way, it was a relief Caesar was doubly careful with conventional and magickal measures. Maybe the hotel gunmen would think twice before mounting any kind of assault on the vampire's home.

Rising to her feet, she hugged the wall as she crept down the stairs. She froze when one tread squeaked under her bare foot. After a few seconds, when no one appeared, she preceded the rest of way down the remaining steps.

So far, so good.

No sooner did the thought materialize when the front door lock rattled. Panic started to overwhelm her.

No, dammit! This is no different than freaking triage! What's the priority?

Hiding, except there were no hiding places in the foyer or front sitting room. The blurring spell wouldn't do any good if she was standing in the middle of a room and someone ran into her. If she went into the kitchen, she could say she couldn't get back to sleep and was looking for tea. But then one of the vamps would shadow her for the rest of the evening as they had last night.

The massive front door started to open.

She dived into the tiny half bath tucked under the staircase and closed the door until a sliver allowed her to watch the hall and kitchen door. Anne stopped short when Alex's shaggy blond head poked out of the kitchen door.

"You're home early. Not enough rogues and gang bangers to beat up?"

An odd expression crossed Anne's face, and her wide, innocent eyes narrowed. Her vamp-out happened so fast, Bebe shoved a fist against her mouth to stop the shriek that bulged in the back of her throat. It was too much like the ugly sons of a bitch who broke into her parents' home. The night her father's head was ripped off.

Anne bared fangs at Alex. "What I do on my personal time is my business." A sneer twisted her grotesque mouth when she added a sarcastic, "Father."

Father? Was Alex Anne's sire? What the hell possessed him to Turn her at such a young age? Bebe struggled to keep her breath shallow and even. If the vamps caught her watching their little soap opera . . .

Alex folded his arms over his chest, his calm look and the dishtowel over his shoulder incongruous with the angry little vampire he faced. "If you're finished with your snit fit, I have the address for that plate number Ptolemy got off the gunmen's van. It took me a while to trace it through several different holding companies, but the final one's Bay Area Consolidated. I need you to shadow the principal shareholder, Lionel Hart."

No.

Bile rose in Bebe's throat. Would Uncle Lionel kill her to insure that her cousin Alice was named high priestess by the Elders? Spots swam in her vision. She leaned her head against the cool ceramic of the toilet. Uncle Lionel had always doted on Alice, and as one of the richest men in the country, he had the means to give Alice everything she desired. Everything except Grandma Petrov's approval.

The split between the cousins had started the day of the funeral for Bebe's parents. Grandma had caught Alice making out with a neighbor boy.

In the family crypt.

Alice had accused Bebe of narcing. The rawness of the whole deal was that Bebe hadn't tattled. But if she had ratted out the real tattletale, their cousin William, she'd be exactly what Alice called her.

From there, Alice had decided since Grandma had called her a whore, she'd act the part. Only Patti Hearst and Paris Hilton had received more press than Alice in the spoiled heiress department. And the weekly pictures of Alice in the tabloids hadn't endeared her to their ultra-conservative grandmother.

The last straw had been Bebe's decision to enter medical school. To Alice, she'd done it only to suck up to Grandma.

Maybe it wasn't Uncle Lionel. But if it wasn't, that left only Alice. Bebe swallowed hard. An innocent man almost died because of this stupid family squabble.

No. Augustine was hardly innocent.

She blinked back the tears that threatened to spill. Goddess, no wonder her old friends avoided her like the plague. How many had Alice threatened?

"Call Stan before dawn so he can cover daytime surveillance of Hart." Alex's voice drew Bebe back to her present predicament. Alice, William and the Elders had been careless enough to lose Grandma's Book of Shadows. Bebe needed to find it while she had the chance and get the heck out of this vampire haven before Augustine dragged her down to L.A.

Anne had calmed down and only a dim golden glow showed in her eyes. "Isn't Hart—"

"Yeah, he's the doc's uncle by marriage. She's going to shit a brick when she hears this." Alex raked a hand through his unruly locks.

"We don't tell her."

Both of the vampires and Bebe jerked at the sound of Ptolemy's voice. How the heck did he manage to sneak into the house?

She cursed herself. She'd been so busy eavesdropping on Alex and Anne that she hadn't been scanning her surroundings. If she wasn't more careful, she was going to get herself caught and maybe even killed. As much as she loathed admitting Augustine was right, she definitely wasn't cut out for espionage.

"What? Why not?" Alex said.

She shared Alex's confusion. After her verbal sparring with him, she assumed Ptolemy would have gotten a kick out of skewering her with her family's homicidal bent.

"Contrary to your opinion of me, Stanton, I've no wish to upset Dr. Zachary. Despite her obvious distrust of our race, she saved my brother's life."

Wow. Who would've thought the brat prince had a soft side?

Then he stepped into view next to Anne, his nostrils flaring. He twisted his head left then right, sniffing like a bloodhound on coke.

"Where is she?" His eyes narrowed, but his gaze continued to flick around, obviously searching for her.

Bebe wrapped her arms tight around her knees. Like once before, a long time ago, whimpers gathered at the back of her throat. *Please don't let them find me. Oh Goddess, please don't let them.*

Alex huffed, exasperation evident in the sound. "She's upstairs asleep. I just checked on her."

Ptolemy stared at Alex for what seemed an eternity before he nodded curtly. "Is Caesar still—"

"No." With his sharp answer, Alex shook his head. "He's awake and in his office with your sister."

Sister? Holy crap! How many vampire siblings did Augustine have running around? Remembering the woman's sharp profile, Bebe wanted to kick herself for not recognizing the new vampire's resemblance to Augustine and Ptolemy.

Ptolemy passed in front of the bathroom door, heading towards the back of the house.

"Why's *she* here?" Anne's voice carried a nasty edge.

Alex shrugged. "Fake sisterly concern and the faint hope that she could fuck Duncan."

Bebe swallowed hard. Who's Duncan? Did she need to worry about another vampire?

A nasty smile crossed Anne's face. "Over or with."

Alex turned his head in the direction Ptolemy had disappeared. "Both probably."

"Too bad someone doesn't accidentally stake the bitch." The venom on Anne's voice made the hairs stand up on the back of Bebe's neck. So much for the vampire's sweet act.

Alex laid a hand on Anne's shoulder and guided her into the kitchen. "Down, girl. Meanwhile, you've got a job to do . . ."

Wetness trickled down Bebe's face, and she swiped a hand across her cheek to eliminate the tears. The family feuds and her old friends shunning her were one thing. Facing the fact that someone really did want her dead was another. Alice's normal weapon of choice had been a well-aimed rumor or a nasty practical joke spell guaranteed to embarrass the hell out of the target, not a physical assault.

No. The vampires had to have known Bebe was eavesdropping. The story could have been concocted for her benefit, to fracture any remaining tie she had to her family.

So why didn't they kick open the bathroom door and kill her? Why all the games? Terror wrapped its ugly hand around her heart and squeezed. No one outside of the vampires knew where she was. They could be playing with her. Was Augustine's claim of flying to Los Angeles just another game?

She shook her head. She couldn't afford the distraction of her wild imagination. She needed to find the wardrobe, retrieve the Book of Shadows and hotfoot it south to the relative safety of Granny E.'s place.

Bebe held her breath and counted to twenty. She couldn't take the chance of reaching out with a mental probe. One of them might feel her.

When none of the vampires reappeared, she toed the bathroom door open. Still nothing. She climbed to her feet and eased next to the door. Faint voices came from the kitchen, but the sounds weren't coming any closer. She eased out of the bathroom. The burning in her lungs reminded her that she was still holding her breath. She released the used air out as silently as she could.

Tiptoeing down the hallway, she passed the clinic and paused outside the next door, which was closed. Laughter trickled out, Caesar's tenor unmistakable. What she wouldn't give to join in the good-humor that laced the air. To share a smile and a chuckle with him, the emotional connection that a good laugh—

Cut the romantic bullshit!

The sharp admonition forced her feet to move to the next room, but a flip of the light switch showed the windowless bare room contained only exercise pads on the floor and an open wooden rack full of hand weapons.

The next room held a grand piano, a bench and a small bookcase full of sheet music. Again, no wardrobe and no place to hide a humungous piece of furniture.

Worry chewed at her. Could the vampires have taken the wardrobe someplace else after it had been delivered here? Even worse, could they have destroyed it, not knowing what was inside?

Bebe hurried around the corner of the hall to the last door and gasped when she opened it. Riotous life overwhelmed her senses, both physical and psychic. What had been a cloak room leading to a massive back porch on the architectural diagrams had been combined and transformed into a gigantic greenhouse. Everything inside glowed with life and beauty. Had she bought into the stereotype of vampires so much she underestimated them?

But stubborn loyalty to the coven overrode the desire to bask in the greenery. Augustine wouldn't store an antique in this humidity.

Bebe jumped at the howl of anger that ripped through the thick atmosphere. It was followed by the distinct crash of the massive front door slamming shut. What the hell was going on? Had the vamps discovered that she was no longer in Augustine's bed? She crossed to the greenhouse door and paused to listen. No other noise presented itself, then the faint shuffling of feet away from her.

She double-checked the integrity of her blurring spell then slid through the door, easing it closed behind her. Her breath rattled in her throat, a harsh noise she was sure the vampires could detect. She peeked around the corner, but no one guarded the hall, waiting to nab her.

Holding her breath, she extended a tentative psychic probe. Only one mind met her mental touch. The rich, beefy essence of Caesar receded upstairs, the pace in time with the faint creak of the wood on the stairs. She released the held air when he didn't react to her probe. That was twice now, and the physician part of her worried at his lack of sensitivity.

Light no longer shone from beneath the door of the room where Augustine and his company had been. The only place she hadn't been since arriving at the mansion. She tiptoed over, listening for any other activity in the house, and turned the knob. A sigh of relief escaped her when she discovered it was unlocked. After closing the door, she thumbed the switch on the wall, and light flooded what was obviously an office.

Bebe's knees trembled, and she hung onto the antique glass knob to remain upright. In a corner between the floor-to-ceiling bookshelves and a leather couch, the dark hulk of Grandma's wardrobe loomed over the rest of the furnishings.

She shook her head at the incongruity. Grandma's wardrobe would have fit in any other room in Caesar's mansion. But no, he sticks it in the one room that had been redecorated in a thoroughly twenty-first century style. Crossing to the desk, she hit the switch on the smaller lamp before turning off the recessed lights from the wall switch. She muttered a silent prayer that no one would interrupt her for the few seconds she needed.

Caution was called for though since Augustine employed half-elves. With all her senses, she examined the wardrobe from across the room. Only the same residual elf magic that permeated the mansion shone in her Sight. No active spells displayed themselves.

Bebe crossed the room and whipped open the old cedar doors. She knelt and reached for the bottom panel of the wardrobe. Probing with care, her fingertips tingled when she found the entrance to the pocket of nymph space within the wood. To most other races, and even most witches, the bottom section would appear to be solid, but the living space of the nymph who had inhabited the tree used to build the wardrobe still existed. With the wards set inside the hole itself, the magick would be invisible to almost anyone.

And it didn't appear than anyone had breached the wards. Relief swept through her. Now, she needed to get the Book out of the mansion before one of the vampires discovered it. Despite her anger at her cousins' and the Elders' behavior, she had no wish for the information in the Book used against them.

Sucking in a breath, her nose filled with the odor of sandalwood, along with Caesar's own distinctive scent. The result sent her heart tripping for reasons that had nothing to do with fear.

She squelched the thrill that ran along her nerves. Caesar may have been friends with Grandma, but could she take the chance he would use the information in the Book against White Rose and their allied covens? No, she had to get the Book out of the mansion.

Except she had no money and no clothes.

Wood moaned overhead as Caesar walked down the hallway toward his room.

Retrieve the damn Book and call Beatrice Flannigan.

The Air Elder was sympathetic to her. Even if Beatrice resorted to guilt tactics to get her to accept the high priestess position, at least Bebe would be away from the vampire's mansion.

She was out of time and out of options. Any moment Caesar would discover she was no longer in his bed.

She whispered the incantation to dissolve Grandma's wards and reached into the compartment. Her fingers found nothing but wood.

No leather.

No paper.

Nothing.

The Book of Shadows was gone.

Chapter 8

Bebe yanked her hand out of the nymph hole. Air couldn't get in her lungs because her heart had shot up and lodged in her throat. She reached back into the wardrobe's secret compartment.

So much for wishful thinking. The Book of Shadows had not materialized in the few seconds since she'd opened the space. Her eyes and throat burned. Both William and Alice had accused her of taking the Book when she returned to San Francisco. Neither possessed the talent to hide their auras so she was pretty damn sure they weren't lying when they said they didn't have it.

Auras. Goddess, she was so stupid. She had the perfect opportunity to check Caesar's aura when she questioned him earlier, but she'd been so angry, all she had wanted was to shove a fireball up his ass. And last night, she'd been so scared all logical thought escaped her.

It didn't matter now. Her real problem was much bigger. Where was the Book? And how the hell was she supposed to find it?

"You really cannot keep your hands off my property, can you?"

Her head whipped around, and she found Caesar leaning against the doorframe, his arms crossed. Her game of hide-and-seek was up. She swallowed hard. It no longer mattered. The Book was gone.

The annoying smirk smeared across his face twisted into concern. He strode across the room, knelt and wrapped his arms around her before she could stand. Cradling her head against his shoulder, his simple gesture loosed the floodgates of her tears.

"Can you tell me what's wrong?" His warm breath brushed against her ear.

How could she trust him? He was a vampire. And yet he gave her more simple acts of compassion in the two days she knew him than she received from her blood kin in the seventeen years since her parents died.

Raising her head, she regarded him. "Why did you outbid me for the wardrobe?"

"Truth?"

She nodded and shifted her visual focus. Scarlet, the color of a warrior, surrounded him, edged by the brick red signature of the virus. She waited for the pulse of ugly gray across his aura that signified a deception.

"On my honor, I did not know who you were. All I knew was that you were from the White Rose coven." He lifted a finger and stroked her right ear, avoiding the sterling silver stud, one of the rose-shaped earrings she received at her Initiation. His light touch sent a tremor through her body. If he noticed her reaction, he gave no indication.

"Since I did not recognize you, I feared you were one of the conspirators. You were the only one from your coven to attend the auction. I suspected there was something valuable regarding the wardrobe by the way you pursued it." He shot her a wry grin. "I was actually trying to preserve it for Bebe since I didn't know you were her."

No change in his aura. She sat a little straighter, reluctant to pull away from his hard, comforting chest, but she needed to distance herself in order to think clearly. "I beg your pardon?"

His left hand still clasped her shoulder. "As I told you, I vowed an oath to Natasha to protect you if her death was untimely. This—" He waved his free hand at the wardrobe and chuckled. "—was of value to you, so I knew Natasha would want you to have it. I planned to give it to you anyway."

His aura held steady. His consideration overwhelmed her, but not enough for her to drop her guard.

"You still haven't told me what's your real connection to my grandmother."

The brilliant scarlet outlining his body darkened and her heart fell. He was considering a lie to tell her. Typical for a man. Just when her opinion of him improves, he goes and does something stupid.

Then his aura flared back. He dropped his hand from her shoulder and shook his head. "There are things I shouldn't tell you." He blew out a deep breath.

The faint prickle of his mental touch sent tingles along her skin but it lasted only an instant. He wasn't trying to read her. Caesar's focus wavered, and she realized he was checking for who remained in the mansion.

A shiver of apprehension rippled down her spine. Didn't he trust his own people?

Amusement quickly followed the heels of that thought. She couldn't talk about trust issues considering the situation with her family.

His golden eyes cleared and his gaze bore into hers. "Since your grandmother's actions have dragged you into danger, I believe you have a right to know. But what I say cannot leave this room. Do you understand?"

She nodded, more than a little concerned. What the hell had Grandma gotten herself involved in?

"Bebe, you must understand that Natasha had your best interests at heart, and she never meant for harm to come to you or your parents."

His sincerity ripped at her. She nodded but silently prayed she could bear whatever secret he was about to reveal.

"I met your grandmother in Paris shortly after she was released from Auschwitz II. She confirmed what Ike and I had suspected during the war—the supernatural breeds had been betrayed by their own kind to the Axis powers."

Horror surged through Bebe. What Caesar said went against every rule and custom in the supernatural handbook—if such a thing existed. Okay, maybe the I.C. code counted. "Wait a minute. Are you saying some of us took part in a Normal war? You took part?"

He nodded. "Once stories reached us here in the U.S. about what was happening in the Old World, we didn't have a choice."

She inched back from him and hugged her arms around her knees. "There's always a choice," she snapped.

His cold expression could have frozen Lake Tahoe all the way to the bottom. "So in your opinion, I should have let the regiment of vampire soldiers Hitler had created decimate Europe?"

"No! That's not what I'm saying! But why would any of us—" She waved her hand to include both of them. "—get involved with someone like Hitler?"

He shook his head sadly. "I honestly don't know. And it wasn't just Hitler. There were pockets associated with the Japanese and Italian military as well. A small team of us, including your grandmother and I, tracked down the known collaborators, but we never discovered their ringleader."

She watched him carefully while he related his story. His aura remained a clear, steady scarlet. She shook her head in disbelief. "And President Roosevelt and General Eisenhower, not to mention the International Council, let you waltz in and play Mossad?"

He chuckled. "Not exactly. Ike is, was, Family. Anyone else within the Allied countries was on a need-to-know unless they were also Family."

She understood his slight emphasis. Family with a capital "F" meant General Dwight D. "Ike" Eisenhower was related to a supernatural by marriage or blood and could be trusted with the secret of their existence. It also meant he was smart enough to leave such matters to the International Council, the supernatural equivalent to the Normals' United Nations.

Except the I.C. had a lot more bite, literally and figuratively.

Her eyes widened as a terrible thought struck her. "Why would the Council sanction hunting down and killing supernaturals without a trial?"

A grim look crossed his face. "All we had to do was read the survivors' minds for sufficient cause."

She had so many questions, but Caesar wiped a hand over his drawn face. The action hit the physician part of her in the gut. How could she forget the doctored bullets ripping into his body last night?

"Damn it, Caesar! When was the last time you drank?"

A wry smile appeared on his face. "You're changing the subject."

She shook her head and climbed to her feet. "I'll let you finish your story after we get some nourishment in you." She didn't miss his wince as he rose from the floor but was smart enough not to mention it. For vampires, strength or the perception of such was paramount in their society.

Nice to know she remembered something from her coven cultures class.

Caesar stopped so abruptly she smacked her nose into his back. He whirled around and caught her as she stumbled, his touch sending warm fuzzy thoughts to places in her body that should know better.

"I'm sorry. I nearly forgot to give you something." He strode over to his desk and picked up a plain, white envelope. Smiling, he returned and handed it to her. "I think this was what you were looking for in the wardrobe's secret compartment."

It wasn't, but she didn't know how much she could trust him yet. She glanced down at the front of the envelope. In Grandma Petrov's neat, tiny handwriting were the words, "For Bebe, in the event of my death."

Chapter 9

Caesar expected Bebe's anger, but from the way her right hand glowed and ozone filled the air, he'd be lucky not to be charbroiled in the next five minutes.

She glared up at him, shook the envelope under his nose and bellowed, "How the hell did you get this?"

Her eyes flashed, red suffused her skin and the ripe peach and ginger smell of her was almost more than his depleted body could handle. Blood rapidly left his brain and departed for parts south. Parts he didn't need to be thinking with when it came to Bebe Zachary. He inhaled in an attempt to clear his head, but the effort only drove the rich scent of ginger, peaches and something that was indefinably Bebe deeper.

"One of my people, Stan Gryffudd, was part of our tracking team. He and your grandmother often left messages for each other in nymph holes during our hunts. When I told him about you searching inside the wardrobe at the auction, he surmised that Natasha may have hidden something in the wardrobe's nymph hole." He glanced at the envelope, which happened to be poking his left nostril. "That's what he found."

She drew back, taking the sharp paper with her. The red glow faded from her right hand as she turned the envelope over and over, examining it from every angle. Ozone sharpened the air again, but so faint that it would not be distinguishable by a Normal nose. He waited for her to finish examining the paper magickally. Patience was the key to winning her trust.

Staring at the envelope, she tapped it against her left palm. With her brows drawn together in concentration, he felt certain the tapping was unconscious on her part.

"It doesn't make sense. Why leave this in the wardrobe and not—" Her mouth closed in an abrupt motion, and her eyes widened.

So, she *was* looking for Natasha's Book of Shadows, but she did not want him to know. It took all of his remaining strength not to laugh outright as her reason for the plans to his estate came into focus. Fine, if she were preoccupied with the Book, she'd have less time to plot an escape from him.

He didn't have to fake the wave of dizziness that rammed his brain with blackness. He grabbed the edge of the desk to stay upright. From the corner of his eye, he watched Bebe's expression shifted from suspicion to concern.

"We were headed for the kitchen, weren't we?" Despite the seven-inch difference in their heights, the petite woman slung his arm over her shoulder and wrapped her own arm around his waist.

Unbidden, images rose of her wrapping other parts around his waist. Her body heat penetrated his robe, despite the thick velvet, to coil in his middle as they shuffled to the kitchen. Despite the pain, her heat and scent wrapped a sensuous cocoon around his brain cells. Thank Horus, the trip to the kitchen was mercifully short.

Once Bebe settled him in a chair, she bustled about the kitchen at his directions, pulling out mugs and warming blood for him and water for her tea. He noticed she didn't show the usual Normal squeamishness at preparing his cup. Nor did she flinch when he sipped.

Instead, she propped her fists on her ample hips, a gesture that nearly had him on the floor, whimpering, and gave him a stern, measured look that contradicted her obsequious tone when she spoke. "I'm not trying to offend you, Caesar, but can vampires take painkillers?"

Her sensitivity, for someone who claimed she hated his kind, startled him. He nodded but didn't say anything. Her exasperated expression was worth the effort of teasing her.

"What can you take and where is it?"

"We can take ibuprofen and aspirin." Barely paying attention to what he was saying, he gripped his mug and tried not to stare at her full breasts jutting against her t-shirt.

"And?" She spoke slowly as if to a child. "Where do you keep it?" Her head tilted and her eyes narrowed. "Again, no offense, but you look like death warmed over."

Humor tugged the corners of his mouth. "To some, we are already dead."

She rolled her eyes and her words come out in a huff. "Oh, please! It's a chronic disease, not a curse. You manage your condition just like a diabetic."

His gaze swept over her, and he inhaled her ginger and peach scent. Her cheeks flushed at his obvious perusal. Regret tinged his purely male interest in her. "Diabetes isn't sexually transmitted, Doctor."

Her face went from pink to bright red in an instant but not from her usual anger. "Why do you have to do that?" she asked, her voice softer than usual.

"Do what?"

"Turn every conversation we have into some sort of sexual innuendo."

He gave a slight shake of his head. "I'm truly sorry if I offended you."

She shrugged. "It's okay."

Relieved that another argument had been avoided, he took a long drink.

She tapped an index finger thoughtfully against her cheek. "But you know there are other methods of satisfaction other than penetration. It involves a lot of latex, but I think we can manage—"

Suddenly, blood was going down the wrong pipe and he couldn't breathe. The image of Bebe on the kitchen table, legs spread like a banquet, beckoning him, didn't help one little bit.

Neither did Bebe banging on the partially healed flesh on his back as he hacked and coughed.

Dragging in a pain-filled lungful of air, he shouted, "Enough!" He reached behind and snagged her waist, pulling her into his lap for a second time. His groin throbbed in response to her well-rounded ass grinding against him.

She stuck her tongue out at him before adding, "Serves you right, jerk-off."

All pain in his muscles and joints faded at the thought of her delicate but strong hands gripping him, sliding up and down his shaft. He grinned at her, the tips of his fangs pricking his bottom lip. "Well, jerking off would satisfy your non-penetration criteria. Were you offering?"

Her eyes widened, but instead of her usual tongue-lashing, her mouth parted in an "O" of surprise. The pink tip of her tongue poked out and slid along her bottom lip, leaving a trail of wetness that he wanted to taste. Her breath quickened, but she made no move to struggle. Like she hoped he would do something. Anything.

Her breath whispered against his skin. He knew he shouldn't be letting the temptation she represented get to him. She may be a witch, but she was mortal. She had a life to live, one that could never include him, not in the way he wanted. She was absolutely, positively, without a doubt, off limits.

And he wanted her like he'd never wanted anyone in his long, misbegotten life.

You can't have her.

But he ignored that silent admonishment by his conscience as he dipped his mouth to meet hers. He explored tentatively at first. With a soft sigh, her lips parted, returning his kiss with a passion that surprised him. Not that he was about to argue when her tongue swirled around his.

He couldn't stop the groan that rumbled through his throat when she shifted against his erection, the sensation sending his system into overload.

This is not a good move.

He had to disagree with his all-too-vocal conscience as he cupped her full breast through the thin t-shirt, his thumb brushing back and forth across her nipple until it tightened. Bebe moaned against his mouth, the sound almost as stimulating as the vibration of her lips. She arched her back, thrusting her breast against his palm, the move totally at odds with his first sight of her in her prim, proper suit. He obliged by dipping his head and tongued her rigid nipple through the fabric.

"Ahem."

He and Bebe jerked apart to find Anne standing in the entrance to the garage, arms crossed and a bemused expression on her face.

"Thank you for waiting until Ptolemy and I were out of the house before you two decided to make out."

Chapter 10

Bebe leapt to her bare feet, a different kind of heat flooding her skin. Except for the coolness of the damp spot on her t-shirt. Sweet Goddess, could she and Caesar be any more obvious? Any more ridiculous? Any more embarrassed?

She glanced down at Caesar. Nope, not one iota of embarrassment on his face. A little irritation in his glowing yellow eyes at Anne's interruption maybe, but definitely not any embarrassment.

Damn vampire.

"I'll go get that ibuprofen," she muttered and walked out of the kitchen with the little dignity she had left. Once in the hallway, she realized she had no clue where it was kept. And she wasn't about to go back in the kitchen to ask.

Alex had said few drugs affected vampires. Therefore, her best choice would be their mini-clinic. She trudged down the hallway and flipped on the lights. She blinked in shock. Her reflection in the mirror over the sink left nothing to the imagination. She watched as her hand lifted of its own accord to touch her kiss-swollen lips. Pink flushed her cheeks, and her wild curls were even more wayward than usual. And taunt nipples poked their own accusation through the borrowed t-shirt.

Goddess! What the hell was I thinking?

She had been so close to doing something so idiotic, so stupid, so—

Forbidden.

Was that why she was so attracted to Caesar Augustine? Because he was taboo? Or because he was the sexiest man she'd ever met?

Bebe was the first to admit that her hourglass figure wasn't the modern standard of female perfection. So what the hell did he intend? To follow through to their lusts' natural conclusion? Recrimination flared in the eyes of her reflection. *That's exactly what you intended,* her image seemed to say.

Just one problem.

Unprotected sex meant infection. She'd been damn lucky not to contract the V-virus last night when she'd touched the blood on his turtleneck with open cuts on her hands. To have sex with Caesar would be asking for disaster.

No matter how wonderful, sensual, exquisite that sex would be.

Her reflection's eyes glittered at the erotic thoughts that rushed through her.

She shook her head sadly at the aroused woman in the mirror.

No sex. No sex for you. Especially not with the hunky vampire in the kitchen. Not unless you want to join him permanently.

Her reflection winced at the mental finger wagging and gave a disappointed shrug of her shoulders. No, vampirism was the best-case scenario. In most cases if a witch survived a Turn, she'd end up nuttier than Grandpa Ben's almond fudge cookies.

Before someone put her down like a rabid dog.

Bebe walked over to the mirror and opened the cabinet behind the silvered glass. Next to the Midol sat a bottle of prescription strength liquid ibuprofen. She grabbed the plastic bottle and closed the cabinet.

Ignoring the pleading look on her reflection's face, she turned for the door, flipping off the lights on her way out.

As soon as she popped through the swinging kitchen door, Caesar and Anne halted their whispered and, from appearances, heated discussion. From the pointed stare Anne shot Caesar, Bebe had no doubt exactly what the discussion entailed. What she didn't understand was why Anne, who'd been overly deferential to the Augustine brothers compared to Alex, would dare give her coven master a tongue-lashing over a witch.

Bebe set the ibuprofen on the table, shoving it over to Caesar with a fingertip. She couldn't meet his eyes.

The tiny female vampire rose from her chair, took Caesar's cup to the counter and retrieved a bottle of blood marked Angus from the refrigerator. Bebe eyed the glassware. Was the marking for her benefit, so she wouldn't think they were drinking human blood?

After pouring the contents into the cup and setting it in the microwave, Anne punched the buttons with a little more force than necessary. The electric hum filled the kitchen, drowning the silence. Then she turned to Bebe, a polite smile on her lips. "Would you like some fresh tea, Doctor?"

Bebe resisted the urge to cringe and nodded instead. Her cup had cooled during the make-out session with Caesar. What seemed like seconds had obviously been long enough for the hot liquid to hit room temperature. And given how warm the vamps liked to keep their mansion . . .

So much for worrying about Caesar penetrating her shields and seducing her. She'd practically thrown herself at him the first chance she had.

Instead of nuking a mug of water, Anne pulled out a teakettle from a bottom cupboard. She filled it from a jug of distilled water from the refrigerator before setting the kettle on the stove.

"You don't have to go to all that trouble," Bebe protested.

Anne flashed Bebe another smile before continuing to spoon tea leaves into one-half of an egg-shaped strainer that screwed together. "No sense wasting the good stuff if Duncan's not here to drink it."

Second time this mysterious Duncan had been mentioned. Like she needed another vampire to worry about. "Who's Duncan? I'd hate to piss off someone by stealing his tea."

"Duncan St. James is my chief enforcer," Caesar said.

Wonderful. The vamp equivalent of a police commissioner.

"You'll meet him when we arrive in Los Angeles." Again, an amused smile spread across Caesar's face.

Bebe resisted the urge to smack him. She was becoming far more acquainted with Caesar's security personnel than she cared. Caesar's humor over her transparent interrogation irritated her, but Anne fiddling with spoons, cream and sugar drove Bebe over the edge.

She had a sneaking suspicion that Anne's fidgeting next to the stove was a stall tactic to keep an eye on them. Like she would let herself lose control again. Her suspicion was confirmed by Anne's next question.

"Are you hungry, Doctor?" Instead of waiting for an answer, the vampire turned to another cupboard and pulled out a bag of English muffins and a toaster.

"You can sit down, Bebe. I won't bite." Caesar's grin was heart-stopping. "Unless you want me to." He waggled his eyebrows.

She didn't know what was worse—Caesar's suggestive look or Anne's reproving glare. Taking the high road, she ignored both and marched to the opposite, and safer, side of the table. Pulling out a chair, she plunked down and crossed her arms. Caesar pointedly stared at the swell of her breasts. His grin widened.

She huffed and dropped her hands to her lap. She sure as hell wasn't going to give him any additional pleasure at her expense. From the sly look he shot Anne, Bebe was sure the female vampire hadn't missed one little bit of their silent exchange.

Anne set the mug of fresh tea in front of Bebe. The aroma alone indicated this brew was far and above the generic tea bags Bebe had found earlier. She took a sip and nodded her appreciation to the vampire. "This is wonderful."

She nearly choked on her second sip when Anne picked up the envelope from Grandma Petrov off the tabletop and asked, "What's this?"

She reached to snatch the envelope out of Anne's hand, but at the last second, she remembered her manners. "It's mine. May I have it back, please?"

Anne shrugged and handed it to her before returning to the toaster, which had disgorged the browned halves of English muffin. Bebe turned it over in her hands again. Still no sense of a witch spell or any other type of magick.

"You could just open it, Bebe."

Her head jerked up and her eyes locked with Caesar's. They no longer held any hint of amusement. Just concern and something else. Worry?

She sighed and looked back down at the envelope rotating between her fingers. He knew her grandmother far better than she ever had, right down to the secret compartment in the wardrobe. What was the sense of hiding the contents of the letter? For all she knew, he'd already steamed open the envelope and read it. "I suppose you're right." Sliding a nail in the corner, she ripped open the top. The envelope contained a single piece of paper. Sucking in her breath, she opened the folds.

> *Dear Bebe,*
>
> *Sometimes the best magic is old magic. I trust you to find your way.*
>
> *Love,*
> *Grandma P.*

What in the Thousand Names of the Goddess was Grandma blathering about? Other than the short, cryptic note in plain old ballpoint pen, the white sheet of average twenty-weight paper was completely blank. There was absolutely nothing special about the note. No, she was missing something. Grandma would have left some kind of clue.

She held it up so the light from the Tiffany lamp suspended over the table could shine through it. Still nothing.

Puzzled, she looked at Caesar. A frown creased his face as he leaned closer to examine the sheet. "What the hell was Grandma thinking?"

He looked at her with a puzzled expression. "I have no idea."

"Well, dammit, you sure seem to know her better than me. Don't you have any idea?"

He shook his head. "I'm sorry. This is strange even for Natasha."

Anne sat the plate of English muffins slathered with butter and honey in front of Bebe. She started to step back but edged closer. "Do you smell something odd?"

"Like lemons?" Caesar said.

Anne nodded, and Bebe drew the paper closer to her nose. Sure enough, the citrusy scent of lemon juice permeated the sheet.

A grin split Bebe's face. Maybe Grandma had made this easy for her after all. Turning the search for the family's Book of Shadows into a treasure hunt would have appealed to the old lady's warped sense of humor.

Or at least the sense of humor Grandma possessed before Bebe's parents were murdered.

She didn't dare use a fireball. It would be too easy to ignite the sheet. Jumping up, she edged Anne aside, stalked over to the stove and flipped the electric burner Anne had used to heat the water back to "On." Carefully holding the paper above the heat, she held her breath. Within a couple of minutes, brown, looping letters appeared on the surface.

Caesar and Anne joined her, each peering over one of her shoulders at the sharp, neat handwriting that continued to develop over the heat of the burner. "I rather had the impression you didn't sense any magick on the paper," he said.

Bebe turned to meet his warm, golden eyes and smiled. "You're right. It's not 'magick' with a 'k,' but 'magic' with just a 'c' as in a Normal illusionist trick. The spelling was Grandma's hint." She couldn't resist adding a jibe. "And really, Caesar, I'm shocked that you didn't suspect this old military trick of using lemon juice as invisible ink."

He snorted. "I'd put my faith in a sword over a box of citrus any day."

"I'll remember that the next time I'm digging bullets out of your hide." She really shouldn't have heated the letter in front of the vampires. What she should have done was play stupid until she had some time alone. She suppressed the sigh of disappointment welling in her chest. What was done was done. And if Caesar knew Grandma well enough to guess her hiding spot in the wardrobe, then maybe he was someone Bebe could trust to help her find the Book.

Even if he was a vampire.

Pulling the paper away from the burner before the page scorched, she shuffled back to the table and read the text that circled the edges of the page.

> *I'm sorry to do this to you, Bebe, darling, since you've made your feelings clear, but you must contact Caesar Augustine at (213) 555-8293. Your life is in danger. Trust no one but Caesar. He can protect you. Take him with you and go to Seven Wonders Antiques in L.A. Ask for the owner. She has something for you. I love you. Blessed Be.*

Bebe raised her head to stare at Caesar. That annoying smirk of his twisted his full lips.

"I'm not going to say I told you so," he said.

"Thank you for not saying it," she replied. She normally didn't resort to sarcasm, but he seemed to bring it out of her.

Anne raised her cup in a shaky salute. "Home it is." She finished her blood in two gulps. "I'll get us packed."

Shortly after sunset the following night, Bebe sank into the plush seat next to Caesar's on his private jet. The gracious host when not making suggestive comments, he insisted that she take the window seat before heading up to the cockpit to speak with the pilots. Alex took the seat behind her while Anne sat across from Bebe, the tiny vamp's hands twisting in her lap, her face even paler than normal. Ptolemy had flopped in the chair next to Anne, totally oblivious to his seat companion's obvious fear of flying.

Bebe took the prudent course of also ignoring Anne's nervous fidgeting and surveyed the interior of the plane. While her family had hardly been poor, the luxury of the Lear met a whole different standard than what she had been accustomed to on Grandma's estate. The accents consisted of real wood, not fake plastic veneer. The leather seats gave a new meaning to the term "butter soft." The whole plane simply smelled of money.

She'd insisted on Caesar waiting the extra day out of concern for her patient, but ten solid hours of sleep had done wonders for her disposition as well. And unpacking the shopping bags Anne had brought home the night before had sent her into ecstasy. She could swallow her pride in order not to wear the men's extra clothes. What had amazed Bebe was the fashionable taste that the little vampire showed in her purchases compared the drab clothing Anne constantly wore.

The rest of Caesar's "gifts" weren't as easy to stomach. Opening the Prada handbag, Bebe found a wad of cash, a bank debit card, a black American Express card and a California driver's license with her picture and the name 'Elizabeth Levi.' In the picture, she wore her white blouse and navy jacket, her lips pursed in an irritated grimace.

She had waved the purse in his face, protesting that she couldn't accept his money and she sure as hell didn't appreciate her picture taken by a cell camera at the estate auction. He took her tirade in his usual maddeningly calm fashion before pointing out that she'd left her purse at the hotel room and that should they become separated then she'd need money and identification.

She had been willing to accede on the money and ID issues, but his last suggestion seared to the core. He opened a Tiffany's jewelry box with a pair of silver ball studs and a pair of large delicate silver hoops.

"You can't wear your White Rose insignia in public, Bebe," he murmured. "No one will question an eclectic in the company of vampires."

She hated to admit he was right. She might as well hang a neon sign around her neck for the assassins that said, "Please kill me." Tears stung her eyes as she removed her rose-shaped studs and the tiny Fabergé-style filigree hoops of her coven. Common sense did nothing to stop the sense of betrayal that washed over her. Differences in opinion within the coven were one thing. Total denial of her heritage was another.

When she had said as much to Caesar, he gave her a sympathetic shake of his head and replied, "Your safety is my sole concern. Someone at the estate auction must have identified you the same way I did, by your coven jewelry." He laid his hands on her shoulders, his touch sending a tremor of excitement through her. "I do understand your need to proclaim your allegiance, but I learned from bitter experience the cost of no prudence in such matters. No one questions my sister's hired witch. No one will look twice when you accompany me, provided you dress the part." She had wanted to argue, but he turned his back and left her bedroom.

In retrospect, he had been right. The vampire pilots had given her no more than a cursory glance when she had boarded the plane with Caesar and his party.

Sighing, she fingered the alien earrings as she watched the last light fade from the San Francisco sky. Forty-eight hours was an awfully short time to have a girl's life turned upside down.

The welcome sense of Caesar's electric aura preceded him moments before he sat next to her and buckled himself in his seat. She gripped the armrest, digging nails into the leather, while the jet taxied toward the runway. The fact that she found his presence desirable was not a good sign. Granted, Grandma trusted him, but that did not mean she had to trust him totally. A nagging sense that he was hiding something continued to plague her.

"We should be at LAX in forty-five minutes." He smiled at her. Not the sad, pitying one or the suggestive leer he deliberately used to annoy her, but a genuine smile. "How about that dinner I promised you?"

In her peripheral vision, she noticed Ptolemy roll his eyes before shoving the earbuds of his iPod into place. His lids closed, and he slouched in his seat, looking for all the world like any other rich, bratty twenty-something.

Anne, on the other hand, frowned but said nothing. At least Caesar's flirtation with Bebe seemed to take the female vampire's mind off her own phobia, but Anne's laser-like attention was unnerving.

"Thank you, but that's not necessary," Bebe murmured.

"Your Grandmother Epstein won't be back in Los Angeles until tomorrow—"

"And if you'd let me talk to her housekeeper, I might have gotten a number where I could reach her," she snapped.

"Do you really want to take the chance of letting the wrong person know where you are?" he fired back.

She crossed her arms and said nothing. Why did this self-conceited jerk always have to be right?

"Since Seven Wonders will be closed when we land, you can call the store when it opens in the morning," he continued in a calmer tone.

"Gee, thanks, Mr. Augustine, for letting me act like a grown-up."

A wicked light gleamed in his golden eyes. "If you don't stop acting like a child, I am going to bend you over my knee."

Retching sounds came from Ptolemy's seat, but the obvious younger sibling act took a second seat to Bebe's shock. Her eyes locked with Caesar's. Heat pooled in her middle at the image of her buttocks bared before this man. Wetness seeped between her legs, and she crossed them in an effort to rein in her reaction. Instead, the pressure added to her agony.

Desperate, she ripped her gaze from his, but not before she recognized the raw need in his eyes. Mercifully, no one said anything else on the short flight.

Chapter 11

The interminably long flight home with Bebe tested Caesar's will in ways that other women never had. The desire in her face when he made the spanking joke had been too much to bear. If not for the three other vampires' presence, he would have lost control and ripped Bebe's clothes from her lush body. The way she kept crossing and uncrossing her legs added to his agony.

Only when his pilot, Kensai Osaka, announced their final approach into LAX did Caesar realize he'd left dents in the steel frame of the armrests despite the thick leather upholstery.

Caesar hung back as the other three vampires and Bebe exited the cabin, each of them shooting a suspicious look at him. None of which stopped him from admiring the good doctor's curves as she climbed down the short stairs of the jet.

"Somehow I doubt you're waiting here just to watch your guest."

Caesar turned to find Kensai with a wry grin on his face. "You'd be right."

Kensai shrugged. "She's not my taste, but I concede where you would find her attractive."

Hades. If his pilot had noticed his interest in Bebe, then he really did have a serious problem. His attention shifted back to Bebe striding across the tarmac to where Duncan waited by an armored SUV, even though his words were addressed to Kensai. "Have Miko and Mai on stand-by." The sisters were Family, Kensai's descendants though Caesar couldn't recall how many generations removed from the ronin.

Jamal, Kensai's life and flying partner, joined them. "You're planning a daytime run back to San Francisco?" The Moor's bared fangs gleamed against his dark skin. "Just what kind of trouble are we in?"

The flashbulb pop behind Caesar's left eye signaled the beginnings of another stress migraine. He rubbed his temple in an attempt to alleviate the pain. Despite some sleep, he still wasn't at one hundred percent. "Ptolemy couldn't keep his mouth shut, could he?"

"He only said that someone took potshots at you, something to do with your solitaire witch." Kensai fixed him with a pointed stare. "He did his job as one of your Enforcers by informing us of potential trouble."

"I know, but sometimes the boy doesn't understand the difference between necessary knowledge and gossip." And Caesar needed to have a long overdue talk with his baby brother concerning that difference. Even after two thousand years, some people refused to grow up.

His irritation must have shown. Kensai shot him a reassuring smile. "The subject will go no further, Master. But I want the girls to wear bulletproof vests for the time-being."

Caesar nodded. "You both should as well. Whoever took shots at us knew I was a vampire. They had explosive rounds and bullets laced with a garlic compound."

Jamal whistled through his front teeth, but Kensai merely nodded and said, "We will take the appropriate precautions."

Reassured, Caesar jogged down the steps and stalked toward the SUV. He couldn't shake the feeling of wrongness about this whole situation. Natasha's extreme measures in protecting her Book and her granddaughter were obviously warranted. But the preparedness of the gunmen bothered him. Did Bebe's assailants know that Natasha Petrov and Ziva Epstein had approached him concerning their granddaughter's protection, or were the assassins merely covering their bases when they tried to kill her? And why murder Bebe when she had no interest in taking over the coven?

Too many questions flew through his aching head with no real answers. If he could figure out the why, then he could discover the who behind this insane scenario. And what the Hades was in that gods-cursed book that Bebe was willing to risk life and limb to get it?

A chill having nothing to do with either his current weakness or the balmy Los Angeles night ran through him. Natasha had been researching the similarities of the V-virus to both AIDS and Ebola. She had truly believed that a cure for him, for all vampires, was possible and had joked that one day she'd take him on noon picnic in Golden Gate Park. Had Natasha found the answer before she died and placed the information in her Book of Shadows?

But that begged the question of who knew about her research besides him. Was Bebe playing him to get her hands on the Book and hold the cure over his head?

He didn't like the ugly suspicion. He wanted to trust Bebe, but it would be unwise to base his trust on a woman he barely knew. She wasn't Natasha, no matter how alike grandmother and granddaughter were. Too many people depended on him to let his guard totally down.

All theories concerning the problems represented by the intriguing Dr. Zachary flew out of his head at the intense argument taking place by the SUV. And for once the good doctor wasn't the one shouting. Instead, she stood to the side, observing his brother's temper tantrum with a bemused smile that exhibited her dimples.

"You are not driving this vehicle! You just got your license!"

The petite Normal teenager Ptolemy shouted at didn't back down one iota. Caesar wasn't surprised. Between her guardians' respective training regimens, Tiffany Stephens could and had killed rogue vampires. She pulled a yellow No. 2 pencil, her weapon of choice, from the pocket of her jean jacket and waved it in Ptolemy's face.

"Back off, Prince of Darkness. I've had my license for a year, and I still drive better than you."

"Tiffany, put the pencil down before someone gets hurt," Duncan ordered his niece.

Ptolemy sniffed in disgust. "She'd barely qualify as a snack."

"He was referring to you getting hurt, Prince Asshole," Tiffany shot back.

The idea of setting Ptolemy and Tiffany on each other tempted Caesar. Such a battle would put the old gladiatorial games to shame. Not to mention he'd reap a fortune on the wagers if he publicized the bout. The two had each done their share of annoying the supernatural community so a profit would be a foregone conclusion.

And maybe it would burn off the mutual attraction Ptolemy and Tiffany felt for each other. Not that his brother would ever touch the girl, much less admit his feelings, but Ptolemy's method of needling Tiffany to circumvent her crush on him drove the rest of the household insane.

Unfortunately, such a plan, no matter how enticing, would add one more straw to the camel-load of issues between Duncan and Selene. Bebe caught his eye. Her smirk indicated she had an inkling of his thoughts without any telepathy between them. He rolled his eyes, and she covered her mouth to smother her giggle.

The simple byplay left him with a warmth that had nothing to do with his cock for once. It had been too long since he'd exchanged such an intimate pleasantry with a woman through a look. But a romantic relationship with a non-vampire was out of the question, and most female vampires looked at him as a means to power.

First things first though. He gathered his mental energy.

Enough!

Everyone except Bebe jumped and whirled to stare at him. Bebe, on the other hand, winced as if in pain. His telepathic shout had probably slammed into her shields like a truck. He'd make it up to her later. First, he needed to play daddy, the part of his position as coven master that grew tiresome.

"If you two are finished, I'd like to leave now." He gave Ptolemy and Tiffany a measured glare. Neither cowered but each had the common sense to lower their eyes and mutter half-hearted apologies.

One of Bebe's eyebrows rose when Ptolemy climbed into the rear seat next to Anne. She gave Caesar a curious look but wisely said nothing. Given the daggers shooting out of little Tiffany's eyes, Caesar did not fault his brother for taking the safer choice. If he rode shotgun, Ptolemy wouldn't resist the urge to comment on Tiffany's driving skills. And Tiffany wouldn't resist the urge to stake him with a pencil in response.

From the dirty look Bebe shot Caesar, she must have noticed his pleased smile when he settled next to her in the middle bench seat. She said nothing and looked out the window next to her. For the first time, he understood Ptolemy's dilemma. It was a bitch to be attracted to someone who was off-limits. Following Bebe's lead, he kept his mouth shut as Tiffany peeled rubber across the tarmac.

Two hours later, Bebe smoothed the skirt of the black dress she wore while Caesar guided his Jaguar through Los Angeles traffic. Once again, she couldn't believe the superb job Anne had done in choosing a wardrobe. The dress hugged her curves in a positive way, and it actually made her short, stumpy legs look long.

She leaned back against the headrest. Everything the vampires had done the last couple of days had destroyed all her preconceived notions. Heck, even Caesar's Brentwood mansion had a modern Mediterranean flair with an incomprehensible number of windows, instead of some dark, gloomy Dracula-like castle.

Despite the chaos of her life had become, she looked forward to some time alone with the enigmatic vampire master. He intrigued her in a way no other man ever had. And it wasn't just because he looked delicious in a suit. If it wasn't for the fact that he was a vampire, she could have enjoyed a date or two with him. Too bad such a relationship would never work out.

Caesar brought his Jag to a smooth stop in front of the famed Anthony's and opened her door before the valet had taken two steps. She complimented his driving when he proffered his arm to escort her into the ritzy restaurant.

He chuckled and said, "Then it doesn't take much to impress you, does it?"

She shuddered. "I was just happy to make it to Brentwood in one piece. Escaping from guerillas in Chad wasn't as hair-raising as Tiffany driving through the remains of L.A. rush hour."

He laughed outright as they followed the maitre d'. Instead of seating them in the main dining room, the prim host led them back to a private room. A cozy, intimate room. One with its own fireplace and a multitude of candles in brass sconces on the walls and in matching tabletop holders. Dark wood paneling and burgundy carpet gave the room a sophisticated and sensual air.

Her first impulse was to protest, but the maitre d' had already whisked out of the room after seating them with a few words in French to Caesar. She settled for giving the vampire the evil eye.

One dark eyebrow raised in a questioning look. "Have I done something to offend you?" he asked.

"Don't you think this—" She waved a hand around the room. "—is just a little too much? Who are you trying to impress here?"

A wry smile filled his features. "Obviously not you." He leaned back in his chair, his fingers steepled as he regarded her. "I thought after the activity of the last couple of days you would appreciate a quieter venue. I, on the other hand, appreciate the solitude with a charming dinner companion."

She grinned back at him. "As opposed to the teen terror?"

His irritated expression left no doubt that he had wanted to ditch his entourage for the peace alone. The vampires had protested, rather loudly, about the lack of security. Tiffany had simply pouted at her lack of inclusion in the dinner plans.

When he didn't appear to want to elucidate, she swallowed hard and gathered what little courage she had left. "Why do you let a Normal girl hang out with your coven?" At his dark look, she reached for her glass and sipped water to soothe her suddenly dry throat.

"Why do you persist in assuming Tiffany is in any danger from us?"

She shrugged and set her glass down. "I'm not. I just can't see any parent, even Family, allowing an underage child to be subjected to a potentially hazardous environment."

He folded his hands and leaned forward until his elbows rested on the table. The similarity to his actions and a lion preparing to pounce unnerved her. Her breath caught, waiting for him to spring.

"I'll have you know, Dr. Zachary, that I haven't been shot at in the last sixty years. At least not until I met you." The glint of humor in his golden eyes belied the dry, clipped tone of his voice. "As for Tiffany's safety, she's fully capable of taking care of herself."

Playing with fire had gotten Bebe into trouble on more than one occasion over the years, but her protective instincts reared up. She waved her hand. "And her parents are okay with their little girl trained to play war?"

Caesar's eyes shuttered and became cold, almost pragmatic. She suppressed a shudder. His look reminded her too much of the rebels who dragged the village children off into the night and turned them into soldiers.

"Not that it's any of your business, Doctor, but Tiffany's parents are dead. They were murdered the same night your parents were. So you see, Doctor, you and Tiffany Stephens have something in common."

Bebe's hand flew to her mouth and gorge rose in her throat. "Oh my Goddess." She'd witnessed the horror the rogues had inflicted on her parents, made worse by her inability to do anything to help them. Had the rogues done the same thing to the Stephens in front of their baby? She struggled to get her memories and emotions under control. She had her grandparents, aunts, uncles, cousins, no matter what pains in the ass they were. For Tiffany to have no one . . .

She dropped her hand and whispered, "Didn't she have anywhere else to go?"

"You mean any Normal family?" He could have sneered, but somehow he understood her manner wasn't condescending. He shook his head. "No. Her only relatives left were vampires or Family not old enough themselves to care for her. As one of her great-uncles, Duncan took her in and raised her as his own."

"How? That had to have been nearly impossible with him, being, you know . . ." For the first time, embarrassment at the way she'd acted toward the vampires consumed her. Heat flooded her cheeks, and she reached for her glass to cover her discomfort.

"You mean, how could a cold, nasty blood-sucker possibly care for a three-month-old infant?" Amusement returned to his voice, and he leaned back once again. "Vampires sharing the night bottles made the job a little easier. It was a joint effort, I assure you. Plus Duncan had help from someone who could bear to go out in sunlight."

Bebe shook her head. "Servants and nannies aren't the same as family." She knew since Grandma often left her in others' care. Goddess, she'd forgotten how much she resented the lack of real attention from her grandmother after her parents' deaths. And poor Tiffany didn't even get the small gift of knowing her parents for the handful of years Bebe had known hers.

Caesar grinned. "Once again, you make assumptions." He reached for her hand, his thumb sliding across her palm in sensual circles. "Duncan had a friend, Phillippa Mann, named as Tiffany's co-guardian. Phillippa took the child to the park, made sure she arrived at school safely—"

"And handled those pesky daytime parent-teacher conferences?" Bebe added.

Caesar laughed, a warm sound from the belly. She had a suspicion it wasn't something he did often.

"That is one assumption that is safe for you to make. There were many. We are all praying that Tiffany manages to graduate from high school this May," he admitted. "Phillippa has a patience with Tiffany that the rest of us often lack."

"This Phillippa must be something special," Bebe muttered under her breath. The wave of jealousy at Caesar's tone socked her in the gut. What claim did she have on him?

None whatsoever, her silent nag chided.

From the glimmer in his eyes, he'd caught her barely disguised cattiness. Instead of his teasing smirk, a wistful expression crossed his features. "Tiffany's the closest any of my household came to having a child we could call our own. Perhaps we all indulge her far too much."

His cool fingers turned her hand over and stroked the sensitive skin at her wrist. How could a touch so slight send a sensual tsunami through her nerves? She clenched her thighs in an effort to concentrate on their conversation.

"So whose smart idea was it to give her an SUV for her sixteenth birthday?"

He laughed again, the sound a viable force that curled through her body. She checked her shields. Nope, still solid. If he couldn't violate her mental barriers, how the hell did he make her react this way?

"The vehicle is Duncan's. Tiffany drives for him when she's not in class. Duncan concluded it was the best solution to keep an eye on the child."

She fingered the crystal stem of her water goblet. "So this Phillippa is Family?"

That sly smile she found so damned irritating appeared on his face. "Why don't you ask her tomorrow morning?"

Figures he would try to distract her. She shook her head. "I can't meet her tomorrow. We're going over to Seven Wonders in the morning. Or are you reneging on your promise?"

"I wouldn't dream of doing so. But that doesn't mean you can't interrogate Phillippa about her relationship with me as well."

The inescapable sensation of being sucked under by quicksand enveloped her. "What are you talking about?"

Caesar took a sip of his own water before answering. "Phillippa Mann is the owner of Seven Wonders Antiques."

Chapter 12

Sweet Goddess, I am such a dumbass.

Bebe blinked, trying to wipe away the shock. He'd lied. Again. Maybe his lies were ones of omission, little facts he refused to reveal, but they were still lies. Her life was nothing more than a game to him. She wanted to fry his butt, teach him not to mess with her. Heat flooded her face, her body, her hands . . .

The wine steward entered, pushing the cart ahead of him with the ice bucket perched on top. She squelched the flames on the edge of her fingertips. Embarrassment at her slip replaced her anger at Caesar.

The steward displayed the bottle and then the cork for Caesar's approval. She settled for glaring at the vampire while the steward poured the white wine. Once Caesar sipped and nodded his acceptance of the vintage, the steward filled her glass, and deposited the bottle in the ice bucket before he scurried out the door. Bebe didn't blame him considering the thick tension in the room.

"I thought vampires only stuck with red liquids." The acid in her voice must have surprised him by the look on his face. Well, what the hell did he expect by not telling her of his connection with the owner of Seven Wonders yesterday? He'd had plenty of opportunities. She toyed with the stem of her glass, but she made no move to taste the wine that she was sure cost more than her plane ticket back from Africa. Instead, she continued to stare at him.

Without flinching, he said, "I like my wine like my women." He smiled before finishing his thought. "A little on the tart side."

Her mouth dropped open at the cheesy pick-up line. It was so incongruous with Mr. Sophisticated Controlling Vampire that she started laughing. Not a polite, social laugh, but a deep belly rumbler that left tears in her eyes.

"Oh, sweet Goddess, where'd you learn to seduce woman? James Bond movies?" She started laughing again, slapping the table until the cut glass goblets sang from the vibrations.

He chuckled as well. "I have to admit a particular fondness for Sean Connery, but nothing beats Ian Fleming's original prose."

Shaking her head between hiccupping gulps of laughter, she said, "No, I gotta disagree. Pierce Brosnan's still the best movie Bond." She swiped her tears away with her fingertips. "You're one sick vampire, you know that?"

Soberness replaced the laughter as she remembered why she was furious with him. And she was letting him distract her. But when was the last time she'd laughed at a man's joke?

No, she couldn't afford to let him off the hook. Too many lives depended on her getting to the Book first, not just hers. "I'm still pissed at you for not coming clean. Why not tell me right off this Phillippa is one of your people? Why all the games?"

He leaned back in his chair, his face still as he probably considered a new set of half-truths to tell her, but his aura remained a clear, brilliant red. "First of all, Phillippa is not one of *my* people as you put it."

"She's not Family?" Damn, what she wouldn't give to read his mind.

He shook his head. "No, Phillippa is not Family."

She leaned forward, elbows propped on the immaculate white tablecloth. "Then what is she? What's her relationship with your coven?"

"Her heritage is her business to share with you if she chooses, not mine." He smiled again, as if he enjoyed their verbal sparring. "As for our relationship, we have done favors for each other over the years. Nothing more."

More dissembling. What else had she expected? But dammit, she was not stooping to his level by asking what kind of favors this Phillippa had performed for him. She sat back with a huff. "In other words, you're not going to tell me a Goddess-damned thing, are you?"

He locked eyes with her, but no feathery touch of his shields against hers came. Instead, he said, "Are you going to tell me what you expected to find in the wardrobe?"

She toyed with the idea of coming clean. Just because he said Grandma trusted him didn't mean that was the truth. And if Grandma trusted him as she said in the letter, why hadn't Grandma ever mentioned that she was friends with Caesar? Maybe Grandma's letter had been a carefully-crafted forgery. There was only Caesar's word that the letter came from the nymph hole. Silence dragged on for a minute, then two, as she and Caesar stared at each other.

The waiter burst into the room, carrying a dish on the tips of his fingers. He ignored the sizzling electricity running rampant and placed the plate before her with a flourish.

She looked up at the waiter. "Wait a minute. I didn't order this."

From the corner of her eye, she caught Caesar's fingertips press his lips when the waiter gave her a haughty sniff.

"I am sorry if Monsieur Augustine did not inform the mademoiselle of the rules for the backroom." The waiter whipped around on his heels and marched for the door, leaving it open a crack as he left.

New horror replaced Bebe's confusion. "What have you gotten me into, Augustine?"

Caesar struggled not to laugh at Bebe's appalled expression. Bebe's leaps of emotion were entertaining, unlike most women he'd known over the centuries. "Unfortunately, the price for using the backroom is suffering through one of Anthony's experiments." He leaned forward and whispered, "Only Zeus knows what he'll do to *my* meal."

She winced before she looked back down at the brown mass surrounded by artfully arranged parsley and a green sauce. She picked up the first tiny fork and poked at the appetizer before she looked back up at him. "What is it?"

"Well, it's definitely not roasted sparrow in honey sauce," he offered.

"Eeewwww!"

He shrugged and leaned forward to inhale the contents of the plate. An all-too-familiar scent from Tiffany's infancy hit his nostrils, making his struggle to keep a straight face that much harder. In all the chaos surrounding Natasha's death, he'd totally forgotten about his bet with Anthony. Leave it to his nephew to pick the wrong damn time. He met Bebe's suspicious gaze. "I'm not sure, but I believe the green sauce is mint."

Eyes narrowed, Bebe laid down the fork. "I think I'll pass. I learned a long time ago, if you can't identify it, don't eat it."

"Bravo! Bravo!" Clapping, Anthony shoved the door open with a hip and strode in. Even though the restaurant owner was forty-five, his beaming, cherubic face and tight brunette curls made him look twenty years younger. He pointed a finger at Caesar. "You owe me a hundred bucks."

Bebe leaned forward. "You were betting on me?" The outraged look on Bebe's face would have been adorable if Caesar wasn't trying to win her trust.

Anthony winced. "Oooo, did I just blow your date, man?"

"We're not dating," Caesar and Bebe said at the same time.

Anthony raised his hands defensively. "Whoa, my mistake, folks."

Bebe's right eyebrow rose. "So what was this bet about?"

"Um." Anthony flicked his gaze to Caesar.

Caesar said nothing. Anthony should have warned him ahead of time. It would serve the child right to sink on his own. A quick glance at Bebe said the ride home would be very unpleasant.

Anthony ran a hand over his unruly curls. "Well, Caesar said I could serve dog food, and no one would know the difference because they assumed expensive meant good. And I bet him a hundred bucks that anyone with common sense could tell the difference between slop and fine cuisine."

The horrified look returned to Bebe's face. "You served me dog food!"

Anthony's expression matched hers, and he waved his hands frantically. "No, no, no!" He pointed at the brown lump. "That's Gerber's ground lamb."

Disbelief replaced horror. "You served me baby food?"

A sheepish grin covered Anthony's mug. "Well, our bet was on the next non-vampire he brought to my restaurant."

Caesar swallowed a groan. He wouldn't be in this predicament if he'd specified the next werewolf. Anthony would have thought twice before serving baby food to the Los Angeles Packmaster.

Anthony shrugged. "For all I knew, he could have brought a health and safety inspector with him tonight, so I played it safe." He removed the plate from the table. "What would you like tonight, Ms.—"

"Elizabeth Levi. She just joined my employ." Caesar ignored the dirty look Bebe shot him. Her safety was his responsibility. He couldn't take the chance that she would, in all innocence, destroy the identity he'd carefully constructed for her.

"So, Liz, what'll it be? I got some fresh scallops in this morning." Anthony winked at her. "Grilled and served with linguini and cream sauce? It's on the house. Come on, what d'ya say? It's the least I can do to make up for you getting caught in the middle of my bet with my uncle."

"Uncle?" She turned to Caesar, and for once, she looked at him with something other than mistrust and suspicion. Her mouth gaped open in confusion.

"Does that surprise you, Ms. Levi?" He couldn't resist baiting her. Again. Even though, he'd mentioned that he had Family, the knowledge apparently was only now registering in her mind.

"Oops, don't tell me I stuck my foot in my mouth?"

Wishing desperately for Anthony to shut up, Caesar dragged his attention away from Bebe's lovely eyes to glare at his nephew. "You do seem to be slipping in the discretion department. I hope you are quite done insulting my guest." He faced Bebe again, who still looked at him with a shocked expression. "Are the scallops and pasta acceptable? If not, Anthony will prepare whatever you desire."

Her mouth snapped shut, and she shook her head. "No the scallops and linguini will be fine."

His attention shifted to Anthony. "Ms. Levi has a fondness for chocolate. I trust you will serve her an adequate dessert." Bebe's mouth dropped open again.

The sheepish look returned to Anthony's face. "No problem. I know just the thing." With the plate of baby food in hand, he strode out of the room.

"How do you know chocolate's my favorite treat?" The suspicion was back in her eyes.

Caesar leaned back in his chair, despite the urge to brush the curl away from her face that had escaped her topknot. He enjoyed keeping the lovely doctor off balance far more than he should. "I sent Natasha a sample box of chocolates from an investment company I was considering. She called me a few days later, saying the company should be sound after she found you asleep on the floor of her wardrobe with the empty box."

Her face flushed a becoming pink, and she could no longer meet his eyes, choosing to stare at the fire. Was she embarrassed by the childhood incident, or like him, did she hate thinking about the innocence that was ripped away from her at such a young age? He wanted to ask but didn't dare, too much history that neither needed to deal with right now.

After a few seconds, she cleared her throat and turned to meet his gaze, all hint of vulnerability gone. "You didn't have to be that hard on poor Anthony."

His eyebrows rose as he regarded her. "He tried to serve you baby food."

"Because *you* insulted him and then made a stupid bet with him." Her lips twisted in a wry grin. "Serves you right that he embarrassed you."

"I was not embarrassed."

She cocked an eyebrow and reached for her glass of wine. "Then why the dressing down?"

Because he had wanted to impress her. Because he'd wanted a quiet place that was reasonably secure to discover what lay behind the cool front she exhibited. Because he wanted time to explore the attraction between them without his household's knowledge or interference.

Not that he planned to follow through on that attraction.

He ground his teeth, searching for a reasonable explanation to give her. One that wouldn't scare her. Or piss her off even more than she already was. "You're right. I was embarrassed."

Instead of the triumphant expression he expected from her at his admission, she sobered and nodded. "It's okay. I won't tell anyone."

For someone who constantly proclaimed her condemnation for vampires, Bebe knew and respected the subtleties of his people's culture.

She toyed with the appetizer fork while she watched him. "Anthony must be one of your sister's descendants."

Her perceptiveness shook him. No one had mentioned Selene in Bebe's presence as far as he knew. "How did you know I had a sister?"

Her face flamed bright pink again. "I, um, well, that is—"

He folded his arms as he waited for her to finish stuttering. How much of the conversation between Selene, Ptolemy and him in his office had she overheard?

"I overheard Alex telling Ptolemy in the hallway that your sister was at the house last night," she finally said.

"When you were snooping through my house, you mean?"

Her face went from pink to scarlet. "Well, if you hadn't outbid me for the wardrobe, I wouldn't have been looking for it."

He smiled at her flustered expression. "Yes, Anthony is one of Selene's descendants. What makes you think he isn't one of Ptolemy's?"

"You're kidding, right? He hasn't been civil to anybody since I've met him, much less any woman."

He roared with laughter at her observation. Despite their parents' vaunted prowess as lovers, Ptolemy had always lacked in the social graces when it came to the opposite sex.

The rest of the meal passed in pleasant conversation. She was remarkably well-read for someone of her generation, and she lavished compliments on Anthony until the young chef glowed with pride.

Later, as they waited for the valet to bring Caesar's car around, she gave a loud sigh.

He glanced down at her. "What's wrong?"

She smiled up at him. "Nothing. That's just it. Nothing's wrong. For the first time in a long time, I feel . . . normal."

Normal.

Something deep inside him responded to her simple happiness in the moment. He leaned closer, giving her plenty of opportunity to avoid him, to step back, to say no. Instead, her mouth opened ever so slightly. He brushed his lips against hers with a feather-light touch.

She didn't back away but eased closer. Her fingers combed through his hair before winding around his neck as she deepened their kiss. Her full breasts pressed against him, igniting a fire that could destroy them both.

A soft moan from her throat was all that was needed to eliminate his fleeting thought. Their tongues met, danced and parted only to meet again. The rich chocolate of her dessert mixed with her own ginger and peach flavor, a taste he couldn't get enough of, would never be able to get enough.

She sighed into his mouth, a sound of both surrender and demand. And gods above, how he wanted to oblige her. Take her to his bed. Tear the clothes from her lush body and love her—

No.

He couldn't love her. Not the way he wanted. Not without destroying her in the process.

He eased out of their kiss, reluctance slowing his movements. She stared up at him, confusion mixed with lust in her huge brown eyes.

In the split second of searching his brain for the right thing to tell Bebe, he caught the scent. Not the ripe apple scent of the Normal staff, but sandalwood.

Another vampire.

The revelation barely formed when a blurred figure rammed them both into the rock-hard pavement.

Chapter 13

Body still reeling from Caesar's kiss, Bebe looked up at him. But something was very, very wrong. His attention was elsewhere, his nostrils flared, like a predator scenting an interloper on the night wind.

Then something slammed them both to the concrete, hard enough to knock the wind out of her. Screams and shouts echoed above and behind them.

Before she could react, before she could even think of reacting, something had a grip on her topknot and yanked her upright. She reached out mentally, and received a psychic slap for her effort.

A female witch.

Pain burned, both through her psychic senses and through her scalp at the manhandling, and she scrambled to get her feet under her. Once upright, she froze at the flesh jammed against her windpipe and the metal grazing the left side of her neck.

Of all the stupid ways to die. Her throat slit in front of an L.A. restaurant by a plain old knife after her first decent date in years.

And that pissed her off. More than any of the posing, politics and plots that had occurred in the week since she'd returned to the States.

Channeling her fury, Bebe stomped on the bitch's instep as hard as she could, throwing her body back at the same time. Caught off guard by the physical defense, her assailant screamed and flailed wildly before they crashed back down on the concrete portico.

The point of the knife sliced across Bebe's cheek as she rolled away from the other witch. Grateful the cut wasn't to her jugular, she continued the roll until her body smacked a potted palm. She swiped her cheek, and reaching up with her bloody fingers, she grabbed a handful of dirt. Using anger and blood as focal points wasn't smart, but she ignored common sense, forced her will into the tiny handful of dirt mixed with her blood, and flung it at the other witch. The glob of mud struck the bitch squarely between the eyes.

More amoeba than humanoid, her hastily constructed semi-golem oozed its way down the other witch's face and into her mouth. While her opponent gagged and choked on the bloody mud, Bebe searched frantically for Caesar. At the sight of him, her inability to catch her breath had nothing to do with the blow to her diaphragm.

He whirled and dodged in a dangerous dance as he fended off three other vampires, obviously trying to draw them away from her. His eyes glowed golden and his bared fangs flashed as he fought. A half-transformed were lay near the curb, its neck broken from the unnatural angle of its head.

The bastard could be pissed all he wanted, but he was outgunned and needed her help. She climbed to her feet, shaky from her own battle. She didn't dare conjure a fireball for fear of hitting Caesar. And there wasn't a damn thing she could use other than the potted palms and the patrons' keys hanging neatly on the valet's rack. Nothing except . . .

Bebe gulped hard. The other witch's knife glittered under the hanging light bulbs that decorated the restaurant entrance. And the witch herself clawed with desperation, trying to breathe past the mud clogging her windpipe. Bebe reached down and snatched up the knife, then cursed herself for not checking if the other witch had bespelled it first.

The bitch hadn't, thank the Goddess. Plain wood met Bebe's palm. Gorge rose in her throat at the thought of what she was about to do. She'd never actually killed anyone. Not even a vampire, despite her years of fear and hatred. She glanced at the writhing witch on the concrete.

So much for doing no harm.

She checked the progress of the vampire battle. Caesar feinted around one of his opponents. He pulled out a push broom hidden behind the valet rack. With a quick snap, he broke off the brush end. A vicious smile lit his face as he twirled the broomstick in his hand, the jagged point whistling in the night air.

The three vamps backed away from Caesar. The one farthest from Bebe met her eyes, noting that Bebe was still standing and the other witch wasn't. The malicious grin he aimed at her disappeared as fast as his legs out from under him when Caesar swept the broomstick under his knees. Only the martial arts kick from one of his buddies kept Caesar from staking him.

The third vampire, an ugly bruiser with a thick shock of brown hair hanging in his face, followed his downed buddy's attention to her. Fangs flashed and an ugly snarl came from his throat.

Then he leapt.

Bebe could only raise her hands in defense before Bruiser slammed her down on the concrete for the third time. Except instead of ripping out her throat, he had a surprised look on his face. She followed his gaze down to where the knife protruded from his chest, her fist still firmly wrapped around the hilt.

"Shit," he said, and his eyes met hers for a split-second before they fell out of the sockets. Skin slid from the vampire's face as he melted. In seconds, Bebe was covered in the gooey, stinking remains of vampire.

She rolled over and, for the first time since medical school, threw up.

"Bebe!"

At Caesar's shout, she swiped congealed vampire flesh off her face. Breathing through her mouth to keep the rotten meat odor from triggering another round of vomiting, she looked up. Distracted, he paid no attention to the vampire behind him. The one that now had a knife in his upraised hand.

"Caesar, behind—"

Before she could finish her screamed warning, the vampire's head rolled across the sidewalk and bounced into the gutter. The corpse collapsed to its knees, the rapid decomposition already sloughing flesh from bones. Behind the melting body stood Ptolemy, a self-satisfied smirk on his face and a bloody sword in his hand.

The last vampire launched himself at Ptolemy, who took a wild swing at him. Having more of a clue than his friends, he ducked and dived underneath Ptolemy's sword stroke, aiming a nasty kick at Ptolemy's knee as he went. Caesar's brother crashed to the concrete.

A solid whack of the broomstick caught the enemy vamp under the chin as he started to rise. He flipped over backwards and rolled left to avoid a jab. When he rose, he clutched the knife of his beheaded friend. With a flick of his wrist, the vampire aimed the steel straight at Bebe and threw.

Before she could blink, the knife went clattering into the driveway. Caesar barely finished the swing that knocked the knife off its flight path when he impaled the vampire on the business end of his broken broomstick. The vampire liquefied even as he attempted to yank the offending wood out of his chest.

Caesar turned and stalked toward her, the expression on his face one of unmitigated fury. His eyes were no longer gold, but shifting rapidly to crimson. Acting on raw instinct, Bebe scrabbled backward away from him on all fours. Her pulse pounded an obscene rhythm as the memory of the night her parents died rushed over her. Caesar's face held the same blood fury as her parents' murderers.

The glow in his eyes faded a fraction. He knelt and held out his hand. "Are you all right, Bebe?"

She eyed his outstretched palm warily before she met his gaze. The red tint disappeared. Neon yellow melted into warm hazel as concern replaced anger. She nodded and reached for his hand, letting him pull her to her feet. Her knees shook as the initial adrenaline rush died. He wrapped an arm around her to support her weight, and she loathed to admit she needed his help. He examined her body, checking for additional injuries.

"I'm fine." She flashed him a weak smile. "I smell worse then I look." She dabbed at the brand new dress. "I'm sorry you wasted the money."

"I'm not."

She looked back up. The glow in his eyes brightened, and this time it wasn't from blood lust. Her breath caught in her lungs and not from her bruised diaphragm.

"The witch's dead."

Ptolemy's voice drew them both back to the present. He crouched next to the body.

"That can't be!"

But Ptolemy was right. She stepped over, and kneeling on the other side of the woman, she checked her pulse and breathing. Or, in this case, lack thereof. She shifted her sight to examine the other witch. The woman's aura had turned black and would soon disappear as the individual cells of her body died. Thankfully, none of their assailants' souls had hung around after their physical deaths. She didn't have the energy to deal with five vengeful ghosts.

Nausea did another queasy journey through her stomach. She'd never killed anyone before. But how? There hadn't been enough dirt to choke the other witch to death. Maybe give her a bad case of pneumonia if any individual dirt particles made it into her lungs . . .

"It's not your fault." Caesar rested a hand on her shoulder. "I'd have preferred to have someone to question, but our attackers were determined. Do you recognize her?"

Bebe shook her head, but then would she recognize anyone from either the San Francisco or Los Angeles covens? Between med school and now, she'd been gone an awfully long time. She tilted the corpse's head. The double piercings in the other witch's ears were empty of decoration. She definitely didn't want to be recognized.

"I think we have a bigger problem." Ptolemy's voice had a worried tone.

Bebe turned to follow his equally worried look. At least twenty Norms were plastered against the huge glass entry doors of the restaurant. In the center of the group stood Anthony, who looked like he was ready to kill someone himself.

"Now's when I really wish I had one of Will Smith's flashy thingies."

"This isn't funny, Ptolemy," Caesar said.

The vampire's attention shifted to his brother. "Who's joking? Between the two of us, we could probably handle the window group, but by now, the entire restaurant knows and someone's sure to have called 9-1-1."

All of Grandma's damage control training prompted an idea. "I could whip something up in the kitchen," Bebe said. "Anthony would have most of what I need. I can wing the rest."

Caesar gave her a wry look. "You can erase everyone's memory before the police arrive?"

She shook her head. "No, but I can blunt it. The customers will know a fight occurred, but they won't be able to remember details or give accurate descriptions. If you two can—" She coughed and nodded toward the two remaining corpses. The remains of the three vampires were already starting to liquefy and dribble across the portico toward the gutter. A good hosing of the concrete would take care of everything else.

"Ptolemy, bring your truck around," Caesar said.

Two hours later, in the back room where she and Caesar had dined, Bebe breathed a sigh of relief, collapsed in a chair and closed her eyes. A mere flicker of thought was all it took to drop the glamour that covered the cut on her left cheek and the bruises on her throat. She didn't have the energy for anything else. Once again, she was totally exhausted and wearing someone else's cotton t-shirt and shorts. Luckily, one of the female bartenders had workout clothes stashed in her bag. A faint wisp of mourning crossed Bebe's mind for her ruined outfit. She had really loved that dress.

For all of the twenty-four hours she owned it.

Her half-assed memory-erasing spell had worked though. Anthony and his staff managed to serve the spell carrier concoction to everyone at the restaurant through free drinks before the police arrived. Thank the Goddess, they didn't have more people there that had witnessed the incident due to the hour and the day of the week. With her reserves wiped out, she wouldn't have been able to make a larger batch of potion. Without decent descriptions of the attackers, who had allegedly escaped, and since no one at the restaurant had apparently been injured, the two officers wrote the fight off as an attempted robbery, gave Bebe and Caesar fake smiles, and said if they learned anything they'd contact Caesar's office.

Bebe gently probed the cut on her cheek. It could have been worse. She could have been one of the bodies Caesar and Ptolemy had loaded in the bed of Ptolemy's pick-up. She didn't have the guts to ask Caesar where Ptolemy had disappeared with the corpses of the witch and the were.

The clink of glassware drew her attention. She opened her eyes to find Anthony collapsing in the chair next to her. A bottle of Jack Daniels and three shot glasses sat in the middle of the table.

"You pour. I'm too tired." He followed his declaration with a gigantic yawn.

"Are you a telepath?" she asked, not that she believed he had breached her shields.

He frowned and shook his head.

She smiled and lifted the bottle. "My favorite." She poured two fingers and had to wait until he finished another yawn before she handed the glass to him. "I'd think you'd be used to the long hours."

He swallowed the entire glassful before she had her own drink poured. "Long hours? Yes. Almost losing my restaurant because some supernatural hit team tries to off my uncle at my front door? No."

Not knowing how to answer him, she downed her own drink, relishing the burn in her throat, before she poured another round for them.

Caesar entered the room and crossed to give her a peck on the forehead, his actions more comforting than she cared to admit. All pretenses of Mr. Dark and Mysterious Vampire were gone. Missing suit jacket, messed hair and rumpled shirt marred his normally immaculate appearance. He pulled a chair closer to hers and dropped into it. Without a word, she poured whiskey into the third glass and handed it to him.

He swallowed it in one gulp and held it out to her for a refill. "They know you're here in Los Angeles."

"No shit, Sherlock." She handed the full glass back to him. Her fingertips tingled at the brush of his touch. How could she be aroused at a time like this?

"You're taking this remarkably well." He eyed her over the top of the glass as he downed the second shot.

"Would you prefer I scream like a girl and wait for you to save me the next time?"

Both Caesar and Anthony grinned at her thick sarcasm.

She took a deep breath, glad for the vague numbness that allowed her to deal with tonight's scare. "I'm not stupid, Caesar. The were and vamps were there to keep you out of the way long enough for the witch to slit my throat. No fuss, no muss, and no way to link anything back to anyone."

She rose and retrieved the knife that had been at her jugular earlier from the plastic sack containing her ruined dress. Returning to the table, she laid the slimy knife on the pristine tablecloth in front of him. "Do you know what this is?"

He looked at the plain, black-handled steel, then met her eyes, his eyebrow cocked and his smirk back in place. "A knife?"

Anthony leaned forward and examined the knife, but he didn't touch it. "It's a sushi knife." He met Bebe's eyes and frowned. "Why would a witch use a sushi knife?"

"Exactly," she said and turned back to Caesar. "It's definitely not an athame—"

"What's an athame?" Anthony said.

"A ceremonial knife witches use to direct energy during a ritual or spell," Caesar answered. "They don't use them as weapons though. It's considered sacrilege."

Bebe raised an eyebrow and glared at him.

He held up his hands. "Sorry, didn't mean to intrude. Please continue."

"There's no spell on this thing, and no residual magick, which means she couldn't have had it in her possession more than a few hours at most." She shrugged. "And why else remove her earrings?"

Caesar leaned his elbows on the table, his index fingers steepled as he considered her words. "The real question is why use the witch to kill you?"

She shot him a nasty smile. "Because vampires are so much more efficient at killing?"

His expression remained deadly sober, which sent a shiver of fear down her spine. "Yes, we are. So are the weres."

Anthony reached for the bottle of whiskey. "Because whoever's after

Bebe wanted someone they could trust to get the job done. Someone with a personal stake in the matter. They just didn't count on how fast she can think on her feet. And the stakes must be pretty fucking high for supes to risk exposure by staging a hit in a public place frequented by Normals, even if it is a Family-owned business."

Bebe and Caesar both turned to stare at the restaurateur.

"Come on, guys. I'm not stupid either." Anthony snorted. "I'm about as much as an eclectic witch as Bebe is. You're one of the White Rose claimants, aren't you?"

She shot Caesar a nasty look and threw her hands in the air. "So much for your brilliant plan. Even a Norm could figure out who I am."

"I'm not telling anyone, Bebe." Anthony grinned, but it wasn't as sparkling as before the fight. "But the White Rose succession has been a big topic of conversation down here. Word around town is Ziva Epstein's been in Africa looking for one of the heirs."

"You are so fucking dead, Augustine." Exhaustion kept her words from packing any real punch. "Europe, my ass. You knew where she was, didn't you? And you didn't bother to tell me?"

Caesar blew out an exasperated breath. "As I told you, I promised Natasha and Ziva to keep you safe."

"And a fine job you've done so far."

Anthony sprayed his third shot of Jack all over the tablecloth at her snarky comment.

"You're still alive, aren't you?" was Caesar's dry reply.

Sticking her tongue out at Caesar, she reached over and poured Anthony another shot. "No thanks to you tonight, but that's not the point. If it wasn't for your brother, we'd both be sushi right now."

An odd frown appeared on Caesar's face. "Yes, we're both lucky Ptolemy followed us."

"Damn straight. Have you actually spoken with Granny E.?" Her eyelids drooped. In fighting to keep them open, she couldn't spare the energy to figure out what his problem was. What the hell happened to all that lovely rest she had gotten earlier in the day?

"No. But I'm assuming that she received my message that you'd returned to the U.S. since her housekeeper said she was expected back tomorrow." He tilted his wrist to check his watch. "Later today I should say." His gaze flicked back to her face. "I'd say it's past time to return home since you can barely remain awake."

"I'm fine."

"Well, I'm not." Anthony rose. "And I have to close, so no offense, Bebe, but get the hell out of my place."

She jerked as she realized Anthony had been calling her by her own name since the fight and not her pseudonym. "How'd you know my real identity?"

Anthony stood and rolled his eyes. "Uncle Jerk-off yelling it on the street wasn't exactly subtle." He held out a hand, which she shook. "It was still a pleasure to meet you. You're welcome back anytime."

"Assuming I live long enough," she murmured as Anthony left the room. Exhaustion wormed its way through her mind.

"You will." Cool, strong fingers encircled her own, Caesar's touch so comforting she didn't want to ever let go.

Except she couldn't relax into the comfort he offered. Something else about the whole attack bothered her, but she couldn't quite grasp the slippery half-thought as it swam through her tired brain. She eyed Caesar. "Is there any way to autopsy the witch? Find out who she is? And more specifically what killed her?"

He winced. "We're trying to identify her from a photo, but the body . . ."

She sighed. "Ptolemy burned it, didn't he?"

He nodded. "There's a jointly owned crematorium that all of us in Los Angeles use for these types of situations."

"And you don't think anyone's going to ask about five missing supes?"

Again, the wry smirk appeared on his face. "Not without tipping his hand."

"Or her hand."

A muscle twitched along his jaw. Damn, he knew Alice was behind this. Was he trying to protect her? Or was he playing a whole different game with the witch community? It took a lot, a lot of money or a lot of threat, for three different races to act in concert as their assailants did tonight, even if the individuals were rogues.

He frowned and rose before helping her to her feet, never releasing his grip on her fingers. "I'm not sure what would be gained by examining her body."

"I want to find out exactly what killed her," she said, grabbing the knife off the table.

He eyed her with concern. "I understand your guilt over her death, but you were acting in self-defense." His gaze flicked down to the sushi knife in her hand. "And I'm afraid to ask why you're keeping that."

Tugging her hand loose from his, she walked over to the corner, dropped the knife in the sack and slung it over her shoulder. "I'll take it with us to Granny E.'s. It might be close to impossible, but we may be able to backtrack where the knife came from." She sighed at the skeptical look on his face. "I know it's a long shot but unless you have a better idea . . ."

He strode across the room to join her at the door and placed his hand on the small of her back as she preceded him out of the room. Despite his lower body temperature, his touch sent a heat through her that was totally inappropriate. She almost stopped just to luxuriate in the sensation.

Instead, they crossed the restaurant's main dining area, empty except for a handful of staff doing last minute cleaning. The employees looked at them curiously but with no real recognition. She should have known. Her spell may have taken care of the customers, but Caesar would have had to erase the memories of the staff while the police interviewed her.

They exited the main doors, and a tall shadow in the corner of her eye made her jump. She whipped around, hand reaching for the knife in her bag because she was, and she hated to admit it, too damn tired to summon a fireball, much less cast any other spell.

The shadow resolved into Caesar's man, Duncan, and she relaxed a fraction.

"What are you doing here?" Caesar demanded.

"Escorting you home, Your Highness." Despite his clipped British accent and deferential tone, steel lay behind Duncan's words. "I was remiss in allowing you to leave the estate unescorted tonight."

She glanced up at Caesar. By the play of emotions across his face, Caesar wasn't happy about needing a bodyguard, but he nodded.

Before either of them could add anything else, Duncan's SUV screeched to a halt in front of them, Tiffany at the wheel. Behind her came Caesar's Jaguar with Anne in the driver's seat, her eyes barely peeking above the steering wheel.

Duncan held the rear passenger door open, and Bebe climbed in and buckled the seatbelt. The last thing she remembered was Caesar pulling her against him and telling her to get some rest. Despite a vague warning in the back of her mind, she snuggled against his chest and sank into the welcoming cocoon of sleep.

Chapter 14

Dense fog surrounded Bebe. She couldn't see anything around her, not even the ground she walked on. Grandma Petrov's voice screamed through the gray mist, whether in anger or pain, Bebe couldn't tell.

"Grandma! Where are you?" She searched in a panic, stumbling because the damn fog obscured everything. Even her spell to disperse the mist failed. "Grandma!" Raw fear squeezed her heart. Something was wrong, terribly wrong. "Grandma? Answer me!" Smoky tendrils swallowed her shout. Grandma wouldn't leave her. She promised.

But the cries faded, and Bebe was alone. All alone. The ground shifted and dipped, then she fell.

Falling through the misty nothingness.

She jerked when her half-asleep brain realized Caesar sat on the edge of the bed. She glanced frantically around the room, the one she'd been shown to by Anne when they had arrived at Caesar's Brentwood mansion.

Except . . .

She didn't remember crawling into bed. A quick glance down revealed someone else's clothes, but then she remembered the bartender who gave the t-shirt and shorts after last night's insanity. Someone must have carried her into the house after she'd fallen asleep in the SUV. And considering who she'd snuggled against in the back seat, she had a good idea who'd tucked her in bed.

So why did the thought of Caesar taking care of her disturb her carefully ordered sense of self?

He's a vampire for crying out loud.

No, the problem wasn't the vampire. It was the man.

A whiff of eggs and toast sent her stomach rumbling, which made sense since the only thing she'd kept down last night had been the Jack

Daniels. Triage. Yeah, triage was a great idea. Deal with the immediate needs first, and worry about the things Caesar Augustine did to her insides later.

Much later.

"I wasn't sure how you liked your eggs, so Tiffany scrambled them." He gestured toward the tray perched on the nightstand, and once again, he had a real smile instead of the usual smirk.

She ran a self-conscious hand over her wayward curls and grimaced. Bits of vampire goo had dried in it, making her hair more impossible than usual. Then she cursed herself. Why should she care about impressing Caesar Augustine? She tried to speak and had to clear her throat before trying again. "What time is it?"

"It's a little after nine in the morning. We can be on the road as soon as you're ready."

"We? You're going out in daylight?"

He chuckled. "Not exactly. Phillippa UV-proofed her place a long time ago."

She nodded, slightly curious about how a vampire traveled during daylight hours.

A half hour, one broken comb, and one loud vampire argument later, Tiffany maneuvered the SUV in a manner Bebe noticed left even Caesar's knuckles whiter than usual. Caesar's entire household had put down their collective foot and said neither Caesar or Bebe were leaving the mansion without an escort. She rather had the impression he wished he'd agreed to one of the other human daytime guards driving them around Los Angeles.

UV film covered all the windows in the SUV so Caesar didn't so much as smoke slightly under the bright California sun, and Bebe realized this was the first time she'd seen him awake during daylight hours. When she asked him about it, he shrugged and said, "It seems pointless to be awake during daylight hours when we can't go outdoors, but occasionally we do venture out." He shot her a heart-stopping grin. "If the cause is worthwhile."

Why did he continue to torture her? She smoothed a hand over the khaki pants Anne had bought for her. It wasn't like anything could ever happen between them. Since she had no idea how to respond to his deliberate flirting, she kept silent and watched the mid-morning traffic.

Soon they were rolling down a quiet street that held a mix of residences and specialty shops. Tiffany swerved down an alley and punched a button on the panel above her head. One of the garage doors framing the alley obediently opened, and she pulled into the deceptively cavernous space.

As the garage door slid closed, a woman opened the side door between the garage and the main building. If Bebe leaned in a different direction, her tongue would be hanging on the floor. The woman was statuesque with sun-kissed brunette hair piled on her head, curves in all the right places, and features that Helen of Troy would have killed for. Except her arms were crossed over her ample chest and a stern frown marred the perfect lines of her face.

"What did you do this time, Tiffany?" she said as soon as the girl popped open the driver's door. "And why aren't you in class?"

"It's holiday break, Phil." The teenage whine came through strong and clear.

"I know, kid. Just giving you shit." The woman pulled Tiffany into a hug. She waved as Caesar came around the vehicle. "What's going on—" Then she caught sight of Bebe and smiled. "Hello, Dr. Zachary. I was wondering when you'd appear on my doorstep."

Bebe couldn't get over Phillippa Mann's kitchen. Blue and white gingham covered the table with matching curtains framing the window over the sink. Pine cupboards with a natural honey stain gave the place a warm feeling. Of course, the freshly baked strudel she served with coffee helped. And she sat serenely in her cream shirt with black linen pants and sandals, a strand of pearls at her throat. The woman made Martha Stewart look positively normal.

Except everyone knew Martha was part daemon.

And Bebe still couldn't figure out what Phillippa was as they sat, munching on delicious strudel and making small talk. Part human definitely. It was the other part that concerned her because the woman practically glowed with power.

When Bebe tentatively probed Phillippa's surface thoughts, nothing came through. Nothing that is but a feeling of sandy beach surrounded by cliffs that blazed in brilliant sunshine. And Phillippa's thoughts were as ephemeral as the afterimages reflected off the limestone cliffs.

Phillippa paused in her conversation with Caesar and Tiffany concerning the merits of UCLA versus Berkeley, turned and gave Bebe a mysterious smile. "I believe Dr. Zachary is growing impatient with us."

Heat flooded Bebe's cheeks. "I'm sorry for my rudeness."

Phillippa merely nodded an acknowledgement and said, "What you're looking for is down there, Doctor." She gestured toward a waist-high stand. An old-fashioned rotary phone sat on top.

Bebe raised an eyebrow for permission, but Phillippa laid a hand on her forearm. "Bebe, dear, if you accept this from me, there's no going back. Do you understand?"

Bebe paused, reminded of Grandma Petrov's mysterious note. "Don't you want to see some ID before you hand it over to me? For all you know, I could be a shifter."

Phillippa laughed, a soft melodious sound. "Tiffany's endorsement is sufficient for me."

Bebe blinked in surprise. Then the realization smacked her between the eyes. The three of them had been discussing her telepathically the whole time, which said something about Phillippa's power. Curiosity quickly followed. "Why Tiffany's word over Caesar's?"

Again, that mysterious smile tilted Phillippa's mouth. "Caesar isn't exactly objective when it comes to you, my dear."

Oh boy, let's make that all public why don't we? Bebe flicked a glance at Caesar and was gratified that he was as irritated as she. Though a small part of her thrilled at the thought he had feelings for her.

She stood, crossed to the stand, and crouched to open the door to the cupboard under the phone. Part of a black leather cover poked from underneath the piles of Los Angeles metro area phone books. Not a real secure place, but Stan had proven that the wardrobe wasn't necessarily safe. Pulling out the various yellow and white pages and setting them aside, she breathed a sigh of relief when the familiar embossed pentacle appeared. Caesar had been telling the truth about finding the letter. She hugged the Book of Shadows to her chest and whispered a prayer of thanks to the Goddess before she returned the phone books to their storage place.

She went to the table and sat, puzzled that she wasn't more excited by finding the Book. The anti-climax was topped when Tiffany gave Phillippa a confused look and asked, "Why the hell did you store that with your phone books? Do you know people are trying to kill Bebe?"

"That's why I asked if she was sure she wanted it." Phillippa smiled and sipped her coffee.

"I'd like to hire you."

Bebe jerked her head up at Caesar's words, but his eyes were aimed at Phillippa, who shook her head. And the look on her face indicated she was someone that not even a vampire should mess with.

Maybe Caesar was suicidal because he didn't shut up. "But Bebe needs to be kept safe while I try to find out who's behind—"

"No," Bebe and Phillippa said at the same time.

Bebe continued, "I don't need—"

"Yes, you do." For the first time, he showed real anger toward her. "Or did you forgot the last couple—"

"No!" Bebe slapped her hand down on the table for emphasis, her fury rising to match his. "I haven't forgotten, but I'm not dragging another innocent person into this mess."

A trace of what may have been sympathy on Phillippa's face as she regarded him. "And this is a witch matter, Caesar, not a vampire situation. I will not interfere, even at your request."

"But you helped Uncle Duncan with me," Tiffany said.

Phillippa's expression softened when she faced Tiffany. "You were a baby. Bebe's a full-grown woman who needs to learn to fight her own battles." She turned back to Bebe. "I'm sorry, Dr. Zachary. I couldn't if you asked me either."

For some strange reason, Phillippa's refusal to help her was reassuring. Bebe smiled. "No apology necessary, Ms. Mann." She wanted to ask Phillippa about Grandma Petrov, how they knew each other, why did Grandma entrust Phillippa with the Book. But something in Phillippa's manner told her that the unusual woman wouldn't answer her questions.

"When your battle is finished, come back and we will reminisce about Natasha."

Bebe's eyes widened at Phillippa's perception, then she nodded. "Thank you." She indicated the book. "For everything."

Ten minutes later as they prepared to leave, Caesar must have sensed her need for privacy because he climbed into the front passenger seat. He wasn't given a choice of the driver's seat.

Bebe hid her smile at his irritation when Tiffany had refused to relinquish the keys. For a teenager, she took her guard duties seriously. Or maybe it was just the power of a seventeen-year-old behind the wheel of a large, military-based vehicle.

Sucking in a deep breath, Bebe flipped open the cover as Tiffany pulled into traffic. The first pages contained the usual recipes, spells and rituals of any witch's Book. She turned to the damning pages to find they were intact. If Phillippa had looked at them, Bebe had no doubt the strange woman would keep the information silent.

Tears blurred her vision, and she blinked them back. What looked like a simple family tree was a quiet network of alliances through marriage and blood that made the acid in her stomach roil. Most of the marriages were indirect, through siblings or cousins, but they left White Rose in control over most of the Western Hemisphere, either directly or through political influence.

And before she died, Grandma had her sights on Europe.

Bebe's index finger traced the thin ink line between her name and that of Alastair Hyde-Smith. The marriage date was still blank. She'd never met the boy so she had no personal grievance against him. But her last real argument with Grandma Petrov ripped at her memory. Even though Grandma's emotional distance since Mom and Dad's murders had bothered Bebe, Grandma had never tried forcing her to do anything until Alastair.

"I'm not attending fucking Oxford so you can shove your claws into another coven! And I'm sure as hell not agreeing to an arranged marriage!"

She had never sworn at anyone in her life until that moment, but Grandma Petrov had merely looked at her with that same imperturbable expression she had worn since the day of the funerals.

"This is not about your personal wishes, Bebe. This marriage concerns the survival of our people. You need to be in a position of strength to succeed me, and Alastair will provide you that strength and more." Grandma didn't even blink, dropping this bombshell on her as if they were discussing whether to have morning tea in the garden or the solarium.

Bebe suppressed a shudder. As a coven's high priestess, she'd have to deal with the leaders of the other supernatural factions. Like the vampires.

She couldn't do it, not without having a nervous breakdown. "Name someone else as your heir. The Elders will rubberstamp whomever you pick and you know it. *I* don't want the job."

Bebe could have been talking to the maid for all the effect her words had on Grandma.

"I've already made the arrangements with his coven's high priestess. You can continue to pursue your medical studies in England with the minimum of disruption."

"You're not hearing me, are you? I refuse to be named your heir, I'm not going to England, and I'M DEFINITELY NOT MARRYING ALASTAIR!" Her scream echoed through the gigantic, empty house. The maid had run from the room when Grandma made her initial proclamation, probably to warn the rest of the staff to stay outside.

"Then you leave me no choice but to cut off your funding." Grandma's cold voice sliced through the remnants of Bebe's scream.

"You wouldn't." But she knew deep down Grandma would and her continuing silence confirmed it. The old woman had done anything and everything to get her way, one of the reasons Grandpa Petrov had left her years ago.

Well, fine. Two could play that game.

"Then I will petition to have the court dissolve the trust, Grandma. I'm twenty-one now, and there's no real reason for it to exist, is there?"

Grandma said nothing, just the slight rise in her left eyebrow her only answer.

Bebe stepped closer. "The only way you can stop it is to have me declared mentally incompetent. Do you really think the Hyde-Smiths will want a nut case in the family? How is that going to look to the rest of White Rose? And even if you manage to retain control of the trust without having me committed, I'll dance naked in a strip joint to pay for school before I let you force me into any kind of marriage."

Calling Grandma's bluff had meant she graduated from UCSF with honors, but Grandma's audacious plan to move Alastair to the U.S. and install him in the mansion following her internship had sent Bebe fleeing to Africa.

Regrets and grief shrouded her. She shouldn't have left things unsaid for so long between her and Grandma. Grandma had been there for her after her parents' deaths, even if her idea of closeness was sending her out for ice cream with the chauffeur. Now, they'd never have the chance to mend their relationship. Maybe Grandma had meant what she said in her letters, that she wouldn't force a marriage if Bebe would just come home.

She flipped back to the page before and stared at the lines showing her parents' marriage. Had Mom been forced to marry Dad too? How had she reacted? Had she been threatened, told she'd be thrown out if she didn't comply with Grandma's demands? Bebe had always believed her mom and dad were totally in love. Were they? Or was it an act thrust on them for political advantage?

Her parents loved her. Of that, she had no doubt. When those vampires broke into their house and the first one grabbed her . . .

Oh my Goddess!

The air in her lungs refused to budge. The viewpoint of her eleven-year-old self crystallized. The rogue vampires had been after her that night!

Dad had managed to get the bastard to drop her. Mom had scooped her up and crammed her into the nymph hole in Dad's gigantic entertainment center before going to help Dad.

Except it was too late.

And all Bebe could do was beat helplessly on the wards of the nymph hole as she watched first Dad, and then Mom, die a horrible death.

The vampires were still shredding the entertainment center, trying to kill her, when Grandma had arrived and blasted them both into the afterlife with fireballs.

She wiped the silent tears from her cheeks. She had been wondering how her life got this screwed up, but she had been fucked from the beginning. Why the hell would vampires target an eleven-year-old, even if they were rogues?

Same reason the three rogue vamps, a witch and a were teamed up to take her out last night. Someone wanted her dead, had wanted her dead for a very long time, and for what? A position of power she didn't desire and a book that proved her grandmother was a power-hungry harpy. What was she missing?

Caesar had said something about a conspiracy to murder Grandma. Why would Grandma trust a vampire and a—whatever the hell Phillippa was—instead of someone in the coven?

And why did Bebe trust Caesar? Because Grandma told her to wasn't a good enough answer. So what was in this for him? He was spending a lot of time and money on her. And a lot of attention.

A lot of attention that she rather enjoyed.

With effort, she wrenched her mind away from his exquisite kissing technique and focused on the more immediate problem.

Had another witch found out about Grandma's master plans? Someone jealous of the power Grandma was amassing? Or maybe someone who resented being forced into a marriage he or she didn't want? If Bebe had been furious, how would William or Alice have reacted?

Except neither of them could have plotted her murder when they were children.

Well, William *had* pushed her out of the tree house when they were eight, and it *had* been intentional. Like it was her fault he sucked at checkers. Her broken arm had healed, but since then, all the therapy in the world hadn't cured her acrophobia.

At least, Grandma hadn't hidden the Book in one of the ancient oaks on the coven's estate. Bebe would never have been able to recover it if she had to climb a tree.

She flipped the Book pages past the proposed future alliances. Maybe Grandma left some clues as to what she knew or suspected. After a few blank sheets, Bebe found more of Grandma's elegant, loopy script.

She stared at the page, squeezed her eyes shut, then looked at the page again. The words on the page made absolutely no sense. The letters were a mix of English letters and what might have been Greek, but the language wasn't one she recognized. Had Grandma placed a spell on the ink or the page?

Extending her senses, she examined the page more closely. No direct magick, just residual power from years of use.

She jolted when the SUV door opened. Caesar stood there with a quizzical look on his face.

"Welcome back to Earth, Dr. Zachary." He must have noticed something was bothering her because his expression changed to one of concern. "What's wrong?"

Her fingers twitched, the urge to slam the Book shut so strong her hands cramped. He was a vampire. He couldn't be trusted.

But Grandma trusted him. Far more than she trusted anyone else in the coven.

Her eyes closed in her frustration. Goddess, nothing made sense anymore. Shoving the fear and worry aside, she listened. To the Goddess for some sign of what to do. To her instinct. To her gut. Her heart.

Her eyes opened to meet Caesar's. "We have a serious problem." She held up the Book for him to see. "I think this has our answers, but it's in some kind of code."

Caesar's gaze flicked to the pages, and his face stilled, that unnatural vampire stillness that never boded anything good for her. His eyes met hers, and her stomach clenched in fear.

"It's Natasha's research," he said.

"What kind of research?" Her stomach tried to crawl back through her small intestine. Maybe she should follow her organ's lead and find a deep, dark hole to hide in from his expression.

"Genetic research. She was working on a way to make witches impervious to the V-virus."

Chapter 15

"What?"

At Bebe's exclamation, any thoughts Caesar had of her holding the cure over his head disappeared. If he'd learned anything over the past couple of days, it was that the doctor wasn't that good of an actress. And he'd met some good ones over the centuries.

He blew out a harsh breath. "Let's go inside. I'll tell you what little I know."

Tiffany, for once, had the intelligence to keep her mouth shut and trailed them into the house. He stopped her at the door of his office.

"Why don't you go to the kitchen and prepare lunch for Dr. Zachary and yourself? Mai should have delivered the grocery order by now," he said.

"Or I could go tell Uncle Duncan about the top secret witch research." She smiled sweetly.

He bared his fangs, letting his irritation show.

Tiffany paled noticeably under her white Goth make-up. "Uh, how does tuna salad sound, Doc?"

"Tuna sounds delicious, thank you." Bebe smiled, despite her fears and concerns that leaked from behind her psychic shields. Her face grew deadly serious as soon as he closed the office door.

She stood there, hugging Natasha's Book to her chest. From the whiteness of her knuckles, the Jaws of Life would be necessary to get her to let go. And the look on her face . . .

He had expected anger, fury, or at the very least, mild irritation from her. Instead, she looked like a lost child as she stood in the middle of the burgundy carpet of his office.

"Would you like to sit down?" He gestured toward the sable leather couch opposite of the huge mahogany desk. Jamal had designed the effect of the furnishings to be both efficient and intimidating, but the room's influence seemed to reinforce the fear Bebe was desperately trying to hide. She remained frozen in place.

He needed a different tactic if he had any hope of getting her to talk. "I'm sorry I don't have any whiskey. Would you like a glass of wine?" He strode toward the mini-bar discretely hidden behind a large potted palm.

"Why would someone want children dead?"

Her voice was so soft, that even with his enhanced hearing, he wasn't sure he'd heard her correctly. He spun on his heel so fast that she jumped back in fear. "Children? What children?" he said.

"The night—" She swallowed hard, as if her thoughts were so terrible that she couldn't give voice to them. "The night my parents died, those vampires, they weren't—" Big, round tears formed, then they began a slow roll down her cheeks. "They were after me."

He crossed back to her, slow so as not to scare her more than she was. Pulling her stiff body over to the couch, he pressed her into a sitting position and lowered himself next to her. "Bebe, the rogues killed a lot of people that night. It was a stupid, senseless power play. Nothing more."

She shook her head, the motion so violent that the clips fell from her hair. Her riotous curls fell around her shoulders. He wanted to bury his nose in the mass just to imprint her smell in his brain forever. If her mood weren't so dire, he would have.

Fool, as if you haven't already done so.

He ignored his chiding conscience and tried to focus on her. "Bebe, it's not unusual for children to blame themselves for bad things that happen. I—"

He caught himself before the confession came spilling out. She was distraught enough. She didn't need to hear his pathetic past. And he had actually done something. He sure as Hades wasn't an innocent like she was.

"This isn't self-blame, Augustine." The fire burned in her eyes again, and she spoke through gritted teeth. "Something else was going on that night. Grandma's genetic research—what exactly was she doing?"

All of his old arguments with Natasha came rushing back. He'd told her that her family wouldn't forgive her for manipulating them, even if it were for their own benefit. Bebe had proven his point succinctly when she took off for Africa. But no, Natasha had dangled the one thing he wanted in his face, and he'd caved.

He rose and began pacing in front of Bebe, trying to gauge her mood, but her face had turned as impassive as the monuments at Karnak. "You have to understand Natasha was doing what she thought was in the best interest of her family."

"Of course, she was." Bebe released the tome and crossed her arms over the turquoise camp shirt she wore. Unfortunately, her position only emphasized her breasts. To the point what little blood left in his body pooled in his cock.

Gods above, she wasn't making this easy, was she? He shoved his fists in the pockets of his Dockers and tried to think of bad sanitation during the Middle Ages. He sucked in a deep breath and plunged into the truth. Or at least as much as he dared to tell her.

"During World War II, a young male witch was captured by the Nazis. He was given to Mengele for experimentation. By then, the Nazis knew about supernaturals, and—" This part still made him sick. "They experimented to find out how various races reacted to the V-virus."

The slight clench of her hands betrayed her anxiety. "Didn't anyone tell those idiots what happens when you Turn a witch?"

He couldn't stop his own ironic smile. Hybrids were prohibited for a reason. If the witch survived the transformation, the virus usually left the witch a bloodthirsty psychopath. And a hybrid was a bitch to kill. "Probably not, hoping any hybrid they created would take the bastards out."

He raked a hand through his hair, forcing himself to continue. "They dumped the witch into a pit with a vampire they had starved. The vampire managed to not suck the boy dry, but the Nazis were shocked when he failed to die or Turn."

Her brow twisted in confusion. "That's impossible with that much contact."

"So the Nazis thought as well, but before they could follow up, the Allies overran the facility where the boy was held."

Her eyes narrowed. "What does this have to do with Grandma?"

"Your grandmother left Auschwitz II with Mengele's documentation of his experiments on supernaturals."

Her eyes widen. "She should have destroyed that stuff!" Disgust etched into her features, she looked down at the Book and shoved. It dropped to the floor, landing with a thud.

He bent and picked up the Book. "She didn't have time. Do you believe she should have left it for the Normals to find?"

Her cheeks flushed, and she stared at her toes. "No" came her whispered reply. Then her head lifted. "But she shouldn't have used that boy's torture to further her own political agenda."

"What political agenda?" Was there something more to Bebe and Natasha's rift than the Hyde-Smith boy?

"She discovered what made that boy immune, didn't she?"

He nodded, concern rising.

She took a deep breath, as if coming to a decision. She took the Book from his loose grip and started flicking through the pages. "This is what I mean about her agenda." She patted the cushion next to her. When he joined her, she pointed to what looked like a convoluted family tree. "All these marriages and children." She traced a branch of great-aunts and second cousins, and he recognized the names. The individuals were members of Nikolai's family who married into North and South American covens. "I thought she was just extending her political power, but she used her knowledge as a bargaining chip to form alliances." She looked up at him through dark lashes. "Didn't she?"

Bebe wasn't a stupid woman, and pretending the entire situation didn't exist wouldn't make things between them any easier. He nodded slowly, then reached for her hand and added, "You have to understand something, Bebe. Natasha believed she was doing the right thing in protecting her people."

She raised her head and stared at him. "And you think I don't understand what this could mean to your people?"

Old anger rose to the surface. Anger at ancient politics that decided his fate when he was about the same age as Bebe when she lost her parents. He rose, took two steps away from her and allowed all the ugliness to come out. He turned to face her and took a step forward. Her eyes widened and she gasped. "Do you really think I would wish *this*—" He gestured at his face. "—on anyone!" He'd seen himself in a mirror once when he was in a "full-blown vamp-out mode" as Tiffany called it. It scared the shit out of him, so he understood the effect on everyone else. "If Natasha found a way to protect the witches, and even better, all the Normals, then I'll be the first one cheering her!"

She flinched at his words. "I-I'm sorry, Caesar. I never thought—" She couldn't meet his gaze any longer.

Harsh breaths ripped at his lungs as he got himself back under control. "I'm sorry, too. I didn't want to scare you, but—"

A soft laugh burbled from her throat, and she looked up at him and smiled. "But I needed a kick in the ass?"

The image of her buttocks sticking out of the wardrobe changed into one of them naked and displayed before him. And the idea wasn't helping him get his bloodlust under control one little bit. He smiled as much as he dared with his fangs fully extended. "Yes."

She pushed a wayward curl behind her ear, and he couldn't stop wondering what her more intimate curls would taste like.

"I would guess that someone knows about her research." She waved a hand at the yellowed pages. "Someone besides you. The bad guys probably assumed I had the Book the whole time." She frowned. "In fact, both Alice and William accused me of hiding it when I called them after I arrived in San Francisco. Even the Elders thought I had it."

She didn't wait for his reply. Not that he knew what to tell her. With two attempts on her life since she returned to the States, he'd wager she was right. Instead, she flipped a couple pages over to the strange writing. "Do you have any idea what language this is? I don't recognize it."

He bent and examined the pages. The letters were a mix of English and Theban, but the words were still gibberish to him. He shook his head. "Her notes disappeared from her office. I had hoped they had been hidden with her Book of Shadows." He glanced at Bebe. "Or that you had them."

Her expression became quizzical. "And I would give them to you?"

He nodded and his gaze returned to the strange script before she could ask why. Hope that Bebe would continue Natasha's research was too much to ask her at this point. "It's definitely her handwriting. It's not a language I know though."

She sighed in defeat. "How am I supposed to know what she was up to if I can't read her notes? Does Granny E. know?"

He shook his head. "Not all of it. And I doubt if she knows Natasha's code."

"Do you have any bright ideas?"

"Not one you'll like."

She raised an eyebrow, a suspicious gleam in her eyes.

"We're going to have to ask for help."

Chapter 16

Bebe laid down the book she'd been trying to read all afternoon, her mind distracted with the waiting. Tiffany had disappeared shortly after lunch, muttering something about shopping. Caesar had disappeared into his office to deal with his private businesses. He poked his head out about three to give her a paper copy of an e-mail from Granny E.

Bebe couldn't help smiling as she had read it. The clipped style was definitely Granny E.'s and seeing today's date reassured her.

To: aha40bcalexandria@augustinecoven.net
From: noreply@google.com on behalf of hpze23842191@silverbear.com
Sent: 19-12-2010 19:23 PM
Subject: Delay

C

Flight delayed. Gatwick fogged in. UnNorm? Rumors flying here. Keep my baby safe!
Be in on Saturday. Will come straight to your place.
Z

Sweet Goddess, could Granny E. be right that the fog in London wasn't natural? Could Caesar have arranged the bad weather to keep her out of the way? The delay nixed any confirmation Granny E. could have given her concerning his story. And the e-mail was from a public terminal.

Bebe had even slipped a telephone handset into the bathroom and tried to call Granny E.'s cell, only to have it roll over to voice-mail. Damn, there was no other way to contact her grandmother directly.

But then, did it matter? Bebe was pretty much at Caesar Augustine's mercy as it was. But he could have drained her and buried her in the back yard at his San Francisco place, so why bother with games?

Pressing her fingertips to her temples, she tried a meditation exercise. The die had been cast when she had shown him the Book. Objective reasoning was what she needed, not her own niggling doubts and childhood terrors.

The fog could be the work of whoever wanted her dead. And despite the fact that Caesar ruled the entire vampire race west of the Mississippi and had money out the ass, his behavior earlier indicated he resented his nature. Did he resent it enough to give up all that power and wealth if the opportunity presented itself? If Grandma had found some kind of antibody to the V-virus, could she have been reverse engineering a cure for those affected?

Giving up on the meditation, Bebe rose from the couch and paced back and forth in front of the fireplace. The huge white brick mantel dominated the formal living room. Her bare feet left faint tracks in the gold Persian rug. Is a cure what he wanted from her? Was that the real purpose behind his innuendo and his wild kisses? String her along until she found a cure for him? She sure couldn't continue Grandma's research if she were dead, so he had every reason to keep her alive.

The deepening gloom in the cherry-paneled room seemed a good place to examine her own motivations for giving in to his attempts at seduction. She could have walked out the front door at any time. Tiffany had woken Anne before she left for her shopping excursion, but neither Caesar or Anne had checked on her all afternoon. Well, other than the e-mail delivery. A thrill had run up her arm and through her body just at the brief touch of his fingers when he handed her the sheet. And the looks he had given her over lunch, like he was stripping off her clothes with his eyes alone . . .

So why was being at Caesar's mercy such an exciting prospect? He wasn't model cute, but then pretty boys had never been her style. His sense of humor, when he wasn't deliberately trying to scare the daylights out of her, was as dry as her own. Over lunch, they had a pleasant conversation concerning the latest books, most of which she hadn't had a chance to read yet. They avoided the unpleasant truths hanging over their heads, and not even his mug of blood bothered her, she realized with a jolt.

Unfortunately, not even Dan Brown's latest best-selling thriller could keep her attention when all she could think about was Caesar's delicious body in those ridiculous cartoon pajamas. She had a sneaking suspicion they were a gift from either Tiffany or Alex, and Caesar, being ever Mr. Etiquette, had politely thanked them before stuffing them in a drawer in his San Francisco house. Even though most of that first night was a blur, she distinctly remembered Alex having to dig for them.

And the pajama bottoms had left nothing to the imagination. Not his finely honed butt. Not his long legs. And definitely not his erection.

"Would you like some hot chocolate? Anne's making some for Tiffany."

Bebe jumped at Ptolemy's voice. Heat flooded her cheeks.

"Anything wrong, Doctor?" he said.

"Um, no." She frantically searched her memory. What had he just asked her?

"I see." He shot her a mischievous grin. "Just lusting after my brother, hmmm?"

Horror engulfed her. Had she leaked her thoughts?

Ptolemy's grin widened, his canines shining dully in the thickening dusk. "I don't have to read your mind, Doctor. Your face tells me everything I need to know."

Something about the way he spoke sent a frisson of uncertainty through her nerves. Caesar may try to scare her to prove a point, but Ptolemy seemed to enjoy head games a little too much for her comfort.

She gave him a wan smile. "I hope my face is telling you that Anne's hot chocolate sounds delicious right now."

He didn't speak, merely gestured for her to go before him and followed her to the kitchen.

Rich cinnamon hit her nose as soon as she pushed the swinging door. Undertones of cocoa drifted in the wake of the spice. Anne pulled a baking dish from the wall oven and set it on a cooling rack. Her long sleeves were rolled to her elbows and specks of flour dotted the front of the baggy slate t-shirt.

Vampires getting domestic?

The more time Bebe spent with them, the more she realized how screwed up her preconceptions were. "That smells delicious. What are you making?"

Anne smiled, a soft, shy look on her face. If Bebe hadn't seen the tiny woman in full vampire mode in San Francisco, she'd never believed Anne was one.

"It's my grandmother's cinnamon bread. She always made it at Christmas." Anne sighed. "I may not be able to eat it anymore, but I still love the smell this time of year. Phillippa, Tiffany and the daytime staff usually enjoy the honors. Would you like some?"

While she spoke, she had pulled off the oven mitts and already had a cup of cocoa, complete with mini-marshmallows, sitting in front of Bebe.

Bebe swallowed. Anne had to have heard her answer to Ptolemy all the way in the living room. Maybe she wouldn't have made it out of the house after all. But her stomach rumbled at the smell of the fresh-baked bread. She perched on the same black, leather-covered stool she had used at lunch and nodded. "That sounds great."

Tiffany burst through the kitchen door, a huge red cloth sack packed full and slung over one thin shoulder and a cell phone glued to her ear with her free hand. "What do you want on your pizza, Doc? It's ringing now."

Pizza? If Bebe's mouth watered from the smell of fresh-baked bread, it practically gushed at the thought of pepperoni and mozzarella. Goddess, she hadn't had pizza since she left for Africa. "Anything, but anchovies." She took a huge gulp of cocoa. The temperature was perfect, and the smooth chocolaty milk slid down her throat.

Ptolemy scowled at the teen. "Tiffany, Mai brought in groceries for you and the doctor."

Tiffany dropped the bag on the breakfast table to flip him the bird while she ordered an "Extra-large Super Deluxe, hold the anchovies and jalapenos." She crossed the room and poked her head in the fridge. "Regular cola okay with you?" she mouthed to Bebe.

Bebe grinned and nodded. Screw the healthy stuff. If she had a target painted on her forehead, she might as well enjoy some decent junk food.

"You'd better not leave that crap to rot in our refrigerator," Ptolemy muttered. Anne smothered a smile as she sat a plate of steaming bread in front of Bebe.

Tiffany clicked her cell shut and dropped it in the front pocket of her jeans. "You're just jealous you were born too early to enjoy real cuisine. And it's not *your* refrigerator."

"Then you'd better not leave that pizza to rot in *my* refrigerator," Caesar said.

Bebe nearly fell off the stool at his sudden appearance. She swiveled around to face him. "Quit sneaking!"

A dark eyebrow rose. "I didn't know it was possible to sneak in my own house," he said. "And you have marshmallow on your nose."

Before she could move, he reached up and swiped the white froth off the tip. Then he pressed his finger against her partly opened lips. Instinctively, she licked the sugary foam from his fingertip. Her entire body flamed at the intimacy of the act. By heat in his eyes, he enjoyed the display a little too much. She could no longer meet his intense gaze and took a sudden interest in the marshmallows. Damn, that didn't help either as her mind replayed what just happened and added its own erotic twist.

Thankfully, he stepped away, putting some distance between his body and her overactive imagination. He paused at the table and tugged the drawstring open to peer inside the bag.

Tiffany raced across the room and slapped his hand away. "They're holiday presents, and you don't get yours until Duncan and Alex come down and Phil arrives."

"I'm here, kid. Now what's the emergency about, Caesar?" Phillippa stood in the doorway leading into the utility room between the main house and Caesar's massive garage.

"I promise I'm not asking you to interfere, but Ziva's stuck in London due to the weather, and Bebe and I needed your opinion on something." Caesar set down the mug Anne had just handed him and disappeared back through the swinging door.

On the door's backswing, Duncan and Alex appeared. And the normally boisterous and smooth Alex Stanton stammered when he saw their guest. "H-h-hello, Phillippa."

"Stanton." A penguin could have skated on her words. But her greeting to Duncan was far warmer, and she positively raved over Anne when the tiny vampire handed her a plate of cinnamon bread.

Interesting. Phillippa's attitude reminded Bebe more of a woman insulted by a suitor than any supernatural rivalry. What could Alex possibly have done to offend Phillippa? A necking session gone awry?

She tilted her head at Alex and Phillippa and raised an inquiring eyebrow as Tiffany handed her the cola. Tiffany grinned and mouthed, "Tell you when the vamps go to bed."

Bebe took a sip from the ice-cold can. This group acted more like a family than her own blood did, and they had welcomed her in their little group with no demands and no questions asked. The realization sent a pang through her heart.

Caesar returned with the Book of Shadows in his hand. "Phillippa, I wanted you to look—"

"No!" Tiffany held up her hand to stop him. "We're opening presents first."

"It's Friday," he said, a hint of amusement in his voice.

"Yeah, and with this group—" Her index finger waved in a circle to indicate everyone in the room. "Murphy is the one, true god, so we're doing presents tonight."

Phillippa grinned. "I kind of thought the same thing." She pivoted to drag in a large shopping bag from the utility room.

Caesar gave Tiffany an indulgent smile as well. "Then I guess we're exchanging gifts before we get down to business." He handed the Book to Bebe.

While the male vampires and Anne disappeared upstairs to retrieve hidden gifts, Tiffany explained the bizarre ritual to Bebe.

"Between the Saturnalia, Yule, Christmas, Hanukah, Kwanzaa, blah, blah, blah," Tiffany said, ticking off each holiday on a finger. "We picked the third Saturday in December for a joint celebration. Anne usually cooks a ham or turkey for me and Phil with all the fixings, but, and no offense, Doc, I just know the shit will hit the fan when your Grandma gets here tomorrow."

Duncan strode into the room, a small pile of boxes in his arms. "Tiffany, watch your language or I will wash your mouth out." He glared at the teen before adding, "Again."

"Sorry."

Bebe placed a hand over her mouth to cover her amusement. Tiffany didn't sound the least bit sorry at all.

Once everyone was back in the kitchen, packages were exchanged, and paper started flying.

Tiffany shocked Bebe by handing her a small navy blue box with an intricate silver ribbon. Her eyes watered at the girl's generosity. "But I don't have anything for you."

Tiffany scowled. "It wasn't right those assholes shot up all your belongings and left you with jack, and as far as I'm concerned, you're part of the family now." Then she shot Bebe a wicked grin. "If you want to do something for me, you could take me to see the new *Saw* movie."

"Tiffany!"

The group cracked up at Duncan's indignant tone as he scowled at his niece.

Bebe ripped off the ribbon and opened the box. Nestled inside was a small silver pentacle on a matching herringbone chain. She met Tiffany's anxious eyes. "You shouldn't have, but thank you," she whispered before wrapping her arms around the girl's frail shoulders and squeezing.

And to Bebe's amazement, everyone else in the room seemed to share Tiffany's sentiment. Except, when the hell could they have done all this? She had just arrived in Los Angeles last night.

Phillippa gave her a small wooden case containing an assortment of herbs and a mortar and pestle. Duncan presented a matching case with small vials of essential oils. Alex's package was the proverbial M.D.'s bag, itself an antique by the wear and tear, but complete with a modern stethoscope, blood pressure cuff, and a digital thermometer. Anne's present was a small suture kit with anti-septic pads that fit neatly into the medical bag.

Even Ptolemy handed her a box. Half-afraid, she pulled the gold ribbon loose and tore off the blood-red paper. Inside the box lay a knife. The ivory handle was inlayed with gold and the bronze edge gleamed under the fluorescent lighting. From the yellowing of the ivory, the piece had to be as ancient as the vampire who gave it to her. Her airways clogged in disbelief. Something like this should be in a freaking museum.

Even Caesar had a shocked look on his face when he saw the contents of the box.

"I can't accept this," she whispered.

Ptolemy's face, however, was gravely serious as he shook his head. "In honor of your first victory over your enemies, Doctor."

She couldn't begin to understand his motivations. One minute he acted as if she were beneath him. The next, he'd protect her.

She nodded, unable to speak. Glancing at the last unopened package, her hands started to shake, and she placed the box with the knife on the counter before her nerveless fingers dropped it.

Various expressions of concern surrounded her, with Anne obviously the most worried. Bebe suppressed a wince. Had the tiny vampire blabbed about catching Caesar and her making out in the kitchen in San Francisco?

"It's very rude not to open your host's gift, Dr. Zachary." Caesar's warm breath teased her ear.

She carefully pulled the ivory ribbon loose and lifted the lid. Cushioned in soft silk lay two exquisite teardrop-shaped pearl earrings. Holding her breath, she picked up one of the gorgeous pieces. The wire loop and setting were obviously handcrafted even to her untrained eye. The jewelry had to be centuries old, if not millennia, just like the knife Ptolemy had given her. Earrings fit for a queen.

Or a princess.

She gulped and looked up at Caesar. His pleased expression faded. The last thing she wanted was to insult or disappoint him, but she couldn't accept these. The money and clothes had been bad enough, even if she intended to repay him, but this . . .

This gift was too extravagant.

Too tender.

Way too intimate.

How long had the pearls been in his possession? Had the earrings belonged to another sister? His mother?

Oh sweet Goddess, was it even worse? Had they belonged to his long-dead wife?

She dropped the earring back in the cushion of silk and slapped the lid back on top. "I can't accept these." She held the box out to him.

He didn't reach for it, just stared at her with that damned impassive look on his handsome face. "As I said, it's rude to refuse your host's gift, Dr. Zachary."

Why did he have to put her on the spot like this? Was it some quirk of vampire culture that escaped her? It was bad enough accepting the clothes and money, but that was sheer necessity. Her lungs burned, reminding her that she'd stopped breathing. She sucked in air, desperately searching for the right words. Anything to get out of this situation.

Why couldn't that damn witch slice her throat properly last night? Then she wouldn't have an insulted vampire in front of her now.

No. With her luck, Caesar would have tried Turning her if her throat had been cut.

Tucking an escaped curl behind her ear, she tried again. "Look, I'm sure in your day this would be a perfectly appropriate holiday gift, but things are different now."

His eyebrow lifted. "Yes, I've noticed how manners are sorely lacking in the latest generations."

Her pulse jumped at his acid tone, and she slid down from her stool and jabbed a finger at his chest. "Maybe the real problem is your arrogant attitude. Maybe you can buy and sell every other woman in California. But you can't buy me," she said through clenched teeth. She slammed the box down on the counter before she stormed through the swinging door. Total silence followed in her wake as she stomped upstairs.

Jerk had to go and ruin a perfectly lovely evening. Damn him anyway.

Not until she threw herself on her bed did she realize she left the Book of Shadows on the kitchen counter as well. The hot chocolate and marshmallows became a lead weight in her stomach.

Grandma's coded notes.

In a room full of vampires.

Chapter 17

Caesar stood still in shock while the entire group stared at him with various levels of disbelief on their faces. What the Hades just happened? Any other woman he'd ever met would have been salivating over such jewelry.

"Smooth move, Ex-lax," Tiffany muttered.

"I didn't do anything wrong!"

"You put her in a difficult position, Your Highness." Anne's soft voice reproached him. "Bebe is a proud woman. It's difficult enough for her to accept your assistance right now, but the extravagance of your gift . . ." She shook her head.

"But Ptolemy—"

"While the knife may be a phallic symbol to some, it doesn't say I'm buying my way into her bed the way multi-million dollar jewelry does, brother dear." Ptolemy smirked.

Caesar dug his clenched fists into his thighs. Otherwise, the urge to punch the shit out of Ptolemy would take over. "I wasn't buying my way into anything."

"Go apologize before she does something stupid," Phillippa said.

A chill stole over his soul. "Like what?"

"Right now?" Phillippa shot him a knowing smile. "She's planning on smashing the bedroom window, shimmying down the portico awning and hitching a ride with the pizza delivery boy."

The intercom clicked on at the same time a resounding boom echoed through the house. Mai's voice crackled through the speaker. "Duncan, please remind Tiffany that security protocol at Master Augustine's precludes pizza deliveries."

Caesar closed his eyes. A familiar pain popped behind his left eyeball. What happened to the old days when it was just him, Selene, and Ptolemy? Things were so much simpler then. Suck on an occasional cow. Stay out of the sunshine. Don't get your head cut off.

Much simpler.

Another boom came from upstairs as Duncan punched the reply button.

"Should one of us go up and tell the doc the windows are made of bulletproof glass before she hurts herself?" Alex said.

"Tiffany's on her way out to the gate, Mai," Duncan replied.

Boom.

"Do you need assistance in the main house?" Mai must have heard Bebe banging on the window, whether through the intercom or from outside didn't matter.

Boom.

"No. Dr. Zachary is exhibiting her displeasure with a Christmas gift. Stay at your post."

Caesar tried to ignore the wry humor in Duncan's voice.

Boom.

"If you want any furniture left, Caesar, you'd better get your ass up there."

He opened his eyes to find Phillippa openly grinning at him. Other than his siblings, she was the only one who dared speak to him in that manner, but he wasn't about to argue with one of the few people who could kick his ass. He pivoted on his heels and marched upstairs to teach the little witch a lesson she wouldn't soon forget.

Bebe was tired. Tired of being manipulated. Tired of being used. Tired of having no control over her life. No, she wasn't going to lie on a bed in a fucking vampire's mansion and be a victim anymore.

Bebe rolled off the mattress. She hadn't bothered with the room's lamps, relying on the hallway lighting to pick her way across the room. Her fingers itched to hit something. Anything to get rid of the anger crawling across her nerves. She needed out of this house. A car horn honked nearby. She threw her psyche in the direction of the sound. Tiffany's pizza delivery boy. If she could just hitch a ride with him . . .

She had to get out of the house first, and she wouldn't make it out any door with five vampires downstairs. Rage gave her strength, and grabbing the chair at the writing desk, she flung it at the window. With a deep boom, it bounced off and landed on the bed.

Damn you, Grandma!

Picking up the antique chair, Bebe swung it against the window with everything her five-foot-four frame held. It only resulted in another deep booming sound that rattled her arms.

I don't need your stupid Book.

Boom.

I don't want your stupid coven!

She threw the chair at the window, and it bounced off again.

And fuck you and your stupid earrings, Caesar Augustine!

Blinking back tears, Bebe heaved the heavy chair against the glass. Muttering a spell under her breath to transform more of the wood's potential energy as well as her fury into kinetic energy, she was rewarded with a sharp *tink*. A thin crack appeared, spider-webbing its way through the window. Except neither the chair or her arms had any strength left. Breathing heavily, she contemplated what to try next.

"What the Hades do you think you're doing?"

She whirled to find Caesar silhouetted in the doorway of the bedroom, his eyes glowing neon yellow amidst the shadows cast on his face. Damn, she'd been so angry she hadn't been "listening" for anyone coming up the stairs. The chair dropped from her nerveless fingers. When it hit the thick carpet, it disintegrated thanks to her spell, its loss of potential energy crumbling the wood to dust. Her fury drained away until only ice-cold fear remained. The air crackled with his anger.

Well, she wasn't going down without a fight. She summoned a fireball, but the magickal energy did nothing to warm her fingertips. "I'm leaving. The witch covens already think you're holding me prisoner." Assuming she was reading between the lines of Granny E.'s e-mail correctly.

Blasting the window would be her only option. She should have anticipated the vampires used reinforced glass. But whacking the chair against the panes had been satisfying. And with a start, she realized she planned to jump out a window, drop to the awning, and let herself fall to the shrubbery below.

What in the thousand names of the Goddess had she been thinking?

She returned her attention to the pissed off vampire. His eyes closed, and he released the metal doorknob he'd crushed. She wasn't sure he realized what he'd done to the device. He rubbed his temple instead of reaching for her as she half expected. When he opened his eyes, they had faded to a soft gold. "You're not a prisoner, Bebe." Even though he made no move toward her, his voice caressed her. "However, if you insist on leaving, would you please use the front door instead of destroying my home?"

His weary tone surprised her. She had expected threats, pleading, even his damn frigid logic, not total capitulation.

Her eyes narrowed. How the hell did his mind work? First, bribing her with jewelry, now letting her leave? Damn, would she ever figure out this man? "And neither you nor any of your people will stop me?"

"There's no reason for you to break your neck in an ill-conceived escape."

"It wasn't ill-conceived." Irritation snapped to life inside her, mostly because he was right.

He crossed his arms, his eyes eerily cat-like in the dimness. "You're afraid of heights, and yet you're planning to jump out a second-story window."

"I—" She swallowed hard. How could this man read her so well without penetrating her shields? "I'm not afraid of heights."

He snorted. "Really? With the death-grip you had on my coat when we were leaving your hotel room in San Francisco?" he said, the weary amusement clear in his voice. He unfolded his arms and crossed the room until he was inches away.

"I was afraid of getting shot that night." Electricity sizzled through her nerves at his presence. Damn, she wasn't about to back away and let him know how much his nearness disturbed her.

"Of course." He reached for her, his cool fingertips stroking her cheek, feeling so good against the half-scabbed knife wound. "I don't want anything to happen to you."

She glanced down at the fireball in her hand. Did she really want to incinerate the man standing before her? After the effort she'd spent saving his life? After all the times he'd saved hers in the last few days? When all he'd done was try to be nice and give her a holiday present? Okay, maybe an incredibly extravagant present. But did that mean he deserved a fiery death?

Dammit, all she wanted was to get out of these stupid political games.

To practice medicine and help those who really needed her aid.

To get her life back.

She clenched her fist to extinguish the witchfire.

Almost as if he knew it was safe, his head dipped to hers. Heat of a different kind flooded her as his lips kissed and nibbled her mouth. His arms wrapped around her waist, tugging her closer.

She didn't object. If anything, she added another want to her list. Her breasts cried for the pressure of his chest against them. Her fingers threaded through the short strands of his hair, seeking any and all additional contact. Tongues tangled and danced.

And before she was ready, he pulled away. Never before had a simple kiss left her so unsatisfied. She wanted more. Far more than she should even dare.

Hesitantly, he released her. "If you insist on leaving, you might want to eat before you go. Tiffany went to the trouble of ordering you dinner." He pivoted and stalked toward the door.

"Wait."

He paused but didn't look at her.

She couldn't stop her words. She had to know.

"Whose earrings were they?"

He froze, the eerie vampire stillness nearly sending her nerves into overload. When she didn't think he would answer, his quiet voice cut through the tension. "They were my mother's. You remind me of her. The same strength to defy everyone to do what you believe is right. I thought you should have them." There had to be more to his story, but he was out of sight before she could dredge up the guts to ask.

Damn, she really *had* hurt his feelings earlier.

Not that the stubborn jackass would admit it.

Never before had she been so unsure of anything. She pressed her fingers to her mouth, only to feel lips swollen from his kiss. She should leave here. She could march out the front door. She had no doubt now that Caesar would keep his word, but where would she go?

Granny E.'s? Her paternal grandmother had always shunned the extra security most high priestesses employed. Since Grandpa Ben was probably with her in London, one elderly housekeeper couldn't protect Bebe from the folks determined to get her out of the way.

And what about the Book? It was still sitting in the kitchen where she'd left it. She couldn't leave it with total strangers.

Okay, maybe not total strangers, but after her little ungracious temper tantrum, the last thing she wanted was to face everyone in the kitchen.

A low rumble came from her belly. She hadn't touched the heavenly scented bread Anne had served her.

Maybe she should swallow her pride.

No matter how big of a lump it was.

She slunk down the staircase. A soft murmur of voices confirmed her sense that everyone was still in the kitchen. The conversation stopped as soon as she touched the door. Taking a deep breath, she shoved it open.

To find everyone staring at her. Was it that obvious that Caesar had been kissing her? Sweat broke out on her palms. What had she expected?

She met Caesar's eyes from his seat at the kitchen table. They had returned to their natural hazel, and they widened at her appearance in the doorway. Then she noticed the Book of Shadows was still sitting on the island where she'd left it. Sucking in a deep breath, she shifted until she found Tiffany, perched on a stool and digging a pizza slice out of the box sitting on the island.

Bebe cleared her throat before she said, "Is the pizza offer still open?"

"Already filled a plate for you." Tiffany scooted the said plate with two slices across the granite countertop until it rested next to Bebe's half-filled mug of cocoa, the now-cooled plate of cinnamon bread, and her soda can.

She climbed onto the stool, took a bite and nearly had an orgasm then and there. Tangy tomato blended with spicy pepperoni, sausage and an array of vegetables, but best of all was the mellow flavor of mozzarella.

"You two had something you wanted me to look at?" Phillippa said from where she sat next to Tiffany.

"Yes. Actually we could use everyone's input." Caesar rose from his chair and crossed to the island. He raised a questioning eyebrow. Bebe nodded, and he reached for the Book of Shadows. Flipping to the mysterious writing, he said, "Do you recognize this?" He pushed the Book across the granite.

Phillippa turned the Book around and frowned while the other four vampires gathered to look over her shoulder. Well, the three guys looked over her shoulder. Anne peered around her elbow.

"It's Natasha's handwriting, but it looks like some kind of code," Phillippa said. Her gaze flicked up to meet Bebe's. "I take it you don't recognize it."

Bebe hesitated. Not wanting to be rude, she still needed to know who or what she was dealing with when it came to Phillippa. She didn't necessarily agree with Grandma Petrov's choice of trusting those outside of the coven, but all the old rules had been thrown out the window the moment she'd returned to San Francisco. "A truth for a truth?"

Phillippa's brow twisted in confusion before she nodded.

Bebe took a deep breath before asking, "What are you?"

Phillippa sighed before answering. "My mother was a nymph, but the sperm donor was an Olympian. I considered your grandmother my friend." She gave Bebe a stern frown. "And that's all of my personal information you need to know."

Demigoddess. Wow. Not what she was expecting. Bebe took a bite of Anne's cinnamon bread, chewing as she considered Phillippa's bombshell. Demigods were rare these days. And due to the rivalries between the pantheons, the few remaining on earth hadn't bothered to band together and demand a seat on the International Council.

Bebe pointed to the strange script. "That section wasn't in the Book of Shadows before I left for Africa, so Grandma had to have added it in the last few years."

"Do either of you know what this text is supposed to be?" Duncan asked.

Bebe bit her lower lip. With the vamps super-hearing, there was no freaking way she could ask Caesar privately. Taking a leap of faith, she dropped her outer shield and sent a tentative probe to him.

Caesar?

To his credit, he didn't jump at the sudden intrusion, but she could sense the surface of his surprise.

Yes?

How do you think your people will handle learning about Grandma's research?

The link was silent as he mulled her question, but his worry came through loud and clear. He'd obviously been questioning the wisdom of informing other vampires of what Grandma was up to. *I don't believe they will overreact, but I cannot guarantee it. However, full disclosure may be necessary to adequately protect you and the Book.*

Time to take another chance. She took a second deep breath and met Duncan's look squarely. "We believe Grandma was doing some kind of genetic research. She had discovered certain witches are resistant to the V-virus."

Six sets of eyes stared at her in stunned disbelief. Several seconds passed before Duncan's dry voice commented. "In other words, the attempts on your life are about more than the White Rose succession."

"We don't know that for sure," Caesar said.

"Who else knows about this?" Ptolemy's tone was more animalistic snarl than human, and his eyes started glowing. Bebe silently thanked the Goddess for Caesar's comforting presence. Otherwise, she had the definite impression Ptolemy would be smacking the shit out of her.

"We don't know. Bebe wasn't even aware of Natasha's research until I told her," Caesar said.

"So she claims," Ptolemy shot back. "Have you read her to be sure?"

Fear rippled down Bebe's spine. She'd managed to keep Caesar out of her head when he tried to read her at the auction and later in her hotel room, but if all five vampires joined forces, she wouldn't have a mind left when they were done.

"That's unnecessary, Ptolemy," Caesar said.

Phillippa twisted on her stool to eye Ptolemy. "*I* didn't even know until now, so you need to calm down, child." She turned back to examine the Book, flipping through additional pages. "It explains why Natasha asked me to keep the Book for Bebe." She looked up at Bebe again. "And if others know about the witches' resistance to the virus, it would explain the cooperation between your attackers at Anthony's."

Bebe popped another bite of bread in her mouth. Something didn't quite make sense in Grandma's plan. She swallowed before she said, "Why not leave the Book in the wardrobe's secret compartment though? She could have warded the nymph hole so that no one but her Confirmed successor could remove the Book." The memory of sitting under the huge oak in the back yard of Grandma's house and reading one of her favorite novels during summer vacation made her sigh. "If she'd left the Book where William or Alice could find it, my two idiot cousins wouldn't have started the asinine court battle."

Caesar and Ptolemy shared an uncomfortable look that irritated her.

"Would you two stop trying to protect me? I'm not entirely stupid. One of my cousins is behind the assassination attempts, and you suspect it's Alice." Her outburst was worth the surprised look on Caesar's face. She tore into the slice of pizza to keep from smiling.

"How did you find out?" he finally asked.

She eyed him with what she hoped was a disdainful stare. "You know the problem with you vampires is that you're arrogant. Unless someone's another vampire or older than dirt—" She shot an apologetic glance at Phillippa. "No offense."

"None taken," Phillippa said with a smile.

Bebe turned back to Caesar. "You think their knowledge and opinions mean nothing."

Tiffany shot a tiny fist into the air. "Go, Bebe!"

Bebe sighed. She could sympathize with the teen, but with too many questions, she needed to focus. "Rather than carving her own life, Alice would rather stew in her jealousy. It doesn't take a rocket scientist to put two and two together. And—" Caesar deserved the truth no matter how much it pained her. "I overheard Alex saying you had traced the hotel gunmen to Uncle Lionel," she finished in a small voice to the stunned looks from the vampires who'd been in San Francisco.

"You'd better watch out for your job, Duncan," Phillippa said, amusement in her voice.

"So it would seem," he answered, but the twinkle in his eyes indicated he shared the demigoddess's humor.

Caesar crossed his arms, a perturbed look on his face. "So is there a point to this besides attempting to embarrass me in front of my people?

Bebe chewed on her bottom lip. Maybe she should have kept her mouth shut, but she was tired of the head games. "Grandma went to a lot of trouble to get the Book out of San Francisco after adding her coded notes to it. She's not the type to do something without a definite purpose. So what was the purpose in putting her notes in the Book to begin with, and why give the Book to Phillippa for safe keeping?"

"The doctor has a point." Phillippa pushed back her plate and propped her elbows on the countertop, her chin resting on her entwined fingers. Her eyes narrowed. "Natasha was sure Bebe would come down to get the book from me."

"Because she left a letter for me in the secret compartment of the wardrobe, where the Book was normally hidden." Bebe slid her own plate aside, no longer hungry even though she'd only taken a few bites. Instead, her stomach ached as worry began gnawing on the contents.

Phillippa tapped the Book with a manicured index finger. "You said yourself, Natasha did nothing without a reason. Why not just give me the coded notes? Why put them in her Book of Shadows?" She raised an eyebrow. "What is it about that wardrobe that she knew you'd find a way to access it?"

"I-I don't know," Bebe said. Goddess, she didn't want to go through the marriages and family trees again. That thought started the acid churning in her stomach.

"Yes, you do," Caesar prompted. "You were determined to pay more than it was worth at the auction."

Bebe snorted. "So says the man who *outbid* me for it." She shook her head then shrugged. "The only thing it meant to me was sentimental. I used to hide in it when I was a child whenever I was upset about something."

"That's where I found you," Caesar said.

She didn't realize she was trembling until his hand engulfed hers and gave a comforting squeeze. She turned to him and understanding dawned. The night of the funerals. He had told the truth the other night. He had been there.

She'd put on the brave face Grandma Petrov had insisted, but as soon as the ceremony finished, she had raced for the comfort of the wardrobe. She wasn't sure how long she'd been in there, weeping, when the dark man had come, offering to take away the pain. Grandma had appeared, scolding the dark man.

When she had asked Grandma about it the next morning, Grandma had said she'd dreamed the whole thing. And like everything else from those horrible days, she'd blocked it from her memory. Goddess, what other knowledge had she forgotten that her survival now depended?

With an effort, she dragged her attention back to Phillippa. "I'm sorry. What did you say?"

"I said," came Phillippa's dry voice, "you need some kind of key to decipher Natasha's code." She tapped the incomprehensible pages with a forefinger. "She knew the Book would be preserved and given to Bebe no matter what. My guess is she destroyed any other notes due to her suspected conspiracy. The only reason I can think of to move the Book is to separate it from the key."

Bebe shook her head. "But Caesar's guard Stan and I checked the wardrobe. We didn't find anything else."

"Whoa, people!" Tiffany waved her hands. "We're making a lot of assumptions here." She jabbed a black fingernail at the text. "This crap may be Grandma Natasha's secret recipe for matzo balls for all we know."

Tiffany's attitude restored Bebe's humor. "If Grandma Petrov ever deigned to enter the kitchen except to castigate our cook, I'd agree with you." Remembering the e-mail earlier, her throat closed in fear. She turned to Caesar. "You said Granny E. didn't know all of Grandma Petrov's plans. Did Granny E. know about the resistance to the virus?"

"She knows your step-grandfather, Ben Epstein, is immune. He—" Caesar started.

Then something happened Bebe never thought she'd see. His pale olive face flamed scarlet.

He gave a little cough before continuing. "Ben's helped certain witch couples who could not have children."

Tiffany giggled. "Talk about donating for the cause."

Caesar regained his composure by glaring at the girl. "I cannot vouch for any other information Ziva might know. Other than the evening of your parents' funeral, the three of us were never alone. I'm afraid we were all occupied with more pressing concerns that night, and Natasha would never have mentioned something like this in front of someone she wasn't sure about. Why?"

A terrible suspicion niggled Bebe's brain. Her heart tried to claw its way out of her constricted throat. She choked out the words anyway. "Are you sure this afternoon's e-mail was from Granny E.?"

He gave a slow nod as her concerns were mirrored on his face, but his attempt at a smile didn't quite reach his eyes. "I'm fairly sure. She's one of the few that has that particular address of mine, other than my sister and the people in this room, and no one could have used her e-mail account without her password. Do you want me to contact Eleanor Hyde-Smith?"

His reassuring smile, though sweet, did not reassure her one bit. She shook her head. "It would be better if I did. You're already in enough trouble with my people from the sounds of it, and a high priestess would respect a request from another witch."

Phoning Alastair's mother ranked right up with being staked on top of a fire ant hill.

Naked.

With honey smeared all over her body.

But protocol demanded that Granny E. notify Mrs. Hyde-Smith of her presence in England.

"Before a vampire, you mean." He checked his watch. "It's two in the morning their time. Are you sure you want to wake her at this hour?"

She couldn't stop her exasperated sigh. "For just once, could we please do things my way?"

He chuckled. "Well, since you did say please . . ."

Two minutes later, he had produced Mrs. Hyde-Smith's phone number and a portable receiver. Bebe said a silent, calming prayer. She didn't relish calling Alistair's mother after refusing to marry her son, but she had to make sure Granny E. was okay.

The phone rang several times before someone answered, "Hyde-Smith residence."

"M-m-may I speak with Eleanor Hyde-Smith, please?"

"Who is this?" The woman's nasty tone indicated she didn't appreciate the late night call.

"Bebe Zachary. I apologize for phoning so late, but this is very important. It's about my grandmother, Ziva Epstein."

"Brigid in a basket! This is Eleanor. Is it really you, Bebe?" Now the woman at the other end sounded positively frantic. "Are you safe? Rumors here are flying that you've been captured by vampires."

Bebe flicked her gaze to Caesar, who listened to the whole conversation with his freaking vampire hearing. She suppressed a smile. Tiffany was the only person in the kitchen who *couldn't* hear both sides.

At her telepathic question, he nodded confirmation that she was speaking to Eleanor Hyde-Smith. Since Eleanor was one of the witch representatives on the I.C., Bebe didn't doubt him.

Deciding not to address the vampire issue, she said, "Yes, ma'am, I'm fine. I'm trying to reach my grandmother. Bad weather delayed her flight out of London, and I thought she might be at your estate."

"She's here, child, along with Ben." Eleanor's tone pronounced trouble. "I'm afraid I have bad news. An unseelie attacked the airport shuttle they rode between Heathrow and Gatwick. Thank Brigid, we were able to extract them from the accident scene before the bobbies arrived. Use of magick such as that alerts every fae and witch in Britain. She's alive, but she's in terrible shape. Been unconscious since we found her. Ben's conscious but not too coherent yet. Apparently the bloody bastard hit him with some kind of confusion spell."

Bebe's heart threatened to explode where it lodged in her throat. "When-when did this happen?"

"Early yesterday morning. About seven our time. I would have rung you . . ."

The rest of Eleanor's words faded as Bebe calculated the time difference between London and Los Angeles. From the shocked look on Caesar's face, he realized the problem at the moment she did. Granny E. was attacked around midnight last night. There was no way she could have sent that e-mail.

". . . hearing all the problems concerning Natasha's succession. Is there anything I can do to help, dear? Are you somewhere safe?"

Bebe forced her mind to register Mrs. Hyde-Smith's words and answered. "When Granny wakes or Grandpa Ben recovers, please tell them I'm all right. I'll call again later to check on them."

"Wait! Where can we reach—"

Bebe clicked off the phone. "We've got to get out of this house. Now."

Chapter 18

A trap.

Caesar cursed himself as he gave orders to evacuate the mansion. He should have known better. Documents could so easily be forged this day and age. Not to mention all of Natasha's fears of an internal conspiracy within White Rose. Apparently, the problem extended to Ziva's coven as well.

No, that wasn't the only problem. He couldn't lie to himself. He had wanted Ziva to tell him to keep Bebe here with him. He wanted the excuse to spend time with the beautiful doctor, to verbally spar with her, to enjoy the fire that coursed through him every time he touched her.

And now his slip in common sense had put her in danger. Kensai and Jamal's arrival to relieve Mai and Miko would be the time to strike.

Which meant they had less than ten minutes to get Bebe out of the house.

He reached out telepathically. *Kensai?*

Yes, Master Augustine?

Where are you?

The ronin confirmed he and Jamal were only two streets away.

We have unwelcome guests outside of the mansion.

Am I to assume you would like an adequate greeting?

Caesar couldn't resist a telepathic chuckle at the eagerness in Kensai's mental voice. *Not just yet. Ptolemy will provide them a distraction. Stay back and observe how many friends we have and how many take Ptolemy's bait.*

Understood, Master.

Caesar released the telepathic connection only to have Tiffany grin at him as she loaded coolers with blood.

"Told you Murphy would strike," she said, slamming the lids shut.

"Now's not the time, Tiffany." The instant the harsh words swarmed out of his mouth, he regretted them. He'd been the one who'd been thinking with his cock when it came to Bebe. Thankfully, Tiffany kept quiet while she started packing two smaller coolers with regular food. Bless Mai and her efficiency with the groceries.

A minute later, Bebe charged through the kitchen door. "Here we go." She tossed the clothing she'd been wearing into Tiffany's outstretched hands. Clean jeans and one of Duncan's black t-shirts from the dirty clothes hamper now clung to her breasts and swam down her thighs.

He bit his tongue to keep from commenting. It would have been preferably seeing her in one of his shirts, but she needed to resemble his chief enforcer's niece as much as possible.

Despite the mixed company rushing back and forth between the kitchen and the garage, Tiffany skimmed out of her own black t-shirt. Ptolemy opened his mouth to harass the girl about her lack of womanly curves.

Don't. We do not have the time for your usual bullshit.

Ptolemy's mouth snapped shut, and he tossed Caesar the sword and harness he'd retrieved from the master bedroom.

Tiffany slipped on Bebe's bra while the doctor wadded paper towels to stuff the cups.

Caesar tried not to remember the heat of Bebe's all-too-generous breasts filling his palms as he checked the blade and harness for his spatha. A replica of his first sword, the steel slid home with a satisfying snick.

"I don't see why she can't glamour Tiffany. It'd be more convincing," Ptolemy muttered. He snapped a clip into his Glock 34.

Bebe glared at him before stuffing one last crumpled towel in Tiffany's borrowed undergarment. "Because any witch or fae will be able to detect a glamour spell. The witches involved will be checking." She stepped back to survey Tiffany's new cleavage and nodded. The girl pulled Bebe's khakis over her own jeans. The result gave the scrawny teenager the illusion of hips.

"And because they've probably been watching my place all day,"

Caesar said, his irritation with his own behavior spilling out in his voice. "They'll have a head count by now." He prayed Bebe's scent on the clothes Tiffany had donned would throw off any were or vampire, no matter how temporary the effect. He pocketed the extra magazines Ptolemy slid across the island countertop to him. Normally, he preferred steel to using a gun loaded with modified bullets. But the weres shared the vampires' allergy to silver, so now was not the time to be picky. He tucked one of Ptolemy's spare Glocks in the waistband of his jeans.

"Ready," Tiffany said, stuffing the hem of the camp shirt into the oversized khakis. She pulled on a baseball cap while Bebe attempted to tuck her unruly hair under another cap she borrowed from Tiffany. The effect wasn't as clean as he would have liked, but paired with the UV film on their vehicles' windows, it would have to do.

I would prefer remaining by your side, and Duncan is not pleased putting his niece in this kind of danger.

Caesar grinned at his brother's continued complaints at acting as Tiffany's escort. *But who else do I have who can play me?* He kept silent on his opinion that Tiffany was more than capable of taking care of herself. Such a comment would only distract Ptolemy further.

Within seconds, both his Hummer and Duncan's Escalade had been loaded with fuel, food, weapons and people. Per their plan, Alex and Anne would escort Ptolemy and Tiffany to Caesar's canyon safe house in his vehicle, while Phillippa followed in her Mustang as an extra precaution. Before Caesar could point out that Phillippa was getting involved in a witch matter, the statuesque brunette shot him an arch look as she climbed behind the wheel and said, "I'm protecting my ward. Nothing more."

The only part that truly concerned him was the fact that Bebe would have to drive Duncan's SUV to maintain the illusion that Ptolemy and Tiffany remained with his Chief Enforcer.

As the garage door rose, Kensai touched Caesar's mind again. *Mai and Miko have slipped out undetected and are on their way to the airport in our vehicle.*

Caesar passed the information to Duncan, but he couldn't resist a chuckle that two Normals had evaded the supernaturals sitting at his door. Maybe this would be easier than he originally thought.

Maybe the foes at the gate knew what he planned and everything was for naught.

Sitting in the garage didn't distract that possibility from his mind. The minutes waiting to see if Bebe's enemies took the bait stretched on for an eternity. Her fingers tapped an impatient rhythm on the steering wheel. Somehow, knowing the interim bothered her too helped his own nerves.

"It is time to go. Do not forget to emulate Tiffany's driving style," Duncan reminded Bebe.

Caesar grinned at the dirty look she shot Duncan. He pressed the earbuds of Ptolemy's iPod in place and slouched down in the second seat.

"How is it you're supposed to be protecting me, but I'm the one who has to drive the five and a half hours to San Francisco?"

Despite Bebe's aggrieved tone, he had the impression she was happy to be doing something constructive. She threw the SUV into reverse and peeled out of his garage. Her two-point turn sent him sliding into the door.

"Any questions about my driving, Mr. St. James?" she said, racing down the driveway.

"None whatsoever, Dr. Zachary," came Duncan's arid reply.

Master? We've counted five vehicles. We cannot confirm the actual number of occupants or their status without revealing ourselves, but there appears to be at least three persons in each vehicle. Three vehicles followed your Hummer.

Thank you, Kensai.

Caesar repeated the information to Duncan, who nodded before he added, "Dealing with only one team will even the odds."

"How do you know we'll only have to deal with one car?" Bebe asked. "Your man said there were two more."

"They'll leave one vehicle to watch my place," Caesar said. "Just in case."

"Yeah, but you're assuming only three occupants in a vehicle. I hate to point out that you boys sent your big guns with the other vehicle. What if the bad guys following us have a demigod with them?" Tires screeched as Bebe whipped the Escalade in a sharp right once she cleared the gates and gunned the engine.

"Do you think so little of the ability of Duncan and me to protect you?"

"Forgive me, oh great and powerful Caesar." She obeyed the stop sign at the first intersection and slammed on the brakes.

If not for the seatbelt, he would have flipped past the front seats and smashed into the windshield. "How can you drive like a maniac and speak with a normal voice?" Caesar asked.

She flashed a grin in the rearview mirror. "Experience is the great teacher, and Chad guerillas provided the ultimate opportunity."

"You were a medic for a mercenary squad? I thought you worked for Doctors Without Borders," Duncan said, incredulity in his voice.

She shook her head. "More than once they made grabs for our medical supplies. When you don't carry guns, you learn to run like hell."

The fourth vehicle is pursuing you, Master.

"We've got company, boys," Bebe said at the same moment Kensai reported.

Caesar eased up to peer over the back of the seat. The blue Taurus rental held back a quarter of a mile, making no move to overtake them. "They don't seem that anxious to make our acquaintance."

"They may only be observers. If they are aware Dr. Zachary is with us, whoever is behind this will wait until they have a more secluded opportunity, such as when we reach your private hangar so as not to attract the attention of airport security."

Duncan's analysis sent a chill through Caesar. He wracked his brain for a way to evade the car following them that wouldn't result in the death of Bebe or an innocent bystander.

"Tiffany would still try to lose them." Bebe's hard tone gave Caesar enough warning to brace himself before she swerved to the left. She headed for a busier street.

Her zigzag maneuvers through the heavy Los Angeles traffic sent a thrill straight to his groin. She showed the same fire she had at Anthony's when they had been attacked, and for some strange reason, her attitude excited him. The zipper of his trousers dug into his growing erection. He slumped back down to ease the bite. The sadist who decided placing metal teeth next to a man's penis should be crucified.

I can't touch her. But the reminder did nothing to quench his desire for the brilliant, fiery woman in the driver's seat.

He tried to focus on the other immediate problem. "Our friends still back there?"

Her big, brown eyes reflected the headlights' glare from the vehicles behind them when she flicked her gaze to the mirror. "Yep. They're keeping their distance though."

As much as he'd rather engage the bastards head on, he couldn't take the chance of Bebe getting injured or worse. He also didn't want an encounter at the airport.

Duncan flashed his cell phone. "Perhaps it is time we use Normal paranoia to our benefit. I could give a description of our friends to Homeland Security?"

Caesar chuckled. "A very good suggestion. Please do."

As Duncan punched the number on the cell, Bebe's eye flashed in the rearview mirror. "Are you crazy? You'd be setting up those poor police to be slaughtered!" She swerved around a semi-truck.

"If our friends are supernaturals, do you think they'd really risk exposure?" Caesar said.

"They did at your nephew's restaurant," she shot back.

"Which was Family-owned. They knew we'd have to clean up the mess to avoid questions ourselves. Natasha's conspirators have worked too hard to destroy all their efforts in a major encounter at LAX. My guess is they will depart at the first sign of the local authorities."

"That's a big gamble on a lot of innocent lives," she said.

"I play to win, Dr. Zachary."

Her slight shudder wouldn't have been perceptible to normal eyes, but she kept silent and her attention remained fixed on traffic the rest of the way. At least until her triumphant shout of "Yes!" as the Escalade maneuvered onto the exit ramp for the airport.

He sat up to look behind them. Red and blue lights blazing, a half dozen LAPD cars converged on the Taurus, effectively trapping their pursuers on the ramp.

Duncan directed her through the back roads to the private areas, security a little heavier than usual thanks to his tip to the Normal authorities. Mai and Miko waited for them in the hanger when they pulled into the cavernous space.

"Did anyone follow you?" Caesar said to the girls. He covered his amusement when Bebe ignored his hand to help her down from the SUV. Her refusal was a good thing. His groin tightened when he detected the scent of her arousal over Duncan and Tiffany's clothing.

Miko shook her head. A couple inches taller than her older sister, she didn't have quite the sternness or dedication to rules that plagued Mai, but it didn't make her any less efficient. "No, the fifth vehicle remains near the mansion. Grandfather will inform you if it departs prior to daybreak."

"Good. File a flight plan to Las Vegas and get in the air as soon as you can. I want you two to stay there until you hear from me or your grandfather."

Mai stepped forward, her bun wound nearly as tight as her whip-thin body. "Master Augustine, are you sure you want us to fly to Las Vegas and stay there without you?" She had to be damned upset to even contemplate questioning one of his orders.

In fact, he didn't recall her *ever* questioning him.

He nodded before glancing at Duncan, who had his cell glued to his ear again. Turning back to Mai, he said, "I need you to buy us some time."

"But, Master—"

He held up a hand. "My orders stand." He softened his voice at the stricken expression on her face. "If you're questioned, and you will be questioned by my sister's people, I don't want you to have any knowledge of our whereabouts."

She gave a slow nod. Even Miko's delicate features twisted in concern. He rarely kept anything from Selene.

And he couldn't even answer to himself his reluctance to let Selene know of the immediate problems. He'd always trusted his twin. His first thought had been to ask for her help. Now, he'd pared vampire assistance down to just Duncan.

Understanding of his own motive hit him like a concrete block.

Because Duncan would be the one vampire who'd understand and sympathize with his desire to find a cure for the virus.

Duncan clicked his cell phone shut. "The police commissioner has verified our friends are in custody. He is concerned however about how long he can keep them. Their attorney is Jimmy Hanson, and he is already down at holding."

"Jimmy Hanson?" Bebe incredulous gaze flicked between the two men. "Wasn't he the one who got off that pedophilic pop star and then the basketball player who murdered his ex-wife?"

"Yes." Caesar's hand clenched. Shit. For Hanson to be down at holding to post bail before the ones following them had even been processed . . .

Now, he had confirmation of how deep this conspiracy of Natasha's ran. And he'd lay his entire fortune it had nothing to do with the White Rose succession. For the first time in centuries, the cold fingers of fear stroked his spine. He couldn't fail Bebe. "We need to leave town before they make bail."

Chapter 19

Hours later, a neck muscle gave Bebe a sharp reminder of how long she'd been behind the wheel. She rolled her head trying to ease the tension. Caesar had driven the first leg until they needed to stop for gas. He finally gave in to her insistence that she takeover the steering wheel. It gave her something to do besides sit and worry in the back seat.

"Pull over at the next exit," Caesar said.

Irritated with him ordering her around like she was one of his minions, she glanced in the rearview mirror. "Why? This was your idea. I told you we should have stuck with the Escalade instead of taking your pilot's Vue." While she enjoyed driving the sporty mini-ute, she had no sympathy for the two large men crammed into the seats.

But she couldn't stifle the yawn that threatened to dislocate her jaw.

"Because you need a break."

At three in the morning, she didn't feel like arguing with him. Besides, she wasn't the one who'd turn into flaming shish kabob if they didn't make it to his San Francisco house before dawn.

A few minutes later, she pulled into a twenty-four hour service station. Surreptitiously checking the other vehicles, she climbed out of the seat and stretched her tight, aching muscles.

"Are you trying to entice every male here?"

She jumped at the warm breath tickling her hair. Turning to glare at Caesar, she said, "You really need to stop doing that."

"Doing what?" he said, a mischievous look on his face. Even though the virus had frozen him in the appearance of a man in his mid-twenties, his true age normally shone in his eyes.

Except when he decided to tease her, which was becoming a constant occurrence despite their predicament. And she liked it. A lot.

Not sure if the irritation was at her behavior or his, she shook her head and stomped into the convenience store to find the ladies' room. Holding her breath, she used the facilities as fast as possible. Damn, she'd used ditches in Africa that were cleaner.

Thank the Goddess, the food area wasn't as dirty. The warm aroma of roasted pistachios cleared her head once she left the restroom, but the siren song of chocolate led her away from the nuts. She paid for the dark chocolate Hershey's bar and found Caesar waiting for her at the door, somehow holding three large coffees. She smiled her thanks as she took the top one and shoved the door open.

Then she felt it. Not a psychic probe but the pressure wave of a search spell.

"What's wrong?" he said, his voice soft in her ear.

A tickle of fear rippled through her nerves. "We need to get back in the SUV. They're looking for us." She started for the gas pumps.

Don't run. We'll attract attention.

His words jerked her out of the instinct to flee. Heat rushed to her cheeks. Not that he had to remind her to remain calm, but that she hadn't reestablished her outer mental shields since she had spoken to him privately in the kitchen earlier. And even more surprising, he had not sent a telepathic compulsion. He spoke to her as an equal. A little thrill ran through her that he took her seriously. At least, he hadn't slung her over his shoulder again.

She took a sip of the scorching java and tried to stroll nonchalantly to the waiting vehicle, Caesar close behind her.

Duncan leaned against the passenger door, but his eyes belied his stance. *What is it?*

Company's coming. The buzz of the spell drew closer, the subsonic energy making her teeth rattle.

Can you perform a counter spell? Caesar asked her as he handed the second cup to Duncan.

She nodded, wishing she had the spell memorized, but she'd never had to worry about hiding something or someone from a magickal search before. Damn, how could they act so calm? Their behavior made her want to kick them both, but that wasn't fair. Caesar and Duncan didn't have the fingernails-on-chalkboard sensation of the nearing spell sparking their neurons.

"Keys." Caesar held out his hand.

Balancing the Hershey's on top of the hot cup, she yanked the set from her jeans pocket and dropped them into his waiting palm. Climbing into the back seat, she set the coffee and candy bar on the floor and leaned over to pull the Book from her bag in the cargo area. Nerveless fingers flipping through the pages of the Book, it took her a couple of precious seconds to find the blocking spell. If she survived this whole mess, she was definitely indexing the damn Book for future generations.

Only one item was listed in the ingredients section. "Oh, fuck!"

Caesar slammed on the brakes, tipping over her cup and flooding the back seat floor with coffee. "What?"

"I need a turtle shell. Pull over there." She pointed to a free parking spot to the side of the building.

The Vue hadn't fully stopped before she flung open the door. Racing back into the store, she grabbed a bag of pistachios and dropped a twenty on the counter. Such an extravagance would have sent Grandma Petrov into an apoplectic fit, but now . . .

Now, everything she thought she knew about Grandma had turned into total bullshit anyway.

Launching herself back into the mini-ute, she yelled, "Go!"

And tried not to think about the very big gun sitting in Duncan's lap.

"Bebe, honey," Caesar said, trying to catch her attention in the rearview mirror and keep an eye on the road at the same time. "I hate to be the one to point out that turtles are animals, not nuts."

"It's sympathetic magick, so I can substitute if I have to." She ripped open the bag and carefully pried open a pistachio with a nail. It went to show how crazy the last two weeks of her life had become when her normally short, immaculate fingernails had grown into talons. "Now, shut up, let me concentrate—" *And don't ever call me 'honey' again!*

His silent chuckle echoed in her mind as she dropped half of the pistachio back into the bag. She placed the remaining half shell-side up on the palm of her right hand and closed her eyes. Envisioning the half nut as the Vue, she murmured the old spell to reinforce the shell protecting the tiny pistachio.

With a warm rush, golden energy snapped into place over the vehicle. She opened her eyes to find Caesar merging onto the interstate, the traffic light due to the early morning hour.

And dead ahead, a boiling wave of red energy flowed southward toward them. Her breath hitched in her throat as they rushed to meet the ugly smear. She braced herself.

But the golden haze of the shielding spell sliced through the blistering energy, a slight pressure in her head the only indication that her protective shell deflected the search around them. She twisted in the seat and watched the red wave pass on into the night. A sigh almost escaped her, but she tasted a bitter, iron tang at the back of her tongue. Icy fear gripped her. Someone had powered the search spell with blood. A whole life's worth of blood.

"Bebe? Are you okay?" Caesar said.

She turned to find him glancing at her in the mirror again. Duncan peered around the edge of his seat. Both vampires had concerned expressions on their faces.

"Yeah, I'm fine." She sucked in a deep cleansing breath.

"Did it work?" Caesar asked.

She nodded and curiosity rose. "Didn't you see the spell coming down the freeway toward us?"

"Truth for a truth?" he said, repeating her earlier question to Phillippa.

As old as he was, what could he possibly not know? But she nodded her agreement anyway.

"If we're close enough to the caster or the subject, a vampire can smell the ozone of a spell's energy, but we can't See the energy itself." He grinned, flashing fang in the mirror. "What is it you see? Natasha would never tell me. Said it was beyond my comprehension."

Bebe smiled. She'd heard something similar from her grandmother in the past, particularly when she had problems mastering a technique. "It is kind of difficult to describe to someone who can't detect the patterns."

Caesar snorted. "Now who's being arrogant about their power?"

She couldn't get angry at his teasing tone. "Would you let me finish? Geez!" She whacked his shoulder. "The energy colors reflect the caster's personal aura, and depending on the spell, the caster's intent." She waved her hand to indicate the vehicle. "My shielding spell would appear as a golden sphere to another witch." She jabbed a thumb toward the rear. "That search spell was a nasty-looking dark red."

"Because of the other witch's aura or the intent," Duncan asked.

"Probably both."

"What aren't you telling us, Bebe?" The reflection of Caesar's eyes glowed in the mirror as his gaze bore into her. Not neon yellow, but getting there.

She sighed and leaned back. Was she that transparent to him? The iron aftertaste left her slimy and wishing desperately for a shower. "Whoever cast it used a blood sacrifice for extra power."

Caesar's eyes narrowed as his attention flicked between her and the road. "Natasha told me witches don't use sacrifices in their spells."

Leave it to fuzzy bunny propaganda to make this difficult for her. She shrugged. "Most won't. And if they do, they use their own blood, not another being's. There are . . . repercussions down the road when using someone or something else's blood without permission. You're taking a part of their life force. And death releases all the energy at once. Someone's pretty desperate to find us to take that kind of risk."

She leaned forward and laid a hand on his shoulder. For some reason, it was important that he understand. "I never have used another person's blood if that's what you're concerned about."

But would you?

I don't know. The question bothered her more than she wanted to admit. She hated to use her own blood in spells, but she'd been desperate last night at the restaurant. Regardless, Caesar deserved nothing less than a straight answer even if it showed her ugly side. *To save someone I loved, I might.* Even if it meant she'd be damned for eternity.

He nodded as if satisfied with her admission. "Thank you for your honesty."

She nestled back into the seat and retrieved the soggy candy bar from the floor. After tearing open the damp wrapper, she bit into the chocolate that was as dark as her thoughts.

What would she do? A few months ago, she would have unequivocally said no blood magick. But then, a few months ago, she'd never pictured Grandma Petrov as a ruthless Nazi hunter or Alice capable of ordering someone killed. Did she have it in her to kill?

The image of the witch, lying on the pavement in front of Anthony's and choking on the blood mud golem, gave her the answer.

Acid crept up her throat. She wrapped up the candy, dropped it in the pistachio bag, and tried not to cry for her lost innocence the rest of the way to San Francisco.

Two hours later, Bebe was still wide-awake without the coffee when Caesar pulled into his garage. A highly irritated Stan met them at the door to the kitchen.

"Somebody want to tell me what the fuck is going on?" The half-elf's deep voice practically barked out his words. "Your sister's been calling here every hour since midnight wanting to know where you are. When I call down to the Brentwood house, Jamal will only say you're out, and he'll take a message." He propped his fists on his hips. "When I call the safe house, Alex gives me the same Morrigan-damned story. And everyone at the Seattle compound says they haven't seen you either!"

"You'll do the same. It's imperative that no one knows we're here for the time being. Do I make myself clear, Stanley?" Caesar's eyes glowed and his fangs extended, sending a tiny shiver down Bebe's back.

Stan held up his hands, his fingers fanned. "Sure, boss, no problem." He cocked an eyebrow. "But if there's something in particular Harry and I are supposed to be guarding against, we need to know."

"Duncan, would you brief the Gryffudds? Have Harry remain on the perimeter watch. Dr. Zachary and I will be in my office when you're finished," Caesar said. Before she could say anything, he hooked a hand under her elbow and towed her through the kitchen.

Goddess, had it been only four days since Ptolemy carried a comatose Caesar along the same path? Too much had happened since then. Too much on her conscience.

She needed a break. Just a little one. Digging in her heels, she said, "Hey, don't I even get a potty stop?"

Caesar halted at her protest, his face contrite. "I'm sorry. I forget you don't have our stamina."

"Stamina's one thing. A full bladder's another." She shrugged out of his grip and shoved her bag into his arms. "Why don't you start a pot of tea while I use the ladies' room?"

She dove into the half-bath without waiting for his answer. She turned on the faucet and lowered the toilet lid. Then she sat and let the tears she'd held in for the last one hundred and some miles fall. As much as she wanted to chalk her weepiness to exhaustion, she couldn't. She was as screwed up as the rest of her family. The real question was how did she convince the Elders they needed to select a new high priest or priestess. *And it harm none, do what ye will.* Yeah, right. The Petrov line really deserved the title the way they upheld the Rede.

She never wanted the H.P. position. She didn't deserve it. And neither did Alice, if her cousin was truly behind the attacks.

But a tiny sliver of doubt remained. Maybe someone was trying to set Alice up. Or was she clinging to the wish that her cousin and she could reclaim their childhood friendship?

Yanking off a wad of toilet paper, she blew her nose and wiped her eyes. Goddess knew William wasn't qualified. He'd rather party with his toadies than deal with the day-to-day administration of the coven.

And she still needed to call Eleanor Hyde-Smith to check on Granny E. and Grandpa Ben. Maybe the London H.P. would have some information on who was responsible for the attack on them. If Grandpa Ben had been hit with a fae confusion spell, the effects should have worn off by now. She couldn't afford to think about what might have been done to Granny E. Not without totally falling apart.

Damn, her life sucked when the only dependable person in it was a vampire. A shiver ran down her spine at the image of Caesar. She brutally shoved it aside as well. Wanting a relationship with him made as much sense as wanting back her friendship with Alice.

No, she needed to deal with a real problem that she might have a chance at solving. Which meant finding Grandma Petrov's cipher key.

She rose and checked herself in the mirror. At least, she didn't have raccoon eyes from her tears. The make-up she'd applied to meet with Phillippa at the antique shop yesterday morning had long since worn off. Splashing some cool water on her face, Bebe tried to make herself presentable. Another look in the mirror as she dried her skin. The red rims around her eyes were weariness. That's all.

She exited the tiny half-bath and walked down the hallway to Caesar's office. Inside, he had already moved the wardrobe to the center of the room. He stalked around the antique, eyeing the piece like a lion trying to figure out if a strange object was edible.

She leaned against the doorframe and crossed her arms. "So have you made it talk yet?"

He smiled at her tiny joke and shook his head. "With your permission, I would like to consult with Stan about the code." His attention returned to the silent wood. "He may have some ideas."

"Sure." She pulled the door shut before she threw her hands in the air. Not that the wood could really stop Duncan from hearing her yell at Caesar, but it'd probably block Stan and Harry. "Would you like to take out ads in the *Chronicle* while you're at it?"

"It was merely a suggestion."

His conciliatory tone made her feel even guiltier for lashing out at him. "I'm sorry. It's been a long two weeks since I first got the telegram about Grandma Petrov's death, and I haven't had much sleep." She tried to knead her neck muscles.

"Here. Let me." He moved behind her, his hands brushing hers aside. Powerful fingers dug into her tight knots.

She blinked in surprise, but the sensation of her muscles loosening under his ministrations felt too good for her to protest. His massage followed the tension lines up along her scalp. She closed her eyes, letting relaxation wash over her.

Then he swept her hair aside, and lips replaced fingers. Cool, sensual lips nibbled and sucked and did so many other delightful things that her skin clamored for more. She leaned against his hard chest with a sigh.

Her conscience niggled in the back of her mind. Necking with a vampire was a bad idea. It could lead to sex. Sex led to madness. Madness led to death.

She smacked her conscience's Yoda imitation aside when Caesar's fingers skimmed her waist. Too many clothes in the way. Her t-shirt disappeared, and the skin-to-skin contact sent heat straight to her pelvis. His hands moved to cup and mold her breasts, tweaking and rolling the nipples through the satin of her bra. His seduction had nothing to do with power or manipulation, but pure male appreciation for a woman. And she reveled in it.

Turning in his arms, she pressed against his solid chest. And even more solid erection. Twining her arms around his neck, she tugged his head down to meet her lips. Yes, that's what she wanted. His tongue still tasted of the extra-strong coffee he'd drank on the last leg of the trip. It swirled and dipped, caressed and tasted her. Hands gripped her rear, lifting and pressing. Automatically, she wrapped her legs around his waist.

She wasn't a virgin by any means, but something about Caesar made desire a living thing inside her. And she wanted him enough to consider risking her life just to ease the burning in her soul.

A loud knock on the office door jerked reality back into focus.

Caesar leaned his forehead against hers while they both fought to catch their breath. *I seriously need to fire my entire staff.*

Unwrapping her legs, she smiled up at him as she slid down the length of his body. Her action elicited a groan from deep in his throat.

She didn't bother to hide her laughter. *That's what you get for starting this*, she sent.

He waited for her to whip her t-shirt on before he called, "Enter."

Duncan brushed the door open and strode into the room, a tray with a steaming pot of tea and several cups balanced in his hands. Stan trailed him into the room. "You wanted to speak with us?" Duncan prompted. He busied himself with the tea.

Bebe resigned herself to the inevitable. She pulled the Book of Shadows out of her bag and laid it on Caesar's desk. "We wanted you to take a look at this, Stan." Flipping to the pages with the mysterious code, she asked, "Do you recognize this? We thought it may have been a code you and Grandma may have used."

The half-elf leaned over and examined the writing, his white-blond brows twisted in concentration before he shook his head. "It definitely looks like Natasha's writing, but it's not a code I recognize." He stood upright, scratching the top of his buzz cut, his gaze darting between Bebe and Caesar. "Must be pretty serious if you're showing all of us a White Rose BOS."

Caesar gestured at the Book. "We believe the assassination attempts on Bebe have something to do with this."

Stan folded his arms over his chest. "It's not going to do them much good without the key to the code."

"That is assuming whoever is after the Book does not already have the key," Duncan countered.

"It doesn't matter whether *they*—" Bebe made air quotes with her fingers. "—have the key or not. My cousins and the Elders are all looking for the Book." She jabbed a finger at the coded notes. "If I don't know what *this* is, I'm not about to hand it over to anyone just to save my own skin."

"And that's assuming your 'they' don't want you dead for an entirely different reason. So where does that leave us?" Stan said. "There's no way the four of us can defend this place against a full-out assault if White Rose comes knocking in force. And no offense, boss," he said, shooting an apologetic look at Caesar. "No matter how quiet we keep, eventually someone's going to figure out you're here with the doctor. Your sister's already in a tizzy."

Duncan stiffened at the mention of Selene. Poor guy. Bebe didn't know how she'd react to the constant reminder of an unwilling Turn. She wished she hadn't gotten quite so much information out of that eavesdropping session.

Caesar must have noticed Duncan's reaction as well because he said, "I'd better call her before she does something we'll all regret." He headed for the door, but stopped short and turned. "Phillippa suggested that the key to Natasha's code may still be in the wardrobe." He disappeared in the direction of the kitchen.

Bebe murmured her thanks as she accepted the hot cup of tea from Duncan. He then excused himself to assist Harry with security. She couldn't blame him for not wanting to be in Caesar's office. Selene's scent must be all over the place.

Facing the confused Stan, she said, "Did you find anything else in the nymph hole besides the letter?"

He shook his head. "No. Caesar was in here when I opened it too. Is there another hole I couldn't find?"

"No." She paced around the wardrobe, willing it to unlock its secrets, but unfortunately, only the heroine in Disney's *Beauty and the Beast* had furniture that talked. So where was the key to Grandma's incomprehensible writing? She did another slow circuit around the wardrobe, sipping Duncan's English brew.

She reviewed the few facts she knew. Grandma had made a point of ensuring that the Book got into her hands by entrusting it with Phillippa. Then Grandma had left the letter in the nymph hole, a letter meant for her, one that relied on an old illusionist trick Grandma taught her to unlock the secret.

Illusions. Normal magic.

A false panel?

Setting her cup on the desk, she started knocking on the outer panels.

"The boss and I already checked for conventional hidden compartments." Stan crossed his arms over his broad chest. He definitely didn't get his build from the fae side of his family. On the other hand, Caesar's chest was perfect, well-defined but not looking like he'd overdosed on steroids. Perfect to snuggle against, perfect for . . .

She clipped that line of thought before she had to change her undies. "I'm sure he did," she murmured.

"I tell you you're wasting your time, Doctor."

She shot him an arch glare. "Thank you for your opinion, Stan, but I'd like to check for myself."

He stalked out of the room, mumbling under his breath. She distinctly caught the word "stubborn."

Well, she'd been called worse. She completed her circuit of the exterior with no luck. Opening both doors, she knelt and felt around the inside of the nymph hole, praying something had been taped, nailed, hell, even super-glued to the interior. Nope, just the same smooth surface.

Oh Grandma, why didn't you tell me you were in this much trouble?

"Why in Hades didn't you tell me you were in this much trouble?"

Caesar held the receiver away from his ear while Selene continued her rant. The volume of her voice would have been painful even to a Normal. And he hadn't gotten past "Hello" before she started.

"I'm supposed to be your second-in-command! And not only do you *not* tell me, you don't even tell Ptolemy. How is he supposed to back you when he doesn't know where you are? I'm coming to San Francisco."

"No. On the off-chance the people after Bebe still think I'm with you in Vegas, I don't want them following you here."

"Have you heard the rumors? Half the supers in the U.S. think you've kidnapped Zachary. If White Rose comes after you, you'll need help." She paused for a heartbeat. "Whether you want to admit it or not."

"I have help," he said through gritted teeth. The dull pulse behind his left eye grew more insistent. He prayed there was still some ibuprofen left in the infirmary.

A short bark of laughter burst through the receiver. "The halfings?" She sighed. "At least Duncan's with you. The Homeland Security tip about the car tailing you to the airport was his idea, wasn't it?"

"Yes. Unless there's anything else you'd like to lecture me about, I need to go." He regretted the curtness the moment the words were out of his mouth.

"Fine. But don't come crying to me when some witch tries to fry your ass." With an abrupt click, the phone line went dead.

Setting the receiver in its cradle, he leaned his head against the cool stainless steel of the refrigerator. Selene was only trying to help. He repeated the mantra a few more times before he stood straight and opened the fridge to snag a bottle of blood. After pouring the contents in a mug, he popped open the microwave, shoved the mug in and punched the buttons to warm it.

The conversation with his twin bothered him. Something he couldn't quite put his finger on around the pain of another stress migraine. No, it wasn't so much the conversation than the implication. His problem was with one witch in particular, and the problem involved keeping his hands to himself and his pants zipped.

"You know, I'm really beginning to like this view of you."

Bebe didn't jump at Caesar's rich tenor as she had at the estate auction. Instead, pleasant heat flooded her, despite the fact he admired the body part she hated most.

"It's not fair that you can admire my chest, but I can't admire your rear end," he said.

You were eavesdropping.

You meant for me to hear you, he sent back.

She ignored his accusation as well as the fact that they were once again alone in his office. Her motives were seriously in question when it came to Caesar Augustine.

A faint brush of air and a more definite sizzle of sexual electricity indicated he had crouched next to her. "I've already checked both the interior and exterior for conventional hidden compartments," he said.

Pulling her upper body out of the wardrobe, she sat up to face him. "So Stan informed me, but what about wood overlays glued to the original panels?" She raised a questioning eyebrow.

From his faint frown, the possibility hadn't occurred to him. It didn't matter though. She hadn't found any such overlay either. But it felt good to know she'd outthought him on something.

He dropped to the carpet and extended his legs, leaning back on his hands. "Have you checked for any enchantments on the wardrobe?"

She nodded and grinned, slightly pleased she was now two steps ahead of him. "Yeah, the first time I was here, but Stan didn't find anything when you had him check either. I'm thinking Grandma may have used something more conventional. She was utterly paranoid about someone or something in the coven. So far, everything she's done to protect the Book of Shadows has been non-magickal. She may have done the same with the key . . ."

No, it couldn't be that ridiculously simple, could it? She cleared her throat. "Caesar, did Grandma tell you to deliver the wardrobe to me?"

He shook his head. "No, not specifically. You were the only heir who was supposed to receive anything. She went out of her way to disinherit your cousins in her Last Will and Testament."

"How do you know what was in her Will?"

He grinned. "It became public knowledge the minute the Elders offered it for probate." He shrugged before continuing. "She definitely intended for you to receive all her possessions under the terms."

Had Grandma gambled that Caesar would remember what the wardrobe meant to her and would find a way to save it?

All of the sudden it was hard to breathe. "Where's the key to the wardrobe?" she said.

His frown indicated he wasn't following her train of thought, which was probably a good thing. She wasn't too sure about her sanity herself at this point.

"I placed it in my safe before we left for Los Angeles. Why?"

"I need to see it." Her whole body shook, whether from anticipation or fear that she was wrong, she couldn't tell. "Why did you put it in your safe?" Had Grandma put a compulsion on him that he was unaware of?

Caesar's frown deepened. "Duncan suggested it when I phoned him that we were flying back to Los Angeles. It seemed like the sensible thing to do at the time." He rose and crossed to the bookcase behind his desk. Tumblers clicked as he rotated the old-fashioned combination dial, and then a deeper thunk when he opened the door. Returning to her, he held out an antique brass key. The patina had dulled from lack of care, but it was the thick, intricately molded key she remembered.

Her fingers shook as she took it from him. Extending her senses around the brass, she didn't detect any magick. If she were right, Grandma had used sleight of hand to fool the conspirators. Just like Normal illusionists entertained their audiences. She bit her lip as excitement and fear mingled.

Bebe twisted the key. It took some effort before the shaft unscrewed from the ornate bow with a high-pitched squeal. A tiny scroll of white paper protruded from the hollow of the key.

"Hades!" Caesar swore and leaned closer.

Pulling the paper gently from the brass, she unrolled it. Her breath released with a rush, and she blinked away the tears of relief that filled her eyes. In Grandma's neat handwriting lay the key to the encoded notes.

Chapter 20

Leaning back in his chair, Caesar stretched before he rose from the kitchen table to grab another cup of coffee. Even his muscles ached after he, Bebe and Stan had spent the last twelve hours translating Natasha's notes.

It was the first time in centuries he'd been awake from dawn to sunset. Once a vampire, he had learned daylight was a one-way ticket to the Underworld. With the advent of UV-film on windows, he found the view of a sunrise wasn't quite the same, and he hadn't bothered after the initial novelty wore off. It reminded him too much of dawn training sessions millennia ago. He never thought he'd miss those, but he did, and the sight wasn't worth the temptation of stepping out into the now deadly sunshine.

Coffee pot in hand, he returned to the kitchen table littered with notepads and topped off Bebe's mug. Her brow knotted in concentration, she didn't even register the fresh coffee as she automatically gulped the contents. If his muscles were tight, hers must be in agony, but she showed no sign. She continued scribbling on the pad in front of her, chewing on her bottom lip as she went.

Forcing away thoughts of nibbling on her bottom lip himself, he caught Stan's eye and raised the pot. Stan shook his head, sat straighter and stretched his hulking frame.

"I hate to say it, but I don't understand ninety percent of what I've translated," the half-elf said.

"It's genome mapping for a recessive gene that triggers the immune response against a certain family of viruses." Bebe didn't look up at Stan. Instead, she continued writing, her gaze flicking from Natasha's notes to her copy of the key and back to the pad she used.

"Oh, that makes a whole lot more sense to me," Stan grumbled.

Bebe raised her head and blinked in surprise when she looked out the window behind Stan. "When did it get dark?"

"At sunset. The same as it does every night," Caesar teased.

In response, she stuck her tongue out at him, which didn't help the carnal direction of his thoughts. He should be thankful for Stan's presence. It kept him from doing anything idiotic, like telling her where to put that tongue to good use.

Duncan stalked into the kitchen, ignored everyone and made a straight line for the refrigerator. He retrieved a pint bottle, emptied the contents into a giant mug, and set the mug in the microwave, shutting the door with more force than necessary.

Caesar swallowed an exasperated sigh. For once Duncan and Selene agreed on something, not that he'd point that little fact out to Duncan. After Selene had finished chewing him out on the phone this morning, Duncan had argued the need for additional personnel when Caesar had ordered him to get some sleep.

Caesar raked a hand through his hair. Considering the rarity of both Duncan and Mai questioning his orders, maybe he was being foolish.

A rhythmic tapping behind him drew his attention back to Bebe, who stared at him without apparently seeing him. The cheap plastic ink pen in her hand banged in an unconscious motion against the last set of notes she'd translated. She jerked out of her trance when he gave her a questioning look.

"It says here the actual test results are at Augustine Research's San Francisco facility." Her eyes narrowed. "Anything you want to tell me?"

He shrugged, slightly uncomfortable with the looks both Stan and Duncan were giving him. "I loaned her the space and equipment for her research. The actual results mean nothing without knowing the original question."

"Does this have something to do with the blood samples you requested from each of us?" Duncan's eyebrows drew together with a suspicious look since his "us" referred to the vampire contingent of the coven employees.

Time to come clean. Caesar nodded before he gave Stan a sharp look. "This information does not leave this room."

"Understood, boss." Stan's eyes glittered with curiosity.

Caesar met Duncan's gaze. "Since Natasha's research concerned certain witches who were resistant to the V-virus, she believed she might be able to develop a cure by reverse engineering the witches' gene."

Duncan's mouth dropped open. Caesar almost smiled, but managed to hold it back. It wasn't too often he could catch his chief enforcer off guard.

"Shit!"

Caesar's attention snapped to Stan. For the first time he could remember, Stan actually looked scared.

"Who else knows about this besides the witches?" Stan asked.

"As far as I know, only the four of us in this room."

Stan shook his head. "This has something to do with the Mengele stuff Natasha retrieved from Auschwitz, doesn't it?"

Caesar nodded.

Stan sucked in a deep breath. "I hate to point this out, but we never found out who was the lead supernatural collaborating with the Nazis. We've got one other person out there who knows about this crap, even if he doesn't have the original research." He waved a beefy hand at the papers strewn across the table. A sympathetic look crossed his face. "And I'm not trying to be a pisser, but the other problem is not every vampire will be jumping for joy at a cure. Not like you two would."

Caesar exchanged a look with Duncan. Were they that obvious?

"He's right." Bebe's eyes didn't shine with fear the way Stan's did. Instead, obvious worry pinched her brow. "Your Nazi sympathizer, if not a member of White Rose, is probably collaborating with a coven member." She pursed her lips while she thought. "It may not be William or Alice behind the assassination attempts. Our conspirator may be using the leadership contest as a cover to get their hands on Grandma's research."

"That's a very big 'if,' and if so, how do we expose him?" Caesar said.

"There's one way to find out."

At Bebe's soft voice, a shiver of apprehension ran up Caesar's back. "I will not use you as bait!"

She winced at his shout, but she squared her shoulders. "We already know some of the supernaturals are working together. If I call the Elders for a Confirmation ceremony, we'll draw out whoever's behind this within White Rose since he or she obviously wants me out of the way." She shrugged. "From there, we should be able to track down their accomplices."

"No." He crossed his arms over his chest and let his nasty vampire side come out. Fangs slid down, but she didn't so much as flinch this time.

Instead, she rose and glared up at him. So much for the intimidation factor of his extra height with fangs and glowing eyeballs. "I *will* call the confirmation for tomorrow night, and I *will* go." She crossed her arms over her ample breasts, sending a different type of heat through his body. "With or without you," she finished.

"The doctor has a point," Duncan said quietly.

Caesar didn't like the implications of Duncan's unspoken remainder of his statement. His chief enforcer would go with Bebe even against a direct order. He swallowed a groan. Hades, he'd been cornered, and he seriously hated that feeling. "Why tomorrow night?"

The smile on Bebe's face was frightening in its own right. "Tomorrow's Winter Solstice. The coven generally conducts major ceremonies on the sabbats unless there's a pressing need otherwise. If I ask for Confirmation and insist on tomorrow night, the Council will assume I've acceded to Grandma's wishes and bend over backward to set it up."

A couple of hours later, all arrangements were in place. Like Bebe planned, the White Rose Elders had fallen over themselves when she called Confirmation, if only to "clear any questions" as it was put. One interesting tidbit in her phone conversation with the Air Elder, Beatrice Flannigan, was that the Elders had bought Grandma's house from the estate representative. Beatrice said it would be a shame if Alice and William's fighting led to the loss of the high priestess's residence, especially since the coven held their major ceremonies in the privacy offered by such a large facility, including a Confirmation. Of course, the fact that the Elders planned to deed over the Nob Hill estate to the new high priestess had been an added incentive in Beatrice's eyes for Bebe to accept her fate.

She smiled to herself while she pulled the soft cotton nightgown over her head. Part of her rejoiced a total stranger didn't have the house where she'd spent half her childhood. The other enjoyed imagining how the Coven would react when she walked into the Confirmation escorted by vampires and fae.

Even better was her conversation with Grandpa Ben. He'd fully recovered from the confusion spell. Apparently, the unseelie's magick had affected the driver of the shuttle, which was why he hit a retaining wall and flipped the vehicle. Granny E.'s injuries had been a result of the accident, and she'd regained consciousness shortly after Bebe had called Eleanor Hyde-Smith. Grandpa Ben couldn't say enough good things about the London Coven's healer, though Granny E. had thrown a fit when the healer ordered her to bed early. Grandpa said it was a good sign, and Bebe had to agree.

Eleanor filled in the rest of the details. Her security had arrived before the dark fae was able to get into the vehicle to complete his job. Unfortunately, the culprit escaped while Eleanor's people rescued Grandpa Ben and Granny E. from the wreckage before the Normal authorities got to the accident scene.

Remembering the end of the conversation, Bebe smiled to herself. Eleanor had alternated between assurances of the Epsteins' safety and dire threats of what would happen to the unseelie if she caught him. The edge in the London High Priestess's voice told Bebe the results wouldn't be pleasant.

Reaching for her brush, she sighed as reality set in. Tomorrow would be ugly even discounting the possibility of another assassination attempt. While she'd like to believe in the inviolacy of the White Rose Elder Council, she wasn't that naïve. Nerves could wait until tomorrow though because she definitely needed the sleep. She hadn't been awake this many hours straight since she'd been an intern.

A soft knock at the door jolted her out of her reverie. The rich, beefy essence left her little doubt who waited on the other side. Snatching her robe out of the open overnight bag, she shrugged it on while crossing the room. She yanked open the door. Caesar halted his fist in mid-knock.

She crossed her arms. "I thought you ordered all of us to get some sleep." Her tone let him know exactly what she thought about his orders.

"I—" His jaw twitched, as if he were working up the nerve to say whatever he came to say. The silence dragged on for several seconds before he bit out, "Could you please put on some clothes so I can talk to you?"

"I have clothes on," she said, swallowing her smile with difficulty. What the hell was bothering him? He had seen Tiffany shirtless for crying out loud.

"I'm not attracted to Tiffany, and your nipples are showing."

She glanced down. Her nightgown wasn't that sheer, but sure enough, her breasts were thriving under Caesar's heated stare. Goddess, she hated admitting what he did to her.

Pulling the edges of her terry robe over the betraying white cotton didn't help one iota. It only served to remind her how sensitized her body became around him. "What's so important it couldn't wait until morning?"

Too much of her discomfiture must have shown in her voice. His annoying smirk returned. He leaned against the doorjamb, his stance easy and confident. Ri-i-i-ght. She'd sooner let one of her many potential assassins in her bedroom.

She must have accidentally leaked because his attitude vanished. He reached up and cupped her face, his thumb stroking her cheek. "That's what I wanted to talk to you about."

"Damn it. I don't need you listening to every stray thought that passes through my head." Men. Give them a bite, and they take the whole freaking pizza. Closing her eyes, she started to raise her outer shields.

"Don't," he whispered. "Please don't shut me out."

Her eyes popped open at his impassioned plea.

"I want you to call this Confirmation off." His gaze bore into hers, and a wave of purple-gray emotion hit her, not an attempt to influence her, but raw, honest fear.

Her hand rose of its own accord to cover his. "We've been through this, Caesar. It's the best way to draw out whoever's behind Grandma's murder and the attempts on my life. You're not compromising your honor or your promise—"

"It's *your* life that concerns me."

His statement touched her. The idea that someone cared about her, not her position, not her power, not what she could do for that person, melted a part of her she thought frozen. Her lips turned upward in a warm smile. Drawing his hand from her face, she twined her fingers through his. She had no doubt he'd protect her through whatever was to come.

"Thank you," she said giving his hand a gentle squeeze. "But we need to end this. Now. Before one of your people gets hurt."

"My people can protect themselves." He bit the words out.

He looked so serious she couldn't resist teasing him. "So a big, bad vampire like yourself—"

He jerked from her hold, his eyes flashing gold. "This isn't a joke! You could get hurt, or—"

His fists clenched, and the scent of burnt flesh rushed through her mind. The conflagration of fear, anger and pain swirled through the corridors of her soul until she couldn't see, couldn't breathe, couldn't think. She swam through the violence he exuded to find herself still standing inside the door of her bedroom.

Before she found her balance, he yanked her to his chest and bent his head. This kiss wasn't the passionate exploration of earlier. No, this one was possessive, demanding. The liquid fire of his thoughts turned into a different kind of heat. Insistent. Penetrating. Claiming.

His body pressed hers against the doorjamb, a wool-covered thigh shoved roughly between hers. Fingers stroked and molded her flesh as if it were soft clay. He left her breathless and needy when his head dipped lower. Shoving the terry bathrobe aside, his mouth latched on her nipple, the engorged tip welcoming his attention.

An electric current shot through her as he sucked and nipped through the damp cotton, the sensation more arousing than if he had access to her bare flesh. Soft cries filled the hallway. It took precious seconds for her to recognize her own voice encouraging him to continue his exploration.

Pushing her nightgown to her waist, his hands palmed her bottom, the motion pressing his covered erection against her core. She would have cursed herself for not putting on underwear after her shower, if the wonderful pressure against her clit let her think. But he didn't give her that chance. His hands and mouth were everywhere, soft touches alternating with the slight scrape of fangs. Not enough to break her skin, but enough to give a thrill of danger, a counterpoint to his rhythm.

Then he lifted her. His strength would have frightened her if she didn't welcome the freedom to wrap her legs around his waist. She clung to him, grinding her body against his.

With her more than enthusiastic response, he didn't waste time. A finger, then two, plunged into her weeping flesh, stroking and pressing the sweetest spot on earth. Every touch made her greedy for more, until the slightest pressure of his thumb sent her plummeting off the edge of the cliff. The inferno of her mind and body exploded.

His mouth over hers swallowed her hoarse cry. All she could do was hang onto his neck for dear life as she shook with tremor after tremor. His fingers inside of her refused to stop until every bit of pleasure had been pulled from her.

Instead of lowering her to the floor as she expected, he swept her into his arms. Striding across the carpet, he deposited her in the turned-down bed. Gently tugging off her bathrobe, he laid it at the foot of the bed before pulling the covers up to her chin. His kiss to her forehead jerked her out of her shock at the reversal in his behavior, but he was halfway across the room before she could find her voice.

"You're just going to leave?"

He paused at her words. For long seconds, she didn't think he would answer even though she could still sense his fiery desire.

When he turned, his eyes glowed with the same intense lust she'd seen the first night in the back of his Hummer. The night he'd been shot saving her life.

"Bebe—" He could have been saying a prayer instead of her name. His eyes closed. Then she noticed his body trembled as well. When he opened his eyes, the golden glow had not diminished.

"If I don't leave now, I'll do something we'll both regret. Goodnight, *amora*." With that, he stalked out of the room, turning off the lights and closing the door behind him.

Bebe took a deep shuddering breath in the darkness. That had been a close call. She burrowed into the blankets, the first tears leaking from her eyes. Caesar was right. She wouldn't have been able to stop herself from saying yes if he hadn't left.

And the fact she wanted him so bad she didn't care if she were Turned or died scared her more than the assassins after her.

Chapter 21

The next morning dawned with a typical rainy San Francisco winter day. The gray, bleary sky matched Bebe's mood. She'd slept little. The times she'd managed to doze, her dreams would start with Caesar doing delightfully wicked things to her body. But just when she was about to climax, she'd hear Grandma Petrov's screams. Then Caesar would turn into one of the rogues who'd murdered her parents. She'd jerk awake when he tore out her throat.

She chalked the nightmares up to her guilt over her parents and for her own unresolved issues with Grandma, but no amount of meditation or prayer helped. The couple of times she'd return to a fitful sleep where once again, the dream Caesar would take her in every imaginable position until Grandma's cries intruded. Finally, she gave up on sleep, but even a session with the guest bathroom's shower massager hadn't taken the edge off her body's neediness.

After putting on jeans and a sweater, she pulled her hair into a loose ponytail and headed downstairs to the kitchen to scrounge some breakfast. Duncan sat at the table, reading the *Chronicle* and sipping from another mug, when he glanced up at her. Him, she could deal with this morning, even with the metallic scent of blood permeating the air. In some ways, he was far easier to figure out than his boss.

And he hadn't given her the most mind-blowing orgasm of her life.

"Good morning, Doctor. Stan left a plate for you in the refrigerator."

"Thanks," she said, crossing the kitchen. "And you can call me Bebe, you know." She found an omelet covered in plastic wrap on the top shelf. Damn, she hadn't been this well taken care of since she moved out of Grandma's. Placing the plate in the microwave and punching the "On" button, she turned, only to have Duncan looking at her with that eerie vampire stillness. Not menacing but unnerving nonetheless.

"Do you mind if I have some of your tea?" Not that she really wanted it, but anything to break the uncomfortable silence. Maybe dealing with him wouldn't be so easy after all.

He nodded, but when he started to rise, she waved him back down. "Would you like some as well?" she asked while measuring out the leaves.

"Please."

A few minutes later, she pulled out the warmed plate and set it on the table before bringing over the cups of tea. Once again quiet fell, punctuated occasionally by the clink of her fork against ceramic. He didn't touch his cup or the nearly empty mug of blood. Those intense green eyes bore into her, but he didn't try to touch her mind.

Finally, she couldn't stand it any longer and laid down her fork. "Are you going to tell me what your problem is or are you just going to continue staring at me?"

He laid aside the paper before folding his arms and leaning his elbows on the table. "Are you going to continue your grandmother's research?"

Okay, that question came out of left field. Pushing her plate away, she leaned her own elbows on the table. "I honestly hadn't thought much past surviving tonight. Why?" And why the one-eighty from his position last night, but she couldn't bring herself to voice that snide question.

"Caesar is gambling our coven's future on his belief that you will continue Natasha's work. I need to know if his faith in you is misplaced." Despite his words, his tone was quiet. Even. Matter-of-fact.

"You were the first on the 'human again' bandwagon last night." She kept her voice as neutral as his. "What changed?"

A small, wry smile quirked his lips. "Too much time on patrol last night to think about my own foolish desires overriding my duty to Caesar."

She nodded. If Caesar prized his honor so much, he'd surround himself with people who thought likewise. "I can't give Caesar the Book of Shadows itself of course, but he has copies of the research notes, both the coded and translated versions. Even if I don't personally do it, he's got everything you need to continue looking for the cure."

Duncan shook his head. "There are not very many people he would trust to carry on the research besides you."

Alex's comment a few days ago about the vampire lack of medical personnel came back to roost. "Surely, someone's willing to get the education in order to finish the project. Goddess, you people live forever!"

Again, he shook his head. "It's already taken Natasha over sixty years to get this far. And after tonight, there is no assurance that anyone from the Augustine Coven will last long enough to start over again. We are about to start a war on your behalf, Doctor. The least you could do is let us die human."

As if Duncan's guilt trip wasn't bad enough, Caesar chose that moment to saunter into the kitchen. He didn't look much better than she felt, between his grayish skin pallor and the dark circles under his eyes. Despite his exhausted appearance, his faux cocky attitude permeated the room.

Good to know his night had been as tortured as hers.

"Good morning." His greeting included both her and Duncan, but his steady gaze held hers. His eyes had a hint of last night's hunger, but a little speculation as well, which meant he'd overheard Duncan's little discussion.

She broke first, reaching for her now cool tea to avoid the looks from both men. The gene-viral research wasn't her project. Dammit, it wasn't even her problem. Grandma's the one who had made the deal with Augustine, not her.

So why do I want to find a reason to stay?

After fixing his own mug, Caesar pulled out the chair next to her and sat down. He took a healthy gulp of his breakfast before he spoke. "Are you planning to return to Africa tomorrow if everything is resolved tonight?" His tone indicted he didn't care one way or the other, and for some reason that cut deeper than his abrupt departure from her room last night.

She lifted her gaze from her cup and met his squarely. "There's no real reason to stay, is there?" Shoving her chair back harder than she intended, she jerked to her feet. "You boys—" She couldn't stop the scathing condemnation in her tone. "—need to give me a personal object, something you'd normally wear that won't arouse suspicion."

"Why?" Caesar's coolness could have frozen the entire bay solid.

"For personal shield charms, unless you want to become a crispy critter the moment someone launches a fireball at your face tonight." A slight shake broke the haughtiness she tried to affect.

Duncan reached beneath the neck of the black sweater he wore and pulled out a locket on a medium gold chain. "Will this do?"

She nodded, and he handed the jewelry to her. Once again, Duncan surprised her. The jewelry was delicate, feminine and very old. A keepsake from his past? But she didn't ask. She didn't want to get in deeper with these people than she already was.

When she turned to Caesar, he stared at her for a long minute before yanking off his gold and onyx ring. When she reached for it, he seized her wrist with a grip that, while not exactly painful, was damn uncomfortable.

"If your spells do not work properly—"

She didn't wait for the rest of his statement. A tiny flare of heat through her hand served as her own warning while she stared deep into his eyes. "I have no intention of anyone dying tonight, Mr. Augustine."

He released her, and a teensy thrill shot through her when he rubbed his overly warm hand against his slacks. Served the bastard right.

"Will you need anything else besides the two cases we brought from Los Angeles?" Duncan said.

She shook her head. "Please don't disturb me for the next hour." Pivoting on her heel, she marched for the kitchen door.

"What about Stan and Harry?"

She turned back to Caesar, an angry smile twisting her lips. "It seems I'm not the only ignorant one in the room." His eyes started to gleam dully in the morning light. Maybe she'd pushed him too far in her horrible mood. Well, he deserved her bitchiness after what he did last night. Especially since he shouldn't have started what he did when he had no intention of following through.

A sigh whistled past her lips. "Elven and witch magicks don't play nice with each other. I'll speak with them, but I'm sure they both will have defensive charms. I doubt if any of the White Roses would be stupid enough to throw a spell at them. If they try anything with Stan or Harry, it would have to be a conventional physical attack."

She waited a couple of heartbeats, but Caesar kept quiet. Damn vampire. It felt good to slam the kitchen door behind her.

Caesar listened to Bebe's footsteps as she climbed the staircase, emotions roiling so bad he wasn't sure what to think or feel.

"I discovered who the eclectic from the restaurant was."

Surprise slammed into him at Duncan's words. "What? How?"

"I . . . borrowed Ptolemy's phone. He had taken pictures of your assailants. The witch was an eclectic named Lily Franklin. Originally from the Cleveland Coven. She had been exiled five years ago for fraud and robbery. She was freelance as far as my contacts know. I am still working on the were's identity."

Caesar blinked in surprise. "When did you do this?"

"I returned Ptolemy's phone before we left Los Angeles." Annoyance tinged Duncan's voice.

"No, I mean when did you have a chance to research her?"

"When you ordered me to bed." The mild reproof hung in the air.

Irritation narrowed Caesar's eyes. "So you're making disobedience a habit?"

"Only because you are being a bloody idiot," Duncan muttered.

"I don't believe I asked for your opinion." Anger rose from the ocean seething through his mind.

"Maybe that is part of the problem." Duncan's voice continued at normal volume. "In the past, you would seek our counsel, weigh the options and take action based on a well-reasoned decision. Those qualities made you an excellent leader, Caesar."

"Made?" The past tense verb kicked him harder in the gut than if Duncan's foot had actually connected.

Duncan raised an eyebrow. "I am your chief enforcer, and I carry Lady

Natasha's Blood Seal on your behalf. I do not resent my service to you. However, you are letting your feelings for Bebe cloud your judgment."

"I don't have any feelings for Bebe."

Duncan's other eyebrow joining the first spoke his thoughts on the subject more eloquently than any words he could have said.

Caesar leaned back in his chair, staring at the tabletop. *Hades.* It wasn't very often Duncan nailed him committing self-deception. Actually he couldn't think of a time the English vampire had forced him to face facts. But Duncan was right. He was in love with Bebe Zachary. He raised his eyes to meet Duncan's. He hadn't been this uncomfortable when his brother-in-law had caught him losing his virginity with Selene's maid when he was fifteen. "Is it that obvious?"

Amusement flared in Duncan's eyes even if his lips didn't curl into a smile. "Other than Anne catching the two of you in here, Bebe's cry of pleasure last night, and Harry's complaints concerning the lack of hot water when he came off duty, no."

Caesar closed his eyes in exasperation. Duncan was right. His behavior when it came to Bebe had been atrocious. And even worse, Ptolemy had been right in abusing him about his choice of Saturnalia gift for her. The sounds of Duncan rinsing his tableware made him open his eyes.

Duncan closed the dishwasher before turning back to Caesar. "What I am about to say, I am saying as a friend."

Caesar nodded for him to continue. The rarity of Duncan's claim of friendship set his curiosity ablaze as to what the other vampire would say.

"Have you considered asking her to join you?"

He couldn't have been more surprised if Duncan had just shoved a garlic-soaked silver stake into his heart. It took a couple of seconds for the shock to die down enough to speak. "You're the last person I'd expect to suggest that she be Turned."

"I am not suggesting you Turn her. I am suggesting you should ask her. First of all, Bebe is much more like Natasha than she is willing to admit. She needs to make her own decisions." A wry smile crossed his face. "Even though we are both old enough to know life does not always allow one's decisions to bear fruit. Secondly, by her answer you will discover how she really feels about you without invading her thoughts."

"No." Caesar shook his head. "I won't even suggest Turning her. The odds of a witch surviving a Turn—"

"Are astronomical at best," Duncan finished. He shrugged. "I know, but she is Nikolai's granddaughter as well as Natasha's. She is stubborn enough to survive the infection if she truly desires it."

Caesar turned to stare at the few brown leaves that clung to the trees in the back yard, dancing under the raindrops. How much of Nikolai did Bebe truly carry in her blood? If she had enough, the question was moot, but she couldn't be with him. At least, not forever.

But maybe she could be Turned. Maybe she could survive. Maybe she'd be one of the rare few that didn't go psychotic. His cock stirred at the thought. Was he willing to risk her life on such a slim chance?

No. Too many maybes. Knowing she was alive somewhere he could deal with, but causing her death would tear his heart apart.

He met Duncan's gaze. "I'm still surprised *you* are suggesting this. Are you sure you're not hoping to give Bebe added incentive to find a cure?"

Again, Duncan shrugged. "I would be lying to say it had not crossed my mind." His attention flicked away for an instant before he cleared his throat and continued. "Love is such a rare thing. I would hate to see you throw it away without finding a way to make things work with Bebe. You both owe yourselves the opportunity to discuss the subject properly before dismissing it." He started out of the kitchen, clapping Caesar on the shoulder as he passed.

"Duncan." His voice made the other vampire stop at the door and look back.

"Thank you for your honesty." His voice wasn't more than a whisper, emotion so thick in his mouth, but Duncan nodded and left the kitchen.

When alone, Caesar buried his face in his hands. Gods above and below, didn't he have enough shit to deal with? He scrubbed the heels of his hands across his grainy eyeballs in an attempt to banish his weariness. Last night was the first time in decades he'd had trouble sleeping. He'd failed miserably in his purpose of speaking with Bebe.

One look at her lush body through the light cotton had destroyed any rational thought. And Bebe's responsiveness to his touch had fired his own lust to the point it took all his strength to walk out of her bedroom. They both needed to be fully dressed before he tried having any discussion of their future with her.

Assuming she wanted a future with him. Such a path would mean no children, no family of their own, and she had never voiced her feelings on having babies, much less if her attraction to him went beyond raw, unadulterated lust. He lifted his head to stare at the barren backyard.

He shook his head at his stream of thought. Had he already given up any hope of a cure? Bebe hadn't really said she wouldn't continue with Natasha's research, but neither did she say she would. And she hadn't specifically said she was returning to Africa either. No, she had said she had no reason to stay. Then he needed to give her a reason.

Two separate problems, for neither of which he had immediate solutions. He sucked in a deep breath and rose to re-warm his mug of blood. After tonight, he'd deal with his emotions where Bebe Zachary was concerned. First, he needed to make sure they both survived the White Rose Confirmation ceremony.

Chapter 22

Anxiety rasped across Bebe's skin as Stan braked the Hummer to an easy stop in front of the Petrov mansion. She tried to remind herself they'd done everything they could to prepare between the protective charms and briefing the men on the coven's major players.

She threw out her senses, but blocking spells rebuffed her efforts. As she had warned Caesar, she had no way to confirm who was inside the building. No doubt, the vampires had already picked up the presence of the hidden security personnel outside of the house. She glanced out the window at the place she'd called home for fifteen years, half-expecting Grandma Petrov to march out the door and scold her for missing curfew. Instead, two black-clad armed guards, a man and a woman, stood sentinel in front of the massive oak doors leading into the house.

Guards who brought their weapons to bear once Duncan cleared the passenger door. He didn't give the White Rose security so much as a glance.

She had to give Caesar's right-hand vampire credit for dismissing the guns so readily. She'd lay odds that the guards' weapons held the same garlic-laced bullets that had nearly killed Caesar a few nights ago.

Duncan opened the Hummer door for Caesar, who in turn, assisted her out of the vehicle, even though she could have easily climbed out in the smart black pantsuit with a matching calf-length jacket Anne had selected for her. As she'd suspected, both guards had been briefed on her appearance, so their mouths fell open when they realized who the vampires were escorting. With all the dignity she could muster, she climbed the steps, her heels tapping smartly on the flagstones. Caesar fell in step on her right, Duncan on her left. The spinach taste of thoughts reassured her Stan brought up the rear. Just as she reached the portico, the female guard regained her composure, shooting nasty looks at the vampires as she stepped to block Bebe.

"I'm sorry, Ms. Zachary, but you can't leave your vehicle here."

"Doctor," Caesar said, his smooth tenor brushing over Bebe both physically and mentally. She hated to admit his support bolstered her flagging confidence.

"Huh?" The woman jerked as if shocked that a vampire would dare speak to her.

"It's Dr. Zachary," Bebe said, giving the woman a saccharine smile. "Don't you think it would be best to start off on the right foot with your new high priestess?"

If possible, the woman's look became even harder. "I'm sorry, *Doctor*. You're not Confirmed yet, and *no* one's allowed to park here for security reasons. You need to park behind the house." She nodded toward the section of the drive that curved around the side of the mansion.

Bebe looked over her shoulder and gave Harry, still sitting in the driver's seat, a single nod. An energy shield, the color of new leaves, sprang over the Hummer. She turned back to the guards, still wearing her sweetly nasty smile. "If you'd like to remove my bodyguard's wards, you're more than welcome to try, but my ride stays here."

Once more, the female guard's mouth opened in shock as she stared at the Hummer now protected by fae magick. Bebe moved to brush by her, but the bulkier male blocked her way. Caesar stepped forward, eyes gleaming and fangs extended, but Bebe held up a single hand.

"You know we can't let *them* in an official coven function, Doctor." The man's brown eyes gave her a sympathetic look that made her wonder just how much the Council of Elders and their security staff knew about the assassination attempts. Could the Elders be in on the scheme?

Raising her chin, she stared the man in the eyes. Well, as much she could when he towered a foot over her. Playing on that sympathy, she said, "It's a sad day when witch kills witch, and I have to depend on outsiders for my safety, don't you think, Mr.—"

"It's Geoffrey, Lady." He nodded, a serious expression on his square face. His abrupt switch in title boded well. "And yes, ma'am, it is." His decision made, he stepped back and waved her forward.

"No! You can't let *vampires*—" The female guard practically spat the word. "—into a Confirmation." She jumped in front of Bebe, but with no support from her partner and a glare from Bebe, her defiance wilted. She stepped back, muttering imprecations under her breath.

Only with supreme self-control did Bebe manage not to sigh in relief. Maintaining her haughty expression, she swept past the woman, Caesar and his men on her heels. The male guard backpedaled to open one of the massive oak doors for her and her entourage, and for the first time in two years, she stepped into her grandmother's home.

The difference between then and now ripped the breath out of her lungs. The heavy, burgundy drapes were the only things that remained in the foyer. The paintings, the sculptures, even the atrocious Napoleonic side table that held Grandma's favorite vase was gone. For the first time, the fact that *everything* had been sold by the estate receiver struck Bebe in the heart. She'd been so angry and so fearful she hadn't let the enormity of the auction hit her.

Until now.

Tears blurred her vision as her gaze swept up the stairs. Even the delicately rendered still life that had perched at the first landing was gone. And thanks to her stupid-ass cousins, she'd never see it again.

No, it wasn't the missing belongings. It was the sterile atmosphere. No joy. No grief. The place held nothing for her.

Bebe, you must collect yourself.

She nodded at Caesar's empathetic urging, literally pulling strength from the surrounding stones in the walls to keep herself upright. She took a deep calming breath just as Beatrice Flannigan charged through the side parlor door into the foyer. Beatrice's warm greeting faded on her lips as Bebe's escort registered. If her salt-and-pepper hair hadn't become completely silver in the intervening years, it probably would have done so in the instant she realized vampires and a half-elf flanked Bebe on the marble tile of the high priestess's mansion.

Flustered, Beatrice tried to speak three times before she smoothed her intricate braids coiled at the nape of her neck and a much dimmer smile stuck to her face. She held out her hands to Bebe. "I'm so glad you came to your senses, dear. It makes things so much easier for all of us."

Bebe threw out a probe before taking Beatrice's hands, but no spell lurked around the other woman. She returned Beatrice's lukewarm smile and double handshake. Now, if she could only make her crazy-ass plan sprout wings and fly. "There are some things I need to discuss with the Elders before we start the ceremony, Beatrice."

The Air Elder's expression grew serious. "Some of us wished to speak with you as well, but I'm afraid Alice and William discovered our plans. They've challenged your Confirmation." She sighed. "If we met with you privately—"

This time Bebe's smile grew genuine. Caesar's information network had done their job. The bait had been scented. For the hundredth time that day, she gave the Goddess a silent prayer that her cousins didn't have the resources to cause anyone significant harm when the trap was sprung.

She patted Beatrice's hand and said, "Don't worry about it. I'd rather have this out in front of everyone, so there's absolutely no questions later."

Beatrice nodded slowly, acting like she seriously considered Bebe's words. "Yes, their accusations have been disturbing to say the least." She met Bebe's eyes, her smile broadening. "Not that I believe a thing. Lady Natasha was so proud of the work you were doing with the children in Africa. I know you had nothing to do with her death, despite your disagreements." She gave Bebe's hand a squeeze as if that cemented her opinion.

At least, now we know what else your family will throw at you during this little hearing.

Bebe inclined her head, knowing Caesar would pick up her acknowledgement even though her words were directed to Beatrice. "My sole regret is that I left things unresolved between me and Grandma. All I can do is make sure her true wishes are followed." She gestured for Beatrice to precede her into the old ballroom where Grandma usually had held her council meetings.

Beatrice ran her hands down the tailored mustard skirt she wore, the motion to collect herself rather than to smooth the non-existent wrinkles in the fabric. She tugged on her matching short jacket before she nodded and headed down the hallway.

Sweet Goddess, why was Beatrice so nervous? Maybe Caesar was right and this whole thing was just another trap aimed at killing Bebe? She shot a glance at Caesar. A reassuring warmth flooded her, and she gave him a small smile in return. She strode after Beatrice, the click of boots behind her. Tomorrow she'd dwell on how upside down her life had become in the last couple of weeks. Right now, she needed to focus on the next couple of hours.

Gasps rippled through the assembled coven members when Bebe and her party entered the ballroom. Shock and outrage, she expected, but there was a healthy amount of curiosity emanating from those who recognized Caesar.

She didn't dare raise her outer shield to block the slurry of wild emotion that threatened to overwhelm her inner shields. Caesar had been right to keep silent communication open in case trouble erupted. Instead, she focused on the bareness of the room.

Once again, everything movable had been stripped but the heavy draperies, which were closed despite the high walls and landscaping that would prevent anyone from observing their rituals from outside. Candelabras, probably borrowed from other coven members since she didn't recognize them and none of them matched, stood at regular intervals to provide light for the proceedings. Good. She wouldn't have to rely so much on her internal resources if a literal firefight broke out.

With all the furnishings gone, the parquet wood strips forming the giant pentacle that took up nearly the entire floor stuck out. The only other object was a makeshift altar in the center of the room. The too-big white tablecloth covering the waist-high table pooled on the hardwood. Each of the ceremonial objects representing the four elements already lay on top of the altar. The chalice, wand, athame and clay plate were the responsibility of the Elders as were the silver and gold bells that represented the Goddess and the God, and therefore hadn't been lost in the asinine estate sale.

An uncomfortable itching sensation of someone staring at her from across the room made her scan the crowd. Ahead and on her left, Alice huddled next to Pierre Le Croix, the Fire Elder. She glared daggers at Bebe.

Amusement rippled through her. For once, Alice wore a sedate black dress, not one of her slinky, sequined party numbers. She stretched up to whisper something in Pierre's ear, revealing a thigh-high slit. So, the dress wasn't that conservative after all. Somehow, it went well with Pierre's flashy burgundy suit.

No sign of Uncle Lionel, but then, he often missed coven events. So why not show up if he supported Alice's bid for high priestess? His absence didn't help Bebe's nerves given the current situation.

She gave Alice a slight acknowledging nod before her attention swept the rest of the room. William stood directly on her right in a semi-circle with three of the Lesser Elders and two others she didn't know. His bland face revealed nothing as he and his little group regarded her, though his associates' distaste for her presence was rather obvious from their expressions. Standing on opposite sides of the room, Alice and William were hardly the portrait of steadfast allies.

As I pointed out, they each could have engineered a separate assassination attempt.

Thanks for that pleasant reminder. It so helps my nerves.

Caesar's soft mental chuckle tickled her brain. *You knew which Elders have thrown their lots in with your cousins.*

Nerves sent the butterflies in her stomach spinning. *I wish your little network hadn't been correct about how many Elders sided with them.* So much of her plan had hinged on convincing the Elders that Alice or William or maybe even both of them jeopardized the entire coven.

Soft ringing cut through the scattered murmurs. The rustling of the crowd replaced the chiming as Beatrice set down the bells and the coven members moved to their positions around the circle. Each of the

Greater Elders took their places at a pentacle tip with their Juniors on their right hand sides. Alice stayed close to Pierre in order to take the spot on his left.

Sucking in a deep breath, Bebe strode across the floor to her place at the northernmost point of the pentacle. The point reserved for the high priestess.

Grandma Petrov's spot.

She'd stopped standing at Grandma's right hand after the second huge fight over marrying Alastair and had left the country a week later. Her feet wanted to carry her one spot over, but reality slammed home. She would never again stand next to Grandma in a coven circle.

She blinked back the tears that threatened and turned to face the assembled coven. Caesar gave her shoulder a quick, reassuring squeeze as he passed her. He, Duncan and Stan ranged themselves behind her. Not part of the circle, but where they could keep an eye on the proceedings.

No one stood in the space to her right. Similar to Arthur's Siege Perilous, it would remain empty until someone worthy could take that place, or in the coven's case, a confirmed h.p. named an heir.

Bebe swallowed the sigh that threatened. Maybe she should accept the Confirmation. With an h.p.'s autonomy, she could institute the democratic conventions so many other American covens had adopted instead of the European hereditary method White Rose had clung to after immigrating to San Francisco.

"Elder Flannigan, I must protest the presence of—" Pierre obviously decided to skip whatever insult he'd originally planned to lob at Caesar by his slight hesitation. "—these outsiders. Confirmations are closed to all but adult coven members."

"Elder Le Croix." Bebe stepped forward, letting her eyes narrow. "Mr. Augustine and his associates are here by my grandmother's request."

"So now we allow the Silver Bear High Priestess to dictate our laws and traditions." An ugly sneer spread across Pierre's sharp features.

Bebe quelled the anger under a veneer of calm. It figured he would try to muddy the issues. "I'm so sorry for your confusion, Elder. I was referring to Lady Natasha Petrov, not Lady Ziva Epstein. Conspirators within our own coven planned and carried out my grandmother's murder."

That little proclamation elicited a number of gasps and exclamations of alarm. Bebe's eyes scanned the crowd, but everyone looked genuinely shocked. Everyone except the Greater and Lesser Elders as well as Alice and William.

Plunging ahead before Pierre could cut her off again, Bebe said, "Suspecting such problems within our coven, she feared for my safety as her heir, and she asked Master Augustine to provide security for me upon my return to the States should any *misfortune* happen to her."

Tension crawled through the room as the initial surprise gave way to anger and fear.

"How do we know you didn't murder Grandma to control the coven?" Alice's low-pitched fury carried through the room. "Everyone here knows you were pissed at her for suggesting that you marry Alastair Hyde-Smith to cement relations with London. Now her Book of Shadows is missing. As the named heir, you are the only other one who knew where it was, and you said you didn't have it."

Game on.

It took all of Bebe's willpower not to clench her fists and march across the circle to beat Alice into a pulp. No wonder she clung to Pierre. She'd always needed her daddy to bail her out of trouble, so now the bitch planned to use the Fire Elder as a substitute.

Well, not this time.

"You know, cousin," Bebe said, letting the sarcasm drip from her words. "I'd suspect me too, if it weren't for a couple of things. I'm not the one who challenged Grandma's Last Will and Testament in court after she couldn't find the Book's hiding place, which, by the way—" She lowered her voice in a pseudo-whisper. "—was the smelly old wardrobe you hated." She raised her voice to a normal volume. "I also didn't get the wardrobe sold along with every other thing Grandma ever owned at an estate auction. Want to guess who bought the wardrobe for me since someone was taking great pains to make sure I didn't get back to San Francisco in time for the funeral, much less the auction?"

She and Caesar had decided it would be best not to mention Phil-lippa's involvement in the safekeeping of the Book. Besides, there was a certain delight in rubbing Alice's surgically enhanced nose in the fact that the Book had been right under it the entire time.

"Then there's the matter of someone trying to kill me ever since I received the telegram from the estate receiver, including a group of gunmen who destroyed my hotel room here in San Francisco." She paused a beat before delivering the coup de grace. "We traced their getaway vehicle to a subsidiary of Bay Area Consolidated. By the way, where is your father tonight?"

Alice's eyes narrowed as the entire assemblage turned and stared at her, but what concerned Bebe more was her aura. The bloody orange energy shifted and flared with Alice's rising anger. The coven hadn't raised a circle yet. If her cousin didn't get a grip, her unchecked magick could kill someone.

Then abruptly Alice laughed, a bitter sound that had the woman next to her take a not-so-subtle step back. "Ooooh, that's clever. Steal a van from one of Daddy's companies so you can pin your power trip on me. What amazes me the most is your pet vampires after the years you've spent trashing them."

Bebe smiled back, a wide one that would have bared fangs if she had them. "It's a lot easier to trust Mr. Augustine after a witch tried to slash my throat two nights ago."

"That's a very serious accusation, Bebe." Morton Sinclair, White Rose's Water Elder, spoke for the first time. "Who do you claim attacked you?"

Somehow, relief flooded Bebe when no one called her an outright liar. Yet. "We've identified the woman as Lily Franklin, a freelance eclectic with no known affiliations." Confusion rippled through the circle at her words. She couldn't blame them. The attempted murder by another witch still shocked her.

Alice made a sound of disgust. "Even if you're telling the truth—"

Aha! The expected slam.

"—who's to say she wasn't someone else you set up, Bebe. And that's no reason for *them* to be here. Our ceremonies and traditions are none of *their* business." Alice sneered at the three men behind Bebe.

"Franklin attempted to murder Dr. Zachary while assisted by three rogue vampires and a packless were in front of a restaurant owned by a member of my Family in the presence of Normal witnesses in my capital. That makes White Rose's Confirmation my business." Caesar's steel voice sent a wave of discord through the coven. The rich, beefy texture of his thoughts enveloped her, a cocoon against the hostility raging through the room, and a sharp boot click said he'd stepped forward on her right, not quite in the circle but in the one spot everyone could see him. He continued his speech as if any coven member's objections meant nothing to him. "Furthermore, Lady Natasha did ask for my assistance in protecting Dr. Zachary. As I explained to her, Augustine Coven will not interfere with the White Rose succession, but I will honor my word to Lady Natasha and ensure that Dr. Zachary survives long enough for a Confirmation hearing to be held."

"Well, you've certainly done your duty." Miranda Doucette's voice carried an oily contempt. Her forest green dress appeared black in the candlelight. "But since this *is* the Confirmation, I hardly see where your services are still necessary."

Bebe suppressed a shiver. The Earth Elder had never disguised her personal dislike of Bebe during their tutoring sessions. When she'd tried to broach the subject with Grandma, she'd been told that Miranda held a potential h.p. to higher standards than her other students. Grandma had added that the Earth Elder had been equally hard on Bebe's mother. Now, Miranda's raw antagonism shone on her pinched face.

"With all due respect, Elder Doucette, I believe the Confirmation has been challenged by Ms. Hart and Mr. Petrov. Until a Confirmation ceremony is actually performed, my duty to Dr. Zachary remains."

Bebe didn't have to see Caesar's face to know his familiar condescending smirk filled his features. It was further confirmed by the ugly look Miranda shot both of them.

"And all we have is your word concerning Lady Natasha's wishes," Pierre said.

"Would a Blood Seal suffice?" Caesar said.

Bebe whirled to face him, her heart pounding. What the hell was he playing at? An h.p. Blood Seal couldn't be faked by another witch. She hadn't seen a Seal on his body the night he'd been shot. Not only had she gotten a very intimate look at every muscle-sculpted inch, he admitted Grandma had not requested him to take the oath.

To her surprise, Duncan stepped forward and shoved up the sleeve of his black leather jacket. He raised his right arm. A wine-dark stain formed a filigreed circle on his pale flesh, the same design the coven used for the earrings worn by its members. Under the multitude of candles, occasional flashes of silver light could be seen in the mark. The Blood Seal promised immolation if a bargain went unfulfilled so it was invoked only in the direst of situations.

"That makes no sense!" snapped Pierre. "If you made the promise, Augustine, why don't you bear the Seal?"

Caesar favored Pierre with an arrogant smirk. "Lady Natasha trusted me to fulfill my promise, but she had concerns that my chief enforcer would not be so willing to assist me with my obligation. He graciously acceded to her wish for insurance."

For once, something Caesar said regarding Grandma made sense. She would have wanted a guarantee of good behavior from the coven master's right-hand man. She already had Caesar on the hook with the lure of a possible cure to the V-virus.

"We have no wish to create a dispute with your coven by preventing you from fulfilling your oath, Mr. Augustine." Beatrice's mouth twitched as she tried to suppress a smile. "Unless any of my fellow Greater Elders has an objection, you and your men may remain until the end of the ceremony."

"If I may remind you, Elder Flannigan, there's still the issue of Lady Natasha's death." Pierre's strident voice rang through the room.

Beatrice sighed, a long exasperated sound.

Bebe bit her tongue to stifle her nervous laugh. Had Beatrice and Morton really expected to force the confirmation through without Pierre and Miranda raising every possible fuss they could? Not to mention Alice and William.

Except William hadn't said a word yet. So what was his motive in all this, or was he waiting to see who survived once the dust cleared?

That would totally be his style. His inherent laziness made her question his role in this charade.

Morton spoke first, his voice soothing and reassuring despite his actual words. "Dr. Zachary, since you brought up the charge of Lady Natasha's murder, please present your evidence."

Bebe swallowed hard, her stomach rebelling at the nervous energy swirling around her. She wasn't sure how much was her own anxiety and how much was the imposed emotions of the people surrounding her. A strange sensation surged up her spine, something she couldn't identify. There was no time to question it. She had no choice but to proceed with the miniscule evidence she had.

"The Elders already ordered an autopsy prior to my grandmother's cremation. They are aware she died from a heart attack triggered by an overdose of nitroglycerin. In that regard, I agree with my cousin, Alice Hart, in that her overdose was not accidental." Goddess, she hated this drama. She pulled a plastic bag from the deep pockets of her jacket and displayed the ziplocked baggie that held a knife.

The gore-encrusted sushi knife Franklin had held at Bebe's throat.

She eyed each of the Greater Elders in turn as she spoke. "Since I believe that the attempts on my own life were orchestrated by the same person or persons who engineered Lady Natasha's overdose, I ask the Elders permission to cast a spell on the knife Franklin used in order to trace who hired her. I would then ask the Elders permission to question that person once the circle's been cast."

And Uncle Lionel wasn't here. How convenient. The stunt could blow up in her face, but Caesar seemed so sure there was more than one member of White Rose involved in Grandma's little conspiracy.

"Wait a minute! How do we know you haven't already bespelled the damn knife to point to whoever you plan on casting as the scapegoat?"

Pierre broke circle, stepping forward, his face red with fury even in the dim candlelight.

"All four of the Greater Elders will examine it at the same time while it remains in Dr. Zachary's hand." A sardonic smile twisted Beatrice's face, and her eyes fixed on Pierre. "I would hate for the knife to be sabotaged to kill her the moment she casts her discovery spell. Is that satisfactory?"

The affronted look on Pierre's face lasted barely a second before he gave a curt nod of agreement. All four Elders crossed the circle and laid their right hands on the knife Bebe had pulled out of the baggie and placed in her raised right palm. Magick tingled and pulsed across her skin as the Elders examined the knife, but no one tried anything.

Beatrice met the eyes of each Elder, and one by one, they nodded their satisfaction that the knife was taint-free. Simultaneously, they pulled away and returned to their places at the other four points.

Beatrice gave a sharp nod. "Please proceed, Dr. Zachary."

Bebe took a deep, calming breath and concentrated on the nasty piece of steel. While the Elders could have performed the same spell, the knife had been intended to kill Bebe. Her connection to the knife would create far more accurate results. It was a saving grace Pierre hadn't disputed that point. She didn't relish the thought of confessing to the coven that she'd killed Franklin. She hoped she wouldn't have to. But it was another degree of relationship that added fuel to the spell, no matter how it turned her stomach.

As she focused, strands of golden energy flowed and danced around the steel, mixing with faint orange-ish wisps, the miniscule revenants of Franklin's power. She called on the bits of information Duncan had pulled about the woman and shaped as complete a picture as she could of the living, breathing person that once existed. Then she murmured the ancient Latin words that completed the circuit of magick.

The knife leaped from her palm to land with a clatter at William's feet.

Chapter 23

Stunned silence filled the room.

Bebe gasped. Not that William wasn't a conniving little weasel, but for him to gather the gumption to have her killed?

She was still trying to wrap her brain around the revelation when William whirled and charged for the closed door, only to crash into Duncan's broad chest. The vampire had crossed the room before any of the witches could react. Her cousin landed hard, sprawling in an awkward heap across the parquet floor.

Duncan reached down to pull the dazed William up by the collar. "I believe Dr. Zachary has some questions for you."

"Let go, you rat bastard." William struggled in the vampire's grip. Not that it did him any good. "I didn't hire that eclectic bitch. Let go!"

"Why did you hire Franklin to kill me, William?" Bebe said. Goddess, she didn't want to hear the answer.

"I didn't! Tim did!" William stopped wriggling and jabbed an accusing finger at Timothy O'Leary. The Lesser Earth Elder.

"No, you just provided the money!"

Bebe blinked in surprise as the Lesser Elder stepped forward, his counteraccusation still echoing through the room. She didn't know the man very well, but he had been in the cluster standing with William before Beatrice called the hearing to order.

Miranda stepped forward as well, her claw-like hand grabbing O'Leary's arm and turning him to face her. "What are you saying?"

Bebe didn't miss the maniacal look that shone in O'Leary's eyes as he faced his senior.

"I'm the one who hired the idiot. We gave that stupid little eclectic bitch everything she needed to slice Zachary's throat, and she still fucked up the job." O'Leary sneered at his Greater. "Come on, Miranda, you're always saying that Zachary didn't have the balls to be high priestess. That we needed new blood. That the Petrovs had no talent. No strength." A smile that could only be described as pure evil leered from his face. "No vision of the future."

"I *never* advocated killing Natasha, much less Bebe." Miranda forced the words through her clenched teeth.

"Hey, what do you mean I have no talent?" came William's pathetic complaint.

O'Leary jerked free of Miranda's grip and sauntered closer to the altar. "You're all idiots." His voice rose as he addressed the coven. "You've merrily followed Natasha Petrov to your own slaughter. Do you have any concept of what our precious high priestess has been doing behind our backs?"

Air caught in Bebe's lungs, electricity racing up and down her nerves. Where did he think he was going?

Miranda stepped back onto her point, met Bebe's eyes squarely, and nodded. That single nod spoke volumes where the Earth Elder's change of mind was concerned. Bebe may not be Confirmed, but she was the acting high priestess.

Each of the Greater Elders followed suit, even Pierre, and for the first time tonight, relief spread through Bebe's soul. Coven members began locking hands with their neighbors, and a slim thread of magick began twirling around the room. Within seconds, only two gaps remained in the circle.

Caesar, step back. A whisper of air told her he'd complied, even though the essence of him didn't leave her psyche. She edged as close to her neighbor on the right as she could without leaving her point of the pentacle. A quick glance showed the woman's outstretched hand, the other witch waiting for her signal.

"She's used her own blood kin to consolidate her personal power, regardless of any benefit to White Rose." O'Leary continued his rant against Grandma, oblivious to the growing tension.

Bebe locked eyes with the vampire across the room. *Duncan, when I tell you, shove William into the circle.*

Like Miranda, Duncan gave Bebe a single nod. The gaze of the two male witches on either side of him flicked from her, to Duncan, and back to her. Their bodies stiffened as they prepared to make the final connection.

She sucked in a deep breath and shouted, "Now!"

In a single fluid motion only a vampire could accomplish, Duncan pushed William forward and leapt back out of the pentacle. The two male witches clasped hands as soon Duncan was clear.

The instant a hot, perspiring palm met Bebe's, a hemisphere of brilliant white energy arced into place over their heads. Except her bodyguards were now on the outside of the shield, and she remained inside with a couple of nutcases.

"You're trapped, O'Leary. Start talking. Who else is in on this plot of yours?" Bebe said. Her anger kept her voice steady.

O'Leary slowly pivoted until he faced her. His leering grin stretched his narrow features into a death rictus. Black danced along his crimson aura. "Would you like to find out, baby?" When she didn't respond to his mockery of her name, he reached toward the altar, his long fingers closing around the athame.

He wouldn't be stupid enough to desecrate the coven's ceremonial knife, would he? She met his eyes. Not stupid.

Insane.

"Put that down, O'Leary," she said, bending a fraction of the circle's magick to lend power to her voice. "You've got no way out. Not with the entire coven, a couple of vampires and a fae between you and the door."

"Who said I was leaving, baby?" he said, and then plunged the athame into his heart.

Chapter 24

For the second time tonight, Bebe found she couldn't make a sound as shock ripped at her.

The psycho had made himself the blood sacrifice.

Black energy bubbled out of O'Leary as his body collapsed. With the circle's shield in place, there was nowhere for his soul to go. The soul energy swirled, collected itself, then arrowed straight toward her, its intent to possess clear.

She couldn't let O'Leary leave the circle. Who knows what innocent person he'd take advantage of in his insanity? No, she only had one choice.

"Don't let go! Don't let the circle collap—"

O'Leary's soul oozed into her, cutting off her words. Sticking a finger in a light socket would have been less painful. She wanted to scream from the agony but couldn't. The blackness filled her nose, her mouth, her throat until she couldn't breathe, much less cry out. It swallowed her vision, sucked away any sound, destroyed any taste, touch or smell.

Her lungs burned, desperate for air. Goddess, was this how Franklin felt when she was dying? Fresh pain seared each brain cell. No, this had to be much worse. Fire scorched every nerve ending as the connection between matter and energy shredded under O'Leary's attack. The bastard was trying to force her out of her own body, ramming his own soul roots into her flesh.

Bebe, fight him! Damn it, woman! Fight!

Caesar was there with her, cocooning her, but he only muffled the pain. Her psychic fingers were losing their grip. Hatred, rage and fear whipped at her, O'Leary's emotions a hurricane wind in her mind, knifing through everything that made her unique.

On the edge of her awareness, chanting sliced through her, but she couldn't spare the power to figure out if the voices were hurting or helping her. It was all she could do to maintain her hold on her body.

C'mon, Busy Be. Don't let that son of a bitch win!

Alice? Her cousin hadn't used that nickname for her in seventeen years. A trickle of energy, like the taste of fresh-picked oranges, flowed through her.

Remember what Grandpa Nick used to say?

Alice's words triggered old emotions, ones Bebe had buried under her grief long ago. *We were his Sunshine Girls, day or night.* He'd compared their auras to sunbeams dancing when they'd played together as children, racing through the gigantic backyard, whether chasing butterflies or lightning bugs. When she found her tears, she'd shed them for the memory of how she and Alice used to be.

No rain, Be, not now. Think sun, think fission, think solar power burning that bastard away.

Fresh rage pummeled Bebe, searing her raw. She couldn't stand any longer against the pain. Hell, she didn't even know if she still had legs.

Bebe, amora. Caesar's sandalwood and steak mixed with Alice's tangy orange. *I love you. Don't you dare leave me.*

Love her? Did he really say he loved her?

Yes, dammit! If you can battle me and a whole cadre of assassins, you can annihilate a measly-assed, cowardly witch!

Caesar was right. She'd faced worse. Her mental hold tightened tenaciously around her body. Hell, she'd done worse. The image of the golem she'd thrown at Franklin sprang into full bloom. But there was nothing to use within the Circle. Nothing except the coven tools.

No, not matter. Energy.

Carefully shaping the memory of the golem she'd created to kill Franklin, Bebe launched the psy-bolt at O'Leary's ghost.

An eerie low-pitched wailing assaulted her suddenly returned hearing. She fell to her knees, pain shooting up her thighs. But Blessed Lady, it was physical hurt, not the psychic agony O'Leary had inflicted. The soul tendrils of the insane Earth Lesser made one last grab at her, but were forced back by the other witches. The tight grips of the witches on each of her hands kept her from totally collapsing to the floor. Kept the circle intact.

The chanting resolved into the voices of the seven remaining Elders, a counterpoint to the keening that rattled her bones and grated her nerves. Bebe blinked, trying to clear her vision of tears that had collected. A white-hot ball of energy surrounded O'Leary's black soul, forcing the miasma into the silver chalice on the altar.

Ashes and despair coated her tongue when the realization of the type of spell hit her. The Elders condemned O'Leary into a Soul Sphere. The ultimate punishment for their people, to be incarcerated for all eternity in a special glass ball. To see and hear everything around you, but to never touch reality again.

Unless someone took pity on you and released you from that horrible prison.

She swallowed the bile that rose at the back of her throat. Someone had placed the Sphere in the ceremonial chalice prior to her arrival, and she hadn't thought to scan the objects on the altar, so unnerved she was by discovering the possible truth about either of her cousins.

The pure white light flared as the dark energy disappeared into the cup with a final scream of desperation and pop of displaced air. The whiteness faded and another type of blackness swallowed the room.

And losing her hold on the two witches, Bebe fell headlong into that other blackness.

Chapter 25

Anger, fear and pain tore a howl from Caesar's throat when the last shred of Bebe's essence slid from his mind. The protective sphere around the circle faded the instant Bebe slipped from the grasp of the witches, landing with a boneless thud. Caesar charged forward and knelt to cradle the unconscious woman in his arms. Blood seeped from both of her nostrils. In the vee of her blouse, the silver pentacle Tiffany had given her had charred to slag though her skin was unmarred.

She couldn't be dead. Dammit, Osiris, it's not her time!

Someone tried to take Bebe from him, but he hissed at the person, bloodrage turning everything around him scarlet. Clutching her to his chest, he bared his fangs. She couldn't be dead, she just couldn't.

"Boss, it's me. Stan."

Caesar blinked hard several times to clear his vision. The pale blur in front of him coalesced into Stan's concerned face.

"The doc's alive, boss, but we need to let the witches check for residual magick from that asshole." Stan's pale blue eyes widened, a pleading look that didn't mesh with his hulking figure crouched on the floor beside Caesar. Stan reached out his arms in supplication, but the half-fae was smart enough not to try touching Bebe. "Please, Caesar."

Swallowing the horrible taste in his throat, Caesar rose, Bebe in his arms. He couldn't leave her on the cold, hard floor. Stan stood as well, and for the first time, Caesar realized the Elders clustered behind the half-elf.

He let his gaze sweep across the candle-lit ballroom. Duncan must have entered the circle as soon as it dissolved too because he had a firm grip on the squirming William. However, Duncan held his eyes and fangs in check, any hunger that might have been triggered by Bebe's or O'Leary's blood well under control. The rest of the White Rose members huddled against the long side walls, as far from each of the vampires as possible, their fear seasoning the very air.

No, from him.

Everyone that was, except Alice Hart. The auburn-haired witch must have been the one he'd snarled at because she wore an expressionless mask on her face, but still stood close to his side. Only a slight tremor of her lower lip showed her unease.

Damn, she was so much like Bebe.

"She needs someplace to rest." Hades, his voice didn't sound human to his own ears.

Beatrice eased forward to stand next to Stan. "There's a donated sofa in the front sitting room." A weak smile lit her face, but she reeked of fear like the rest of her coven.

Fear of him, of what he'd do next.

He gave a slow nod, as much because he barely clung to his own self-control than to reassure the frightened witches.

"Pierre—" Beatrice pointed to O'Leary's body, the tainted athame still sticking out of its ribcage, his dark blood staining the center of the pentacle.

The Fire Elder gave a curt nod of his silvered head. "I'll take care of all three items."

Stalking after Beatrice, Caesar paused and speared Duncan with a glare. "Natasha has a windowless room upstairs. Second floor, third door on the right. Keep the little bastard there until I come up." He let his eyes settle on the cowering witch in Duncan's hands, who noticeably shrank to the floor in a desperate attempt to evade his gaze.

Beatrice started at his instructions to Duncan, whipping around to stare at him. Her eyes widened in alarm. "William is not your responsibility."

He allowed a small smile to cross his face. "I'm not disputing your authority, Elder. However, he hired three rogue vampires to attack me while one of your people tried to slit Bebe's throat. I will be involved in his questioning."

The Air Elder flushed bright red, but instead of arguing, she pivoted on her sensible heels and marched from the ballroom.

Good. He didn't know if he could maintain his control if she'd chosen to pick a fight while he was in this condition. As he followed Beatrice, the soft click of heels indicated Alice trailed behind him.

The front sitting room was a bare as the rest of Natasha's house except for two worn chairs and an equally shabby couch. He carefully laid Bebe on the threadbare cushions, then knelt next to her, keeping her small, delicate hand in his. In his peripheral vision, Beatrice stood near Bebe's feet and clutched her hands together. Anxious worry added more wrinkles to her visage. Alice sidled next to the Air Elder, almost as if the younger woman wanted comfort but was afraid to ask for it. He had no sympathy for the girl after the way she'd treated Bebe.

"Master Augustine."

He cast a baleful glare at Morton Sinclair, who crouched next to him on the right.

The elderly witch gave him a sympathetic look and laid a hand in Caesar's shoulder. "I need you to step aside so I can examine her."

Caesar continued giving Sinclair a nasty look. Trust was something he had in short supply right now when it came to any White Rose member.

Stan leaned over the arm of the couch where Bebe's head rested. "Boss, I can watch him. He makes a move I don't like—"

"You're perfectly within your rights under the Blood Seal to rip my throat out, Master Augustine," Sinclair finished smoothly. His scent carried only the faintest trace of his nervousness, which could easily be attributable to his concern of what he might find lurking within Bebe. Brown eyes gazed serenely out from under bushy white eyebrows.

Caesar gave the slightest of nods before laying Bebe's hand down on her waist and stepping out of the way.

Sinclair rested one palm on Bebe's forehead and the other over her heart before he closed his eyes and mumbled a few words. An electric sensation rippled through the sitting room, and sharp ozone filled the air. Seconds seemed to drag into hours before he opened his eyes.

It took Sinclair another second before his eyes found their focus, and he looked up at Stan. "Do you detect anything I might have missed, Master Fae?"

Apparently, the old witch knew and respected fae culture enough not to say Stan's name. No fae, even a half-breed like Stan, would give a possible foe a weapon to use against him. And in magick, knowing a being's true name was the most powerful weapon of all.

But he'd given the witches his personal name in his efforts to draw Caesar out of his bloodrage. The enforcer's sacrifice rattled Caesar.

Stan shook his head. "Nothing magickal I can See." He met Caesar's gaze. "The doc's clean as far as spells, but she could have some internal bleeding from the sheer power forced through her body. We should get her to a hospital to double-check."

The acrid smell of ammonia assaulted Caesar's nostrils. His hand shot out and nearly broke Sinclair's fragile mortal bones when he grabbed the Elder's wrist. "What are you doing?"

The old witch seemed unperturbed. "Just smelling salts, Master Augustine. I agree with your fae though. I didn't detect any internal damage, but I'd prefer a second opinion. And if we can't wake her up this way, she may need an M.D."

Caesar released Sinclair's wrist. The Elder broke the capsule, but a single pass under Bebe's nose was all that was needed. She jerked up so fast she nearly knocked heads with Sinclair.

"For the love of the God and Goddess, get that shit out of my face."

Her voice was a bare whisper, but the sound of it sent a wave of relief through Caesar. Shoving Sinclair aside, he bent and pulled her into a giant hug, murmuring, "Thank Isis," over and over again.

"Ouch! Hey! My nose! Caesar, let go!"

Wetness trickled down his face in his joy. He eased up on his hold to examine her. Pins had fallen from her hair, strands escaping to curl wildly about her face. Dark smudges remained under her eyes, but her all-too-familiar annoyance blazed out of her gaze.

She reached up to shove at his shoulders. "Let me up, dammit! I need to go kill that no good little shit."

"O'Leary's dead, Bebe," he gently reminded her.

"I don't mean him." Her words came out in a gruff snarl, her throat scraped raw by her earlier screams when the traitor had attacked her. "I mean the son of a bitch I have the misfortune to call family."

Bebe struggled against his hold a second before her face dissolved into tears. "He killed her, Caesar. He killed my grandma." She repeated the words in between hiccupping sobs, clutching Caesar in her grief.

Sinclair disappeared for a moment, but before Caesar could send Stan after the witch, he returned with a glass of water that he pressed into Bebe's hand.

Caesar stared at the Elder, who just gave his benevolent smile and said, "Your fae can assure you it's safe, Master Augustine."

Caesar glanced at Stan, who nodded at the same time Bebe whispered, "It's okay, Caesar." She wiped her eyes with the heel of her free hand then took a huge gulp of water, nearly choking in the process.

Caesar rescued the glass and held her tightly as she recovered her breath. "You all right?"

She nodded but grief still shone in her eyes. He could only imagine what the confirmation of William's involvement in the conspiracy had torn inside of her.

"W-what—"

He and Bebe both turned to find tears streaming down Alice's face. She cleared her throat before trying again.

"How did he do it, Be?" The expression on Alice's pale face contained the same morbid look of someone who'd seen a horrible accident but couldn't stop staring at the carnage.

"He swapped out Grandma's normal dosage of nitroglycerin with capsules at ten times her dosage mixed with Viagra," Bebe said. She gave a wry smile. "Whoever did the autopsy probably didn't bother to check for blue diamonds in a 102-year-old woman." Her smile disappeared and she shuddered. "O'Leary knew about the plan for Grandma, but William did the deed. Someone outside of White Rose was helping them though. William insinuated it was a woman to O'Leary, but never introduced O'Leary to her or mentioned her name."

"You got all this from O'Leary?" Caesar asked.

Bebe nodded, and another shiver took her. "He was too intent on killing me to guard his own mind. Or what was left of it. We need to question William."

"In a minute, *amora*." He gently pushed her back down on the cushions when she tried to rise. "You need to rest, and Duncan will make sure William stays put. We also have other concerns." He cast a nasty look at Alice. Running his tongue deliberately over his canines made the young witch take an involuntary step back.

"I-I-I didn't—" Alice said at the same time Bebe laid a hand on his shoulder and said, "She didn't have anything to do with William and O'Leary."

He swung his head back to face Bebe. "How can you be sure? William could have lied to O'Leary that the woman helping them was an outsider." He gave Alice another glare. Bebe was far too forgiving, and he wasn't about to let the other witch verbally attack her, much less physically. "I noticed Lionel Hart wasn't present."

Alice couldn't meet his eyes, focusing on her toes instead. "Daddy refused to support my challenge and wouldn't come tonight. He said I—" She swallowed hard before continuing. "He said I was a spoiled idiot."

A tug on his arm brought his attention back to Bebe. A gentle smile spread across her face. "Trust me. I'm sure Alice and Lionel aren't involved in William's plan." She looked up at Alice. "Thank you for your help in the circle."

Caesar turned back to the other witch to find a mix of surprise, regret and embarrassment in her expression. A little confused himself, he asked, "Help? What help?"

"Didn't you feel Alice in the link?" came Bebe's bemused voice.

Red crept up Alice's cheeks. "I didn't realize you and Be—" She coughed before continuing. "I mean, I didn't know you and she . . ." She twisted her fingers, looking everywhere around the room but at him and Bebe. "I didn't mean to eavesdrop. I'm sorry."

She'd "heard" his declaration to Bebe during the battle with O'Leary.

He looked back to Bebe, his lips twisting in a wry grin. This was definitely an opportunity he couldn't let pass. "I believe I said something to you to which you have not responded, *amora.*"

She blushed and opened her mouth, but whatever answer she had disappeared in Duncan's shout.

Caesar, get up here! Now! Alarm tinged Duncan's mental tone.

Caesar rose, but Stan had already jumped up and raced for the door. Bebe's eyes widened, and she swung her feet to the floor.

"You're staying here," Caesar said.

"Like hell, I will." Her expression promised fury and brimstone. "William's my problem."

"Our problem," he countered.

"Do you two want to stand here arguing?"

He and Bebe both turned to find Alice standing with her arms crossed over her chest, the response similar to Bebe's but not as delightful.

"Or find out what our son of a bitch cousin is trying to pull now?" Alice finished.

Caesar shook his head in resignation and held out a hand to help Bebe up off the couch. He led the way out of the sitting room, Bebe and the other three witches following close on his heels.

Stan already stood next to Duncan inside the door to the windowless room. He looked at Caesar, shock on his face. "Someone's possessed him, boss."

Caesar pushed past his men to see William for himself. The witch sat on the floor, back propped against the far wall, no longer the sniveling, broken man Duncan had hauled upstairs. William's head tilted at an angle, a sly smile on his face.

The expression was all too familiar, and Caesar's gut clenched in confirmation when William began to speak.

"Hello, brother dear. Still slumming with the witches, I see."

Chapter 26

Bebe sidled into the room next to Caesar and stared at William, the change in him too confident and too secure to be the skunk who ran for the door when the magicked knife fingered him. She shifted her sight to find a riot of dark color surrounding him instead of his normal blue-tinged orange aura. Stan was right. Someone else was inside William's body. More than one someone from the psychedelic rainbow that surrounded his body.

"Well, Selene, at least I'm not pretending to be one of them." Caesar's cool voice carried a hint of wariness.

A vampire couldn't possess a person. She would have to be channeled through a witch. It was the how that made her stomach cramp. More blood magick. Her jaw clinched so tight the muscles hurt. She shot a look at Alice, who had edged into the room beside her.

No hint of black marred the sunshine orange aura. A baffled expression appeared on Alice's features. *Who's Selene? Another vamp?*

Yes. Now be quiet. When Alice's aura remained clean, Bebe's last shreds of suspicions regarding her cousin dissolved, but an uglier thought replaced them. Selene had to be William's mystery woman. Bebe's stomach did a nauseous flip that had nothing to do with O'Leary's attack. Did Caesar know all along? Had the conversation concerning Alice's involvement she'd overheard between Alex and Ptolemy been a set-up after all? Cleaving an already strained relationship so no one discovered the truth until it was too late?

"Sorry for the unconventionality, but we need to talk, brother," William/Selene said. "Alone."

"Anything you need to say you can say in present company," Caesar said.

Bebe's head spun, trying to puzzle out what was happening. If Caesar knew of Selene's involvement, he wouldn't want everyone to hear it, would he?

"Fine." William, or Selene that was, gave a dramatic sigh. "You still don't get it, do you? Petrov played you. Kept you all nice and tame while she plotted to destroy our people."

"The only person playing games here is you, Selene. Did you provide William with the doctored nitroglycerin pills?" Caesar's voice carried a harsh undertone.

"Stupid bastard was so eager to do it, but he didn't have the balls to get his hands really dirty. He just couldn't wait to get his mitts on his granny's money." William/Selene giggled. "Got a little too greedy, and he still blew it, didn't he? Should have taken both of the girls out when he had the chance."

Bebe swallowed the bile in the back of her throat. Oh sweet Goddess, everything Alice and she had accused each other of doing, and William had been behind it all along. And from her conversation with Caesar in what seemed like eons ago, Caesar knew, or suspected, William's involvement in the overdose-triggered heart attack.

"That explains William's motives, but it doesn't explain yours," Caesar said.

"Do you know what that bitch was doing?" Selene's shriek using William's male vocal cords set nerves on edge. He/she beat fists on the floor in fury.

"Yes," came Caesar's quiet reply. "I do. She was looking for a cure for the V-virus. Is that why you had her killed?"

A frozen mask of anger fell over William/Selene's face. "Has it occurred to you that her 'cure' was a mutated version of the virus that would slag us before we had a chance? What do you think the newborn witches are carrying in their modified genes? One sip from a blood bag with that crap and that's it. No more vampires."

Bebe sucked in a breath. That's not what Grandma's notes specifically said, but Selene was right. It wouldn't take much alteration for that odd little gene to do exactly what she said.

"I don't know who you get your information from, but you might want to do a breathalyzer test on your snitch." Caesar crossed his arms, his expression one of total disgust.

"Really?" The sly smile returned to William/Selene's face. "Why don't you ask you little pet witch beside you?"

Bebe shivered at the murderous look Caesar cast her. "You were with me, Caesar. You saw her notes in the Book. You know that's not where Grandma was going with her research."

"Ahhhh, so the bitch's notes *were* in her Book of Shadows." William/Selene's cackle would have scared the piss out of the Crone herself. "She led us on such a merry chase." He/she leaned forward. "Tell you what Bebe, darling. You give me the Book of Shadows, and I'll let you have your precious Grandma's soul back."

"What are you talking about?" But deep in her gut, she knew. She'd had the nightmares for nearly three weeks now, but she still didn't want to hear it. She'd seen it done to O'Leary moments ago. But condemn someone to that fate without a trial, without a real reason? No one could be that cruel, that amoral, that evil.

"Don't play stupid, dear. It doesn't become you." William/Selene held out a hand, and the image of a brilliant purple Soul Sphere appeared to float just above the palm. Not the white of a sealed sphere. A purple the same shade as Grandma Petrov's aura. "Miko is waiting for you at San Francisco International." An obnoxious smirk spread across his/her face. "I'll be generous and allow for traffic or any delays by Homeland Security. We all know what a bitch they can be." He/she scowled. "You have three hours to get to the Karnak for the exchange. You don't show or you bring any other witches and Granny dearest goes poof."

An expression appeared on William's face that Selene probably thought looked seductive, but was just downright creepy. "You know, Duncan, since you don't like me as a woman, maybe you'd like to take a spin with me as a man."

The disgusted look Duncan gave him/her was all the vampire needed to make his feelings clear.

"Oh well, maybe some other time then."

The insane rainbow surrounding William faded. He slumped over and proceeded to vomit all over the dusty maple floorboards.

This cannot be happening. Bebe reached behind for a wall as dizziness swept through her overloaded body. Not finding any support, she landed unceremoniously butt first on the floor. The sphere was the only explanation for the bizarre nightmares of Grandma, trapped and screaming for help. The witch who cast it hadn't sealed the thrice-damned thing properly, allowing Grandma to touch her subconscious. And it had to be Selene's eclectic.

Goddess, how could any witch do something like that to an innocent? "Bebe."

She blinked away the tears of despair to find Caesar crouched next to her, concern lining his normally marless forehead.

"I'm so sorry, *amora*," he whispered. "I'll go with you to Las Vegas and try to talk my sister out of her foolishness."

"Foolishness? Is that what you call what she did to my grandmother?" Fury replaced shock, igniting a fire that needed to strike out at someone, anyone. And Caesar was the closest target. "That bitch engineered my grandmother's murder." She jabbed a finger into his granite chest, her voice rising. "Someone who was your friend, or so you say. And worse, your sister is holding my grandmother's soul for ransom. And all you want to do is *talk* to her?"

Caesar stood, his expression icy. "I'm tired of you blaming me for everything that's wrong in your life just because of what I am. In case it hasn't occurred to you, Doctor, my sister needed one of *your* people to curse Natasha's soul into that sphere when she died."

He spun on his heel and stalked toward the door, his fists tightly clenched at his sides. But he paused at the door and turned back to her, his face devoid of emotion. That lack of anything scared her more than his anger.

"One more thing, Doctor. I saw from the look on your face that my sister was telling the truth about the possibility of converting the gene. If that was your plan—"

"Stop it!" Alice screamed the words at the same moment Duncan shouted them.

"Alice?" Bebe scrambled to her feet. Her cousin may have four inches on her, but that only meant Alice's head came to Caesar's nose instead of his chest. And now, Alice shoved every inch she could in Caesar's face.

"If you were friends with our grandmother, you are not walking out of here with that attitude." Alice shook a fist beneath his eyes, setting her silver bangles jangling. "And you are not treating my Be like shit and think you'll get away with it."

Caesar quickly suppressed a flinch and took a step back, though probably more concerned over the metal touching him, not from the fist waving beneath his left nostril. "You seem to have a rather abrupt change of heart for someone who accused Bebe of murder less than an hour ago," he said, his voice leaden.

"Ms. Hart is right. Both you and Dr. Zachary—" Duncan paused to give Bebe a meaningful look. "—are letting your pride consume you. This is a time to make a rational plan." His right eyebrow rose a fraction of an inch. "In the Hummer on the way to the airport. Selene does not bluff."

"We're coming, too."

Bebe looked over her shoulder. Miranda stood outside the room, a look of murderous fury on her face. A look that for once wasn't aimed at Bebe personally. Pierre, Beatrice and Morton crowded next to her. From the looks on the Elders' faces, they'd heard every word of her exchange with Selene.

She shook her head. "I appreciate the offer, but you heard Selene's terms. If I show up with any of you—"

"Then the bitch shouldn't have left a loophole in her terms," Stan said. "We're coming with you."

Turning, Bebe saw him and Duncan wearing the same terrible grin, grins that promised death and destruction to whoever got in their way. She found herself clutching Caesar's coat sleeve to keep her hand from trembling.

"You and your coven are not the only ones with a stake in this," Duncan said.

Chapter 27

Now, Caesar's world was literally falling apart in front of him. Selene's betrayal was catastrophic, but how dare Stan and Duncan volunteer their services without his authorization!

Duncan faced him, and the other vampire's expression sobered. "Caesar, think about it. This is only partly about Natasha's research. If Selene were behind the attacks seventeen years ago—"

Old habits jumped into place, despite his own heartbreak. "Duncan, I've heard enough of your accusations against her." Caesar bit out the words through gritted teeth. "I understand your personal feelings regarding Selene, but you have no proof—"

"Then why the hits on both you and Lady Petrov, boss?" Stan's quiet voice cut through the tension between Caesar and Duncan. "On the same night at the same time? I saw the doc's family tree. If Selene's that pissed off about the witches' immunity, then the hits on Natasha's people make sense. Eliminate anyone who might be carrying the gene. But why the attacks on us?"

No. Caesar felt his intestines knot. Selene was his twin. They'd shared their mother's womb for gods' sakes!

Stan didn't stop his relentless analysis. "Without you here, Ptolemy would side with her out of blood loyalty. With both you and Duncan gone, the rest of us would have been mincemeat for those loyal to her. None of the other supernatural leaders would have interfered with an internal vampire matter, but if you had asked Natasha for assistance, she'd give it. You know it, boss. Selene had to take you both out at the same time. She just didn't count on both you and Natasha reacting as fast as you did that night and foiling a majority of the attacks."

"She knows you'll insist on accompanying Dr. Zachary to Las Vegas.

She will use this opportunity to remove both of you from the picture," Duncan said.

"Permanently," Stan added. "Which is why we're going with you."

Bebe's fingers twined between his, the gesture oddly comforting in his numb insanity. How could he have been so blind? If Duncan and Stan were correct, Selene's involvement went back more than seventeen years.

Gods above! It had. The teasing puzzle of thought snapped into place. Selene knew about the research, just as she had known about Duncan's stunt with Homeland Security, when Caesar had spoke with her on the phone. And he hadn't told her. Stan had pointed out that the only person who knew was the Nazi conspirator. Oh, sweet Isis, what had he done?

All those people. Dead. Because he hadn't wanted to see what evil Selene was truly capable of committing.

"Caesar?"

He looked down. Beside him, Bebe peered up, concern on her features.

"We have to go now. Are you coming?"

How can you still want me?

She smiled, a tremulous one that struggled through the tears welling in her eyes, but it still managed to light her face brighter than the sun he hadn't seen in centuries. "This started with both of our families. We need to end it. Together."

His promise to Natasha must be kept, for Duncan and Bebe's sake if not for himself. At his nod, Bebe gave his hand a squeeze.

As the group strode down the hall after leaving William in Pierre's tender mercies, Bebe named Alice as her heir, even though her Confirmation hadn't been completed. Thankfully, the Elders weren't questioning her decisions or her orders. Being the high priestess was what she'd been trained for since she was eleven.

On the way downstairs, the Elders decided Alice, Miranda and Beatrice would accompany Caesar's group to the airport.

Bebe hid her grin at the female guard's dismay to the camaraderie between the vampires and the Elders. Morton waved Miranda and Beatrice off at the door of the mansion with a thumb up, saying he'd contact all the other High Priests and Priestesses and alert them to the possible danger.

With Harry behind the wheel and Stan hexing the traffic lights to keep them green, the Hummer raced toward the airport. Caesar and Duncan twisted to face the four witches crowded in the third seat.

"What if we buy a book at the airport and spell it to look like the BOS?" Alice said.

Miranda whacked the younger witch in the back of the head, earning a nasty look. "Why the hell do you think that vampire has an eclectic working for her?" She turned to glare at Bebe. "You couldn't name someone brighter to replace you? You damn well better not get yourself killed, girl."

"She wants the White Rose family trees as much as she wants the Book of Shadows," Duncan said. "She needs it to make sure all the lines are wiped out to prevent the genetic engineering she fears."

"She's going to know if I rip out any pages." Bebe shook her head. "I don't see anyway out other than not give it to her."

"You're not seriously considering leaving Grandma in that bitch's hands, are you?" Alice's face held a horrified look under the passing streetlights.

"No!" Appalled that Alice would think her capable of such an act, Bebe struggled to complete a plan. "I need to let her have it long enough to set Grandma free, and then steal it back."

"You have one thing on your side." Caesar let his fangs show in his smile. All the witches, but Bebe, recoiled.

You are so wicked. Bebe's smile took the sting out of her admonishment.

You have no idea, amora.

"Natasha's notes are in code," he said aloud. "The key isn't in the Book. If we can exchange the Book for the Soul Sphere before she realizes she's been duped—"

"I could 'port the Book to Harry before Selene's witch could do anything. The eclectic wouldn't dare to stop my spell for fear of destroying it," Stan volunteered from the front seat.

Harry glance at his partner before returning his attention to the road. "Hey, I'm coming with you guys!"

"No." Caesar leaned forward to give the younger man a reassuring squeeze on the shoulder. "I appreciate your desire, but I need an elf back-up on this end as well as a witch back-up. Stay with Alice Hart at all times unless you hear orders from me otherwise."

"I don't need a fucking babysitter."

Caesar chuckled at Alice's complaint and glanced at Duncan. "I thought we left Tiffany in Los Angeles."

Duncan nodded, his expression serious. "The similarities between Ms. Hart and my niece are disturbing to say the least."

All conversation ceased as they made their interminable way through the security checkpoints to the private hangars. Caesar checked his watch for the thousandth time. He'd lay money that Selene had called in the latest terrorist tip that had the guards in an uproar, retaliation for Duncan's tactic when they left Los Angeles two nights ago.

He clenched his fist in frustration. No, he didn't need money. Natasha's soul was already on the table.

Harry slammed on the brakes the proscribed distance from the Lear. A dark figure stood next to the entry ladder, someone too tall for either Miko or Mai.

Caesar narrowed eyes. It couldn't be. Wasn't anyone around him listening to him anymore? He charged out of the Hummer. "Ptolemy? What the Hades are you doing—"

Ptolemy pulled both hands out of his pockets. The Glocks in each fist froze Caesar's blood.

No, not his baby brother too.

"We've figured you'd come with her." Ptolemy shifted to aim the right gun at Duncan. "Don't try it, St. James."

"Like that piddly piece of shit could do anything," Duncan said, his voice a snarl of rage.

Caesar risked a look at his chief enforcer, whose eyes glowed neon green with his fury. "Don't do it, Duncan. He's loaded with garlic-laced bullets."

"Caesar can tell you how bad they feel, and I don't want to kill you." Ptolemy actually had the balls to look regretful.

"No, just me." Bebe stepped around Caesar before he could stop her.

"No, I don't, Doctor. Just give me the Book and I'll let you walk."

"Not without my grandmother, you snake," she hissed.

Ptolemy nodded, weariness in his eyes. "I figured you say that." He gestured at the plane. "Just you and Caesar."

"You can't—" Stan started.

"This is a family matter, Gryffudd. Stay out of it." Ptolemy met Caesar's gaze, even though his other gun was now pointed at Stan. "We don't have a lot of time. You know she'll destroy the Sphere without blinking."

Caesar sucked in a breath. He'd counted too much on Stan and Duncan's backup when they reached Las Vegas. Without Stan along to keep Selene's eclectic in check, it would be up to Bebe to magick the Book back to Alice. Once she did, and that was a big assumption on his part that a witch could pass objects through Otherwhere like a fae could, he didn't know how he was getting both of them out of the Karnak alive. None of his usual sanctuaries in the city would be safe, and it would be too close to dawn for him to reach any of the mountains surrounding Las Vegas, much less find a deep enough cave or crevasse.

We've got to go, Caesar. Your brother's getting an itchy trigger finger. Bebe started for the ladder.

Deliberately ignoring his brother, Caesar faced Duncan. "Get Alice back to the witches' mansion and stay with her. It's spell-protected. Contact Los Angeles and Seattle and keep them apprised of the situation."

Duncan stiffened but nodded.

Caesar stalked to the jet and climbed in after Bebe. He'd have to trust Duncan to ferret out those vampires who were loyal at the other compounds. Anyone in Las Vegas was suspect. Once he reached the cabin, Miko's quiet sobs from the cockpit were audible over the roar of the engines. He threw his senses forward, but Mai was noticeably absent.

"Put your sword in the closet and lock it."

Caesar gritted his teeth at Ptolemy's words. He might as well walk into the Coliseum and try petting a pride of starving lions without his spatha.

"Do it." Ptolemy shifted until the barrel pointed at Bebe's head. Something flickered in his eyes for a moment.

Regret? But the emotion wasn't enough to risk Bebe's life on. Slowly, Caesar pulled off his jacket, unlatched the harness and shoved the leather and steel into the tiny luggage locker.

"Sit down and buckle up." Ptolemy had pocketed one of the Glocks, but the other gleamed in his right hand.

Caesar ground his teeth in frustration. What had Ptolemy done to Miko, and where was Mai?

Bebe laid a soft hand on his and shook her head. Damn, she was right. Now was not the time, but gods help his siblings if Mai was dead.

Dropping into the seat next to Bebe, a sense of déjà vu stole over him. Three days ago, they had been sitting in these same seats on their way to Los Angeles. Now, his life was as inside out and upside down as Bebe's. The irony forced a chuckle out of him.

Ptolemy shot him a suspicious look as he made his way to the cockpit but didn't say anything.

Care to share what's so funny? When he turned to her, Bebe's delicate black brows were twisted in concern. *Because if you're having a nervous breakdown, a little forewarning would be nice.*

He lifted her hand, basking in her scent as his lips brushed her delicate skin. *Merely reflecting on the Gray Ladies' sense of humor. You were right,* amora. *Three nights ago aboard this very jet, I arrogantly believed I could protect you. Now I find we share a similar position with each of our blood kin.*

She smiled at him, a sweet, loving smile he desperately wished he deserved. *You're right about something too. You bared your heart to me, and I never answered. I—*

"Oh, for the love of Venus, can you two stop making googly-eyes at each other for two seconds?" Ptolemy threw himself into the seat across from them and scowled.

"Jealous?" Strange how their positions had been reversed in more ways than one. Normally, he was the one chiding Selene for baiting Ptolemy. But he needed any information he could get, which meant playing nasty.

Ptolemy snorted. "Hardly."

No one spoke as the Lear rolled toward the designated runway, pausing only for a moment before gravity and momentum shoved Caesar deeper into his seat. Leaping into the air, the jet performed a slow sweeping arc before orienting southeast.

Caesar's stomach rolled along with jet. They were committed to Las Vegas. A silent prayer to Neith rose from his mind. If ever he needed divine inspiration to come up with a strategy, now was the time.

"You know, Ptolemy, I never pictured you as the greedy type. When did you and Selene decide to kill me?" he said.

Ptolemy's eyes widened. "This isn't about taking over the coven." He waved the gun at the bag Bebe had shoved under her seat. "Natasha's notes need to be destroyed before anybody else gets the bright idea of using the information against us."

"So what are you saying? I accidentally got in the way of the gunmen you sent after Bebe? Gunmen using bullets specifically designed to—" He turned to Bebe. "What's the strange gesture your generation makes with their fingers?"

"Air quotes. Also known as bunny ears." She demonstrated.

He smiled. "Thank you, *amora*." He faced his brother again, widening his smile. "Kill vampires?" Using his index and middle digits, he repeated Bebe's gesture. He deliberately left the middle digit in the air when he was finished.

Ptolemy's cheeks flushed only the faintest of pinks. Interesting. Did he not drink enough before leaving Las Vegas or had Mai and Miko put up more of a fight than he anticipated and drained his strength?

"I tried to stall you that night, but you were too intent on reaching Dr. Zachary." Ptolemy grimaced. "And the men William hired were late. You weren't supposed to get to the hotel until after they'd stolen the Book."

Who was lying to whom here? The men at the hotel were definitely there to kill Bebe. Caesar made a soft *tsk*-ing sound. "It's so hard to hire good assassins. I would have thought you would have learned a thing or two from Octavia."

Ptolemy sneered, but his grip tightened slightly on the gun. "I learned plenty. Maybe not as much as you, *Alexander*."

"Alexander?"

Caesar turned to meet Bebe's questioning look. "My birth name. I gave it up centuries ago." He faced Ptolemy again. "My so-called siblings like to throw it in my face."

"I'm not the one who brought up the past," Ptolemy shot back. "Or sick enough to take the name of our parents' murderer."

Ptolemy's verbal strike hit far deeper than he realized. What would happen if he knew the truth? That Caesar had helped their mother die?

Taking a slow, deep breath, Caesar forced his muscles to relax. He needed to hang onto his control and swallow his ancient guilt, or he and Bebe both were doomed. Letting his fingers form a steeple, he peered over the tips at his brother. "You're right, of course. Forgive me. So let me guess? You came to Anthony's Thursday night to make sure the second team succeeded."

To his surprise, Ptolemy shook his head, a morose look on his face. "Selene sent the second team, even though I told her I'd be able to get the Book from Phillippa. So I followed, and when it looked like you were—" He sucked in a harsh breath and couldn't meet Caesar's gaze any longer.

Hades, curse him for a fool! Caesar wasn't sure what made him angrier, his own blindness or the unnecessary guilt his brother had inflicted on Bebe. "You didn't give a shit about me. When you saw Bebe take out two of your assassins, you killed Franklin so neither of us could question her."

Ptolemy's head jerked up, his eyes blazing gold. "And it should have ended there. I told Selene she'd gone too far, but she still sent a squad to the Brentwood mansion to retrieve the Book."

"If the Book is all she wants, why is she trying to kill me?"

Ptolemy jerked at Bebe's soft voice, a look of shock on his face. After a moment, he shook his head violently. "She's not, I swear."

"One of the White Rose witches tried to kill Bebe tonight during their Confirmation ceremony. And then Selene had Bebe's cousin William possessed in order to demonstrate her power," Caesar added.

Again, Ptolemy shook his head, a firm expression of denial planted on his face. "No. That had to have been William's idea, not hers." He faced Bebe. "In case you haven't noticed, Doctor, your cousin is nuts."

"Then why was Selene killing our people seventeen years ago?" Caesar didn't let his voice rise above a soft murmur. His heart ached too much to make the effort. Ptolemy was still defending her, just as Caesar had to Bebe earlier before heading to the airport.

The ragged disbelief on Ptolemy's face gave way to a slightly hysterical laugh. "St. James's using the current trouble to make a case against her, isn't he? When is he going to give up his insane need for retribution? Selene screwed up by fucking him, but she's paid her fine."

"If it was only the situation with Duncan, I'd agree with you. But I have reason to believe she was the supernatural who collaborated with the Nazis as well," Caesar said.

Ptolemy's mouth fell open.

Caesar willed himself to stay still. His brother couldn't dissemble to this level. On one hand, he was relieved Ptolemy wasn't involved deeper than he was. Selene used the same line of bullshit on their baby brother she had tried feeding him through William. And she'd nearly succeeded.

"Where on earth did you get that idea? From her?" Ptolemy pointed the gun at Bebe, waving it uncomfortably in the direction of her all-to-vulnerable mortal heart. "Selene's our sister, and you believe someone you've known a week. Or is this more of St. James's bullshit?"

"Why don't you ask her when we arrive in Las Vegas? Ask her why it was necessary to hold Natasha's soul prisoner. Ask her why Bebe needs to die." Caesar couldn't look at his brother any longer.

His chest hurt, and it wasn't from his gunshot wounds of the other night. He almost wished it were. Something physical would be so much easier to deal with. He closed his eyes against his seething emotions. Despite Mother's best efforts, the three of them had ended up plotting against each other, just like she and her siblings had done. Was the Ptolemaic dynasty doomed to repeat the same pattern until the end of time?

The subtle shift of air pressure indicated Miko had begun their decent. They needed a plan before they reached the Karnak.

Bebe, don't react. We can't let Ptolemy know we're talking.

Okay.

He breathed a soft sigh of relief that no sound of her shifting in her seat came to him. *Can you transport the Book and the sphere to Alice magickally?*

The Book, yes. The sphere, no.

I thought witches could transport objects, but not living things through Otherwhere.

Her silent laughter fluttered against his mind. *Sounds like Grandma left something out of the translation.* Deadly sobriety came with her next thought. *The key is whether what's being transported has a soul. Technically, I could transport a dead elephant if I have the power to move that much mass. But the sphere with Grandma in it? I might as well slap a strobe on it with a sign saying 'Blue Light Special' for all the nasties in the Otherwhere.*

Damn. He was running out of ideas. The landing gear sliding into place made a soft grinding beneath them.

Caesar, where would your sister be keeping Mai?

He barely suppressed his start of surprise. Slitting his eyes open a fraction, he checked Ptolemy. His brother wiped his free hand along his thigh, as though trying to wipe blood and remorse off on his jeans. *She may be dead. Miko was crying when we first boarded.* And had stopped at some point, though the occasional sniffle came from the cockpit. He didn't dare touch her mind. Ptolemy would be waiting for such a tactic, but the deep connection he'd forged with Bebe in the circle passed under his brother's radar.

If she is, Ptolemy doesn't know it, and I can't see Selene killing Mai until she was sure Miko had delivered me.

How do you know what Ptolemy's thinking? Can you get into his mind without him realizing it because he's sure acting guilty?

Again the soft fluttering like a butterfly's wings. *No, silly, his aura. Yeah, it's gray around the edges, probably subconscious regret at setting me up for Franklin's death and being conned by Selene. But there's no black.*

Which means?

He has no involvement in a murder.

But Franklin—

Wasn't a murder in his eyes. To him, he was saving your life.

Amora, you scare me.

The fluttering sped up until it became a buzz. *Good, maybe you'll stop treating me like a porcelain doll. Is there any place we can get a UV-protected vehicle?*

There's a small, private area located in the main parking garage. The keys will be in the security office. The odds of us reaching Los Angeles—

No, she'll expect that and have the airport and any routes to California blocked. Do you have any other compounds east?

That I trust right now? No.

What about the other vampire masters?

He punctured his tongue with a canine to keep from laughing outright. *No, amora, Virginia and Jean-Pierre will consider this situation my problem to clean up.*

Fine. Her snort of derision was audible. *We'll hole up in a hotel in Utah before dawn—*

"What's your problem?" A harsh note buzzed in Ptolemy's voice.

Caesar opened his eyes to find his brother staring at Bebe suspiciously.

She turned from the window. "I'm continually amazed how you big, bad vampires get your rocks off by beating up defenseless girls."

"I haven't touched you, Doctor." Ptolemy's lips peeled back from his fangs. "Yet."

Unfazed, Bebe stared back, anger twisting her full lips. "I meant Mai and Miko."

Again, Ptolemy flushed the faintest pink. A Normal wouldn't have even noticed.

She must have seen something in his aura because her lips tilted in a nasty smile. "Leaving aside me and Caesar, what do you think Kensai will do when he finds out?"

Whatever retort Ptolemy planned to throw out was swallowed by the sharp series of jolts when Miko touched the jet down on the runway.

"Sloppy," Caesar remarked. He gave the same nasty smile to his brother, releasing some of his pent-up fury. "I'm sure Selene will leave Miko's punishment in your capable hands."

Instead of answering Caesar, Ptolemy clenched his free fist against his thigh and addressed Bebe. "Last chance, Doctor. Give me the Book, and I'll let Miko fly you back to San Francisco."

"My terms have changed. I want Mai, Miko and my grandmother in return for the Book." Her expression would have done any professional poker player proud.

An exasperated sigh blew from Ptolemy as the jet pulled to a stop in front of a hangar. He didn't take his eyes or the gun from them when he yelled over his shoulder. "Miko, shut everything down and get in here!" He unclipped his seatbelt, rose from the chair and pulled the second Glock from his coat pocket.

A moment later, the cockpit door opened. Miko limped into the main cabin with only one eye red from crying. The other sported a shiner that had nearly swollen the orb shut. But both eyes glared naked hatred at Ptolemy.

"Let me guess. Mai wasn't in any shape to fly." Bebe's voice dripped with sarcasm.

Ptolemy stepped back behind Caesar's chair. With some amusement, Caesar noted his brother was out of the reach of Miko's legs as well.

"Open the door, Miko."

"I just hope I'm there when you get your evil heart staked, you bastard," she spat, but she moved to obey him.

Ptolemy nudged Caesar's back with what definitely felt like one of the Glock muzzles. He must have poked Bebe too, because they unclipped their seatbelts and stood as one. Bebe reached beneath her seat and pulled out her shoulder bag that contained the Book of Shadows. Without a word, they followed Miko down the ladder.

Caesar scanned the area. No one waited to meet them. He resisted the urge to smile. Selene had spread her people too thin in the effort to seize the Brentwood mansion, and Ptolemy must not have been able to notify her in time or tip off the Los Angeles assailants without revealing himself to those who were loyal to Caesar.

Ptolemy avoided the ladder altogether and leapt down, landing lightly next to Caesar.

"Show-off," Caesar muttered under his breath.

Ignoring him, Ptolemy waved toward the SUV parked on the tarmac. "Doctor, you'll drive. Everyone else in the back."

Caesar's heart skipped a beat. No, Ptolemy wouldn't shove Bebe out the door while she was driving. It would attract too much attention. Still, being that far away from her left an antsy feeling that Caesar found annoying. His fingers automatically moved to stroke the pommel of his spatha, and he was reminded that it sat locked in the Lear.

Ptolemy waited until Caesar and Miko had climbed into the rear bench seat, then he flicked the child safety locks on the door before shutting it.

Well, on the plus side, he and Miko weren't getting tossed from the moving SUV either.

"You're going to have to give me directions, asshole," Bebe said.

Again, Ptolemy gave an exasperated sigh, but surprisingly made no comment on her insult. "Follow the signs out of the airport, then make a left at the light and then another left at the Strip."

The good doctor deliberately squealed the tires as she accelerated away from the hangar.

Caesar laid a hand on Miko's arm and winced at the way she flinched from him. "Where's Mai?"

"She was still at the Karnak the last time I saw her." Miko's voice trembled, whether from anger, fear or exhaustion he was uncertain. "The bitch deliberately broke her leg. I'm sorry, Master." Her breath hissed in pain. "I shouldn't have—"

"It's all right." He gave the girl's forearm a gentle squeeze. "I'm not thinking very generous thoughts about my sister either."

A single tear rolled down her cheek. "I shouldn't have left her there. Selene had her arm wrapped around Mai's neck and threatened to pull her head off. If she—" She choked back a sob.

"Where else are you injured?" he said at the same time he sent *I have a plan, but are you well enough to help?*

She nodded and for the first time tonight, hope shone in her good eye. The injured one was now completely swollen shut. "A sprained ankle and I think my cheek bone may be broken." A wry smile curved across her lips. "The bitch needed me well enough to pilot the plane."

Bebe braked at the first traffic light, tapping a fast rhythm on the steering wheel as she waited for the left arrow light.

"So Ptolemy, how did you manage to ditch everyone at the safe house?" Caesar pitched his voice to carry over the bass of the truck that had pulled up next to them. When his brother ignored him, he laughed. "Oh, come on. You can tell me. Aren't you the one saying the younger children don't know shit?"

Ptolemy refused to look at him.

He leaned forward to rest his folded arms on the back of the bucket seat in front of him. "Let me guess. You claimed you would try to lead them away in order to let the others make a break for San Francisco. You then left the safe house, but the idiots Selene hired were too stupid to follow you, so you couldn't warn them where I'd taken Bebe and the Book."

Ptolemy whipped his head around to glare, but the vampire glow of his eyes was washed out in the bright streetlights and neon signs. "You should have told me where you were going."

"It seems now I had good reason not to."

The gun came up, pointing at Caesar's head, but it quivered in Ptolemy's grip. "I'm fucking sick and tired of you treating me like I'm stupid."

Keeping his voice even, Caesar said, "What are you talking about?"

"You just think you're all superior, don't you? 'Look at me. I'm the coven master. I know everything.' " The glow faded from Ptolemy's eyes. "Guess what? I'm tired of living this fucking existence, too. But I'm not letting some half-assed witch plot to kill me without even a fight. I am *not* turning into our parents!"

Caesar stared at his younger brother, words clogging in his throat. Today was the first time Ptolemy had spoken of their parents' deaths since they were children. Old guilt rose up, threatening to swallow him whole. What would Ptolemy say if he knew the role Caesar had played in their mother's suicide?

"We're here. Or would you boys like me to find a playground where you can duke it out?" Bebe turned into the Karnak's long curving driveway and headed for valet parking.

Ptolemy jerked before shoving the guns in his pockets, but his hands remained inside, hanging tight to the metal by the tension in his shoulders.

The valet opened the front passenger door. "Welcome to the—" Eyes bulging, he stammered for a few seconds before finding his senses. "Mr. Antonius, why aren't you—"

Shoving past the poor valet, Ptolemy said, "My brother wanted to do a spot inspection, and frankly you are sorely lacking at this point."

If the man's eyes were bulging before, they jumped out of their sockets when he caught sight of Caesar. He gulped loud enough to be heard over the crowd of pedestrians on the Strip and the constant dinging of the slot machines from the casino inside.

"M-M-Mr. Augustine! My apologies. We didn't know you were coming." He scrambled to open the rear passenger door, and Caesar climbed out.

"That's the point of a spot inspection, isn't it?" Ptolemy said, his snarl scaring the valet even more.

If you didn't want the entire staff to know we were here, you should have instructed Bebe to drive around to our private entrance.

Slightly amused at his brother's nasty glare and silence despite the circumstances, Caesar turned and assisted the limping Miko down from the SUV. Bebe already stood next to him, her knuckles white as they clenched her bag.

The valet still shook from Ptolemy's reprimand. "Shall I get a wheelchair for your friend, Mr. Antonius?"

"That won't be necessary." Ptolemy shot Caesar a pointed look. "If you'd lead the way to the private elevator?"

Sucking in his breath, Caesar lifted Miko's left arm around his shoulder and wrapped his right around her waist to support her. Sharing a look with Bebe, they entered the hotel. Straight into an encounter either he or his twin wouldn't be walking away from.

He just had to make sure Bebe and the girls walked out with him.

Chapter 28

Any other time, Bebe would have stared at the sheer opulence of the Karnak, the newest of the Vegas hotel/casino resorts at the south end of the Strip. Despite the late hour, or early morning depending on how one viewed it, noise blared in the casino, crowds of tourists talking, laughing, and gambling. The difference between here and the African villages where she worked would have boggled her mind. All that food and money wasted.

But now . . .

Now, she wondered how the hell they were getting out of the hotel alive, despite Caesar's assurance. She glanced at Miko hobbling along with Caesar's help. The swelling in the girl's lower leg matched the swelling on her face.

Miko needs to get off that ankle and get some ice on it.

Caesar glanced down at Bebe, a half-amused and half-irritated expression on his face. *I won't undermine her confidence by carrying her through the lobby.*

Grimacing back, she sent, *Neither of which will matter if we all die here.*

He neither said nor thought anything, just gave a look that clearly proclaimed, "Thanks for the vote of confidence."

She followed as he led the way to a private alcove where a man stood, dressed in the stylistic black of expensive private security. A quick shift of Sight confirmed the guard was a vampire. Selene wasn't taking any chances.

The guard nodded to Caesar and pressed the "Up" button.

Tightening her grip on her bag, she risked a peek behind her. The minute her eyes met Ptolemy's though, he found a sudden interest in the huge statue beside him, the one that blocked the alcove from most scrutiny.

Interesting. She dredged up the basics she'd learned in her psychology classes years ago. Good to know Ptolemy wasn't entirely comfortable about this whole situation, but would she have a chance to use that knowledge?

The elevator pinged and its doors slid open. Bebe let a soft sigh of relief escape when the muscle-bound vampire didn't step on board with them. Instead, Ptolemy pressed "P1" and the car stated to rise.

Clearing her throat gained Ptolemy's attention, but she'd have to tread carefully. "What has my grandmother done to you?" When he didn't answer, she shrugged, trying to make it seem as nonchalant as possible. "I ran away to Africa because she tried to make me marry Alastair Hyde-Smith." She gave a self-deprecating chuckle. "She threatened to cut off money for school too. So whatever she did, I would probably sympathize."

Bebe, what are you playing at?

Ignoring Caesar's warning, she focused on Ptolemy and allowed her sincerity to shine through. "No matter what happens, I want you to know that I appreciated your Saturnalia present."

An emotion flickered across his features so fast she wasn't sure it happened, much less what it represented until he spoke.

"I meant what I said in Los Angeles."

Had it occurred to the idiot that he may be the next enemy she had to vanquish? Bile rose in her throat. What if he did? What if all this was an elaborate charade to get someone else to kill him? Did he hate himself that much? His tirade in the SUV suddenly made sense. The elevator halted and the doors slid open once again before she could respond.

"Welcome to the Karnak, Dr. Zachary."

The smooth, velvety tones belonged to the female vampire who'd arrived at Caesar's San Francisco house the night after he'd been shot. She stood in front of one wall that was nothing more than floor-to-ceiling windows. Any other time, Bebe would have admired the view of the Las Vegas skyline.

Instead, she focused on the vampire. As before, she dripped in designer clothes and expensive jewelry all the way down to her snakeskin stilettos, but this outfit shouted business. The rose shell top and medium gray pantsuit set off her olive complexion. Her black hair was wrapped into a no-nonsense French twist, not a strand out of place. She exuded control, but unlike Caesar, her attitude carried a nasty, oily taste.

The black sparks in Selene's orange and red aura confirmed Bebe's impression.

"I'd feel a lot more welcome if your brother wasn't holding guns on us."

Selene laughed, a sound she probably meant to sound musical and ladylike, but it sent shivers down Bebe's spine.

"Ptolemy won't hurt you, Doctor. In fact, my baby brother spoke rather highly of your fighting abilities." Her gaze shifted to Caesar. "Why don't you help Miko over to the couch? I'm sure standing cannot be comfortable on that injured ankle of hers. Lucien, would you get some ice for Miko?"

Bebe looked over in surprise. Standing near the wet bar was a witch. For some reason, she'd assumed Selene's eclectic was a woman. Dressed from head to foot in black, he had pulled his greasy brown hair into a queue at the base of his neck. Obviously, Selene kept her witch well in check. This guy reminded Bebe of a pit bull. A very dangerous pit bull that would only respond to his mistress's command.

Another chill ran down Bebe's back. Now she knew who'd been teaching William and his friends how to cast sacrificial blood spells. No hint of the original color of his aura remained, and what existed was so black that it blended into his designer suit.

And his eyes bore into hers.

She had the barest instant to fling up her outer shields, but even then, she staggered under the psychic blow. Only a firm grip on her elbow kept her from falling to the plush carpet.

"Lucien! Behave yourself. Dr. Zachary is my guest." The obscene pressure disappeared at Selene's reprimand.

Bebe didn't believe for one instant that the attack hadn't been sanctioned. Blinking away the tears that had sprung to life at the pain, she found it was Ptolemy keeping her upright, not Caesar. She swallowed hard, pulled herself erect on shaky knees and muttered, "Thanks."

Once again, Ptolemy had the strange look on his face. This time it stayed long enough for her to identify a mixture of regret and pain. When she tried to shrug his hand off, he kept a firm grip on her, but not with the effect of intimidation.

"Why don't you sit down, Doctor?" He steered her over to the armless chair next to the couch where Miko sat with her injured ankle propped on pillows.

Closer to Caesar, Bebe realized with a start. She reached up to finger the pentacle Tiffany had given her, but it was gone. Incinerated in the magickal battle back in San Francisco, and in the frantic drive to the airport, she hadn't had the chance to replace it. She was down to raw strength and the protection charm she'd placed on Caesar's ring. Goddess, she hoped it would be enough.

"Where's Mai?" Caesar's voice held a touch of anger underneath its surface calm. He strode toward his sister from where he'd arranged Miko on the couch.

"Resting in one of the guest bedrooms." Selene sauntered forward and looked up at her twin, but the stilettos put her close to the same height so she didn't have to look far. "Don't worry. Her leg has been set, and she'll recover fully." She gave a mock frown. "Though I'm afraid she isn't as comfortable as I would like. She refuses to take anything for the pain."

"How does she know you aren't trying to poison her, you treacherous cow!" Fury rolled off Miko in waves.

Making a clucking sound with her tongue, Selene shook her head. "You girls brought this on yourselves by disobeying my direct order and then attacking me." The smile she gave Miko would have made the nastiest predator on the planet tremble. "But I keep my word. You and your sister may leave."

Another male security vamp appeared from the hallway, pushing Mai ahead of him in a wheelchair, her broken right leg propped up. A grimace of pain twisted her ashen face. It was all Bebe could do to remain seated and not check on the girl.

A small cry sprang from Miko's throat. The security vamp parked the wheelchair next to the elevator. Caesar made no move to stop Miko when she scrambled off the couch and hobbled to her sister.

Mai's anger-filled eyes sought out Caesar. "I'm sorry, Master. We failed you."

"No, you didn't, Mai." He glared at his sister.

Selene ignored him. "Marcus, please call the motor pool and have one of the Normal drivers take the Osakas back to Los Angeles." The guard nodded, pressed the down button and moved to wheel Mai onto the elevator.

"Marcus."

The guard paused, a glint of fear in his eyes at Caesar's sharp tone.

"I'd make sure that the girls arrive in Los Angeles intact if I were you. Kensai will not take kindly to his granddaughters disappearing or suffering any additional harm en route."

Marcus's Adam's apple bobbed before he nodded at Caesar's veiled warning. A whoosh of air announced the arrival of the elevator. He pushed the wheelchair through the open doors, Mai limping along behind. The doors closed, and a hum indicated the car's steady descent to the lobby.

Bebe's hands dug into the leather of her bag. Damn, if only she and Caesar were leaving with the girls.

Selene turned to her brothers and Bebe, clasped her hands together, and grinned. "Let's get down to business, shall we?"

Chapter 29

Caesar willed his hands to relax at his sides. Any other time he'd play his opponent like a puppet. But this time . . .

This time he was definitely in deep horse manure. If anyone on this planet could read him, it would be his twin. The reek of steel and garlic coming off Ptolemy next to him clogged his sinuses. The harsh *chunk* of the elevator locking in place thirty floors below sent his stomach plummeting.

"We want to see the Sphere before we discuss anything," he said.

"We?" Selene raised an eyebrow, mocking him.

"You've been going out of your way to make enemies, my dear sister." He smiled, giving her a full view of his extended canines. "Smacking around Family members is not the way to win best coven mistress."

Eyes narrowed, she said, "I warned you that taking sides in the witches' dispute was not in your best interest."

"Especially since you'd already taken sides." He laughed outright at the sheer irony. "All of Mother's efforts to build a strong family, and you've ended up just as backstabbing as our aunts and uncles."

"At least I'm not getting dragged around by my dick like Father." She practically purred the words.

"Maybe so, but unlike you, I didn't turn into a power-hungry whore. And that was one of the nicer insults the good citizens of Rome threw at Mother."

In two quick strides, Selene crossed the carpet, but he didn't bother evading the slap. A slap that would have dislocated his jaw if he were Normal.

He didn't give her the satisfaction of rubbing away the sting. "What's the matter? A little too close for comfort?" He seized her wrist millimeters from his face as she tried to slap him again and gave her a vicious smile. "Sorry, sister dearest. You've had enough free shots."

"Stop it! Both of you!"

Ptolemy's shove took Caesar off guard, and he stumbled back against the couch where Miko had been moments ago. Apparently, he wasn't the only one surprised from the stunned look on Selene's face. Unable to catch her balance on the obscene modern shoes she wore, she landed on the cushions with a soft *whoof*.

His brother stood there glaring at both of them. Even though Ptolemy's face was flushed with anger, the color was even paler than during the flight here. "Give Bebe the Soul Sphere." When Selene paused for the barest instant, he snapped, "Now!"

Selene climbed to her feet taking a few healthy steps back from both Caesar and Ptolemy. An analytical expression appeared on her face. Did his baby brother realize he'd just made himself a target of Selene and her lackeys?

A sly smile replaced Selene's strategic look, and she waved at her eclectic. "Lucien."

From behind the wet bar counter, the witch produced the pulsing glass ball, brilliant purple swirling and shifting inside it. He practically slithered over to where Selene stood.

She took it from him and fixed Bebe with a nasty look. "I want to see the Book first."

Caesar glanced down at Bebe. Huge brown eyes stared up at him, filling with tears. What was the worse crime? Condemning Natasha to non-existence or unleashing whatever horror Selene twisted the research into?

It's your play, amora.

Giving him a slow nod, Bebe stood and crossed over to Selene. Reaching into her bag, she pulled out the Book. She paused, looking for all the world like the innocent child who had been orphaned years ago.

Then Bebe swung the Book with everything in her tiny frame at Selene's arm that held the sphere. The glass ball flew into the air.

Catch it, Caesar!

But he was already moving before Bebe's telepathic shout. Leaping over the couch, his fingers extended and wrapped around the surprisingly heated glass.

"Hand it over or so help me, I'll kill her." Selene clutched Bebe by the throat with one hand, holding her high in the air, the other hand held out to him. The Book of Shadows lay underneath Bebe's wildly swinging feet.

"You have what you want, Selene. Let her go."

"Not everything. Give the sphere back before your little girlfriend strangles to death."

"Let Bebe go," Ptolemy said, taking a step toward Selene. "We have the Book and the notes that were in Caesar's possession. There's no reason to kill her."

No. Horror rippled through Caesar. The translated notes he'd left at the San Francisco mansion.

A smirk twisted his sister's lips before she dropped Bebe, who lay gasping and choking on the floor.

If he'd known Ptolemy was in on this little conspiracy, he'd have changed the combination on his safe. He should have had Stan lock them back in the wardrobe's nymph hole. Or given them to Duncan for safekeeping. But it was far too late for any regret now. He stared daggers at his sister.

In that second, all Selene's schemes shone in her eyes.

And sorrow filled his soul. For Ptolemy's naiveté. For not listening to Duncan all these centuries. For finding an excuse for every stunt Selene pulled. For putting his beloved Bebe in danger.

He faced Ptolemy. "If you wanted control of the coven, why didn't you ask for it? You're my brother. I would have given it to you, dammit!"

A stunned look filled Ptolemy's features. "What in Hades are you talking about?"

"The attempted coup seventeen years ago." *Bebe, crawl away from Selene.*

Bebe, her face still blotchy, gave a slight shake of her head, tendrils of escaped hair making the most miniscule of motions. The pins that originally secured her knot gleamed dully from where they clutched the haphazard curls. And he wanted nothing more than smooth those wild strands out of her face and reassure her.

I don't need any reassurance.

The sound in his mind was more growl than words. Her right hand clenched in front of her, a slight red glow surrounding her tiny fist.

"Rogue vampires were responsible for those deaths." Uncertainty filled Ptolemy's voice.

Caesar's attention returned to his siblings. "I have to give credit where credit's due. You almost had me fooled on the jet." His lips curved into a slight smile, and he held up the sphere. "I'd applaud if I didn't have my hands full. Killing two birds with one stone. And if both birds manage to survive, then make sure the birds blame each other for the damage. Ingenious." He propped one hip casually against the back of the couch. "You learned well from Hitler, kids."

"We didn't have anything to do with that bastard!" Ptolemy's eyes glowed golden from his anger.

"Come on. The jig's up. He knows."

Selene's predatory smile sent a wave of rage down Caesar's spine. The bitch had him on the ropes, and yet, she still was trying to make Ptolemy look like one of the bad guys.

Other witch . . . dangerous . . . Bebe out . . .

The faint words whispered through Caesar's brain. Except the familiar voice didn't come from any person standing in the room, but seemed to come from the pulsing amethyst light in his hand. No. Was such a thing possible?

"I'm sorry you found out." Selene pulled the tiny pistol from her pocket, aiming at his heart. "Good-bye, Alexander."

Then she screamed in pain and fury as a fireball exploded in her face.

Chapter 30

The second the witchfire left her fingertips, Bebe clutched the Book of Shadows tight against her chest and launched herself away from Selene. Gaining her feet, she scrambled toward the elevator. She turned to see if Caesar followed her.

The world shattered in a knife-edged wind. Caesar and Ptolemy dived below the deadly hail, but the wind did nothing more to Selene than blow out the flames in her hair. Bebe's vision caught every detail before she thrust the Book in front of her, shouting the Latin spell to raise a shield. It wasn't enough to stop the wind though. Gale forces slammed the energy bubble into the elevator doors. Raw inertia smashed her against the inside of the shield.

But Blessed Goddess, the multitude of fragments that had been penthouse windows couldn't penetrate her shield. Shards slid around her and embedded themselves in the plasterboard or shattered against the steel elevator doors.

With an abrupt shift, the wind disappeared, and the protective bubble dropped to the floor, dragging her and the Book with it. Glass tinkled all around her as she landed hard, her left ankle bending at an unnatural angle until bone snapped. The shield failed with the wave of agony. Tears spilled down her cheeks, but she swallowed the cry of pain. She wasn't about to give the asshole the satisfaction.

A wild roar sounded, but not from the wind. Caesar charged over the couch and tackled Selene. A wrestling match ensued as Ptolemy joined the fray, each of the siblings trying to grab the woman's pistol.

The other witch didn't even lend his mistress a hand. His attention was focused solely on Bebe. With a sharp gesture and muttered words, he summoned a miniature whirlwind.

The dirt devil sucked up shards of glass and aimed straight for Bebe.

The idiot had to be totally loony-tunes. If that thing sliced her to shreds, it would set off the vamps' blood lust. They were already pissed off, and he was the only other meal in the penthouse.

She shoved the pain of the broken ankle into a mental compartment and focused. Calling up a wind as well, she used to it slide her and the book along the tile floor. If she could get behind the bar, she'd have a little protection and maybe find something to use as a weapon.

Seeing her tactic, Lucien dropped the tiny tornado and added his magick to hers. Her gentle slide became a headlong rush through the blown-out patio doors. She tried grabbing anything to stop the wild trip, but it was next to impossible with only one free hand, and she didn't dare drop the Book.

She managed to angle her path toward one of the heavy iron tables decorating the ledge. A cry ripped from her throat when she slammed back first into the wrought iron. Fire shot through her broken ankle. Eyes closed against the wind and glass shards, she reached blindly for a table leg and held on.

The wind cut off, and glass tinkled against the tile. She opened her eyes. A new fear rippled through her as she stared at thirty stories of empty space below her. In answer to her phobia, the building groaned as the decorative latticework and concrete of the balcony bent and pulled apart, leaving a person-sized hole next to her. Vertigo wove through her brain, making the tiny dots of light below spin.

"So, the little witch is afraid of heights." A maniacal gleam in his eyes, Lucien stood inside what was left of the patio's sliding glass doors. "Give me the book, and I won't shove you over the side." He held out his hand. The malevolent blackness of his aura stretched from the tips of his fingers toward her.

Every cell in her screamed to take the offer, even though deep down, she knew he'd shove her over the side as soon as the Book was in his tainted hands. He'd use her violent death to fuel his spell to destroy Caesar. With no one to stand against Lucien and Selene, the world would become a nightmare.

"I'm not asking again, child." Lucien flicked his wrist, and the concrete underneath the tile she lay on rumbled and bucked. Cracks appeared and spread around her.

A faint tickle came from the back of her mind. So ephemeral and familiar, and for a weird, wild moment that stretched on forever, Grandma's voice, clear as a bell, said, "He's given you the ammunition, darling. Use it."

And Bebe knew. Earth and air and blood.

Releasing her death grip on the precarious safety of the table leg, she snatched up the nearest piece of dirty glass. The shard sliced into her thumb, the pain and blood searing and coalescing with the energy she drew. Muttering the words, she threw her intent into the surrounding fragments, and as one, they shot through the air carried by a current of wind.

In that split second, only the slight widening of his eyes gave any indication that Lucien realized his fate. Glass shredded his flesh, the largest piece ripping through his throat. The words of his spell died stillborn as his jugular sprayed the white carpet with sticky red droplets.

For the second time, she had harmed someone using blood magick. A mixture of filth and sorrow swept through her.

Lucien's momentum brought him stumbling yet another step toward her before his heavy body collapsed on the broken tiles of the patio. Pitch boiled out of the corpse.

Oh, Goddess, she couldn't do this again!

The miasma twisted. A feeling akin to maggots on her skin rolled across her as it focused on her. Soul energy pooled and spread across the damaged floor, cutting off her escape.

A scream perched on the edge of her bruised throat.

Scarlet hooks poked up through cracked concrete and tile. They latched onto the dark ooze, pulled and stretched until it tore. Too much like her father's flesh under vampire teeth. A bass note rattled the lime chips and hunks of glass beneath her legs. The tone rose and rose until she clamped her hands over her ears.

What in the Thousand Names of the Goddess had Lucien bargained with? She managed to raise another shield, but it couldn't block all of the harmonics in that obscene noise. Her very bones thrummed with the note until she thought they would shatter too.

With a final burst of sound, the hooks dragged the soul fragments apart and disappeared back into the floor of the patio.

Her shield dropped. Blackness edged across her vision from the effort she expended. She needed to get back inside. Goddess only knew how much Lucien had weakened the structure, not to mention those things that had ripped his soul apart. But she couldn't summon the physical energy amidst the throbbing in both her head and her ankle.

"Bebe!"

Strong hands lifted her and carried her away from the traffic sounds and back inside the penthouse. Caesar's clean sandalwood scent engulfed her. Tears of relief coursed down her cheeks now. A hot smooth ball was shoved into her hands. A reassuring heat. A familiar mental warmth accompanied the physical sensation.

Grandma was safe. She slipped the sphere into her left pocket. Relief washed through her.

Until the soft snick of a safety being released made her eyes open.

With her clothes hanging in strips and her hair haloed like the snakes on Medusa's head, Selene glared at Bebe. "Get away from the bitch, Alexander." One of Ptolemy's Glocks shook in her two-handed grip. "Now!"

Somehow, the pistol was less scary than the bugged-out glowing eyes and fangs. Bebe's heart sank. No doubt, the vampiress would rather tear out her throat, and she had nothing in her to hold Selene off. Killing Lucien had drained the last of her energy.

Careful not to jar her ankle, Caesar lowered Bebe until she stood on her good leg. Ptolemy lay sprawled on the floor next to the couch. A black wooden handle stuck out of his chest.

"This is over, Selene." Caesar's voice was barely human. He shifted to cover Bebe's body with his.

Bebe clutched his jacket, more to keep upright than for comfort. It wouldn't matter if he took a bullet for her. Selene would just wait for the garlic to kick in, shove him out of the way and blow out Bebe's brains.

"All I want is her. Stand aside." Selene waved the gun, naked fury turning her patrician features ugly.

"You didn't have a problem with shooting Caesar earlier. What changed?" The fear and anger made Bebe's voice sound alien to her own ears. "Got your rocks off by killing one brother already?" Damn, they needed a plan.

Caesar must have heard her. *The charm you placed on my ring?*

It's our only shot. Keeping the book tucked under her right arm, she linked the fingers of her left hand with his, touching the gold and onyx. It pulsed with the magick she laid on it yesterday.

A wet cough from the floor grabbed everyone's attention.

"I wouldn't worry. Her aim sucks." Ptolemy used the coffee table to pull himself upright. A little gasp of pain escaped when he pulled the knife free from his chest. He tossed the offending steel aside and dragged himself to his feet. "F-Y-I, Selene. The heart's on the left side."

"I wasn't trying to kill you. I just needed to borrow your gun for a moment." Selene smiled, a vicious grin that reminded Bebe too much of the bastards that had killed her parents. "There's one witch I want dead."

A clap of thunder filled the penthouse. Caesar's coat and the Book were ripped from Bebe's grip. She found herself crashing to the floor and smothered underneath a broad chest. Fire burned in her ankle as the broken bones grated against each other. She swallowed the tears spurred by the scorched nerves. It didn't matter. Once Caesar's body dissolved, Selene would finish off Bebe, smash the sphere and still have the Book of Shadows. Bebe wanted to scream in frustration as well as pain. There wasn't a damn thing she could do to stop any of it.

An all-too-familiar scent of rotten meat filled her nostrils.

No. Tears brimmed under her closed lids. *Not like this.*

The weight holding her down disappeared, and she blinked before wiping slime from her face. She wanted the bitch to see her eyes when she died. But it was Ptolemy standing there beside her, a sad look on his face.

Except she could clearly see the light fixture through his head.

Oh, Goddess! The puddle she lay in was what was left of his body.

An animalistic roar of fury burst from Caesar's throat. He charged Selene, tearing the gun out of her hands. She fought back, but she was no match for his rage-fueled strength. Seconds later, he dragged his struggling twin to the crumbling balcony.

Bebe carefully placed the Book on an overstuffed chair. The she pulled herself to her feet, a difficult task between the goo-coated marble and her broken ankle. She carefully picked her way across the debris to the balcony where Caesar stood, dangling his sister over the edge and shouting at her in a language Bebe didn't recognize. Fear made her hesitate at the frame of what had been the sliding glass door. She wasn't sure what was worse, this side of Caesar or the thought of going out on a damaged balcony over three hundred feet above the ground.

A faint glimmer shone out of the corner of her eye. Oh Goddess! Despite the stars shining high above, pale blue spread across the eastern horizon. In the insanity, she'd lost track of time.

"Caesar!"

The man who turned to face her wasn't the man who'd kissed her so tenderly, who'd told her truths that were agonizing but that she needed to hear, who'd told her he loved her. The dark man who'd promised to take away her pain had disappeared. No, this man was just like the monsters from her childhood.

And she couldn't bear letting him take that fall into absolute blackness by killing his sister.

Releasing her death grip on the frame, she inched forward, as much from her own vertigo and pain than to prevent him from dropping Selene. "Caesar," she said, keeping her voice low and gentle. "You need to put her down."

He growled at her, actually growled, but he didn't let go of Selene. Probably a good thing since a thirty-story drop would smash even a vampire into sidewalk jelly.

Bebe sucked in what was left of her courage. *Caesar, please, you don't want to do this.*

"She-she—" He fought for the words, like he could barely remember English.

"I know what she did, but this isn't going bring anyone back." Her voice broke. She struggled to draw a breath. "Not my parents or Tiffany's. Not Grandma." Glancing back at the putrid remains slowly being absorbed by the carpet and the sad-faced phantom still standing next to them was all it took for the tears to cut loose. "And not Ptolemy." She choked back a sob. "Don't become as warped and twisted as she is. This isn't what your parents would have wanted." Holding out a hand, she whispered, "Please."

His panting slowed, and his head shifted back to look at the sister he held by the throat. A deep-throated growl emerged, and with a sudden violent throw, Selene went sailing through the air to slam into the beige concrete above the missing doors before landing with a sick thud on the patio.

Her head rose, blood pouring from her nose and a nasty cut in her scalp. Black hatred boiled from her aura.

Caesar's hands flexed, but he didn't move toward his sister. "I declare you rogue, Cleopatra Selene Antonius. You are a non-entity to the Augustine coven."

At Caesar's pronouncement, Selene's eyes widened. "I didn't mean to hurt Ptolemy. You know I didn't. She's the threat!" A shaking finger pointed at Bebe.

"You will have no comfort, no succor, no shelter from any member of the Vampire Nation," Caesar continued in a monotone, ignoring Selene's pleading tears. "Harm to any sentient will result in the death penalty."

You would choose her over—"

"You made your own choice when you tried to kill me. When you—" Emotion flared in his voice. His fists clenched at his sides. "When you killed our brother." An ugly smile spread across his features. "But you are my twin. We shared a womb, so I'm being far more generous than I should." He glanced at the brightening sky before turning back to Selene. "You have until sunrise to get out of my territory."

The vampiress scrambled to her feet. Naked loathing twisted her sharp features. "You have no idea—"

"Go to New York. Maybe Virginia will be more generous to you than me."

Selene's face blanched at his taunt. Limping awkwardly on a broken stiletto, she backed up until she was inside the penthouse. Keeping her eyes fixed on Caesar, she inched toward the slime that had been Ptolemy.

"And don't even think about reaching for one of those guns in there, sister dear. You won't survive."

She stiffened for the barest second before she dashed for the stairwell door and disappeared.

"Caesar?" Bebe whispered.

His attention returned to her from somewhere else. She wasn't sure she wanted to know where. A small quiver of relief spread through her aching body when his fangs began to recede.

"You need to get inside," she said, but he didn't seem to hear her. "Now, Caesar. Is there a secure room further inside?"

He nodded, a weary motion, and held out his hand. When she took it, a small sigh escaped his lips. He swung her into his arms and entered the trashed penthouse. Skirting the broken furniture, smashed glass and the two sets of remains in the living room, he carried her down a dark hallway and shut them in a bedroom as the first rays of sun peeked over the mountains.

Caesar set her gently on the bed and wrapped his arms around her. She didn't resist his soul-searing kiss. At least, she didn't until he hit a tiny cut on her bottom lip, and she jumped at the new pain.

"I'm sorry, *amora*," he said and pulled back a few inches. "We need to get you a doc—"

Bebe let out a little yelp of surprise. Phantom Ptolemy peered over Caesar's shoulder, rolling his transparent eyes and making a gagging motion with his index finger.

"What?" Caesar's head whipped so fast to look behind him it was wonder he didn't give himself a kink in his neck. "What's wrong?"

"It's okay. I—" She bit down on her lip, and fresh pain reminded her of the cut. How the hell did she broach the subject of his brother with Caesar?

Ptolemy gave her pleading look. He may have unfinished business with Caesar, but after the last several hours, she sure didn't have the strength to deal with a permitted possession. At least, Ptolemy wasn't trying to force his way into her body, and she sighed at that small grace.

The glass in her pocket warmed to a near uncomfortable temperature. Something else she needed to deal with. The heat faded and flared again. Yes, she had the strength to complete this one small act.

She met Caesar's concerned gaze. "There's a couple of things we need to take care of."

His eyes shifted to take in the amethyst sphere she pulled out, and he nodded as he rose. "Of course. I'll give you your privacy."

She laid a hand on his arm, stopping him from retreating from the room. "I need you here. I want—" She swallowed hard. What she was about to ask him would require the most intimate contact. When they were done, he'd know her heart and soul, the inner face she'd never shown anyone. "There's something you need to see."

His eyes narrowed. "What's going on, Bebe?"

"Nothing bad," she said, more to reassure herself than him, and gestured with the sphere. "We need to say our good-byes, and by linking with me, you'll be able to See."

She wouldn't bother casting a circle. It wouldn't be needed in this case. Instead, she patted the bed next to her. Confusion filled his expression, but he climbed carefully next to her on the bed, trying not to jar her ankle.

Reaching out with her senses, she double-checked that Lucien was in fact gone. Phantom Ptolemy must have understood what she was doing because he nodded confirmation that it was just the three of them. The glass gave a little pulse of heat. Okay, four of them.

Reaching for Caesar's hand with her own, she twined her fingers with his until palms met. The touch sent a tremor of heat through her that had nothing to do with the magickal energy she summoned. Then she shifted to her Sight and dropped her shields.

All of them.

The effect amazed and stunned her. It was like looking through two different sets of eyes at the same time. She *was* looking through two perspectives at once. And the loving cocoon she'd felt in the circle at Grandma's mansion enveloped and surrounded her. Hints of Caesar's fury at Selene's betrayal and his grief over Ptolemy swirled through her emotions, but the majority of his feelings held relief that she was safe and alive.

"Ptolemy?" he whispered, and his jolt of surprise rippled through her.

It's all right, Caesar. I wanted . . . I needed to say I'm sorry. So sorry. For everything. I shouldn't have listened to Selene. Ptolemy's voice held an odd dissonance.

Caesar shot her a worried glance, and she gave him a reassuring squeeze. He turned back to his brother. "You've got nothing to apologize for. You saved Bebe. I—"

The words clogged her throat as if they were her own, not Caesar's. Tears trickled down her cheeks at the double portion of pain and regret.

Ptolemy's gaze shifted down. *I know I don't have any right to ask this . . .*

Caesar coughed softly. "Y-you can ask me anything."

Keep an eye on Tiffany. She— Ptolemy raised his head to meet his brother's eyes, a fierce determination in his expression. *She'll try to go after Selene once she knows the truth. I don't want anything to happen to the kid.*

A wry smile curved Caesar's lips. "I'll try. I can't guarantee anything."

Matching amusement twisted the ghost's visage. *That's the reason I didn't make you swear by the Styx.*

Another pulse of heat warmed Bebe's palm, reminding her of her own promise. Raising the Soul Sphere to eye level, she whispered the words to dissolve the glass. The freed energy shifted, misted and finally coalesced into a familiar form. Wrinkles gone and standing straighter than Bebe had ever seen, a much younger version of Grandma gazed down at her and smiled. It was a broad, genuine smile, the kind she hadn't seen her grandmother wear in over seventeen years.

I knew you could do it, my baby. And I'm sorry too. Please understand. I wanted to protect you. I never meant to hurt you.

Bebe nodded, tears clogging her throat again, but this time her own.

A brilliant white light appeared behind the two ghosts, spilling and flooding everyone with a nearly tangible glow. Caesar had to turn his head away, and even Bebe had to raise her left hand to shield her eyes. Grandma glanced over her shoulder, then back at Bebe. The soft flutter of wings filled the bedroom.

We have to go. I love you.

The strange resonance of the words coming from both ghosts at the same time made Bebe shiver. Grandma blew her a kiss and disappeared into the light. Ptolemy turned to follow, but he paused to look back at his brother.

Don't let her go.

Then he too was gone. A flash and almost audible snap closed the doorway between the living and the dead.

Tears trickled down Caesar's face. He pulled her into his lap and kissed her, a gentle loving kiss. "Thank you," he murmured against her hair.

And they sat like that for a very long time.

<h1 style="text-align:center">Chapter 31</h1>

Two days later, Bebe hung up the phone and cradled her head in her arms on top of the writing desk. If she weren't so damned exhausted, she'd collect the energy to call room service for some dinner. Her rumbling stomach reminded her that she'd missed lunch hours ago. Adding its own complaint, her ankle throbbed in time to her pulse.

"That bad?"

She lifted her head to find Caesar standing before her, a glass of water and her bottle of painkillers in his outstretched hands. "Any food with that?"

He grinned. "Crabcakes are on their way up. The vegetable of the day was asparagus, but I can call for something else for you."

"That sounds like heaven to me," she said before she took the bottle of pills and popped a couple into her mouth. Then she took the glass from his proffered hand. The simple brush of his skin shot a wave of heat straight to her pelvis. Choosing to ignore it, she sipped the water, swallowed the meds and leaned back in the executive chair he'd appropriated for her temporary "office" in a spare bedroom of the Karnak penthouse.

"To answer your original question, no. Alice and I shoved our compromise solution down the Elders' collective throats. It's pretty sad when we're being the reasonable ones."

He tried to hide his chuckle. The scent of wine mixed with the metallic tang of blood meant he'd had his dinner already. "Beatrice wasn't happy about your abdication," he said.

A sigh escaped her lips. "In her mind, she lost face backing what to her was the losing side." She shook her head in disbelief. "Even though I'm Alice's named heir until her first child is born. Alice is going to try to amend the coven by-laws to switch to American-style elections instead of European succession, but . . ." From the pensive look on Caesar's face, he doubted her cousin's success as much as Bebe did. Alice's political acumen left something to be desired. Especially after she called Miranda Doucette a dried-up hag during one discussion/argument.

Bebe rubbed her temple at the dull pain that had plagued her the last several hours. Somehow, the headache overshadowed the rest of the bruises, breaks and other assorted damage to her body. The hotel's Normal doctor had offered to give her a Vicodin prescription, but she needed her wits a little sharper in order to deal with the White Rose mess. Now, she almost wished she'd taken him up on the offer.

"At least, our tentative truce is holding now that she's realized just how much William manipulated her. In the meantime, I'll pray to the Goddess every day that Alice doesn't get herself killed before she pops out a kid."

A frown creased Caesar's face. "You don't think Pierre and Miranda flushed out all of William's co-conspirators?"

Sitting face level with the zipper on his pants was not helping her concentration one bit. Her thoughts keep turning in a direction they shouldn't be going. One that involved the bed less than a yard away. She could seduce Caesar. That would accomplish her plan. Hell, it'd be the fastest way to heal her broken ankle too.

No, she wouldn't stoop to those tactics. The poor man had been yanked around enough by his own family the last few years. She couldn't do that to him.

The chair squeaked when she shoved away from the desk and stood. "I just don't know." She shook her head as Caesar handed her the crutches. "He was more than willing to spill his guts in return for having his magick bound and making a conventional plea bargain with the D.A." A smirk spread across her lips. "Given his fate if left in the hands of the coven that was the smart road for him to take. The Elders questioned him under a truth spell before they turned him over to the police, but there's the possibility Lucien altered his memory."

Caesar raked a hand through his dark hair, leaving the short strands standing on end. "Given Selene's alterations to the Karnak's books, I wouldn't be surprised if she had Lucien do so."

"Any idea where the money went?" She took another sip of water, just a small one to calm her nerves. The problems they discussed seemed insignificant compared to what she wanted to propose to him. She didn't want him to think her idea was drug-induced bullshit.

Propose. What a funny way to put it, considering that was what she would be doing. Another nervous gulp of water caught in her throat and resulted in a major choking fit.

Cool fingers plucked the glass from her, and then she was being patted on the back like she was an infant. Goddess, was that what he thought of her? A baby that needed to be cared for? He'd been caring for her enough the last few days.

"Are you all right?"

"Went down the wrong pipe," she muttered before she gave a final racking cough and wiped her eyes. "What were you saying about the money?"

"Duncan tracked it as far as a series of transfers made to a private account in the Caymans." An exasperated huff indicated his annoyance. "After that, it disappears." Caesar's handsome features grew pensive. "If it were just the couple of million, I wouldn't be worried, but . . ."

Except it wasn't just the Karnak Selene had stolen from. His people found altered records going back at least a century. The current estimates of the siphoned funds he'd received from his various businesses were closer to the mid-ten digits. A rogue vampire with a fortune at her disposal could wreak havoc.

And nearly every vampire loyal to Selene had disappeared when she did. The ones who couldn't escape committed suicide before they could be questioned.

Without another thought, Bebe propped the crutches against the desk, wrapped her arms around Caesar's waist and hugged him. "You did the right thing by letting her go. It would have destroyed your soul to have killed her."

Strong arms held her in turn, and he nuzzled her hair. "I don't know what I would have done without you the last couple of days."

The passionate heat emanating from his psyche erased any doubts she had what she wanted most in the world. She knew who she wanted and where she wanted to be. Her only fear was his reaction.

Pulling back a fraction, she gazed up at him and cleared her throat. "I've been thinking about what you asked." The words clogged in her throat, and she drew a deep breath. "About continuing Grandma's research."

A hopeful light flared in his hazel eyes. "And?"

"I'm worried about not completing it before I die." She held up a hand when he opened his mouth. "Please let me finish before you say anything else. The learning curve I'm facing is bad enough, and even if I trained someone else, there're so many other things that could happen. But I've been doing some research myself and—"

Her body trilled in anticipation. This was it.

"I want you to Turn me."

Caesar jerked away from her embrace so fast she had to grab the desk edge to keep her balance. Anger and disbelief mingled on his face. "You want me to what!"

Wincing at the pain in her eardrums, she held out her hands. "Listen to me. Caesar, please. I've been doing some research, and I believe there's a common reason that some of the hybrids survive—"

"No! I won't. Don't even ask me such a thing." He whirled and stalked from the bedroom.

"Wait! Caesar!" Bebe cursed her broken ankle and her emotional ineptitude. Could she have handled this conversation any worse? "I know what I'm getting into." Snatching the crutches, she hobbled after him.

She caught up to him in the living room when he pivoted so fast she crashed into his chest. Grabbing her by the arms, he lifted her in the air. The crutches dropped and her feet dangled. Glowing neon yellow eyes bore into her, his pupils shot with blood red.

"You have no clue of what you are asking of me." His words were low, dangerous, full of his raw masculine power.

And she wasn't afraid. Despite his appearance, despite her past, despite everyone else's schemes and lies. She drew a deep breath, and said, "Yes, I do know what I'm asking. Please put me down."

He set her down as if she were a porcelain doll. Then he backed away from her, staring at her like she'd grown a second head. "You were lucky that night I was shot. If—" He shook his head fiercely. "And you're injured now. No, I can't—"

Bebe took a tentative hop toward him, reaching out mentally as well but his shields were tight. "Caesar, listen to me. I know—"

"No, you don't!" His howl still echoed in the air when vampire speed made him seem to disappear in thin air.

"—I love you," she finished to the slamming stairwell door.

Chapter 32

It was close to midnight before the door to the rooftop garden creaked open. Bebe's scent reached Caesar long before she did. The thump-slap of the crutches and her one slipper made a sobering counterpoint to the shouts and laughter of the holiday revelers on the Strip. He stood at the ledge surrounding the garden and stared at the lights of the city. He couldn't face her, not sure of what stopped him. Pain? Guilt? Love?

Or a combination of all three?

"Watching the skies for Santa Claus?"

That made him turn around. "I beg your pardon?"

Neon lights from thirty-one stories below cast a soft light on her face. "Santa Claus? St. Nicholas? Father Christmas? The fat guy in the red suit with flying reindeer?" A sad, sweet smile spread across her face. "You do realize it's Christmas Eve, don't you?"

Christmas Eve. That meant in a span of minutes it would be the twenty-fifth of December. His and Selene's birthday. And for the first time he could remember, there would be no family celebration. No phone call to Selene if they couldn't get together. Not even wisecracks from Ptolemy about their age.

The loss ached deep inside of him. How could their relationship have shattered so thoroughly?

Because it had been stressed over his failure to protect Ptolemy when they were barely more than children. Because it had been cracked for centuries when he refused to see Selene for the conniving bitch that she was. Because it had been fucked up from the beginning when their mother had seduced two married Roman generals in the desperate hope of retaining Egypt's independence.

And what did he have to show for it? He couldn't love the woman in front of him, not the way she deserved.

"So you're still not going to talk to me?"

He raised a quizzical eyebrow at Bebe's question until her original query rushed back to the forefront of his thoughts. "I'm sorry. I was just surprised you celebrate the holiday." For some reason, it hadn't dawned on him that she would. Good to know Nikolai had some influence on her upbringing before he and Natasha divorced.

She shrugged, a slight gesture, before pulling her jacket tighter against the cold desert air. "My family's just as mixed as yours when it comes to religions." Reaching for her throat, she tugged the silver chain, all that was left of Tiffany's holiday gift to her, and said nothing else as they both turned to stare at the cityscape.

Family. Maybe that's what his strange little household was. He'd never before considered that concept. Alex was nearly as annoying as his nephew, Anthony. Anne had become the daughter he'd never sired. Even Phillippa was closer to him than Selene ever truly was. And Duncan reminded him so much of his older brother, Caesarion. So serious, so intense, so capable.

He didn't force any of them to live in the Brentwood mansion, even though everyone had their own room for those times they spent the day there. They all had their own houses, apartments or condos. Well, except Tiffany, but he had no doubt she'd find her own place as soon as she graduated. And she'd dropped enough hints that she wanted to be an enforcer, despite Duncan's well-intentioned objections.

Some coven masters were far more controlling than he was, but he'd viewed the room arrangement as convenient. The younger vampires didn't drive him crazy and vice versa. In fact, he wasn't that demanding of any of the vampires in his territory. As long as they registered their presence, paid their taxes for group services like the blood banks and didn't kill anyone, he let them do as they wished.

Sure, he employed his household staff and enforcers, but that didn't account for the little traditions like their winter holiday present exchange, celebrating birthdays and the personal joking. Even Tiffany's repeated attempts to egg Ptolemy—

A hard lump rose in his throat at the thought of his brother. Hades, he couldn't even bury Ptolemy's remains properly, no mummification, not even a coin for Charon under the tongue. He'd failed Ptolemy so many times before, but this time sat like ash in his mouth.

Even worse, he'd taken his anger at himself out on Bebe. Thank the gods he hadn't harmed her. A soul as beautiful as hers didn't deserve his crap. What she deserved were children, a real family, a life without constant turmoil. So much more than he could offer her. It had been millennia since he'd felt this powerless.

He had to clear his throat twice before he could speak. "I apologize for handling you so roughly. You didn't deserve such ill treatment."

She hobbled closer to him, quiet and sure. Her tiny, soft hand reached up and cupped his cheek, her thumb stroking as soft as a butterfly. "There's something you need to get through you thick skull, Caesar Augustine. I love you, and you're not getting rid of me so easily." A gentle smile replaced her somber expression. "No matter how far you run, I can still limp after you. Or were you planning to break my other ankle to get away?"

A few days ago, his heart would have leapt at her words, but now? Now, he couldn't be a selfish bastard, no matter how much it broke both of their hearts. He took her petite hand from his face and held it in both of his. "Listen to me, *amora*. I will not condemn you to my fate."

She sucked in a deep breath. "Caesar, I didn't propose this lightly. Every hybrid who has survived and remained sane, did so because they had a vampire mate helping them through the Turn. I'd survive because I want this. I want to be with the man I love. Knowing you would be with me the entire time—"

"And we'd break every law of the International Council."

"If we petition the Vampire National Congress for my Turning, they'd be required to say no. If we do it, then tell them . . ."

Hades, he was tempted to go along with her insane plan, but there were too many other factors, too many things that could go wrong, too many enemies against them. He shook his head. "No, we'd have the witches crawling down our throats as well."

She smiled, a look so wicked and enticing at the same time, he wanted her right there on the roof. Pulling her hand free, she ran her fingers down his chest. His gut clenched in anticipation when those tempting digits paused at his waist.

"The only one who can officially object would be the White Rose High Priestess, and she's already given her *unofficial* approval," she said.

A snort of derision escaped him. He didn't know what was worse—Bebe's naiveté or Alice's blatancy. "Of course, she'd approve. Has it occurred to you it's the most convenient way for her to get rid of you?"

She huffed, grabbed her right crutch and whacked him on the shins. "Has it occurred to you that she was in that link with us back in San Francisco? She Saw how we both felt about each other. You wanted a declaration from me. Well, here it is, buster." Dropping both crutches, she flung herself at him. He caught her before she toppled them both into the raised flowerbed next to them.

Her broad grin shone with its own light. "I love you, and I'm sure as hell not leaving you."

He pulled her closer until her body was snug against his, her heat radiating through him. He returned her embrace, inhaled her sweet scent and wanted the night to never end. Wanted what she offered. Wanted her warmth. Her laughter. Gods above, he wanted her.

Guilt poured through him. No. He'd already caused the deaths of his mother and Ptolemy. If anything went wrong, if Bebe came out of the Turn dead, or worse psychotic, he'd be required to kill her. And he'd never forgive himself.

"No." He tried to let go, needed to walk away, but his limbs refused to obey him.

Her body tilted slightly until her dark eyes met his. "Talk to me. Tell me what it's like, so I know what to expect."

A lot of things blurred together after two thousand plus years of living, but that gods-awful nightmare remained crystal clear. "What happened to us—" Shifting his attention to the neon-lit skyline, he sucked in a lungful of crisp air before he could face her again. "I never want to hurt you, Bebe, but you need to understand something. Ptolemy and I weren't supposed to be Turned. They came for us with the intent to kill, but then that was common practice in Rome. Assassinate your enemies before they get you. How much do you know about the early Roman empire?"

"A little." She shrugged, and again the slight smile appeared. "I've already figured out you weren't on the good side of one of the emperors."

Her wry tone elicited a chuckle. "Actually, that would be my parents. My misfortune was worse. I got on the wrong side of Father's ex-wife, who happened to be the sister of an emperor." Soberness hit him. "My parents were Marcus Antonius and Cleopatra VII of Egypt."

Shock filled her features, and she leaned away from him to examine his face. He could practically see the cogs turning in her head.

"Mark Antony and Cleopatra? The Antony and Cleopatra?"

He nodded.

She covered her mouth for an instant to get her obvious humor under control. "Oh, you poor thing."

He rolled his eyes. "See? This is why I don't tell people."

She laughed outright this time. Waving a hand, she said, "No, no. I'm sorry. It's just—" Another spate of laughter shook her. "You're the only one I've met who has more family issues than me."

"Thanks. That makes me feel much better." But no real acrimony filled his words.

Without a word, Bebe took his hands in hers and pointed over to a bench. He swung her into his arms. Already petite, she weighed practically nothing since she barely had a chance to eat over the last couple of weeks. Once at the bench, he settled her gently on his lap, and they huddled on the sun-weathered wood. Soft quiet filled the private garden, blocking out the cheers and shouts from the streets below. The warm cocoon of her spirit filled him as he continued.

"We were taken to Rome after our parents' deaths, and Octavian gave us to his sister to raise as proper Roman citizens. Octavia had been humiliated by Father and—" He suppressed a shudder at the memories. "—took her displeasure out on us. No physical marks on Selene, of course, since she could be used for marital alliances. But that didn't stop Octavia from—" He clenched his hands at the old pain. "She used little things against Ptolemy and me. Barely enough food, no blankets or heat in the winter. Working us like servants hoping we'd get sick and die. She was sorely disappointed when we didn't comply."

Bebe said nothing, merely rested her head on his shoulder. The spicy ginger of her hair filled his nostrils, and the heat of her arms wrapped around his neck warmed his soul. He didn't think he'd be able to get the words out if she looked at him.

"After three years at her tender mercies, Juba of Numidia asked for Selene's hand. One of Octavian's stipulations was that Juba take responsibility for Ptolemy and me, keep us contained. As far as the great Caesar Augustus was concerned, that ended the matter." He snorted at the memory. "You'd think Octavia would be happy not having to look at us, not having everything rubbed in her face. But sending us across the Mediterranean didn't appease her.

"There was a lot of unrest in Numidia. Octavian had raised Juba, so the locals resented the 'Romanization' of their king. When the typical attempts at poisoning us failed, she sent vampires. It was easy for assassins to slip into the palace."

Slim fingers stroked his hair in comfort. He didn't deserve it, but Gods above, it felt good.

"They found Ptolemy first. I'd borrowed his saddle while mine was being repaired. I stumbled on the attack when I went to his room to return it. I threw the saddle at them and shouted for the guards, but before I could draw my knife . . ." He closed his eyes as the past and the present blurred together. "The odd thing was how little blood there was." Blinking away the wetness collecting in his eyes, he drew a deep breath.

"Did you even know what was happening to you?" Bebe raised her head to look him in the eye.

He shook his head. "They had nearly drained Ptolemy. He was already slipping into the Turn coma by the time the guards arrived, not that we knew what was happening. We didn't think he'd live through the night. As far as we knew I just had a couple of odd bites on my forearm."

Old guilt mixed with new and spilled out of him in a bitter torrent. "I failed to protect him that night. Just like I failed three nights ago. Just like I always fail everyone I care about."

"You can't blame yourself for Selene's actions. She's a big girl. Big enough to make her own choices. She's the one who shot Ptolemy, not you."

Hades, how did he make Bebe understand? "I can't do this to you! I can't be responsible for—" The words caught in his throat, ancient pain and new grief choking him.

Understanding dawned in her eyes. "Who was she?"

Bebe needed to know the truth. Maybe then, she'd walk away from him. So what if she'd take his heart with her? Gods knew he deserved having it ripped out.

"My mother," he whispered. Silence weighed down the night. The winds paused, and the stars held their breath, waiting as he did for her reaction. There was a reason the Kindly Ones kept a special place in Tartarus for those who murdered their mothers.

But confusion twisted her brows. "Did you try to Turn her?"

He shook his head.

"But how—"

"I'm the one who smuggled the asp to her."

"Oh."

He found himself holding his breath along with the rest of the universe. She leaned her head against his shoulder, and her arms wrapped around his neck again.

Tears were in her voice when she spoke. "She had no right to ask that of you."

"I would have done anything she wanted." Bittersweet love filled him. "You simply didn't question her orders."

"But you were what? Nine? Ten?" Anger tinged her voice. "You don't ask a child to help you commit suicide."

"She didn't ask me that," he said softly.

Bebe sat up straight, eyes blazing when she met his gaze. "Did you know what she planned?"

"No, but—"

"Then quit blaming yourself because she conned you into helping *her*. It wasn't your fault."

Somehow, Bebe's quiet, furious defense of him sent a wave of comfort through him, but it didn't change things between them.

The butterfly touch of her thoughts lit his mind. *Yes, it does change things.*

Gods help him, she was stubborn. He stared at her. "How?"

"I'm asking you straight out to Turn me. No tricks. No manipulation. I love you, and I want to be with you."

Her face was so earnest he wanted to believe her.

Then read me. Defiance flared in her eyes, daring him to Look.

With a tentative mental probe, he reached for her. And Saw blinding radiance. Love, nearly a tangible thing, spilled out of her. No shields blocked him. Warm yellows and golds caressed him, washed through him. This was Bebe's soul at its purest, and it made him want to weep. He pulled her close and hugged her.

"Now tell me what to expect," she said, her voice muffled by his chest.

He sighed. "You're not going to let this go, are you?"

"Nope." A slight giggle followed the word. "You should know by now I'm just as stubborn as Grandma." She raised her head from his shoulder. "And if you don't do it, I'll find someone else who will."

He didn't have any doubt she'd do exactly that. Another wouldn't have the incentive to make sure she survived the Turn. Staring up at the few stars that pierced the light pollution brought him no alternatives. Finally, he looked at her and said, "All right. We'll do it your way. But if this goes wrong and you haunt me, so help me, I *will* have your ass exorcised."

A wide, triumphant grin spread across her face. "I understand."

He shook his head, wondering what the hell they were both thinking. He kept the explanation clinical. There was no fucking way he'd romanticize it. "You're looking at fever and vomiting within the first thirty-six hours of exposure to the virus, followed by coma. Onset of coma depends on the initial blood loss and the location of the contamination. The length of the coma depends on the age and general health of the person as well as the amount of blood lost. Seventy-two hours is the average."

He paused, making sure he had her attention. "It hurts Bebe. You may be in a coma, but you're going to remember the pain. Selene—" His throat closed at the mention of his sister, but he forced the words past. "Selene compared it to giving birth to all three of her children at the same time."

Bebe gave a small, dry laugh. "Well, I've never been pregnant so I couldn't say."

"You will *never* be able to have children if we do this, *amora*."

She sobered and seemed to give it some thought before she shrugged. "We could always adopt." Another grin lit up her face. "Or we could ask Tiffany to be a surrogate." The grin flipped to a frown. "Wait. Bad idea. There's a chance the kid would be exactly like her."

That statement ripped a belly laugh from him, only to be replaced by worry and fear for Bebe's life.

"Caesar, I can handle this. Honest. And you'll be here with me every step of the way." But a tiny hint of fear flickered in her eyes.

"We don't have to do this," he repeated.

"It's just . . . I mean, when you were bit—" She licked her lips. "D-did the bites hurt?"

He couldn't help smiling at the trepidation in her voice. "I don't *have* to bite you, you know."

"I know." She swallowed hard before returning his smile. "I was kind of hoping to do it the other way."

He laughed. He couldn't help it. No one had ever made him so angry and so happy all at the same time the way Bebe could. And it drove away the morbid melancholy of the past. "Are you trying to seduce me, Dr. Zachary?"

A scowl darkened her lovely face. "I know I suck at it. You don't have to rub it in." She squirmed in his lap, struggling to escape his hold.

He swallowed a groan at the effect of her warm, round ass on his body, but he wasn't about to let her go hopping across the roof and break her other ankle. Actually, she didn't seem to be fighting him as hard as she could have. She finally gave up though, probably because she realized the effect her movement had on his cock, which very obviously poked her hip. She pursed her lips and huffed a curl out of her eyes before she glared at him.

"This is not fair. If you're not going to succumb to my feminine wiles, at least let me make a dignified exit."

His right eyebrow rose of its own accord. "Explain to me how a slipper and a cast equate to dignity?"

She stuck her tongue out at him in response.

"I can think of a better use for that tongue."

Her winsome smile lit her face. "So can I."

The groan that rolled from his throat was fully audible this time. He buried his nose in her hair. "You have no idea how I want you, *amora*."

Wriggling her hips, she giggled. "I have a pretty good idea."

"Are you absolutely sure? Once we do this, there's no going back," he whispered into her hair.

A deep sigh shuddered through her body. "I'm tired, Caesar. Tired of being alone." Her voice hinted of tears. "And so are you. We have some-thing good here. Why do you want to throw it away on maybes and what-ifs?"

A chuckle rolled through his chest. "Have you been talking to Dun-can?"

"No. Why?"

"He suggested that I use the same reasoning on you."

"Really?"

The incredulous note her voice made him look at her. "Why are you so surprised?"

A wry smile twisted her lips. "Guess I never pictured him as a roman-tic. Smart man though. Maybe you should listen to him."

Amora, you need to think carefully about this. Right now, there is no cure. There's no guarantee you will be able to find one. You will never feel the sun on your face, never taste another morsel of food—

So I have to give Tiffany all my silver jewelry. And I was never a big fan of garlic anyway.

What happens when you accidentally immolate yourself with one of your own fireballs?

She laughed, a joyous sound in the glittering night. *I will trust you to have fire extinguishers in every room.*

He didn't know what else to say to convince her this was a very bad idea. He couldn't convince himself that it was a very bad idea anymore. It wasn't just the thought of making love to her every night for an eternity. She was right. He wanted someone to love, wanted someone to call his own, and wanted that someone to be Bebe and no one else.

A sigh whispered past her parted lips as she stared at him. Not intruding on his thoughts, though the awareness of her hovered on the edge of his mind, but giving him the space to make that commitment.

He couldn't resist any longer. His lips sought hers of their own accord. His tongue swept hers, peaches and ginger invaded every breath he took, and his arms pulled her tighter against his chest. The kiss was exquisite, not full of want, not demanding, but a promise.

Her hands and mouth urged him on, but he broke the contact and simply watched her face. Gold, red and blue neon reflected from her pale skin. A slow smile spread across her dimpled cheeks, and she nodded once. No words, verbal or otherwise, passed between them. Caesar stood, Bebe's petite frame cradled in his arms, and he headed for the staircase.

He paused, looking from the narrow passageway to her. "How'd you get up the stairs with the crutches?"

Brown eyes sparkled as she laughed. "I defied gravity."

Groaning from her bad joke, he treaded down the stairs, careful of the cast on her ankle.

Bebe had been in Caesar's bedroom twice in the past few days since coming to the Karnak, but this time the golds and browns that decorated the room shimmered and moved as if alive. Depositing her gently on the king-sized bed, he moved with a contained grace while he lit the candles stationed on various surfaces.

Excitement and fear warred along her nerves. He'd given plenty of chances for her to change her mind, to back out of this. No, she wanted him, accepted what the Turn would do to her, even made peace with the pain and problems that would come with their defiance of the International Council's laws. Then her real worry hit her.

It'd been an awfully long time since she'd had sex. And he had over two thousand years of experience.

Goddess, please don't let him be disappointed.

"*Amora.*" He sat next to where she sat propped on the gold and chocolate pillows. "Are you sure—"

"Yes," she snapped. And immediately regretted her tone, though his arrogant smirk mitigated her guilt. "I'm sorry, but you're ruining the mood when you keep asking."

His dark eyebrow cocked upward. "Gods forbid I should ruin a lady's mood."

A heartfelt sigh escaped her lips. She laid two fingers on his soft lips. "No more words."

He complied by wrapping his lips around her fingers, tongue stroking the pads. The effect bypassed her brain and flooded her pelvis. A soft gasp followed as his mouth released the fingers, kissing and stroking its way across her palm.

Ripples of pleasure swept through her at the slight scrape of a fang on her wrist's pulse, the hint of danger adding to the tension in her body. Even with lids hooded, his eyes shone gold when he left her wrist and looked at her. Grasping the clip holding her hair up, he tugged it loose. Curls fell, tickling her cheeks, until he brushed the wayward strands back. He cupped her face, his lips meeting hers for a soul-searing kiss.

Shields gone, their desire mixed and danced. Mental and physical touch melted together until Bebe wasn't sure where she stopped and he began. His lips found her earlobe, nibbling and sucking along her neck. Her back arched of its own accord, and she couldn't get enough sensation.

His cool flesh was the only thing that contained the fire threatening to destroy her. When that touch disappeared, a whimper rose in her throat. In a flurry of motion, her sweater and bra vanished.

Except he didn't touch her. He sat there, looking at her. Not the unnatural predatory stillness of a vampire though. His jaw muscles clenched and shifted under his skin, but he made no move toward her.

"Caesar? What's wrong?"

A slight smile creased his face. *Nothing. You're just so beautiful. I want to remember you like this.* His aura flared brilliant scarlet. He wasn't lying.

A mixture of embarrassment and pleasure burned her skin at his words. No one she'd been with had ever called her beautiful. For the first time in her life, she felt truly desired and desirable.

Not breaking eye contact, his head dipped and lips grasped a hardened nipple. She nearly came from his rough tongue brushing the sensitized skin. Her eyes closed as she luxuriated in the heady feelings.

Cool air hit damp skin, raising gooseflesh, and her eyes popped open. Easing sweatpants and panties over her hips, he tugged the knit and lace down her legs and gently stretched the fabric around her cast before tossing the clothing over his shoulder.

She reached for his face, but he caught her hands and pressed them to the comforter. "No, *amora*, this is my time."

He gently pushed her legs apart. She sucked in a harsh breath, feeling more exposed than she'd ever had. Rough fingers stroked the soft flesh of her inner thigh. Gold cotton and stuffing bunched in her fists as she resisted the urge to touch him. Lying down between her legs, he gave a tentative lick across her hot, wet center. A sob ripped from her throat at the electricity that fried her nerves.

A soft chuckle hummed across her clit before he began kissing and sucking her in earnest. His want wrapped around her in a soft cocoon of love. Desire flew back and forth between them.

Her eyes closed again as she sank into the sensations, mind and body. Her hips matched his rhythm, and the pressure and heat built until it had nowhere else to go. She screamed while her body shuddered and convulsed under his touch.

She blinked away the tears that had collected under her lids. By the time, her vision cleared and her senses returned, he'd shed his clothes. Muscles, defined but not overdone, shifted under the candlelight as he climbed into the bed and lay beside her, pulling her close. He kissed her, a delicate, sensual exploration that left her breathless. She clung to his neck for a moment, trying to collect her scattered thoughts.

Last chance, amora. *I won't be able to hold back this time.*

Laughing softly, she reached down and stroked him in answer. His groan rumbled against her ear. The sound sent a surge of wickedness through her. Kneeling proved awkward with the cast, so she wiggled around until she could prop herself on her elbows. The maneuvering caused them both to howl with laughter, but the amusement gave way to his moan with the first swirl of her tongue.

The heady scent of him penetrated her brain, spurring on her boldness. Salty, sweet taste met her tongue as she ran it up and down his length. A glorious feeling of power enveloped her at giving him pleasure. Nothing else matched in her life, and she didn't want it to end.

He grabbed her upper arms, drawing her up beside him but still careful with her injury. His action tore a whimper of disappointment from her throat.

"Not this time." Brilliant yellow lit his face as he settled her on her back and nudged her knees apart. His tip pressed against her entrance, and she lifted her hips in response, wanting, needing him. She couldn't bite back the squeak of impatience.

"I love you, *amora.*" He entered her, slow and steady letting her body adjust to his, filling her until she thought she would burst. There was no going back now.

The friction against her already sensitized flesh sent a frisson of erotic energy bouncing between them. Wet heat enveloped hard strength until she didn't know who she was anymore. She just knew she never wanted it to stop.

The tempo grew, ebbed and crested again until it exploded in a wash of light. Muscles seized as waves of pleasure and heat flooded her. Just as she started drifting back to earth, he went rigid in her arms. His climax sent the waves crashing through her again, and her body echoed his release.

Caesar rested his forehead against hers as they both sought a calm breath. *You can't leave me,* amora. *I couldn't live without you.*

Tears blurred her vision as she reached up and cupped his face. *I won't. I promise.*

He withdrew and shifted them both around until they were huddled under the covers, clinging together.

Neither said anything. Bebe realized there was nothing more to say. It was a long time before Caesar relaxed into sleep, though his hold on her waist was just as secure as before. But despite the boneless satiation and deep weariness, sleep eluded her. Not from regrets, but from concern over the next stages that would change her life forever.

Goddess, please, oh please, grant me the courage to survive the next few days.

No answer, no sign, came though Bebe didn't really expect one. Finally, exhaustion claimed her, and for once, no nightmares of her parents or grandmother intruded on her slumber.

Chapter 33

The horizon above the Muddy Mountains gradually shifted through the spectrum from midnight blue to rose. Bebe bundled the blanket tighter against the chill and took another sip from her mug. Mint chocolate swirled around her tongue while she waited for the first sliver of Sol to peek over the distant range.

No twinge of discomfort nudged her, no urge to run and burrow in the loose desert soil. She would have known by now, from the need for the wool encircling her if nothing else. Vampires had more resistance to environmental changes.

A sliver of scarlet poked over the black mountains. Liquid orange flared to blinding yellow-white. She closed her eyes to the caressing rays. No frying of skin, other than the standard UV messing with her lily-white nose. No screaming in agony. No spontaneous ignition into flames.

Nada.

Nothing.

She sighed, not sure if from disappointment or relief. On the plus side, the energy from all the sex over the last three days had channeled itself into healing her ankle. The new walking cast could probably come off by the end of the week.

She chugged the cold remains of chocolate and limped from the rooftop garden back down the stairs to the penthouse. Shedding blanket, coat and her one boot, she made her way back to Caesar's darkened bedroom where she ditched the rest of her clothing before crawling under the comforter with him. He pulled her tight against him, and she listened to the ultra-slow beat of his heart.

"Still nothing?" He sounded amused.

She shook her head. "What's the point of sacrificing yourself to the dark side if you don't become one of the undead?"

He chuckled in earnest and kissed the top of her head. "I'm not dead." As if proving his point, his cock pulsed against her thigh.

Irritated, she turned and socked his chest as hard as she could. Not that it made any difference. He only laughed harder. She propped herself on one elbow and glared at him.

"I appreciate your attempt, *amora*." Those eyes, the soft stroke of his fingertips on her cheek were almost enough to make her forget her annoyance. No wonder his parents were considered the most famous lovers on the planet.

She sat up and the comforter and sheet dropped from her chest. With anyone else, she would have been scrambling to cover herself, but with him, her nakedness felt—wonderful. "We need to try again."

He blinked in surprise before he answered. "We've been *trying* for over three days now. Not that I'm objecting." To prove his point, he raised his head enough to pull her right nipple into his mouth, sucking almost to the point of pain before releasing to it with a slight pop.

She swallowed hard against the erotic warmth pooling in her center and struggled to remember the thought she'd been trying to verbalize before he distracted her.

"I know. It's just—" She huffed an exasperated breath and brushed fingers over the bites on her left breast and neck. They weren't as unintentional as the one on her inner thigh. And they'd turned her on more than she cared to admit. "We obviously screwed something up, or I'd be a vampire by now."

"No, we didn't screw anything up" he said. He tugged her arm until her head fell to rest on his chest. "You read Natasha's work."

She gave up with a deep exaggerated sigh and snuggled in the crook of his shoulder. He was right. Within four generations, there would be no way in hell he or any other vampire would be able to Turn any witch.

The realization hit her like a two-by-four. She popped upright and socked Caesar in the chest again. This time must been hard enough because he grunted. Rage engulfed her at his betrayal. "You knew!" She punctuated each sentence with a blow. "You knew Grandpa Petrov was the boy the Nazis found! You knew your bite wouldn't affect me. You knew I wouldn't Turn!"

He blocked her next swing and flipped her on her back before she could take a breath to protest. By the time she took that breath, he had pinned her wrists above her head with one hand and straddled her legs. "That will be quite enough Dr. Zachary."

He grinned, fangs and all, while his free hand cupped a breast. A few weeks ago, she would have found the sight terrifying. Now, her anger melted into need. She moaned and closed her eyes to the sweet sensation of the pad of his thumb brushing her nipple ever so lightly.

She bucked and pleaded, but he extended the torture with lips, tongue and fingers, before switching his attention further south. Then he released her wrists and plunged his fingers into her dark, tight curls until she screamed with a different kind of release.

Boneless, she whispered, "Not fair."

"What's not fair?" Raw desire flared in his golden eyes when he rose to position himself between her thighs.

"Changing the subject using sex." She wrapped arms around his neck and legs around his waist, feeling the pent-up tension in his corded muscles. He plunged into her with a hiss. The sensation of him sliding home nearly sent her into orbit again. He whispered something that her overloaded brain couldn't translate, but his magical hands could.

Damn, they don't call Latin the father of the romance languages for nothing.

An age-old rhythm seized them both, and her petty grievances flew from her mind on the waves of the second orgasm. He collapsed on top of her, spent as well. Rolling off, he tugged her snug against him once more.

"Still not fair," she murmured in the drowsy aftermath. He wound and unwound a curl of her hair around his index finger for so long that she believed he wouldn't answer her.

"I—suspected that might be the case."

The situation was so ludicrous she laughed. Not a girly giggle, but that deep belly laugh you hit when you realized how ridiculous the universe is.

When she could finally control herself, she propped up on her elbow again. Caesar scowled, irritation and—was that hurt feelings?—on his aristocratic features.

She kissed the tip of his nose. "There are easier ways of getting my undying declaration of love. But—" She frowned and wagged an index finger to emphasize her point. "If you *ever* use me as a guinea pig again, I'll stake you."

He sat up and nailed her with a glare. "Is that what you think? That I'd risk your life to satisfy a curious whim?"

"Didn't you?" Her heart stopped. She wasn't sure she could handle it if his answer was yes.

He seized her shoulders, yanking her up until their eyes were inches apart. "I had to be sure you wanted to be a vampire. If Natasha had miscalculated, if something went wrong—" He dragged in a deep breath and pulled her into his arms, squeezing her tight against his chest. "I didn't want you to hate me if you did Turn."

"Grandma wouldn't have made that kind of mistake," she whispered into the hard muscle smashed against her face. She pulled back to meet his eyes. He had to understand without any vampire or witch tricks, only the simple honesty of a man and a woman who care for each other. "And I wouldn't have hated you. I chose my own path. I always have."

He cupped her face in his hands. "And I chose you." An expression of raw emotion crossed his face. "If you will have me."

"What are you saying?"

"Marry me, Bebe."

"No."

The stricken look on his face made her realize how harsh her answer was.

"Goddess, I'm fucking this up again." She closed her eyes, praying for strength before she opened them and her mind to him. "I mean, not yet. Let me find the cure first."

His thoughts reached for her, but underneath the assessment was affection and sexual desire. "You weren't sure you could find it in your lifetime."

"I've got incentive now, don't I?" She shrugged. "I figure I've got a hundred, hundred-ten good years unless I have some early onset senility problem."

"So you'll stay in Los Angeles?" Apprehension filled his features, a look so contrary to the arrogant smugness she'd become accustomed to.

She grinned. "Try to get rid of me."

He cocked an eyebrow. "I meant, live with me in Los Angeles."

"And I said, try to get rid of me."

"For how long though?"

"Till death do us part?"

His eyes flared with annoyance. "That's not funny."

"Oh, come on, it is."

His eyes gleamed yellow.

She gulped. "A little."

He began tickling her, but her shrieks of laughter soon turned to something else much more enjoyable.

Snow fell in a quiet blanket outside Selene's Boulder safehouse. The one her brothers didn't know existed. It had been a better investment than she ever dreamed.

Leaning back in her chair, Selene twirled the crystal goblet of blood, curious of the reaction of the man sitting across the table from her. Tyrone Mallory didn't recoil, not so much as flinch. Good. Maybe this was a Normal she could deal with. She leaned forward and handed the copies of the research notes Ptolemy had taken from Caesar's safe to Mallory.

He glanced through them before looking back up at her. "This was all you could retrieve?"

"Yes." A frown tugged at the corners of her mouth. Once again, no obvious reaction from the man. His heartbeat remained constant. She skimmed the surface of his mind. Just deadness. No spark of hope remained. She couldn't even find a vague sense of despair. He'd already given up on life.

"I don't want my daughter to become a vampire," he said.

"That's why I brought this to you. With your research facilities and our combined capital, we could find a way to help your daughter."

"And what do you get out of this, Ms. Antonius?" For the first time, curiosity flared in his eyes.

"What all good little Romans want, Mr. Mallory." She sipped her blood and smiled. "Revenge."

Turn the page for a sneak peek of the next Bloodlines novel, *Zombie Love*.

Zombie Love

Chapter 1

My transformation into the undead started with a pregnancy test stick.

A used pregnancy test stick.

Not mine, thank you very much.

I slammed the plastic zippered baggie, used pregnancy test stick enclosed, down on my boss's desk in triumph. "Here's your proof. Jessie Alton is knocked up. Her housekeeper confirmed it."

Ralph O'Malley recoiled in disgust. His blue eyes narrowed, and he snarled, "Jesus, Ridgeway, get that thing off my desk!" He poked at it with his pencil, pushing it away from him, until I scooped it up in my filthy hand.

I didn't blame him. I wasn't thrilled about dumpster diving for the proof just because a major TV star peed on the damn thing, but I also didn't want my editor destroying valuable evidence. Legal would want the little stick for DNA testing in case Alton sued.

The A/C kicked on, but the weak circulation did nothing more than stir the lingering cigarette smoke in Ralph's tiny windowless office. Despite the ban on indoor smoking in Los Angeles, the publisher of the *National Scoop* ignored Ralph's predilection for cancer sticks.

"Have the copy on my desk in an hour." He eyed my grime-laden clothes. "Make that two. Get a shower first."

I hesitated a moment.

Ralph guessed at my question. He shook his head and said, "When I told you and Bill I'd have my decision on the assistant editor position on Friday, I meant *on Friday.*" He snatched up the cigarette smoldering in the overflowing ashtray and took a puff before he added, "You've got one hour and fifty-nine minutes."

That wasn't the question I was going to ask, but a cheap thrill filtered through my aching muscles. Bill hadn't bested me out of the job.

Yet.

I focused on my pitch. "I want to do a follow up story on the *private investigator*—" With the baggie still in one hand, my fingers made awkward bunny ears. I suspected the man was a mercenary, not a PI. "—Brent Poole hired to rescue his girlfriend—"

"No."

My watering eyes blinked under the double assault of his smoke and my clothes. "What?"

"I said no." Ralph's bulging orbs and quivering jowls resembled his bulldog, Emerson. At least, Ralph didn't drool all over my leg when he visited my desk.

My boss could have knocked me over with the test stick. Alton and Poole could sell more issues in an hour than any other celebrity could in a week. I glared back. "This guy rescues the highest paid, most popular actress in television history who's knocked up by the highest paid, most popular movie actor—"

"You got garbage in your ears, Ridgeway? I said no." Pink crawled up Ralph's neck and invaded his cheeks. "Now, have you and Agnes discovered what rehab center Sierra Mallory's holed up—"

I ignored his blatant change of topic. "She's kidnapped by some doomsday cult and saved—"

Ralph rose to his feet, teeth chewing on the butt of the cigarette.

I ignored the warning. "—by someone Poole hired, and you don't want a follow-up?"

A growl filled the room. My editor was actually growling at me. I couldn't ignore that fact. I took a careful step away from the desk.

Twin columns of smoke blew from his flared nostrils. "I said no, and I meant no."

The gray haze quivered as we matched glares. Then air seemed to whoosh out of him, and he collapsed back into the ancient leather chair.

Glancing at his watch, he muttered, "You've got one hour and fifty-five minutes if you want the fucking cover for this week."

He knew how to push my buttons. Sheer pride kicked in.

"Fine, boss." I pivoted and charged out the door, careful not to slam it on the way. What the hell was going on? Ralph never nixed one of my ideas. Okay, that wasn't true.

He had.

Once.

Two years ago, I'd snapped the Sabretooth's power forward and the lead singer of a certain boy band having very good time in a hot tub. Even though Ralph ran my initial story, he refused to let me pursue the rumor of a stalker threatening the outed basketball player. His negation now made about as much sense as it did then.

A smile stretched my lips. Good thing I'd already started on the story, or maybe I would've walked away like I had at the time. I may be a slow learner, but I did learn.

I strode through the bullpen, ignoring the gagging and retching sounds in my wake. Everyone backed away from my aroma, except for . . .

Damn. No way could I dodge the lanky woman headed straight for me. Agnes Durley, AKA Agnes of God, because the rest of the staff agreed only the Almighty could love the crazy bitch.

"Samantha, I need to talk to you." Agnes' idea of a whisper carried through the huge room. The snickers started close to us and quickly spread. At least she wasn't wearing her tin foil hat today.

"I'm kind of in a hurry." I tried to slide past her, only to be nailed by Agnes's claw-like grip and the pungent scent of garlic. I swallowed my impatience and a little nausea as the garlic aroma mixed with the cigarette smoke and garbage wafting from my clothes and hair. She may be missing a few screws, but no one could match the woman's research skills. And she had saved my ass on more than one occasion. Besides, Ralph needed someone to write the Elvis/alien baby stories.

"This is serious, Samantha." Agnes lowered her voice only a couple of decibels. "You need to be careful. The streets are dangerous."

"So's Ridgeway's smell," someone muttered from behind a cubical wall.

Tell me something about Los Angeles I don't know. Too many disappearances and murders had been happening lately, way too many for even Los Angeles, and no one knew what prompted the new round of turf wars. Two of the more notorious gangs had actually called a truce through a network affiliate in order to proclaim their innocence.

I breathed through my mouth since the combination of smells overwhelmed even my junk-food-hardened stomach. "Agnes, please, can't this wait? Ralph wants my story now." I patted the hand digging into my upper arm and tried not to wince. The woman had a grip that rivaled the Governator's. "I promise I'll come talk to you in two hours."

Agnes leaned closer. "People are vanishing. Kidnapped by bad vampires."

Great. Another one of her conspiracy stories. The last one involved the FBI covering up the fact the former vice-president had been possessed by doves. "Agnes," I began while prying her fingers off my bicep. "Vampires don't kidnap people. They eat them."

Agnes shook her head, the greasy, graying strands whipping wildly. It was hard to believe she'd once been a beauty queen contestant. The porcelain skin over gorgeous cheekbones didn't counter the wild-eyed look she gave me.

"The good ones don't eat us." She yanked a strand of garlic bulbs out of her safari jacket pocket and thrust the aromatic veggies at my head. "Wear this. It will protect you."

"Ridgeway doesn't need those. Her reek would drive away any self-respecting vampire." Bill Morton, my office nemesis, hung over his cubicle wall, smirking at us. A noticeable silence fell over the bullpen.

Eyeing the forty-something definition of kiss-ass, I mustered a bored look. If the rest of the guys saw me getting pissed, their jibes wouldn't stop. I didn't have time to deal with their crap. Not with a deadline in less than two hours. "Geez, Morton, just because *you* didn't get laid last night doesn't mean you have to take it out on the rest on us." Gales of laughter followed my comeback, and Bill slunk back down in his chair, his lips pursed in a sour grimace.

I turned back to Agnes and tried to give her a reassuring I'm-taking-you-seriously smile. Otherwise, Agnes would hound me the rest of the afternoon, and I wasn't about to miss my deadline. Not with the cover bonus. I needed that cover bonus. "If I wear my grandmother's silver cross, I'll be okay, won't I?"

She eyed me suspiciously for a couple of seconds, her gaze boring into my skull. I tried not to flinch. Maybe Agnes really could pick up thought waves without the damn foil hat on and knew I was lying.

Finally, she nodded and said, "Silver should be sufficient." She grabbed my arm again. "Just be careful on the streets at night. They have Normal help." With her bizarre statement, she released me and marched back to the closet that served as her office. It was sadder than her hat. She'd requested the damn closet and had lined the walls with foil too.

Then her words registered. Normal? As opposed to what? Zombies?

I sighed and shook my head. It wasn't worth the effort to figure out what the heck Agnes was blathering about. Not to mention I had to plan a way to convince Ralph to print the follow-up on Poole's hired gun.

I headed for the ladies' room amid another round of chuckles and snickers.

Selene Antonius strode down the antiseptic hallway of Mallory Labs toward the section converted into an ICU. The staccato clicks of her heels echoed against bare tile. The vampire guard at the door bowed slightly, but she ignored him in favor of the man standing vigil at the observation window. The set of Tyrone Mallory's shoulders was one she recognized.

One she remembered all too well despite the passing of the last two millennia.

A death watch.

"How'd the trials go?" he asked as she halted by his side. He didn't look at her.

She folded her arms and stared into the room at the still figure on the bed. The girl's pale neck blended into the white blankets covering her. It might as well have been a funeral shroud. Despite the airlock, Selene's sensitive hearing could pick up the soft beeps of the EKG unit and the muffled hiss of oxygen. "When did they put her on the ventilator?"

"An hour ago." The despair in his voice nearly drowned the last remnants of his hope.

She could feel Mallory turn his piercing grey eyes away from his only child. "You didn't answer my question."

"The results with the chimpanzees look promising." The last thing she wanted was to lose the gifts the vampire virus had granted her. Unlike her asinine brother, she wasn't throwing her immortality away on a cure. Someday, he'd learn his lesson the hard way when his little witch whore staked him in the back. And if she found a way to let Duncan walk in daylight again, maybe he'd forgive her.

"Promising?" Mallory stepped closer to her. "My daughter has days, maybe hours, and all you can say is *promising*? This research is the only chance she has."

She turned to face Mallory. The guard flicked a questioning look. A slight shake of her head deterred him. A Normal could hardly be considered a threat to her. Mallory's lack of fear where she was concerned was one of the appealing things about him.

"Do you want to use Sierra as the human test subject?"

The stubborn set of his jaw gave her his answer. His gaze shifted back to the dying girl. "You could—"

Her sigh whispered through the air. It always came down to that request, didn't it? "Is that what you really want for her?" She waved her hand between her and the guard. "To be one of us?" She shook her head. Pain stabbed through her heart. The girl couldn't even give permission. Another lesson learned the hard way. "There's no guarantee she'd survive the Turn, Tyrone." *There's no guarantee she'd still love either of us if she survived.* But there was no gain in burdening him with that knowledge. She knew from bitter experience he wouldn't listen to reason at this stage. No grieving family member ever did. "It's been two years since we started the V-Prime Project. Give the team a few more days."

"Fine." His attention returned to the girl struggling to hang onto life. "But if Sierra dies before they're ready, I'm feeding the entire science team to the prisoners."

Acknowledgements

I'm indebted to so many people for making this book possible:

To Darling Husband (DH) and Genius Kid (GK) for supporting the dream.

To Able Benevides and his staff at the Greenspoint IHOP in Houston, Texas. Thanks for the encouragement and the constant ice tea refills!

To my Panera Pals: Nancy Bowden, Christie Craig, Jody Payne and Teri Thackston. Thanks so much ladies! And the purple penis will remain legendary.

To John Foxjohn, Linda Krzywicki and Theresa Lehr for bravely reading the first scribblings of what would become this novel.

To Stephanie Bond, Rhonda Morrow and Colleen Thompson. Your professional advice has been invaluable, ladies.

And last, but definitely not least, to my fellow members of the Northwest Houston and West Houston Chapters of the Romance Writers of America. You folks rock!

About the Author

Suzan Harden transitioned from writing information technology manuals for companies and legal articles for a law enforcement magazine to her first love, fantasy and science fiction in all their forms. She's the author of the Millersburg Magick Mysteries, the Soccer Moms of the Apocalypse series, and the Books of Apep series.

Contact Suzan Harden
Facebook: Suzan Harden
Email: suzan@suzanharden.com
Website: www.suzanharden.com

Sign up for Suzan's Mailing List